LIGHTS OUT

JASON STARR

St. Martin's Minotaur
New York

www.minotaurbooks.com

Library of Congress Cataloging-in-Publication Data

Starr, Jason, 1966–
    Lights out / Jason Starr.
        p. cm.
    ISBN-13: 978-0-312-35973-7
    ISBN-10: 0-312-35973-X
    1. Baseball players—Fiction. 2. Triangles (Interpersonal relations)—Fiction. 3. Brooklyn (New York, N.Y.)—Fiction. 4. Canarsie (New York, N.Y.)—Fiction. I. Title.

PS3569.T336225 L54 2006b
813'.6—dc22

                                                                    2006045057

First published in Great Britain by Orion Books,
an imprint of The Orion Publishing Group.

First St. Martin's Minotaur Paperback Edition: July 2007

10 9 8 7 6 5 4 3 2 1

LIGHTS OUT

PART ONE

One

The day Jake Thomas came home to Brooklyn, Jake's parents, who still lived three houses down from Ryan Rossetti and his parents in Canarsie, hung out a huge banner connected to trees on either side of the street, which read:

WELCOME HOME JAKE, OUR HERO

Ryan had to drive right under the banner on his way to work, which wouldn't have been such a big deal if 'J.T. fever' hadn't been sweeping through the neighborhood all week. It seemed like everyone was wearing THOMAS 24 jerseys and Pirates hats, and hundreds of cars proudly displayed BROOKLYN LOVES JAKE bumper stickers, a giveaway from a Ralph Avenue dealership. Some stores had posted eight-by-ten glossies of Jake in their windows, and Pete's Barbershop on Avenue N was giving free shaves to anyone who showed a Jake Thomas baseball card. Pizzerias, restaurants, bars, delis, and even a nail salon had their own Jake Thomas specials, and the *Canarsie Courier* was running a cover story about Jake called 'Brooklyn's Son Returns,' so Ryan had to see an annoying picture of Jake – smiling widely with his fake choppers – in newspaper dispensers everywhere.

Ryan cranked the volume on his Impala's CD player, shouting lyrics of Nelly's 'Hot in Herre.' A few minutes later he double-parked in front of a deli on Flatlands and went inside for his usual ham-and-egg on a roll and black coffee with four sugars. At the register, Andre, the high school kid who worked there, said, 'Jake Thomas home yet?'

'Dunno,' Ryan said, shaking his head as he dug into his pocket for money, although he'd already put a five on the counter.

'Yo, you hear? There's gonna be a block party for him later.'

3

'Really?' Ryan said, playing dumb. Jake's mother had been planning the surprise party for weeks and Ryan's mother had been up late last night cooking five trays of her famous lasagna.

'Yeah. Eighty-first Street's gonna be closed off. Gonna be free food, music, dancing, all that shit.'

'Oh, right,' Ryan said. 'I think I did hear something about that.'

'I'm goin', man,' Andre said. 'Gonna meet J.T. up close, shake his hand, get my picture taken with the NL batting champ. Yo, you think if I bring him a bat he'd sign it for me?'

'Why not?' Ryan took his change and returned to his car. Several minutes later he pulled into the driveway of a house on Whitman Drive in Mill Basin. Leaving the CD player on, he ate his breakfast, but when he was finished eating he didn't get out of his car. He always told himself that if he turned off the CD player or radio in the middle of a song it would mean bad luck. So he waited for the last lyric of the Mobb Deep joint and then, timing it perfectly, shut the ignition.

Carlos and Franky were already setting up the drop cloths downstairs when Ryan entered the house. In the bathroom, Ryan changed out of his street clothes – a sleeveless T-Mac jersey over a plain black hooded sweatshirt, baggy Pepe jeans, a San Antonio Spurs baseball-style cap worn sideways over a black do-rag, and not new but very clean Nike Zoom LeBron IIs – into his white painting clothes and old paint-covered sneakers, and then returned to the living area and started helping Carlos and Franky with the wall repair.

It was the second day on this job, and it was going to be a tough one. The house was average-size – three bed, two bath – but the old owners must not have painted in years, because there was peeling paint everywhere, and lots of bubbles needed to be sanded down. Ryan and the other guys had spent all day yesterday scraping and spackling and they'd gotten through only half of the downstairs. The upstairs wasn't in as bad shape so there was a shot they could start laying on the primer by the end of the day.

Ryan got to work, spackling, when Carlos said to him, 'Jake Thomas come home yet?'

Carlos was Ryan's age – twenty-four – with a thin mustache and

4

tuft of hair on his chin. He'd been asking Ryan about Jake all week, and Ryan had been trying not to pay too much attention.

'Dunno,' Ryan said without looking at Carlos.

'But he's coming today, right?'

'Guess so.'

'What?'

'I think so,' Ryan said, louder.

'Hey,' Carlos said. 'If I bring you a ball in tomorrow, you think you can get J.T. to sign it for me?'

'Don't bust chops,' Franky said. He was a big guy, a few years older than Carlos and Ryan.

'It ain't for me, man,' Carlos said. 'It's for my little cousin – he loves baseball. I told him I work with Jake Thomas's homeboy, he was like, "Hook me up, yo."'

'There's gonna be a party for him later on my block,' Ryan said. 'Why don't you stop by if you want an autograph?'

'I don't know the guy, man,' Carlos said. 'I don't wanna go up to him and be like, "Gimme your autograph." Come on, man, do me this one favor. It ain't for me – it's for my cousin. He's, like, eight years old and shit.'

'He can't get everybody autographs,' Franky said. 'He probably's gotta get autographs for a thousand guys already, right, Ry?'

'It's all right,' Ryan said, working the scraper hard against the wall. 'Bring the ball in tomorrow and I'll ask Jake to sign it.'

'Thanks, man,' Carlos said. Then he said to Franky, 'See? It ain't no big deal.'

They worked for a while without talking. Carlos's box in the corner was playing top forty – Avril Lavigne's new song.

Then Franky said, 'So where's he coming in from?'

Ryan knew Franky was talking about Jake, but he pretended to be lost.

'Who?' Ryan asked.

'Jake Thomas,' Franky said.

'Oh,' Ryan said. 'Pittsburgh, I guess.'

'He got an apartment there or something?'

'I think he rents a house,' Ryan mumbled.

'What?'

'He rents a house,' Ryan said louder.

'Probably a friggin' mansion,' Franky said. 'The guy's gotta be making, what, a couple mil a year now, and wait till he's a free agent – he'll break the fuckin' bank. The Pirates sucked this year, but Jake was freakin' spectacular. What'd he end up at, three fifty-three?'

'Three fifty-one,' Carlos said.

'Three fifty-one,' Franky said. 'Jesus, that's like a DiMaggio number. And he had, like, twenty-five homers, hundred ribees.'

'He got twenty-two jacks,' Carlos said.

'Twenty-two home runs,' Franky said. 'And what'd he get last year, twenty?'

'Seventeen,' Carlos said.

'That's all right,' Franky said. 'At least the numbers are goin' up. And the guy steals bases and's got that rifle arm. You see that one they showed on ESPN last week, when he threw out the guy trying to go first to third on that ball in the gap?'

'Yeah, 'gainst the Cubs,' Carlos said.

'The guy's got a fuckin' gun,' Franky said. 'I swear that ball was, like, five feet off the ground the whole way. I bet he could've been a pitcher if he wanted.' He turned to Ryan and said, 'Hey, J.T. ever pitch in high school?'

'Little bit,' Ryan said.

'Who was better, you or him?' Carlos asked.

'Me,' Ryan said confidently.

'You ever pitch to him in a game?'

'Little League, intrasquad – shit like that.'

'You struck him out?'

'Sometimes.'

'But he got some rips off you too, right?'

'Sometimes.'

'Hey, you think J.T. is gonna make the Hall someday?' Franky asked.

'Keeps playin' the way he is he's gonna,' Carlos said.

'Look at the numbers he's puttin' up,' Franky said. 'You gotta admit those're Hall of Fame numbers. Guy hits what, three fifty-one last year? Jesus.'

Carlos and Franky continued talking about how great Jake was, and Ryan tried to block out the noise, thinking about Christina. She looked so beautiful last night in the backseat of his car, with

6

the lamppost light in her eyes. But then, before he dropped her off, she started crying. He really should throw her a call to make sure she was okay.

Then he snapped out of his thoughts when Franky said, 'Hey, Ry, you think J.T. is gonna come play in New York someday?'

'How the hell should I know?' Ryan said, wishing they'd shut up already.

'I don't know,' Franky said, 'I thought maybe he said something about it to you or something.'

'We don't talk a lot these days,' Ryan said.

'Still,' Franky said, 'the guy musta said *something*. I mean, any guy grows up in Brooklyn, his dream's gotta be to play for the Yankees or the Mets. And after next year he's gonna be a free agent.'

'Pass the spackle, will ya?' Ryan said.

Ryan tossed his finished container of spackle aside, then took the new one from Franky. Carlos started telling Franky about how he went to get his car fixed yesterday and the guy tried to charge him three hundred bucks for an oil change and a new muffler, and Ryan thought, *Good, no more talking about goddamn Jake.* Then, after Carlos said he was thinking about selling his car anyway, putting an ad in *Buy-Lines*, Franky said, 'That'd be something, having a guy from the neighborhood playing for a New York team. I bet he'd be the best player in the history of Brooklyn.'

'What about Sammy Koufax?' Carlos said.

'*Sandy* Koufax, you fuckin' moron,' Franky said, 'And he was a pitcher. I'm talkin' about a hitter. What hitter in the history of Brooklyn is better than Jake Thomas?'

'Nobody,' Carlos said.

'That's what I'm talkin' about,' Franky said.

Ryan couldn't take it anymore. He left the scraper and the spackle on the floor and headed toward the front door.

'Where you goin'? Franky said.

'Taking a break,' Ryan said.

'But you just got here.'

Ryan left the house. He went to his car and took out a pack of Camels from the glove compartment. He lit up, leaning against the side of the car, when he saw Tim's pickup coming down the block.

Tim O'Hara, the owner of Pay-Less Painting, was only thirty-five, but he was doing pretty good for himself. He had four crews of three guys doing painting jobs around Brooklyn, and he'd recently bought a nice house – three bedrooms, a garage – near Marine Park. He used to help out painting, but now he was a pure contractor, going out and bidding on jobs, and getting guys to work for him for ten bucks an hour. Tim was a good guy, and he and Ryan always got along, but Ryan still planned to start his own business someday. He figured he could put ads in papers and bid on jobs as easily as Tim could, and he could be just as successful. All he needed was a chunk of change to start out with. He'd already put away two thousand bucks, but he felt he needed at least five as a cushion and for start-up costs. He was also saving to move out of his parents' house and, eventually, buy a ring for Christina, so he expected to work for Tim for at least a couple more years.

Tim double-parked the pickup, then got out and approached Ryan. Tim was about Ryan's height – five-ten – and his reddish-brown hair was receding on the sides.

'Gotta quit that shit,' Tim said.

'You only live once,' Ryan said.

'So you wanna live to forty?'

Ryan took a long drag on the cigarette and let the smoke out very slowly through his nostrils.

'So how's it going?' Tim asked.

'Good.' Then Ryan realized Tim meant the painting job. 'Coming along.'

'You think you guys can finish up in three days?' Tim asked.

'That's pushing it,' Ryan said. 'There's a lot of wall repair to do in there – 'specially downstairs.'

''Cause I got another job for you to do – three-story house, Midwood – big job. Might be a four- or five-dayer. How about four days?'

'Dunno,' Ryan said. 'Talk to the guys.'

Tim went into the house and Ryan stayed outside, finishing the cigarette. It was a nice fall day – sunny, in the sixties.

A few minutes later, when Ryan went inside, Tim was in the

8

living room saying, 'but it looks like you guys're doing a really great job in here. Seriously, you're putting my other crews to shame. I was just at this other job in Sheepshead Bay, and Jimmy, Rob, and that new kid I hired, Benny – they're goin' on a week and they're just putting on the second coat today. And it's not a big job neither – two bedrooms, one bath. Benny – I swear to God on my grandmother's grave – he painted himself into a closet yesterday.'

'You're shittin' me,' Franky said.

'Cross my heart, hope to die,' Tim said. 'Jimmy told me all about it. He comes back from his lunch break and hears the kid screaming, "Lemme outta here, lemme outta here!"'

Franky and Carlos started laughing. Ryan thought it was funny too, but he wasn't in the mood to laugh. He got busy spackling.

'They had to use the scraper to get him outta there,' Tim said.

'What a fuckin' idiot,' Franky said.

'Nah, Benny's a good kid,' Tim said. 'He just doesn't have all the seeds in his apple, if you know what I mean.'

'But come on, to paint yourself into a closet,' Franky said, 'you gotta be a fuckin' retard.'

'He's lucky they found him in there,' Carlos said. 'It was five o'clock, his ass coulda been stuck there all night.'

'Imagine that shit,' Franky said. 'They show up the next day and find the stupid kid there, still screaming to get out. That woulda been a fuckin' riot.'

Franky started laughing. He had a loud, infectious laugh, and Carlos and Tim joined in. Even Ryan smiled a little.

'But seriously,' Tim said, 'what I was saying before – you guys are the best crew I have. I really mean that. You always do quality work, and I know when I assign you a job you'll finish it on time.'

'So you gonna give us a bonus, boss?' Carlos asked.

'Yeah, how 'bout a not-painting-ourselves-into-a-closet bonus?' Franky said.

Franky and Carlos laughed again.

'Tell you what I'll do,' Tim said. 'You guys finish this job in four days so you can get started on that new one in Midwood, I'll give you an extra fifty bucks apiece.'

'Aw right!' Carlos shouted.

'A Hawaii five-O sounds cool to me,' Franky said.

9

'But don't rush it,' Tim said. 'Remember, it's quality over quantity. I'd rather do ten jobs well than twelve jobs not so well, you know what I mean?'

'Don't worry,' Carlos said. 'We'll do a good job *and* we'll get it done in four days.'

'What about you, Ry?' Tim asked.

Busy smoothing out spackle, Ryan said, 'What?'

'You think four days is doable?' Tim said.

'Yeah,' Ryan said. 'Why not?'

'Way to go, guys,' Tim said. He started toward the door; then he stopped and said, 'Jesus, I almost forgot. Hey, Ry – your buddy Jake Thomas come home yet?'

Ryan waited a few seconds, grinding his back teeth, then said calmly, 'I really don't know, Tim.'

'I think he's gettin' sick of that question,' Franky said.

'What're you talking about?' Ryan snapped. 'I'm not sick of anything. I just don't know if he's home yet, that's all. Who'm I, his mother?'

'Testy, ain't we?' Franky said. 'You sound like my friggin' girlfriend. What's it, that time of the month again, Justine?'

Carlos laughed.

Tim said to Ryan, 'I don't wanna impose on the guy or anything, but you think if I give you a baseball card tomorrow you can get it signed for me?'

'Sure,' Ryan said. 'I mean, I'll ask him to.'

'Damn,' Carlos said. 'My man Ryan's gonna have a lotta shit to get signed!'

'Hey, if it's too much trouble . . .' Tim said.

'It's no big deal,' Ryan said. 'Bring in the card tomorrow, I'll give it to Jake.'

'Cool,' Tim said. 'And great work here again, guys.'

Tim left, then Carlos said, 'Come on, man, let's get our asses to work – I want that fifty bucks.'

'Don't worry,' Franky said. 'All we gotta do is finish the wall repair by lunchtime and we could have the whole house primed by tonight. We do the first coat tomorrow, the second coat the next day, and we still got a whole day left over.'

'I'm not rushing the job,' Ryan said.

'Who said we gonna rush it?' Carlos said. 'We just gonna work fast, that's all.'

'What's the matter,' Franky said to Ryan, 'you don't wanna get the bonus?'

'It's fifty bucks,' Ryan said. 'It's nothing to get a boner over.'

'So if I gave you a fifty-dollar bill you'd rip it up right now?' Franky asked.

'That's not what I'm talking about,' Ryan said. 'You heard what Tim said – quality over quantity. I'm not gonna slap on the paint for fifty fuckin' bucks.'

'What's wrong with you anyway?' Franky said. 'All day – no, all week – you been acting like you got a big fat dick up your ass.'

Ryan dropped the scraper and took a step toward Franky. He wasn't really going to go after him; he just wanted to make a point.

'Come on, chill, y'all, chill,' Carlos said. 'Yo, maybe Ry's right. We'll take it easy, yo – do up all the wall repair today and get on the primer. If we just don't fuck around and bullshit, we'll get this house down in four days, no problem. So just everybody let's just chill and get to workin', what y'all say?'

For several seconds Ryan and Franky remained facing each other, and then they started working again. Usher was singing 'Yeah,' and Ryan climbed to the top of the stepladder to work on a big crack near the ceiling when his beeper went off. He glanced at the readout – CHRISSY WORK – and got down off the ladder and headed toward the front door.

'Another fuckin' break?' Franky said.

Ryan went outside, took out his cell, and called Christina.

'I was so glad it was you,' Ryan said. 'I was thinking about you before.'

'Where are you?' Christina asked. She sounded like she'd been crying again.

'Work – where do you think? You okay?'

'Is Jake home yet?'

'You know how many times I got asked that question today?'

'Is he?'

'I have no idea.'

'I'm scared.'

'Don't be. You're gonna do great tonight – I guarantee it. And just remember – I love you.'

'Shit, I gotta go. Dr Hoffman needs me for a root canal.'

'Hey, I just said I love you.'

'I love you too.' Christina waited a few moments, then said, 'I don't think I can do it.'

Ryan rolled his eyes. 'You gotta do it, Chrissy – it's the perfect time.'

'Why? I mean, why can't you just come over tonight and we'll stay locked in my house till he leaves? I'll leave a message at his parents' house, say I'm sick – I have the flu.'

'We're not doing that.'

'Why not? I'll take off from work tomorrow and we can stay in my room all day and—'

'We gotta take care of this thing tonight, get on with our lives.'

'I know, I know, but—'

'You're not gonna chicken out on me, are you?'

The line was silent for a while, and then Christina said, 'Come by my house after work – I have to see you first.'

'You wanna do this or not?'

'Of course I wanna do it.'

'Then just go to Jake's tonight and—'

'Let's go together.'

'I really don't think that's a good idea.'

'I need you there with me. Just show up with me, then you can leave.'

'Why can't you—'

'Please,' she said. 'If you're there ... I don't know ... I'll feel more comfortable. You don't even have to come in. You can just wait outside. He won't even see you.'

Ryan shook his head, knowing he'd give in, but waited awhile anyway before he said, 'Fine, but then you're gonna do this tonight, just like we planned it. No backing out.'

'Coming,' Christina said to someone. Then she said to Ryan, 'I'll see you later ... I love you so much.'

'I love you too,' Ryan said, but Christina had hung up.

Ryan remained on the stoop, lighting another cigarette. After taking a couple of long drags he stomped out the butt and went back into the house.

Two

Exiting the gate and heading into the United terminal at LaGuardia, Jake Thomas didn't want to be recognized. Usually he didn't mind getting stopped – he wasn't one of those asshole celebrities who punched cameramen or started fights with reporters – but today, with all the shit that had been happening in his life lately, he just wanted to be left alone.

He flipped down his Gucci shades and no one seemed to notice him, not even a good-looking blonde sitting off to the right. She must have been foreign or something because she definitely didn't seem to know who he was. She was just staring at him in a way that said, *Ouch, he's hot*, and why shouldn't she? Jake knew he was styling in a beige Helmut Lang suit and a black Armani shirt. The suit jacket was open and the top few buttons of the shirt were undone, showing his custom-made gold-and-diamond JT nameplate necklace from Jacob the Jeweler. He had a Louis Vuitton carry-on bag over one shoulder and was wearing black Ferragamo loafers, a Charriol watch, Neil Lane rings, and a Tiffany two-carat princess-cut diamond stud in his left ear.

Continuing through the terminal, passing a gift shop, Jake saw a kid up ahead pointing at him. At the ballpark he was always friendly with kids, flipping them balls in batting practice, signing as many autographs as he could before and after games – and even outside the ballpark or in the hotel lobby. Jake loved making kids' days, but he did it mostly for PR. At the ballpark, he never knew who might be watching. Reporters could see him blow off a kid and it would make the papers the next day. Or the kid could be the GM's son or nephew or whoever, and if word got out that Jake Thomas was blowing off little kids, the ad guys at Nike and Pizza Hut and wherever would start freaking and it could turn into a big-time headache. By always being Mr Nice Guy, smiling widely, asking kids their names and chatting with their parents, Jake had developed a rep as being one of the most accessible pro athletes in the country, which boosted his profile with the ad agencies. He already had the perfect look for the marketing world. His father was black, and his mother was half-Italian, half-Irish, so he had that whole light-skinned, melting-pot, Derek Jeter/Tiger Woods thing happening. He also had a great smile – recently porcelain-veneered sparkling-white choppers, contrasting perfectly with his complexion. All of this contributed to his ninth-place position on *Forbes*'s list of the top fifty most marketable athletes in the world – and that was as a member of the Pittsburgh Pirates. He knew he'd make the top five easily, maybe even beat out Tiger for number one, once he started playing for a big-market team.

The kid, probably ten years old, was tugging on his father's sleeve, and Jake could read his lips: 'It's Jake Thomas! It's Jake Thomas!'

When they reached Jake the kid asked, 'Hey, are you Jake Thomas?'

'Nope,' Jake said, and kept walking.

He bypassed the baggage claim-area – he'd had his luggage overnighted to his parents' house in Brooklyn – and approached a squat, bearded guy who was holding up a card with RYAN ROSSETTI written on it. Since he'd made it to the majors, Jake had been using Ryan's name with limo drivers and at hotels, airports, and restaurants, so he wouldn't get harassed.

'Mr Rossetti?' the driver asked Jake. He had a Russian-or-something accent.

'Yeah,' Jake said. Then the driver led Jake over to a Lincoln Town Car and opened the back door for him, and Jake said, 'Whoa, what's this?'

'What do you mean?' the driver said. 'I bring car to drive you to Brooklyn.'

'I didn't order a Town Car,' Jake said. 'I ordered an SUV limo.'

'Yes. But this is car I bring. Come, get in car. It's okay.'

Jake was going to insist on an SUV. Then he saw a few kids noticing him, and he knew that if he stood around waiting for the SUV he'd get swarmed.

'Whatever,' Jake said, and got in.

As the car curved around toward the terminal's exit, Jake took out his cell and called his agent in LA.

'So you don't return my calls anymore, huh?' Jake said.

'I called you twice,' Stu Fox said.

Jake didn't know if this was true or not, because he hadn't checked his messages.

'Where are you?' Stu asked.

'Backseat of a Town Car.'

'Moving down in the world, huh?'

Jake laughed, although he didn't think it was funny, then said, 'So did Ken get back to you yet?'

'Yeah, he won't give. He says if they let your PT into the clubhouse next year it'll damage team morale.'

'What morale? We finished thirty out.'

'I'm just telling you what he told me.'

'Did you tell him that if I don't get my own trainer, *in* the clubhouse, I'm not showing up to spring training?'

'Come on, Jake, nobody gets a PT in the clubhouse after all that Giambi shit.'

'He says no, ask him who else but Jake Thomas is gonna get asses into the seats next year. Ask him whose face he's gonna put on the yearbook cover. Ask him what player on his team's gonna be starting in the All-Star Game, and what player will probably finish in the top five in the MVP voting this year, if I don't win the damn thing. Without me, I bet the team gets contracted, has to move to San Juan or Monterey, and you think Ken doesn't know that?'

'I hear what you're saying,' Stu said, 'but it may not make sense to get confrontational right now. I mean, the season just ended two weeks ago and—'

'Jesus,' Jake said. He tried to flex his legs, his feet hitting the back of the front seat. 'You should see me right now – I'm curled up like a goddamn pretzel. Which reminds me – I want my own SUV limo on the road next year.'

'I think that's out of the question.'

'With fish tanks.'

'What?'

'I want fish tanks in the limo, and DIRECTV and a fully stocked bar. Oh, yeah, and I want room upgrades on the road –

suites *with* Jacuzzis.' He heard his call-waiting beep, then said, 'Call me,' and took the other call. 'J.T.'

'Jake – Robby.'

'We get the *GQ* cover?' Jake asked.

'Not quite,' Robert Henderson, Jake's publicist said. 'But some other great things came down the pike this morning. Dave Shaw from *TSN* wants to do a sit-down with you next week.'

'Next.'

'He said he'll come to your—'

'Next.'

'Mike Winter from *SI* wants to ask you a few questions for an article he's doing.'

'Is the article about me?'

'Well, no, not really. I mean, it'll include quotes from—'

'Who's the article about?'

'Albert Pujols.'

'Next.'

'We're talking about *Sports Illustrated* here, Jake. Can't you just talk to the guy for five minutes? He'll do it on the phone, or e-mail you the—'

'Next.'

'ESPN talked about doing a segment about you in a couple weeks, but it's not solid yet.'

'What's the deal at *GQ?*'

'They're still featuring you in next month's issue, but they haven't made a decision about the cover yet.'

'Who'm I up against?'

'Ben Affleck.'

'*What?*' Jake said. 'You're telling me that I'm gonna get bumped for Ben fucking Affleck?'

'The *GQ* cover's a tough nut to crack.'

'Come on, man. After the year I had I should be on the cover of *SI, TSN, Details, and GQ* in the same month. My on-base percentage was four-seventy, I stole thirty-four bases, plus I hit three fifty-one, knocked in a hundred six. You know what my average was with runners in scoring position?'

'Three ninety?'

'Four-oh-two. But you know how many *SI* covers I've got in my career?'

'One.'

'Bingo – when I was a fucking rookie! It's a disgrace is what it is. If I was a mutt like Randy Johnson, okay – but Jake Thomas should be fending off the covers.'

'I got you on the cover of *Details*.'

'Fuck *Details*. I want *GQ*, baby. Make it happen.'

As the Town Car exited the airport and was zipping along the Grand Central Parkway, bouncing over potholes and grooves in the tar, Jake played his voice mail. He skipped through messages from his lawyer and his accountant, but listened to the entire message from Natalie – a European model, maybe from France or Italy, but who lived in LA – whom he sometimes saw when he was on the coast. Natalie sounded sexy on the phone, with her European accent, talking about how much she missed him and wanting to know when he was going to be in LA again. He skipped through messages from his personal shopper, his stylist, then listened to one from Max Manikowsky, the Pirates' PR guy, who wanted to know if Jake was interested in appearing at a fund-raiser for the Juvenile Diabetes Research Foundation this December. Jake loved doing medical benefits and visiting sick kids in hospitals – shit like that was great for his image. He called Manicocksky back and left a message on his voice mail to definitely count him in. He listened to a couple more messages, including one from Cheryl, a cocktail waitress from Phoenix, and then clicked off.

'Tell me,' the driver said. 'Your name – it's not really Ryan Rossetti, is it?'

Jake looked up and saw the Russian's big dark eyes in the rearview mirror.

'I know who you are,' the driver went on. 'I hear you on phone and I see you on TV. You're that baseball player on Pittsburgh Pirates – the one from Brooklyn. You're Jake Thomas.'

'My name's Ryan Rossetti.'

'Come on,' the driver said, smiling. 'I hear you say your name's Jake Thomas. You're famous baseball player, right?'

'Just drive the car, Vladimir.'

'My name is not Vladimir.'

'Whatever,' Jake said.

As the car continued along the Van Wyck Expressway, Jake

relaxed, zoning out, thinking about Patti, the stewardess on his flight from Pittsburgh. She was thin with long, straight blond hair and looked kind of like a low-budg Cameron Diaz. When the plane was going into its descent, she leaned over Jake's seat and brought her face up to maybe an inch in front of his and told him that she was going to be at her place on the Upper East Side for a few days and that he should give her a call. Then she slipped a United business card into his hand with her name and number written on it, a little heart instead of the dot on the *i* in Patti.

Jake remembered Patti mentioning that she lived with 'a few other girls,' and he wondered if 'a few' meant three, four, or even five. If it meant more than four and the other girls were anything like Patti, that meant there would be a significant possibility of getting into a six-way. Jake had never been in a six-way. His personal record was four girls at once, and the record had an asterisk next to it because two of the girls had been in pornos and one was a stripper-slash-prostitute.

Jake flipped open his cell phone, ready to leave a message for Patti. He'd tell her, *I'd love to get together tomorrow night, and maybe your friends would like to meet me too?* He'd leave it vague and polite-like, but still make it obvious what he had in mind. He took out the business card and started to punch in the digits when he realized, sadly, that arranging to meet Patti – especially over the next few days – was out of the question, since the main reason he was coming home to Brooklyn this weekend was to finally set a wedding date with Christina, his high school sweetheart.

Although Jake had been engaged to Christina for six years, nowadays they barely spoke. It was weird, because when he started going out with her during the summer before sophomore year he didn't think he'd ever even want to date another girl. She was beautiful, without a doubt the best-looking girl in Canarsie, maybe in all of Brooklyn, and he was positive he was going to marry her someday. As high school went on and things started getting crazy, what with the big-league scouts chasing after him and all of the national media attention, he became even more convinced that Christina was the one for him. He knew she was his rock, that she loved him before he made it big, and that she'd love him forever no matter what. Yeah, he fooled around a little bit on the side, but how could he resist? Girls were throwing themselves at him left and right, and he was only a teenager. He figured he'd sow his oats for a few years and then marry Christina and live happily ever after.

After high school, he used part of his signing bonus to buy her a fifty-thousand-dollar, two-carat emerald-cut diamond ring from Harry Winston, and then he proposed to her on the Canarsie Pier, but they didn't set a wedding date. They both agreed it would be best to get married in a couple of years, when they were older and things were more settled. His first year in the minors he saw Christina as much as he could. Then, when he got called up to Pittsburgh, he still talked to her on the phone a lot, but they rarely saw each other. There were more girls too – a lot more girls. They'd line up for him after games, or just show up at his hotel rooms. He was the new golden boy of baseball, he was just starting to make it big, and he was having the time of his life. He still had it in his head that he'd marry Christina someday, but he thought about her less and less. Although he kind of liked the idea that she was waiting for him, after a couple more years went by he decided it wasn't right to keep leading her on this way. He was planning to break up with her last summer, and probably would've if it weren't for a fourteen-year-old Mexican girl named Marianna Fernandez.

When Jake met Marianna in June at that club in downtown San Diego he had no idea she was in junior high school. Yeah, her braces and kind of young-looking face should've been dead giveaways, but a lot of adults wore braces these days, and she definitely didn't look like jailbait. She had a curvy Latina body and was wearing something low-cut with her cleavage all pushed up and a skirt that must've shown ninety percent of her ass. Jake figured she had to be at least eighteen.

And it wasn't like he didn't try to figure out her age. In his hotel room, before they started going at it, he said, 'So how old are you?' and she said, 'Twenty.' Not even eighteen or nineteen, so Jake figured he had a couple of years to play with even if she was lying.

A few weeks later Marianna's father called Jake's agent, Stu Fox, accusing Jake of statutory rape. When Stu broke the news to Jake, Jake said, 'Who the hell is Marianna Fernandez?'

Stu explained and then Jake said, 'Oh, her. What do they want?'

'Fifty grand,' Stu said.

'They go to the cops yet?'

'Nope, but he said they will if you don't pay.'

Jake started to realize how serious this situation was. A conviction for statutory rape meant jail time, but even getting accused would scare the hell out of the ad nerds and cost him millions. He considered giving the Fernandezes the money. People had probably seen him and the girl sucking face on the dance floor, and guests at the hotel had definitely seen them together, and they might've even been caught on security cameras. On the other hand, making a payment would make him look guilty as hell, so he decided to gamble and ignore the whole thing and hope the guy backed off. The strategy seemed to work until a month later – this was August now – Stu got another call from Mr Fernandez, asking for a hundred Gs. Now Jake knew there was no way he could pay. How did he know Fernandez would stop at a hundred? He could ask for another hundred, or a million. Next year Jake would become a free agent and was planning to sign a blockbuster two-hundred-million-dollar deal. He couldn't get caught up in paying off a greedy blackmailer when he was on the verge of making that kind of dough.

So Jake told Stu to ignore Fernandez again and see what happened, but that Mexican bastard didn't give up. He made more calls, demanding the hundred grand, continuing to threaten to take the story to the cops and the newspapers. Then, during the last week of the season, Jake tried to make a deal. He had his lawyer draw up papers, agreeing to give the Fernandezes the money in exchange for signing a document swearing that Jake and Marianna had never had sex. Jake didn't know if they'd go along with it, but if they balked he had a plan B anyway – marry Christina. The good PR of setting a wedding date with his high school sweetheart would have to offset the bad PR of getting accused of rape. If setting the wedding date wasn't enough, Jake had a plan C. Two days ago, in Pittsburgh, he had hired a PI to dig up some dirt on Marianna Fernandez. Maybe she had a drug problem, or a sex addiction, or her father had tried to blackmail other people. If they found something on the family, Jake would hire a PR guy to do a major smear campaign, totally discrediting them, and the problem would be solved.

Jake was confident that everything would work out for him somehow. He'd marry Christina next December, and they'd move to Hollywood Hills, Beverly Hills, or some other hills where the houses went for at least ten mill a pop, and he'd become the new right fielder for the LA Dodgers. Jake's goal was to pull a Shaq – go play for an LA team for a few years, then branch out of sports into movies. He'd already acted in commercials, and the next step was to break into real acting. But he didn't want to be a joke, like O.J. and Jordan. No, none of that *Naked Gun, Space Jam* crap for Jake Thomas. He didn't want to be in movies, he wanted to be in *films*.

Jake was jolted from his thoughts by the stench of raw sewage drifting across the highway. He pulled up his suit jacket to cover his mouth and nose, then said, 'Vladimir, can you close the fucking window up there? Jesus.'

The driver shut his window, but the odor lingered, and it reminded Jake that he was on his way to Brooklyn. Sometimes he couldn't believe he was actually *from* Brooklyn, that he'd spent eighteen years of his life living in such a hopeless dung heap. His neighborhood, Canarsie, had been built on landfill, and that was exactly what the neighborhood was to him – a big pile of garbage and dirt. Every time he visited it seemed to get worse – infested with gangs and drugs – and he thought his parents were out of their minds for still living there.

All of a sudden Jake felt claustrophobic and not nearly as pumped as he had before. Maybe it was the idea of going back home, or maybe it was because he was trapped in the backseat of this coffin on wheels. Or maybe it was his parents – the fact that they'd been married for thirty-one years and they seemed more boring each time he saw them. What if the same thing happened to him and Christina? While Jake liked the idea of setttling down and having kids – being known as a family man would be great for his image and would probably bring him more lucrative endorsement deals – the idea of being committed to one woman scared the hell out of him. It had nothing to do with Christina herself, because he knew he couldn't do better for a wife. She was caring and loving and beautiful, and he knew she'd pump out some great-looking babies. The only problem with Christina was that she was one person. If he could split her up into, say, twenty

Christinas and spread them out over the country, maybe he could handle being married – *maybe*. Otherwise, he didn't know how he'd stay faithful.

Vladimir Pain-in-the-ass-ovich exited the Belt Parkway at Pennsylvania Avenue and drove through the Spring Creek Towers housing complex. Brooklyn always looked bad, but it looked worse after being away for a long time. Tall, cramped-together, project-style buildings prevented the sunlight from reaching the street, and kids in do-rags stood huddled on corners, protecting their turf. When the car turned down Flatlands things didn't get much better. There were more projects, burned-out buildings, and empty lots overrun with garbage. The avenue itself looked narrower, more run-down than Jake had remembered. An angry mother was pulling her sloppily dressed kids along the sidewalk, a homeless guy was sleeping in a refrigerator box, and burnouts sat on stoops and garbage cans, staring at nothing. Awnings, brick walls, and bus shelters were filthy and covered with graffiti. When Jake was growing up, the neighborhood had been a working-class mix of blacks and whites; now it was almost all black, and it didn't look as working-class either. Maybe it wasn't the worst neighborhood in the city, but give it a couple of years and it would be another East New York.

Jake decided it was time to get his parents the hell out of Brooklyn. He'd buy them a fucking condo in the city and send them the key. Or maybe move them out to LA, get them digs on the beach in Santa Monica or somewhere out there. Meanwhile, he'd keep it mellow this weekend – stay inside most of the time, set the wedding date with Christina, then split. Hopefully after this weekend he'd never have to visit his old neighborhood again.

As the car turned onto East Eighty-first Street, Jake was getting that closed-in feeling again, probably because the street was lined with butt-ugly attached brick houses with tall stoops and no front lawns. He couldn't wait to get out of the car, to stretch, and then he saw the crowd ahead. There were maybe two hundred people on the street, and tables set up with food and drinks, and a big banner hung over the street that read, WELCOME HOME JAKE, OUR HERO. The car double-parked, and a swarm of kids, most wearing THOMAS 24 jerseys and Pirates caps, surrounded it, cheering as if it

22

were bottom of the ninth, bases loaded, two out, game seven of the World Series.

Thinking that he was going to kill his parents for this, Jake got out of the car, giving the crowd his best Hollywood smile.

Three

The paint job was going much faster than Ryan had expected, probably because he and the guys didn't screw around all day the way they usually did. Actually, they didn't talk much at all, and, without talking, there was nothing to do but work. By five o'clock they had finished all the wall repair and laid on the primer in the entire house, and Carlos had even put on a first coat in the dining room. Ryan was cleaning his brushes in the kitchen sink when Franky came in.

'Hey, just wanted to say sorry for before,' Ryan said.

'Sorry for what?'

'All that bullshit I pulled. It's got nothing to do with you. I just have a lot on my mind – personal shit, you know?'

'Eh, forget about it,' Franky said, smiling.

Driving home, Ryan listened to rap on a college station at the end of the dial. An ad came on for a Ja Rule concert at the Garden next month, and Ryan decided he'd go online later and buy two tickets. Christina hated rap – unless it was Will Smith or, after she saw *8 Mile*, Eminem. She'd definitely bitch about going to the concert, but Ryan knew he could convince her. Maybe they'd make a weekend of it – rent a hotel room in the city, like they sometimes did. But in the past Christina had had to tell her dad she was going to spend the weekend at her friend Nancy's in the Village, and Ryan would make up some story for his parents, and then they'd meet in a hotel room in Midtown. This time they wouldn't have to make up any lies or worry about being seen together. Finally they could be a real couple, able to hold hands and kiss in public, do whatever the hell they wanted. Ryan would pick her up at her house, then they'd drive into the city and spend most of the weekend in bed, making love, except on Saturday night, when they'd go catch Ja.

Ryan couldn't imagine a better two days.

At Flatlands Avenue, Ryan turned right, passing South Shore High School. As usual, he tried not to look to his left as he drove by the athletic field; sometimes he drove home a different way, looping around on Glenwood Road and back to Flatlands on Seventy-ninth Street, just to avoid it. He managed not to turn his head for most of the way, but then he stopped in traffic, and he noticed the back of the car in front of him and the BROOKLYN LOVES JAKE bumper sticker.

'Shit,' he said. Then, looking away from the car in disgust, he turned toward the field and saw himself on the mound, on that raw April day, pitching against Wingate.

When the game started there'd been a small crowd, maybe twenty people, watching. Later, when word got around the school and the neighborhood that Ryan Rossetti had a perfect game going, more people showed, and by the last two innings there must've been a hundred fans there. Jake had hit two monstrous solo homers, giving Ryan all of the run support he needed. He had awesome command of his pitches, striking out practically every batter he faced. In the last inning there were two outs, and Ryan was pitching to Wingate's cleanup hitter. It was a three-two count, and Ryan didn't want to walk him and ruin the perfect game, bringing the tying run to the plate. He also knew the guy was expecting a fastball so he threw him a sharp breaking curve, which sliced the outside corner for the final out.

Ryan remembered how great it had felt being mobbed by his teammates, getting carried off the field on Jake's and the catcher's shoulders. A short article in the *Daily News* the next day said it was probably one of the best games ever pitched in Brooklyn high school history. Ryan had struck out seventeen of the twenty-one batters he had faced, and the other four outs had been on weak ground balls.

At the time Ryan had thought that the perfect game would be the beginning of a perfect career. Although he'd always been shorter and skinnier than other kids his age, he'd worked his ass off to get where he was. Most kids played baseball only in the spring and summer, then turned their attention to other sports, but Ryan was different. Ryan played some basketball and roller hockey to stay in shape, but he focused on baseball year-round. If he couldn't get into a game or find somebody to have a catch with, he'd go to Canarsie Park and self-hit a bucket of balls, or he'd go to a schoolyard with a rubber baseball and pitch to a spray-painted box against the side of the wall. In the dead of winter, while other kids were playing in the snow or sitting home watching football or basketball on TV, he'd shovel out a big area in a parking lot or a schoolyard or a dead end, and pitch to a backstop. Instead of blowing his allowance on video games and comic books, he used his money for baseball equipment and sessions in the Gateway batting range on Flatbush.

When he wasn't playing baseball, Ryan was usually thinking about it. Sometimes he lay awake at night, or stared out the window in school in a daze, imagining pitching in the World Series at Yankee Stadium. He had a perfect game going, and when he blew away the last hitter – usually Mark McGwire – with a blazing fastball, his teammates mobbed him and carried him off the field on their shoulders. He took baseball cards of Ryan Klesko, and old ones of Ryan Sandberg and Nolan Ryan, and whited-out the Kleskos, Sandbergs, and Nolans, and wrote in *Rossetti*. Then he pasted the cards onto the wall next to his bed and stared at them every night before he went to sleep.

Ryan was the superstar of his team in the Joe Torre Little League. He was a good hitter, but his pitching stood out. When he was eleven years old he had better poise on the mound than most high school kids, and he had great movement and outstanding control. But Ryan knew that if he wanted to pitch in the big leagues, his height would be a major obstacle. Most big-league pitchers were at least six feet, and most successful ones were taller than that. The tallest person in Ryan's family, his uncle Stan, was five-ten, and Ryan's father was only five-eight. Ryan's Little League coach told him that if he was serious about making it as a baseball player he should focus on playing second base or shortstop where height wouldn't be as much of a factor. Ryan was thinking about it, but then, when he was fourteen, he saw an Olympic gymnast interviewed on TV. The gymnast had some childhood disease that she'd overcome to make her dream come true, and she said she'd made it because she didn't quit; she knew in her heart what she was meant to do, and she wouldn't let

26

anything stop her. Ryan felt the same way, and decided either he'd make it as a pitcher or he wouldn't make it at all.

During junior high and all through high school, Ryan did yoga stretches and hung upside down on gravity boots, and took vitamins and minerals and drank protein drinks with brewer's yeast, bee pollen, and soya lecithin, trying desperately to increase his height. But when he was seventeen, he stood at only five-nine and three-quarters. His lack of size didn't seem to have much of an effect on his pitching, though, because he was still the most dominating high school pitcher in New York, and maybe the whole East Coast. Although he didn't throw particularly hard – his fastball peaked in the low to mid-eighties – he still had great movement on his pitches and uncanny control. Most games he walked at most one or two hitters – remarkable for a teenager. He also threw a great hook. You weren't supposed to throw curves until you were finished growing, because it could tear up your elbow, but Ryan's curveball broke so sharply, and he had such great control of it, that he couldn't resist tossing at least a few of them every time he pitched. He'd wait for the key spots in the games, when he was ahead in the count and really needed a strikeout, and then he'd let one fly. The batter would usually duck out of the batter's box, thinking the ball was heading right toward his head; then a stunned look would appear on his face as the pitch nailed the inside or outside corner and the ump called him out.

During the spring of his senior year of high school, scouts became seriously interested in Ryan. They watched every game he pitched, and there was talk that the Dodgers, Cubs, Indians, and Astros wanted to sign him. But while the scouts were very impressed with Ryan and viewed him as one of the top prospects in the country, Ryan was always 'the other guy' scouts came to see on the South Shore team. The guy they were really drooling over was Ryan's South Shore teammate, Jake Thomas.

Unlike Ryan, who'd worked his butt off to get where he was, baseball came easy to Jake. His father, Antowain Thomas, had been a star running back in high school and college, and Jake had inherited a perfect athlete's body. He never had to work out or do anything extra to improve his game. While Ryan was living and breathing baseball as a kid, Jake played other sports, and after school and on weekends he spent his time doing things that other kids did, like playing video games and going to movies and chasing girls. Jake played in Ryan's Little League, and, although Jake never showed up for practice and didn't seem to care very much about the games, the coach always put him in the cleanup spot in the order, and every time he came to the plate he seemed to hit monstrous home runs or screaming line drives.

During their sophomore year of high school, the *Canarsie Courier* did an article about Jake and Ryan, calling them 'The Dynamic Duo,' and the nickname stuck throughout their high school careers. Additional articles in the *Courier* and other local papers made a big deal about how Jake and Ryan had grown up on the same block, had played Little League baseball together, and were a sure thing to make the majors. Even *Sports Illustrated* did a small article about them, calling the two Brooklyn kids 'hugely talented,' and 'can't-miss prospects.'

Although the press made out as though Jake and Ryan had been best friends all their lives and that making it to the big leagues together would be a dream come true for both of them, this was far from the truth. Ryan and Jake had never been friends. When they were kids they played together all the time because their mothers were best friends and they lived three houses away from each other, but they'd never gotten along. There had always been a rivalry between them, a competitiveness about everything they did. It didn't matter if they were playing Wiffle ball or stickball or having a footrace on the street on the way home from school – they always tried their hardest to beat each other.

Jake and Ryan dominated in high school, breaking most of the Public Schools Athletic League's hitting and pitching records. Jake was pegged as the surefire number one pick in the nation. While the scouts were impressed with Ryan's control, toughness, and competitive spirit, they were concerned about his size. Ryan tried to convince them that he was still growing, that he'd have a growth spurt while he was in the minors, but the scouts had researched the heights of people in Ryan's family and knew the chances that Ryan would ever be taller than five-ten were slim.

It helped Ryan's cause that he was pitching so lights-out. In his senior year, his record was eleven and oh, he averaged thirteen strikeouts and less than two walks per seven innings, and he tossed five shutouts and the perfect game. Despite his lack of size, Ryan got drafted, in the fourth round, by the Cleveland Indians. At best he had hoped to be drafted in the sixth or seventh round, so he was thrilled. Meanwhile, Jake got drafted as the first overall pick in the nation. The night of the draft Ryan and Jake and most of their teammates stayed out all night partying. It seemed like the fairy-tale story of the two kids from Brooklyn was going to have a fairy-tale ending.

But things didn't work out so well – or at least, they didn't work out so well for Ryan.

While Jake tore up the minor leagues from the get-go and got on the fast track to the majors, Ryan struggled in his first season in instructional ball at Winter Haven. He got blown out in his first two starts and was demoted to the bullpen. After a few solid outings, he made it back into the rotation and pitched well the rest of the year, including tossing a two-hit shutout. The next season he was promoted to A ball at Kinston. After a couple of rocky starts, he settled down and became the team's number two starter. His career seemed to be moving along. His goal was to make it to double A the following season, or even triple A, and then make it to the majors within two to three years. He was pitching in his last game of the season, a Carolina League play-off game against Lynchburg, when it happened. The funny thing was, he never even felt it. He had just completed what was probably the best inning of his minor-league career. He had struck out the side on nine pitches and, although he wasn't being clocked at the time, he felt like he was hitting the low to mid-nineties – a good five miles per hour faster than he'd ever thrown in his life. Then he took the mound for the next inning and he heard a pop. He was pulled from the game and taken to the hospital for an MRI, and it was determined that he had torn the ulnar collateral ligament in his left elbow. The doctor explained that the injury could have happened that day, but more likely it was cumulative. Ryan realized that all of those curveballs he'd thrown in high school had finally caught up with him.

Ryan was finished for the season and had Tommy John surgery about a week later. The procedure, which replaced the ligament in his left elbow with one from his right forearm, was considered a success, and the surgeon told Ryan that, assuming everything went well with his rehabilitation, there was no reason why he couldn't pitch again next season.

But a few weeks after the surgery, Ryan knew something was wrong. He felt tingling and numbness in his pitching arm that didn't seem to be getting any better. His surgeon explained that he probably had some mild nerve impairment, which was normal, and told him to have patience, that most pitchers eventually returned to full strength. Ryan rehabbed over the winter at the Indians' spring-training complex in Winter Haven, but by March he still felt weakness in his arm. He continued to work out vigorously and pitched in a few simulated games. Although he didn't have any pain in his elbow, he had lost velocity on his fastball – velocity he couldn't afford to lose. His top heater maxed out at eighty-one miles per hour. Even worse, his bread and butter, his great control, was gone. His fastball didn't hit locations and his curveball didn't break nearly as sharply. With the loss of speed and a lack of movement on his pitches, he wasn't much more effective than your average batting-practice pitcher.

In May he was sent back up to Kinston. In his first start he got rocked, giving up nine runs in one-and-two-thirds innings. He started developing another problem – stiffness in his shoulder – and was placed on the disabled list. When he came back he made a few more equally ineffective starts, then was demoted to the bullpen. Pitching in relief, he continued to get beaten up, his ERA ballooning to over ten, and in July he was released.

Ryan returned to Brooklyn, where he worked out every day and paid out of pocket to receive treatment from a physical therapist. He hired a kid on the Canarsie High baseball team to catch for him every afternoon, but he couldn't get his speed or control back. A year went by with no change in his performance, and it finally set in that his lifelong dream of pitching in the major leagues was dead.

Ryan was crushed and disillusioned. He decided that what that gymnast had said was total bullshit. Nobody had worked harder or spent more time and energy chasing a dream than Ryan Rossetti. But in the end all those hours of dreaming and working his ass off had gotten him a big fat nothing.

Broke, living in his old room in his parents' house, Ryan had no idea what to do with the rest of his life. His mother pushed him to apply to college, but he had no interest. The only thing that had ever interested him was baseball and without that everything seemed pointless. His mother suggested that he could get a degree in physical education, and maybe coach a high school or college baseball team someday, but the idea of spending his life on a baseball field, being constantly reminded of how his dreams had gone to pot, seemed like torture.

Ryan didn't have the energy or the desire to look for a job. He spent most of his time at home, locked in his room, watching TV. He watched anything but baseball. Just the thought of baseball made him sick. He couldn't even read the sports section of the newspaper anymore without getting depressed. The worst thing was hearing or seeing anything about Jake. Whenever the Pirates played the Mets, people would huddle around the big-screen TV at the Thomases' house, like they were watching the fucking moon landing. It killed Ryan to see this guy who'd always had a take-it-or-leave-it attitude about baseball making it so big. Ryan knew that should be *him* on TV, and Jake should be the one stuck in Brooklyn.

One day Ryan went into his backyard and burned all of his old baseball cards and baseball magazines and programs and year-books and anything else he could find in his house that had anything to do with baseball and was flammable. His mother wanted him to go to a shrink, talk to somebody, but he didn't see the point. He started drinking beer and put on a gut. He also started listening to a lot of gangsta rap. He'd never paid much attention to music – especially rap – but he suddenly identified with the raw anger of rappers like Nas, 50 Cent, DMX, and Canibus.

But even rap couldn't get him out of the dumps. When he was bitter he spent his days snapping at people, or in his room alone, cranking his stereo, getting pissed off at the world. When he was depressed he couldn't get out of bed. Sometimes he got so down that he thought about killing himself. He had several plans for how to do it and might have actually gone through with one of them if it hadn't been for Christina.

Ryan had had a crush on Christina for years. They went to kindergarten through sixth grade together at the Holy Family School, and then they went to the same junior high and high school. In eighth grade Christina was so beautiful that Ryan, like most of the boys in the school, was too intimidated even to talk to her anymore, but she was also his biggest masturbation fantasy. Practically every time Ryan jerked off – which meant about three times a day – he imagined that Christina was standing in front of him in her school uniform, unbuttoning her blouse, letting her short plaid skirt fall to her knees. Before he could imagine any more he'd start coming wildly all over his stomach.

In high school, when Jake and Christina started going out, Ryan was jealous as hell. It just didn't seem right to him that an asshole like Jake should get a great girl like Christina. From the very beginning Jake treated her like dirt, always bragging to guys on the baseball team about other girls he'd fingered or fucked. Ryan wanted to tell Christina the truth about Jake, but he didn't want to upset her, and he didn't think it was his place to get involved.

After the Pirates selected Jake in the first round of the amateur draft and Jake got his five-million-dollar signing bonus, he bought Christina a huge rock and popped the question. Then he went off to play in the instructional league, and Christina stayed in Brooklyn and went to the New York City College of Technology and studied to become a dental hygienist. They saw each other a lot during the off-season, but most of the year they got together only once in a while, or just talked on the phone. Christina was upset that she couldn't see Jake more often and that he kept putting off setting a wedding date, but it was hard to leave a guy she'd been with for so long, who was making millions of dollars a year, and was bound to make even more.

One night Ryan decided that without baseball he had absolutely nothing to live for. He was about to swallow a handful of Advils and end his miserable, pointless, stupid life, when he realized that OD'ing on Advil might not kill him – it might just fry his brain, make him into a retard or something – so he decided to jump in front of a subway instead. He was in his car, driving toward the Rockaway Parkway station, imagining the great relief he'd experience as the subway wheels decapitated him, when he decided he was hungry; so he pulled over in front of Flatlands Bagels and ordered an everything with chive cream cheese and a cup of black coffee. He had no logical reason to do this, because in a few minutes he would be dead, his head severed by a speeding L train, and a bagel with cream cheese wasn't much of a last supper. Later, he decided that stopping there must have been fate, or God must have stepped in and made him do it, because he knew that if he hadn't pulled over at the bagel store he definitely would've killed himself.

He took the bagel and coffee to go and headed back toward where he'd parked, around the corner on Ninety-second Street. It was starting to rain, a stiff wind coming in off Jamaica Bay. He was thinking about how he'd stand at the far end of the platform to catch the train at its fastest so the conductor wouldn't have time to see him and brake, when he saw her. He felt like he was in one of those romantic scenes in movies, when the guy and the girl see each other in slow motion. She was walking toward him, starting to smile, those great eyes lighting up. She looked even more beautiful than the last time he'd seen her, at a party after high school graduation. As they started talking, Ryan discovered that he was as nervous around her as he had been when he was a teenager, his mouth getting dry and his heart beating out of control, as if he'd just run a forty-yard dash. When she asked him where he was going, he couldn't say, 'To jump in front of a subway,' so he said, 'Oh, no place – just back home.' She told him how great it was to see him, and about how most of her old friends from high school had moved out of Brooklyn, and suggested that they get together sometime. Ryan said that sounded great to him, and they exchanged numbers.

Ryan returned to his car, suddenly realizing that for the first time since his baseball career ended he had a reason to live.

He called Christina the next day, and they arranged to meet at the Arch Diner for dinner. Although it wasn't a real date, because Christina was still with Jake, Ryan had never had a better time with a girl. They stayed at their table for over three hours, getting refills on their coffees and talking about people they knew from the neighborhood. Christina talked a little bit about her strained relationship with Jake, which made Ryan happy, and Ryan told her about how his baseball career had ended. She offered support, telling him that he just had to find something else he loved, and Ryan looked at her, smiling, because he knew he already had.

Ryan and Christina started getting together all the time, going to diners or bars, or just watching TV at each other's houses. Ryan became as absorbed in Christina as he used to be in baseball. He couldn't stop thinking about her when they were apart, and he wanted her as badly as he used to want to be a major-league starter. Whenever she started complaining about how unhappy she was with Jake, Ryan prayed she'd announce she was going to break up with him so he could have his shot. Sometimes he watched Jake on TV, talking to a reporter after a game, acting like Mr Nice Guy, with that phony game-show-host smile, and it killed him inside that Christina was still with him. Ryan could have told Christina stories of how Jake had cheated on her and lied to her, but he didn't see the point in telling her what she already knew but just didn't want to admit. Obviously Christina liked the idea of being engaged to a famous baseball player – even if he was the world's biggest dick – and Ryan knew that if he tried to convince her to break up with Jake it would only work against him. If she was going to leave Jake, she had to do it on her own.

Ryan called her a lot, sometimes four or five times a day. He just liked to hear her voice and see what she was doing. Whenever she mentioned Jake's name or said that they'd talked on the phone, he'd get jealous as hell. The times when she flew to Pittsburgh or some other city to be with him were unbearable. Ryan would lock himself in his room and listen to rap, trying to get hold of himself, but he couldn't stop imagining Christina and Jake together.

One night Ryan was at Christina's, watching TV, and her father was out playing poker. Christina hadn't heard from Jake in over two weeks and he wasn't returning her calls, and Christina was more pissed off than Ryan had ever seen her. At some point there was a lull in the conversation, and they looked into each other's eyes. A moment later Ryan was kissing her. At first she kept her lips tightly shut and Ryan thought, *Fuck, I blew it,* and then her mouth opened and she started kissing him back in full force. A few minutes later they were in her bed, making love. It would've been perfect, like a dream come true, if it weren't for his damn control problem.

Ryan had never had trouble lasting before, but he could hold out for only about ten seconds with Christina. He thought it was first-time jitters, but the next time it happened again. Sometimes he couldn't last long enough to *start* making love to her, and he'd come while taking down her panties, unhooking her bra, or just kissing her. He thought it might have to do with her incredible beauty – maybe he was *too* attracted to her – but even thinking about disgusting things – a pile of shit in a toilet bowl, the gray hair that grew out of his father's ears, or his ninth-grade algebra teacher, Mr Finklestein – didn't help. He thought doing it outside might relax him, so he took her to Manhattan Beach one night. It was romantic under the stars, with the waves crashing, but he came all over the sand.

Ryan decided that Christina and Jake's engagement was stressing him out, affecting his ability to relax and be himself in bed. But after tonight that would all be history. Jake would be officially out of the picture, and Ryan would be able to make love to Christina the way he knew he could.

The drivers behind Ryan were honking their horns and yelling out their windows, and Ryan realized he had caused a traffic jam. He stepped on the gas a little too hard, and the car sped forward. Then, as the light turned red at the next corner, he had to hit the brake and the car jerked to a stop.

A white minivan pulled up alongside Ryan's car. The driver-side window opened and the driver, a fat guy in a suit, screamed, 'The fuck's your problem, shithead?'

Ryan, staring straight ahead, lost in thought again, didn't bother answering. Then the light turned green and he drove on.

Four

After Jake got out of the Town Car, he grabbed the pen and baseball that one of the fans was thrusting in his face, and signed the ball, continuing to smile widely with his thirty-five-thousand-dollar choppers. As he made his way slowly toward the stoop leading to his parents' house, the crowd kept cheering and chanting his name, and he tried to keep up the charm, saying 'Hey,' 'Yo,' and 'How's it goin'?' and promising that everyone would get an autograph. It was hard to see far ahead with all the flashes, but he made out his mother's proud, smiling face off to the side. As usual when he hadn't seen her in a while, he was surprised at how old she looked. There was gray in her hair, and her face looked thinner and more wrinkled than he remembered. He was still pissed off as hell at her for planning this stupid block party, but he didn't want to blow the great photo op. This shit always looked great in newspapers – the superstar baseball player who loved his mother. It would really kick up his heart-of-gold image.

He kissed his mother on both cheeks, then hugged her tightly and whispered into her ear, 'What the hell is this bullshit?'

'What's wrong?' Donna Thomas whispered back, concerned.

'I told you I wanted this weekend to be low-key,' Jake said.

'Oh, don't be a party pooper,' Donna said.

Smiling, with his arm around her waist, Jake said to the crowd, 'I'll be back in a few,' and the crowd chanted, 'Jake, Jake, Jake' as if he were Rudy, that midget football player from Notre Dame.

Jake and his mother reached the stoop where his father was waiting.

Antowain Thomas was six-four, two-eighty, but he had more fat than muscle these days and receding, close-cropped, salt-and-pepper hair. He gave Jake a once-over, looking him up and down, and Jake knew the old man was thinking, *Why you dressin' like that? Just 'cause you got it going on don't mean you gotta show it off.* Meanwhile, Antowain was wearing old brown corduroys and a yellow-and-red wool sweater he must've had for twenty years. He always wore mismatched outfits and kept his clothes until they ripped or moths ate holes into them.

Jake shook his father's hand, and then smiled and gave him an extra-warm hug because the flashes were still going off and he knew it was another prime photo op.

Walking between his parents, with his arms around their waists, Jake headed up the stoop toward the front door.

When they entered the house, Jake was ready to chew out his parents for planning this party behind his back, but the lights went on and people shouted, 'Surprise!'

The house was packed. Jake recognized a lot of his old friends and classmates, going back to elementary school at P.S. 276, and some of his parents' friends and people his father worked with. Some of his relatives were there too, including his sister, Michelle, and her accountant-dork husband, Roger.

Jake acted happy about the surprise and shook hands and gave people warm hugs. Then, with his usual charm, he gave the room a speech about how 'unbelievable' this was, and how great it was to see everybody again.

After about fifteen minutes of pouring on the bull, he took his mother off to the side and said, 'I can't believe you did this.'

'Did what?'

'I told you I wanted a mellow weekend, and this is what you do? See? And you wanna know why I don't come home to Brooklyn anymore?'

'I'm just so proud of you, that's all,' Donna said, 'And I want the whole world to know it.'

'But you can't do shit like this to me,' Jake said. 'I mean, I'm a major celebrity now. I can't just be around a crowd of people without advance notice. I need security.'

'Security from who?'

'Kooks, stalkers, psychos. God knows who the hell's out there.'

As if on cue, the crowd on the street started chanting, 'Jake, Jake, Jake . . . !'

'Just try to relax and enjoy yourself,' Donna said. 'Why don't you have a drink or something to eat?'

She tried to put her arm around his waist, but Jake avoided it.

Then his cousin Bobby came over and said, 'Hey, Jake, they're asking for you outside.'

'Yeah, I hear,' Jake said. 'Do me a favor, will ya? Tell them I'll be back outside in a few.'

'Sure,' Bobby said, and walked away.

'See? Now I'm gonna be out there all day,' Jake said to his mother. 'I should just duck out the back door and stay in a hotel.'

'Oh, don't act so spoiled,' Donna said. 'Some people would kill for what you have.'

'You don't get it,' Jake said. 'I wanted to take a break from my life this weekend. I thought I'd see you and Dad, and get to spend some time with Christina. Where is she, by the way? I didn't see her in there.'

'She had to work,' Donna said. 'But she said she's gonna be by later. Look, Jake. You don't get a lot of opportunity to see your family and friends nowadays, so why don't you just try to have some fun with it? It'll just be a few more hours; then you can relax the rest of the weekend.'

'I don't have a choice now, do I?' Jake said.

Back in the living room, Jake was cornered by his uncle Alan, Donna's brother. Alan was a thin, bald guy with thick glasses who lived in Nowheresville, Pennsylvania, somewhere out near the Delaware Water Gap, and he always bored Jake to tears. Jake wasn't sure what Alan did for a living – something to do with marketing or sales, or computers, or maybe something with drugs or chemicals – but he went on and on about his job, and Jake had to back away a couple of feet because Alan was a close-talker, and his breath smelled like sardines. Alan continued talking about whatever, and Jake smiled at other people in the room and said things like, 'Hey, how's it going?' 'Yo, what up?' and 'Hey, look at you,' and shook hands with people who were passing by and had little conversations with them, telling them how great they looked and how good it was to see them, even if he had no idea who they were. Some old guy came up to Jake and said, 'The Mets need you in right,' and Jake said, 'Let's see if they can afford me,' and the guy walked away laughing. A black guy with a shaved head came over and said, 'Great to see you again, man,' and Jake said, 'Yeah, you too, bro,' and then they shook hands and slapped each other's backs, and Jake figured the guy was somebody he went to school with, although he didn't look at all familiar.

Five minutes must have gone by, and Alan was still yapping away. Then Jake heard the words *keynote speaker* and *an hour or two tops* and he knew he had his chance to escape.

'Love to, man,' Jake said. 'I'll tell my PR guy to buzz you. If it fits into my schedge, I'm there, bro.'

Jake walked away but didn't get far before he heard a high, nasal voice say, 'Jake, wait, I wanna talk to you.'

Jake recognized the voice right away. He had known Rose-Marie Rossetti his entire life and she and his mother were still best friends.

Rose-Marie came over and gave him a kiss; she had a lot of lipstick on so he knew there was a big mark on his cheek now. Hoping he wouldn't get a zit there, Jake said, 'It's so great to see you. How's it going?'

'Everything's going great, and it's great to see you. It was such a great idea your mom had to throw this party.'

'Yeah, it was,' Jake said. 'So where's Ryan?'

Jake didn't really care where Ryan was, but he realized for the first time that he wasn't at the party.

'He'll be here later,' Rose-Marie said. 'He wouldn't miss this for the world.'

'Cool,' Jake said. 'I'd love to see him.'

Jake didn't expect Ryan's father, Rocco, to be at the party, so he didn't even ask about him. Rocco and Jake's father had hated each other for years; they'd never set foot in each other's houses, and they never would.

'So,' Rose-Marie said, 'you look handsome as always.'

'Thanks,' Jake said, pretending to be flattered. 'You look great too.' Then he took a closer look at her and saw that she was still overweight and had that dark mustache. Growing up, the kids in the neighborhood used to make fun of Rose-Marie – behind Ryan's back – walking around with their forefingers over their upper lips.

'I heard you had another great season,' Rose-Marie said.

'That's true, I did.' Jake looked beyond her, waving to his aunt Joanne.

'We're all so proud of you.'

'That's great to hear. Having support at home means a lot to me.'

'You know, I see a lot of Christina these days.'

'Yeah?'

'Ryan and her have become very friendly. He has her by the house sometimes.'

'Yeah? That's cool.' Jake smiled at the kind-of-familiar-looking woman across the room who he thought might be an old friend of his mother's but who could've been his second- or third-grade teacher.

'Christina's a great girl,' Rose-Marie said. 'When are you gonna marry her already?'

'Stay tuned.'

'Really? You set a date? Donna didn't tell me anything about that.'

'We didn't set a date *yet*.'

'Well, you better not do it too soon. I'm gonna have to go on a diet before the wedding.'

Jake rested a hand on Rose-Marie's shoulder playfully, then said, 'You kidding? You look beautiful just the way you are.'

'What a charmer. No wonder all the girls go so crazy over you.'

'Great seeing you again.' Jake started away.

'Oh, and I made my famous lasagna especially for you,' Rose-Marie called after him.

'Great,' Jake said. 'Can't wait to have some.' He smiled until Rose-Marie looked away, and then he winced. He was off carbs, and besides, he hated Rose-Marie's lasagna. It was always too dry, and something in the sauce gave him the runs. She had to be the only Italian woman in the world who couldn't cook.

His sister waved him over, and they talked for a couple of minutes. Michelle was two years older than Jake and taught economics or business or something like that at some college on Long Island that he always forgot the name of. Jake could never think of things to talk about with his sister, so he was glad when Bill and Wanda, neighbors from up the block, came over and joined the conversation. As soon as he had the chance, he slipped away.

After talking with some more neighbors and relatives, Jake finally made it to the stairwell and he didn't blow his chance for a getaway. He went up the stairs two at a time, then down the hallway to his old room, since converted to a guest room. Glancing around, he saw that the bed was covered with coats, and Steven and Ellen, some old friends of his parents', were there. Before he was seen, Jake made a U-turn and went through his parents' bedroom, into their bathroom, and locked the door.

He took out his cell and called Christina at work. A receptionist answered, and Jake said, 'Yeah, Christina, please.'

'She's with a patient. Who's calling, please?'

'Tell her it's her little itty-bitty cuddle bear.'

'Little what?' The receptionist was suspicious, as if she thought this might be a crank call.

'Itty-bitty cuddle bear,' he said slowly.

She asked him to say it a third time, and he did, spelling *itty* and *bitty*.

'Wanna leave a number?' she asked.

'It's an emergency; just put me through.'

The receptionist deep-breathed, then said, 'Hold on.'

About a minute later Christina came on and said, 'Hello.'

'Hey, baby, hey, baby, hey,' Jake said to the tune of the No Doubt song.

'What's up?' Christina asked, sounding pissed off.

'That's the welcome I get?'

'I'm really busy. What's the emergency?'

'I wanna see you.'

'Where are you?'

'Hell . . . I mean my parents' house, hiding out in the bathroom . . . Hey, you didn't know about this party bullshit, did you?'

'Kind of. Look, I really have to go. I'll see you later, okay?'

Still looking in the mirror, Jake noticed a short, very thin hair on his forehead, below his hairline.

'Shit,' he said.

'What?'

'Nothing.' He opened his parents' medicine chest to look for a pair of tweezers. 'So when am I gonna see you, baby?'

'I just told you – later. When I get off work.'

'I can't believe you're gonna keep me waiting so long.' Jake made a disgusted face, looking at his mother's diaphragm and at a bottle of wart ointment, and then he found the tweezers.

'Look, I really have to go,' Christina said.

'When do you get off?'

'Four thirty.'

'I'll come pick you up.' Jake plucked the hair.

'No,' Christina said quickly. 'I mean, I gotta go home and change and . . . I'll just see you at your house like around six.'

'Cool,' Jake said. 'I've got some good news for you.'

'What is it?'

'I'll tell you when I see you.'

'I better go.'

'Can't wait, baby.'

After plucking another stray hair from under his right eyebrow, Jake replaced the tweezers and realized he was feeling bummed. For a second he thought it had to do with the party and the whole Marianna Fernandez mess, but then he decided it was Christina. In high school they used to have great times together, talking and laughing, but now he felt like they had nothing to say to each other, and he wondered if this whole getting-married idea was a big mistake. Maybe his lawyer could talk the Fernandezes' lawyer into getting Mr Fernandez to sign that paper and settle. Or, if they couldn't settle, and they needed some distraction PR, maybe he could start dating Paris Hilton or Lindsay Lohan or an Olsen twin. Getting linked with some trendy chick would get him tons of photo ops and mentions in the gossip columns, and it would save him from having to marry a dental hygienist from Brooklyn.

Nah, Jake decided. The big sports star hooking up with the movie-star type was a cliché – marrying his high school sweetheart was the right move for his image.

Jake left the bathroom. In the hallway outside his parents' room Jake met his father, who'd just come up the stairs. Antowain Thomas gave Jake the same once-over that he'd given him outside, looking him slowly up and down, and then said, 'You spend so much time getting dressed, no wonder you got no time to return your father's damn phone calls.'

'You called me?' Jake said, taking out his cell.

'Not now,' Antowain said. 'I'm talking about during the season. I get your voice mail every time.'

'Sorry,' Jake said. 'I—'

'I called you three times right after that game against the Astros. The one you went oh for five and struck out three times.'

Jake squinted, as if trying to remember, but he knew exactly what game Antowain was talking about.

'Right,' Jake finally said. 'The pitcher had good stuff that day.'

'Bullshit,' Antowain said. 'The Pirates scored seven runs that game, knocked the starter out of the box in the fifth. It was only you looked like you was swattin' flies up there.'

'So I had a bad game.'

'You had a bad *month*. I saw your other games too. You were pulling out with your shoulder on the off-speed stuff; your timing was all messed up. That's why I called you – was gonna give you some pointers.'

'Thanks,' Jake said, 'but that's why we have a hitting instructor on the team.'

'Your damn hitting instructor didn't stop you from hitting two fifty-eight in September, one forty-two with runners in scoring position. See, I know all your stats. Your average dropped seventeen points that last month. You only had one homer, nine RBIs. That's pitiful.'

'What the hell are you talking about? I had my best season ever. I ended up at three fifty-one. I won the freakin' batting title.'

'That satisfies you?'

'Why shouldn't it satisfy me?'

'You could've hit four hundred, you set your mind to it. You got the same problems you always did – you don't stay focused; you quit when your team gets too far ahead or too far behind. Just 'cause your team's out of the race, you don't show up to play no more.'

'I don't need this shit.' Jake tried to get by, to go downstairs, but Antowain wouldn't get out of his way.

'And how 'bout all them strikeouts?' Antowain asked.

'I only struck out, what, eighty times this year?'

'That's too much for a guy who only hit twenty-two homers. How come you don't have your power numbers up? You got the height; you got the extension. You could've hit forty homers this year if you just went to the gym instead of the nightclubs. Yeah, I read the papers – I know how you been gallavantin' 'round town with the ladies.'

'The papers lie,' Jake said, thinking that he'd never heard his father use the word *gallavantin'* before.

'And how come you only had twenty-seven doubles?' Antowain went on. 'Guy with your speed should've had thirty-five at least. You don't hustle outta the box, that's why. You just stand there, watching the ball, just like you did in Little League.'

'So let me get this straight,' Jake said. 'I put up awesome numbers this year, I'm probably gonna get MVP votes, and that's still not good enough for you?'

'You're not reachin' your potential.'

'Bullshit. Nothing I do's ever good enough for you. If I had a year like Babe Ruth or Barry Bonds, you'd still find something wrong with it.'

'You can always do better.'

'See? And you wonder why I don't return your calls.'

'You just don't wanna listen,' Antowain said. 'You think you got all the answers.'

'Whatever you say,' Jake said, and he pushed by his father and went downstairs.

The party was still going strong; there seemed to be even more people in the house. Jake was scanning the room, looking for Christina, when Donna Thomas came over and said, 'Having a good time, honey?'

'When Christina comes I'm outta here,' Jake said, glancing at the NO NEW MESSAGES display on his cell phone, wondering why nobody was getting the fuck back to him.

'Come on,' Donna said. 'You have to stay until at least eight o'clock. People want to see you.'

'People always want to see me,' Jake said.

He went outside and the crowd gave him a thunderous ovation, as if he'd just slammed a game-winning homer. As he signed some kid's glove, the crowd pressed closer to him, jostling for position. It was mostly kids with their dads, but there were a lot of other adults there too, including reporters and photographers from the *Post* and the *News*. And, of course, there were also a lot of girls, screaming, 'I love you,' and 'Will you marry me?' or just screeching the way girls always did when they saw Jake. He had groupies in Pittsburgh, and in most other cities, and he had been on the cover of *Teen People* twice.

Jake posed for pictures with the girls, and most of them kissed him on the lips, blushing, as if this were the biggest thrill of their lives, which it probably was. Most of the kids asked him to sign only a ball or a baseball card, but others had brought bats, balls, gloves, cards, yearbooks, eight-by-tens, and other shit for him to sign. They told him that he was their favorite player, that they wanted to grow up to be just like him, and about ten different people said to him, 'You rock.' Although Jake remained polite, smiling for the cameras, signing everything, he knew that most, if not all, of these people were full of it. The ones wearing THOMAS 24 jerseys and Pirates caps were the biggest phonies. Seriously, how many Pittsburgh Pirates fans could there really be in Brooklyn? Most of the stuff he signed today would probably wind up on eBay.

As Jake continued signing, reporters interviewed him, and he told them how much being a role model for kids meant to him, and how flattering it was for him to get so much attention from the hometown fans. Tomorrow all of this would pay off when the articles ran about how Jake had tirelessly signed autographs for hours and how unselfish athletes like Jake Thomas were an endangered species.

A pretty, light-skinned girl who kind of looked like Halle Berry handed Jake an eight-by-ten glossy, the one where he was wearing the short-sleeved Van Heusen linen shirt, with his arm muscles bulging. Jake asked her what her name was, and she said Jasmine. While he signed the picture, *To Jasmine, love always, Jake Thomas*, Jasmine told him that she had a poster of him hanging up in her room.

'You do?' Jake said, as if this surprised him.

'Yeah, I look at it every night before I go to sleep. Can I get a picture with you?'

Jasmine squished up close to him, wedging her head under his armpit and putting an arm around his waist. She was wearing Tommy Girl, which reminded Jake of what's her name in Denver, and also that girl in San Francisco – Donna, or Debbie, or Diane, or something with a *D*.

Jasmine's friend snapped the picture, and then Jasmine said to Jake, 'If you ever wanna, like, go out and have some fun sometime, here's my number.'

Jasmine handed him a folded-up piece of paper; then she kissed him on the lips. The crowd oohed as Jasmine winked at Jake and walked away with her friend.

Someone brought out a chair for Jake to sit on, and he continued signing until the sun began to set. Then he heard a familiar voice call out his name. Even in Gap boot-cut jeans, some old brown leather bomber jacket, and kind of ratty, out-of-style long hair, Christina was a goddess. She was a natural beauty, the type of girl who could look great without trying, who could throw on dirty laundry and look awesome, and Jake remembered why he'd gone so nuts for her in high school and why she was going to become Mrs Jake Thomas. Okay, so maybe he'd have to polish her up for LA – hire her a stylist, encourage her to lose a few LBs – but then she'd be perfect.

As Jake headed toward her, the crowd parted to let him pass and he imagined all the great press the wedding would get – 'Superstar Marries High School Sweetheart,' 'Jake Thomas Weds First Love,' 'Beauty and the Best.' He'd probably be able to renegotiate his Nike and Pizza Hut contracts, get on a Wheaties box.

When Jake reached Christina he lifted her up, holding her like that for a few seconds to let the photographers get their pictures, and then put her down and laid one on her. Now he knew he was making the right decision. If he married somebody else he'd never know if the girl just wanted to be with him for his wallet and his image – because he was Jake Thomas. But Christina had known him before he was Jake Thomas, or at least before the name Jake Thomas meant anything. Of course, he'd make her sign a prenup in case the marriage fell apart, but it was still good to know that their love was real.

'I missed you so much, baby,' Jake said.

He kissed her again. She must've started smoking cigarettes, because he felt like he was sucking face with an ashtray, but for the first time all day, he was glad he came home to Brooklyn.

Five

On East Ninety-fifth Street, Ryan pulled into a spot and put the car in park, bopping his head to the beat of 'Candy Shop,' one of his favorite 50 Cent joints. He listened to the whole song; then, timing it exactly with the last lyric, he shut off the CD player.

As he walked up the sidewalk, a kid, maybe ten years old, pulled up next to him on a dirt bike and mumbled something Ryan couldn't make out, but he knew it was an offer to buy drugs. Ryan shook his head, and the kid said, 'Fuck you then,' and rode away.

Christina and her father lived in a small two-story, two-bedroom house. It could have been much nicer than where Ryan lived – there was a front yard, it was on its own lot, and there were a lot of trees on the block – but the place wasn't kept up. It needed a paint job desperately, gutters were hanging down off the roof, siding was missing, and the lawn was mostly weeds.

Ryan rang the doorbell, then heard slow, creaking footsteps. Seconds later, Al Mercado opened the door, smiling, but when he saw it was Ryan, his usual bitter expression returned.

'Oh,' he said, 'I thought it was gonna be Jake.'

Ryan entered the house, breathing in the odor of must and mildew, which probably came from the old carpeting. As always, the house was dark and the shades were drawn.

'Christina's upstairs getting dressed,' Al said, and then he settled back onto the couch and stared at the horse race on TV.

Ryan was about to say something when Al raised one hand, making the *stop* sign, and continued to stare intensely at the screen.

Ryan couldn't believe that one of Al's sperm had helped to create Christina. If Ryan didn't know Al, if he just passed him on the street, he would've figured he was some sick, homeless nutcase. Al was bald except for some gray hairs he combed from the back of his head over the top. He had a scraggly gray beard, wore old, dirty clothes, and he usually looked filthy, like he didn't bathe. The funny thing was, Al was a bright guy. For years he taught social studies at Hudde Junior High. Christina claimed her father was different back then – he took care of himself and dressed better; you could actually sit down and have a conversation with him. Then Christina's mother died when Christina was nine, and Al had a breakdown. It got so bad he had to take a leave of absence from work, and Christina's aunt Mary had to come live with them for a while because Al was so depressed. Al went back to teaching the next year, but he still hadn't recovered. Then, as he was leaving school one day, crossing Nostrand Avenue, he stepped into a pothole, fell, and broke his hip. Even though he made a full recovery, he got one of those crook lawyers to claim that he was experiencing pain and emotional distress and worked out a hundred-thousand-dollar settlement from the city. Then he got a doctor to say that teaching was impossible in his condition, and he went on disability. Instead of putting away money for the future, he pissed it away on poker, horses, and weekend junkets to Atlantic City. Within a couple of years all of the money from the settlement was gone, and now he was living on his monthly checks and the money Christina brought in. Meanwhile he spent just about every day parked on the living room couch, watching the racing channel and gambling on his OTB phone account. Ryan hated the way Al used Christina. He was always hassling her to set a wedding date with Jake, probably because he figured that Jake would give him more money to blow at the track. After tonight, the old man was going to be in for a pretty big shocker.

Ryan stood to the side, near the staircase, waiting for Christina as the race continued. Al didn't say a word, still focused on the TV, and then suddenly stood up and started screaming at the top of his lungs, 'Stick 'im! Stick 'im! Stick 'im! Come on, stick 'im! Stick 'im, you fuckin' munchkin! Stick 'im!' Then Al just stared at the screen again, until the announcer said, 'Divine Lady holds on by a head!' and Al screamed, 'Goddamn piece of shit! What do you think the whip's for, to put up your fucking ass? The whole fuckin' race he doesn't lift the fuckin' whip. Fucking cocksucker!'

'Did you win?' Ryan said, just to bust balls.

Of course Al didn't catch on to what Ryan was doing, and said,

'That horse gets up I get the exacta *and* the double. Was paying a hundred and change. Fuckin' munchkin can't use his goddamn whip. Un-fuckin'-believable.'

Al settled back down onto the couch, muttering curses.

'Ryan!' Christina called from upstairs. 'That you?'

'Yeah,' Ryan said.

'Come on up!'

Ryan went up the narrow, creaky staircase and met Christina on the landing. Her hair was wet and she had no makeup on, but she still looked great in jeans and a little light blue top – the same blue as her eyes. Over the past few years she'd gained some weight, maybe fifteen, twenty pounds, mostly below her waist, but Ryan thought that the extra weight made her even sexier. She had wavy light brown hair that used to be shorter, but she'd grown it out, and now it went halfway down her back. As Ryan approached her his stomach muscles tightened, his back heated up, and his palms began to sweat. He didn't feel as awkward as he did as a kid, when he couldn't even speak to her, but he still felt nervous.

Ryan smiled, then kissed her. As usual, it felt great to hold her close and to smell her hair, which today smelled like a strawberry lollipop. He let go of her and ran his hands down her back, settling them on her great J.Lo-esque ass.

Ryan pulled away slightly, staying maybe an inch away from her face. Looking into her eyes that seemed to have little lights in them, especially when he and Christina looked at each other, he whispered, 'I missed you so much.'

'Me too,' she whispered back.

They continued making out; then Christina pulled Ryan along the hallway into her room and closed the door behind them. The stereo in her room was on – Enrique Iglesias – and Ryan pushed Christina back against the door and started kissing her neck, his hands moving up under her top, then over her small, firm breasts. She had a bra on, but he could still feel her nipples against his palms. She moaned softly as he kissed the spot that drove her crazy, where her neck met her jaw near her ear. He continued to caress her breasts with his left hand while his right moved to her waist and unbuttoned her jeans. Then, as he pulled down the zipper, Christina said, 'We can't.'

'Why not?' Ryan said, grinding his hips up against hers as he continued kissing her neck with his half-open mouth.

'Not with him right downstairs,' Christina said.

'We'll be quiet,' Ryan said. 'I promise.'

He finished unzipping her jeans and moved his hand against her panties. She let him touch her for several seconds, then pushed him back slightly. 'We can't – seriously.'

Ryan backed away and Christina zipped her jeans.

'I'm sorry,' Christina said. 'I didn't mean to get you all worked up, but you know how I get. I just can't do it with him in the house.'

'Come on,' Ryan said. 'His eyes are Krazy Glued to that TV. You could set the house on fire and he wouldn't know what was going on.'

'Sorry, Ry, I really am, but I just can't.' Christina sat down at the makeup table and started putting on her blush.

'I'm so sick of all this sneaking-around bullshit,' Ryan said.

'You think I'm not?'

'So what're we gonna do about it?'

'What do you mean? I'm breaking up with Jake tonight.'

'So when can we start acting like a normal couple?'

'Right away . . . I guess.'

Ryan watched Christina fake-smile to push up her cheeks while she put on her blush. Now Iglesias was singing 'I Have Always Loved You.'

'You mean that?' Ryan asked.

'Mean what?'

'That after tonight we can be a normal couple.'

'Of course I mean it.'

'So after tonight we don't have to have car sex anymore? We can start doing it in our beds whenever we want, even when our parents are home?'

Still facing the mirror, Christina opened a lipstick. 'Well, not after *tonight*.'

'Then when?'

'Soon.'

'How soon?'

Christina pursed her lips, finished applying her lipstick, then said, 'I don't know, okay?'

'Come on, I want a date,' Ryan said. 'A week, two weeks, a month, six months, a year . . . ?'

'After we get engaged.'

'So let's get engaged tonight.'

Remaining deadpan, Christina looked at Ryan's reflection. 'You're joking, right?'

'Why would I joke about that? You don't need a ring to get engaged. I'll give you something else – my school ring or something. You can wear that till I get you a diamond. Come on, let's just do it. That's what you want, right?'

'Of couse that's what I want.' She stood up and went toward her dresser. She opened a jewelry box and took out a necklace.

'So then what's the problem?'

'There's no problem,' she said. 'I just don't wanna rush right into any . . . I mean, wouldn't it be more romantic if we waited – you know, built up to it?'

'I'm not talking about getting married – I'm just talking about getting engaged.'

'Let's not talk about this now.'

'Why not?'

'Because I'm nervous enough already about tonight.'

'Why does talking about getting engaged make you nervous?'

'Can you just stop it?'

'Stop what?'

'Look, we can't get engaged that fast, all right? I mean, how's that gonna look?'

'Look to who? To Jake?'

'To everybody.'

'So you're not even gonna tell him about us tonight?'

'No. I mean, I don't know. I mean, maybe, but—'

'But what?'

Christina went through her jewelry box again and took out a pair of silver hoop earrings.

'I'll see how it goes.' She held up the earrings to her lobes, looking in the mirror. 'I mean, we don't want to cause a whole big scene, right?'

'He's gonna find out about us eventually,' Ryan said. 'Why not just get it over with?'

Christina made a face and put the earrings back, and then took out the pair of diamond studs that Jake had bought her.

'Because,' Christina said. 'I mean, what's the point in making him think that . . . or get angry about . . . I mean, I don't want to hurt him – I just want to break up with him.'

Christina put in the first stud.

'You have to wear those earrings, huh?'

Christina looked in the mirror.

'What difference does it make which ones I wear?'

'None, I guess.'

'Fine.' She removed the stud, then put the pair away and took out the hoop earrings. 'You don't want me to wear them, I won't wear them.'

'You can wear whatever you want.'

'Can you stop getting so fucking angry at me?'

Ryan shook his head and went toward the window, which looked out on the street. That drug-dealer kid was still riding up the block and back on his bicycle.

'Look, I'm sorry, all right?' Christina said. 'I'm just scared, that's all. I mean, this isn't easy for me. Me and Jake've been together a long time and . . . Can't we just stop fighting?'

Ryan remained facing the window. The song had ended, and for a few seconds the only noise was the faint sound of Al screaming at the TV downstairs. Then the next song came on.

'Please,' Christina said.

Ryan didn't budge.

'Pretty please. With sugar on top . . . and cherries . . . and pickles . . . and anchovies . . . and peanut butter . . . and broccoli . . .'

Ryan finally turned around, smiling. Christina came over to him and kissed him softly on the lips.

'I love you so much,' she said, 'and I can't wait till we can be together all the time.'

'If you really love me,' Ryan said, 'will you turn this shit off?'

Christina laughed, then went over to her dresser and picked up a hairbrush. She held it up to her mouth like a mike and started singing along.

'Mercy, mercy,' Ryan said, playfully trying to grab the brush.

Christina sang some more. Laughing, Ryan finally grabbed her hand and pulled her back toward him. He kissed her a few times, running his fingers through her slightly damp hair. He pulled back and said, 'I'm the one who should be sorry, taking everything out on you. It's just all this Jake-coming-home shit – it's driving me crazy.'

'Yeah, I know what you mean.'

'Today at work nobody would shut up about it. And all the guys – they want to bring in crap for Jake to autograph.'

'Dr Hoffman wants me to get him an autographed bat. And my cousin Brenda called last night – her daughter wants a signed picture of Jake to bring into show-and-tell.'

'You know what's gonna be great?' Ryan said. 'A few days from now we'll be able to walk around, go to the supermarket or the deli or wherever, and we won't have to hear his name every two seconds.'

Glancing toward the mirror, Christina said, 'You messed up my lipstick.'

Ryan pulled her back toward him and started kissing her again, harder, and then he moved his right hund swiftly down along her stomach, then under her jeans.

'Down, boy,' Christina whispered.

'Come on,' Ryan said, 'just this one time.'

'We shouldn't.'

'Please.'

Christina was moaning, breathing faster. Then she said, 'You promise you won't make any noise?'

Ryan guided her back down toward the bed and unzipped her jeans. As she pulled them, and then her panties down, he took his sneakers off quickly, then his jeans and boxers. Christina lay on the bed with her legs apart, waiting for him. Ryan knelt down over her, suddenly feeling too good. He forced himself to think about a big pile of shit, his father's ear hair, rats crawling through sewers, Osama bin Laden, roadkill, but it was hopeless. He ejaculated in several weak spurts onto the bedspread.

'Damn it.'

'It's okay.'

'Fuck. It's just that we were trying to do it so fast and—'

'Don't worry about it.'

'Shit.'

'Stop it.' Christina moved a few strands of hair away from Ryan's eyes. 'We would've had to be too quiet anyway.'

'We always have to be fuckin' quiet.'

Christina kissed Ryan; then he started going down on her. Christina leaned back, letting Ryan go on for several seconds, and then she said, 'You don't have to do that.'

Ryan looked up at her and said, 'I want to.'

He started again, trying his hardest to get her off.

Christina shifted back away and said, 'We should really just get going.'

'You sure?'

'I can't now anyway.'

'I'm really sorry, Chrissy. I promise later I'll be able to—'

'It's okay – really. Just hand me a tissue, will you?'

When Ryan and Christina went downstairs, Al was still gripped, watching the racing channel.

'Bye, Daddy.'

Distracted, sneering at the TV, Al didn't answer for a few seconds. Then he said, 'What?'

'Ryan's taking me over to Jake's.'

'Oh, right,' Al said, 'the party for him.'

'Yeah, you should go. Ryan's mother made her great lasagna, and there's gonna be other great food and music and—'

'Can't make it,' Al said, his gaze shifting back toward the TV.

Christina leaned over and kissed her father on the cheek.

'Don't wait up for me, Daddy.'

Christina and Ryan were heading toward the door when Al said, 'Hey, Ryan.'

'Yeah?' Ryan stopped but didn't look back.

'You still paint houses, right?'

'Right,' Ryan said extending the *I* sound, as if saying, *Yeah, and what's it to you?*

'My cousin Arnie's finishing his basement and's lookin' for a painter,' Al said. 'You interested?'

'Tell him to call my boss,' Ryan said.

'What's the name of your company again?'

'Pay-Less Painting. It's in the book.'

Ryan and Christina left the house. The late-afternoon sun was bright in Ryan's eyes, making him squint.

'Where're you parked?'

Ryan jutted his chin toward his car up the block, but didn't say anything.

Ryan went around to the driver-side door and let himself in. Christina opened her own door, making a face because Ryan hadn't let her into the car first.

'Sorry,' Ryan said.

Christina sat down, still looking pissed off, as Ryan started the engine. They pulled out of the spot and drove up the block in silence.

'What's wrong?' Christina asked.

'Nothing.' Ryan turned onto Avenue M.

After a few more seconds o silence, Christina said, 'You're not still upset about—'

'No,' Ryan said quickly.

'You're sure? Because I swear it really doesn't bother me. I mean, I know how much pressure you're under and—'

'I'm just sick of your fucking father dissing me all the time.'

'He wasn't dissing you.'

'See? That's why I can't tell you what's wrong. 'Cause you always get like this – defending him.'

'But he didn't do anything wrong.'

'How about all that housepainter bullshit? He disses me like that every time I'm over your house.'

'He was just offering you business.'

'Bullshit. He knows I don't own the fucking company. He was just looking for a chance to get a couple licks in.'

'Licks in about what?'

'My baseball career falling apart. He thinks it's a big joke, saying, "You still paint houses, right?" with that big smirk on his face.'

'I don't think you're being fair.'

Ryan rolled his eyes, then shook his hear and bit down on his lower lip in frustration. He should've known better than to talk negatively about Al to Christina. Although the guy was a lazy bum and was obviously using Christina for the money she pitched in for bills and to clean up after him like a fucking maid, she couldn't see any fault in him.

Ryan slowed at the stop sign. A bunch of kids in do-rags passed in front of the car. One of the kids glared through the windshield at Ryan and Christina. Then he said something to his friends and all of the kids laughed, looking back toward Ryan's car.

Ryan hit the gas and drove on.

'I'm so sick of this,' Christina said.

'You started it, not me,' Ryan said.

'I mean all these gangs – not being able to go out at night. You know a lady on my block was raped in her own house last week? I didn't wanna tell you about it 'cause I was afraid you might get worried about me. It was one of those home invasions. Two guys just broke into the house, raped her, and stole everything. It's so scary – I can't wait to get out of Canarsie.'

'You can't run away,' Ryan said.

'What're you talking about?' Christina said. 'You said you wanna move to Long Island or Jersey. . . . Now you wanna stay?'

'I didn't say that.'

'Then what're you saying?'

'I didn't say anything.'

Ryan hit the brake at another stop sign and Christina, not wearing her seat belt, jerked forward. She gave Ryan a look, then put on her belt as Ryan drove on.

'You know, you don't have to be ashamed of what you do,' Christina said.

'Who said I'm ashamed?'

'I didn't mean *ashamed* I just . . . I mean, it's not your fault that you can't play baseball anymore. A lot of people can't make it in sports. You just have to move on – find something else you like doing. . . . Besides, it's not like you're gonna be working for Pay-Less forever. You're gonna start your own business soon, right?'

Ryan didn't like the sneaky tone in Christina's voice, as if she were really saying, *You're not gonna be making ten dollars an hour forever, right?*

'As soon as I can,' Ryan said.

'"Cause I've been thinking,' Christina said. 'You know how I still have Jake's engagement ring, right?'

'Yeah.'

'I was just wondering if like, maybe I could, like, you know, sell it. He must've paid a fortune for it, and it's in perfect condition. I could probably get twenty or thirty thousand for it, and then I can give you some money to, like, I don't know, get your business started.'

'Why would you want to do that?'

'Why wouldn't I?

'Look, you wanna sell the ring, sell it,' Ryan said. 'I don't need handouts.'

'I'm just trying to help you.'

'I don't need your help, all right?'

'Listen to you screaming at me,' Christina said. 'I don't know what the hell's wrong with you.'

Christina grabbed the pack of Camels from on top of the dashboard and took out a cigarette and the lighter that Ryan had stuffed inside. She lit up and took a long drag, looking away.

'Shit,' Ryan said. He'd overshot the turnoff onto East Eighty-second Street.

'So we'll go around the corner,' Christina said. 'What's the big deal?'

Ryan drove around the corner, and Christina continued to smoke, opening the window slightly to let the fumes out.

'Look,' Ryan said, 'we both know I'm never gonna have the Jake Thomas kind of money. I'm not gonna be able to buy you the big house and fancy jewelry, so if that's what's important to you—'

'That's not what's important.'

'But if it is, I just want you to know I'm not gonna hold you back. I mean, I want you to be happy, so if you change your mind and wanna stay with him—'

'How can you say that? I don't care about the money. I want you.'

'You mean that?'

'Of course I do.'

They turned off Flatlands onto Eighty-first Street. Ryan steered the car around the police barricades, which were partially blocking the street, but he couldn't get much farther. There must have been a hundred people near that goddamn welcome-home banner.

Ryan double-parked and cut the engine.

'I can do this,' Christina said, trying to psyche herself up.

'You're gonna kick ass,' Ryan said. 'I promise.'

Christina took a last long drag on her cigarette, then tossed it out the window. Ryan leaned over to kiss her, but she didn't move at all in his direction, and he knew it was because Jake was close by. This got Ryan a little pissed off, but he did his best not to show it. He rested a hand on her thigh and squeezed it gently, and then they got out of the car.

As they approached the center of the party, Ryan recognized people from the block and the neighborhood, but there were a lot of strangers too. Fans had come with bats, balls, gloves, and other memorabilia that they hoped to get signed, and everyone seemed to be having a great time, eating from plates of plantains, meat patties, Ryan's mom's lasagna, and hot dogs and hamburgers, and drinking soda and keg-beer. Beyoncé's 'Naughty Girl' was blasting from the big speakers that Jamal, a guy who lived across the street from Ryan, had set up. Ryan nodded at Jamal as he passed, and Jamal acknowledged Ryan by pumping a fist in his direction.

'Let's go back,' Christina said nervously.

'Don't worry, it'll be okay,' Ryan said.

The crowd got denser and louder as they approached the Thomases' house. As they wove around people, Ryan kept saying, 'Coming through, I live here, coming through.' Finally, through a space in the crowd, Ryan spotted Jake holding court, posing for a picture next to some teenage girl. *Jesus, what an asshole*, Ryan thought. Who did he think he was with those sunglasses and all of that jewelry and that expensive suit? Jake was smiling in his usual phony way, showing off those stupid fake white choppers.

'Does he see us?' Christina asked.

She was a few inches shorter than Ryan and couldn't see Jake yet.

'Nah,' Ryan said.

Christina and Ryan continued to make their way through the crowd, and Ryan was getting that same sick, angry, jealous feeling he always got when he saw Jake. Ryan knew it should be *him* standing there, signing autographs for the kids, getting all that attention.

Christina called out Jake's name, and Jake must have heard, because he smiled widely and started heading in her direction. Jake didn't make eye contact with Ryan, acting like Ryan was invisible. Then, when Jake reached Christina, he wrapped his arms around her and pulled her toward him, lifting her off the ground slightly. When her feet were back down, his hands still on her hips, he leaned in and kissed her on the lips. It didn't surprise Ryan that Jake went to kiss Christina – she was still his fiancée, after all. What surprised Ryan was the way Christina was kissing him back, with her mouth open and her hands wrapped around his waist.

Six

All the cameras going off and the people whistling and cheering must have been making Christina uncomfortable or something, because when Jake tried to kiss her again she put her hands against his chest, pushing him away, and said, 'Okay, that's enough,' sounding all pissed off.

'It's okay, baby, don't worry,' Jake said, and he said to the photographers, 'Guys, how 'bout cooling it for a while, huh?'

Jake put an arm around Christina and kissed her gently on the cheek. People in the crowd whistled, and one guy shouted, 'Go for it, Jake!' and some kid yelled, 'Kiss her again! Kiss her again!'

Christina said to Jake, 'Can't we go inside?'

'Sure, baby, sure,' Jake said, and he took Christina's hand and led her back toward the front of his parents' house.

The crowd moaned.

'Sorry, I have to go inside for a few, but I'll be right back!' Jake announced. 'And don't worry – everybody who wants an autograph is gonna get an autograph – I guarantee it!'

The crowd cheered. Then, as Jake and Christina entered the house together, the people inside started applauding and cheering. Flashes from cameras went off, and Jake was smiling, hamming it up, but Christina still seemed pissed off.

She squeezed Jake's hand and whispered, 'Can't we go somewhere?'

'No *problema*,' Jake said. 'Lemme just get my coat and my bags.'

'No, I mean upstairs,' Christina said, 'or someplace we could be alone.'

'Cool,' Jake said, smiling, figuring that Christina wanted to have sex. She used to be kinda shy that way, never wanting to do it in public or when other people were around but hey, maybe she'd changed. The only problem was that they had no place to go. The guest room had been converted into a coatroom for the party, and doing it in his parents' bed would be a major downer.

'You wanna go upstairs?' Christina asked.

'Why not?' Jake said, thinking they could do it in a closet.

Christina walked ahead of Jake toward the staircase allowing him to get his first good look at her ass. It used to be about as narrow as her hips, and had a cute little heart shape, but now there was flab on the sides and the heart shape was gone. It was still a nice ass, an above-average ass, but once they got married he'd have to watch it closely.

When Christina reached the stairs, Jake's mother rushed over and grabbed her hand.

'Christina, wait, I have something for you,' Donna Thomas said.

'It's really not a good time, Ma,' Jake said.

'Don't worry; you can have her back,' Donna said. 'I just want to give her her birthday present.' Then she said to Christina, 'I called you on your birthday last month and left a message with your father. Did you get it?'

'Yeah, I did,' Christina said. 'Sorry I didn't call you back, but I've been busy with work and everything and—'

'That's okay, I understand,' Donna said. 'Come on upstairs for a sec and I'll give you your present.'

'Ma, can't you do that later?'

'We'll be right back.'

Donna and Christina went upstairs. Jake looked away, cursing to himself; then he saw Ryan standing a few feet away.

Jake's first thought when he looked at Ryan was, *Man, what a loser.* Jake hadn't talked to Ryan much since high school, and had seen him maybe once or twice since the Indians had cut him. He heard about him all the time, though, through his mother, who was best friends with Ryan's mother. So Jake knew that Ryan had had some kind of breakdown after his baseball career fell apart, then got some kind of job painting houses. His life sounded depressing as hell, and the guy looked like hell too, like he'd been in a war or something. And what was the deal with the do-rag, the T-Mac jersey, the gang-style jeans, and the LeBrons?

'Hey, buddy, where did you come from?' Jake asked, smiling pleasantly as if he were happy to see Ryan.

'Outside,' Ryan said, not smiling at all.

Ryan and Jake did the handshake they'd made up as kids – tapping the sides of their raised fists twice, then, with the same hands, clenching the tips of each other's fingers and pulling their hands away simultaneously, making a loud snapping sound – but it didn't help break the ice.

For a few seconds afterward Ryan didn't say anything. He just stared at Jake in a weird, lost way.

'So how you been, bro?' Jake asked.

'All right,' Ryan said.

'That's cool, man. That's real cool.'

Jake didn't know what else to say. He felt like Ryan was jealous of him and his baseball career and that he had to walk on eggshells, make sure he didn't say anything that might rub Ryan the wrong way and make him feel bad about his life and dreams going to shit. Meanwhile, Ryan had never had any real talent. Yeah, he practiced hard when he was growing up, had big dreams, but he was deluded, believing a guy his size could make it to the major leagues, as a pitcher no less. Jake must've told him hundreds of times to give it up, to learn another position, maybe second base or even shortstop, if he wanted to have a shot at making it in the show, but Ryan wouldn't listen. Then, when Ryan blew out his elbow, he used that as an excuse, acting as if his 'great career' had been cut short. But the fact was, he would have hit a dead end sooner or later. He had mediocre stuff – bottom line, end of story. His fastball didn't have any pop, and his curveball broke the same way every time. Just because he could get high school kids to back out of the box and duck their heads didn't mean the pros would go for that junk. If he didn't fuck up his arm, he would've been cut in another year or two anyway. Best-case scenario, he would've made it to triple A for a game or two, and then he would've been back in Brooklyn, living with his parents and painting houses.

'So you came here straight from work, huh?' Jake asked.

'Yeah,' Ryan said. 'Kind of. How'd you know that?'

'You got some paint . . .' Jake pointed to Ryan's goatee.

'Oh.' Ryan picked out the clump of paint with his thumb and forefinger and flicked it away. 'I guess I do.'

Ryan still had that weird, shell-shocked thing going on, and Jake thought, *Man, what a fuckin' freak show.*

'So how's all that going – the painting houses?' Jake asked.

'Pretty good,' Ryan said. 'I'm starting my own business.'

'Cool. That's real cool, bro.'

Jake looked over his shoulder, hoping to see Christina coming down the stairs to save him, but she wasn't there.

'So how long you in town for?' Ryan asked.

'Just a couple days,' Jake said. 'I was hoping to have a low-key weekend, you know, chill with Christina, but then they hit me with all this party shit. But I just gotta take the good with the bad, I guess, know what I mean?'

'Yeah, well maybe I'll stop by tomorrow,' Ryan said. 'I mean, if you're around. I promised some guys at work I'd have you autograph some stuff for them.'

'*No problema*, bro,' Jake said; then he turned again and saw his mother and Christina coming down the stairs. Christina was wearing some ridiculous-looking pink sweater with blue and red flowers around the neckline.

'So,' Donna Thomas said. 'What do you think?'

Seeing how uncomfortable Christina looked in the sweater, with her arms stiff at her sides, almost made Jake crack up. Managing to keep a straight face, he said, 'Wow, Ma. That looks really beautiful. Did you knit that yourself?'

'I certainly did,' Donna said, and she put an arm around Christina's waist as she kissed Jake on the cheek. Then she said to Ryan, 'Aren't they the best-looking couple in the world?'

Ryan, staring in that lost, psycho way, didn't say anything.

'Well, excuse us,' Jake said, as he took Christina's hand.

'Where you going?' Ryan said.

'We're just gonna have a little talk,' Jake said, swirling his tongue against his inner cheek for a moment, making sure that Ryan, but not his mother, saw it.

'You're not going anywhere,' Ryan said.

'What're you talking about?' Jake said.

'It's okay,' Christina said to Ryan.

'No, it's not okay,' Ryan said.

'What the hell's your problem?' Jake said.

'Why don't you come with me?' Donna said to Christina. 'I

want to show Rose-Marie the sweater. She helped me pick out the wool.'

'Come on, Ma,' Jake said.

'It'll take two seconds,' Donna said.

'I'll be right back,' Christina said to Jake, then followed Donna into the living room.

Ryan turned and watched as Christina modeled the sweater for his mother.

'What the hell's wrong with you, man?' Jake said to Ryan.

Ryan, still watching Christina, didn't answer.

'Seriously, that shit was very uncool,' Jake said. 'I mean, I understand how hard it all must be for you – I mean, seeing me on *Sports Center* every night – but I've had a long, shitty day and I really need to get my pipes cleaned.'

Ryan turned back toward Jake and shouted, 'Shut the fuck up!'

'Whoa, dude,' Jake said. The house was noisy, with people talking and music playing inside and outside, but Jake's brother-in-law, Roger, who was standing several feet away, must've heard what Ryan said, because he was looking over.

'Talking about Christina like she's some ho,' Ryan said. 'Fuck you. Christina's a beautiful woman and she deserves to be treated with respect.'

'All right, bro, relax, relax,' Jake said, fake-smiling, not wanting to cause any more of a scene, making out like he and Ryan were just two old friends kidding around. Then, when Roger stopped looking over, Jake said to Ryan, 'You better chill with this shit, man.'

Ryan had turned back toward Christina, who was looking back at Ryan and Jake.

'Oh, I get it,' Jake said. 'You got the hots for my girl.'

The way Ryan was glaring, without blinking, Jake knew he'd hit on it.

'See? You can't slip one past J.T. I remember how you used to get in high school, when me and Christina started going out. We'd be at a party or whatever and you'd just start staring at her with your mouth hanging open, like you were catching flies. You got good taste, bro – I'll give you that much.'

Jake laughed, but Ryan's expression didn't change.

'Look, if you're just hard up and wanna get some why don't you

chill and come outside with me later?' Jake said. 'I'll get you a
hot-looking girl on your arm in two minutes. That's if you don't
mind taking my sloppy seconds.'

'You're such a fucking asshole,' Ryan said, and he walked away.

Jake shook his head, deciding that Ryan was too far gone for
help, then went into the living room toward Christina, his
mother, and Rose-Marie Rossetti. A kid he didn't know cut him
off and asked him to sign a Pirates batting helmet and a Topps
rookie card; then his cousin Sheila came over and he had to
bullshit with her for a couple of minutes. After posing for a
picture with his parents' friends the Petersons, and signing some
more shit, he finally reached Christina. He took her aside and
said, 'Let's just get the hell out of here, baby.'

'Why?' Christina said. 'I mean weren't we gonna go upstairs
and talk?'

'There's too many people here. I can't walk five feet without
getting stopped.'

'Where do you want to go?'

'Anywhere to be with you, baby.'

'How about we go outside?' Christina said.

'How about we go to the city? I'll get us a suite at the Plaza and
a reservation at Nobu. Don't worry – we'll stop at Barneys and
buy you some new clothes to change into.'

'No. I mean why can't we just go to the backyard or the
basement or something?'

' 'Cause I wanna be alone with you.' Jake held her hand and
tickled the underside of her wrist with his middle finger and
pointer.

Christina moved her hand away and said, 'Jake, we really need
to talk.'

'So what're we waiting for? Let's go.'

'Why can't we talk right here? Go into a room or something,
or—'

'How about we go back to your place?'

'My place?'

'Yeah. I mean, it'll be nice and quiet there, right?'

Christina looked over toward a table where Ryan was standing,
pouring a glass of soda.

'All right. I mean, maybe it is a good idea to get out of here . . .
I'll be right back.'

'Where're you going?'

'My jacket's upstairs.'

'You can get it later. Besides, you got that beautiful sweater to
keep you warm.'

Jake smiled, but Christina didn't seem to think it was funny.

'I'll be right back,' she said, and hurried toward the staircase.

Jake was immediately cornered by his cousin John, some kid
with bad acne, and a tall, bearded guy who looked kind of familiar
and might have been a second or third cousin on his mother's
side. As he signed a Pirates yearbook, some baseball cards, and a
cap for them, they asked: 'Do you know Carlos Beltran?' 'Who's
the best pitcher in baseball?' 'What's the longest home run you
ever hit?' Jake tried to answer all their questions as patiently and
as politely as possible, but he was distracted, suddenly thinking
about Patti, that United stewardess.

'What?' Jake asked, lost.

'Who'd you rather play for, the Yanks or the Mets?' the kid
with the acne asked – for, Jake figured, the second or third time.

'Yankees,' Jake said. 'I mean, with all that tradition, it would be
a dream come true.'

Jake turned his head and saw Christina coming down the stairs,
wearing her jacket and holding the sweater over one arm. He felt
like running out the door and going right to Patti's place, but he
managed to control himself. It was only one weekend for
chrissakes, and after he set the wedding date and left Brooklyn
he'd be a free man again.

Before Christina could reach Jake, Ryan came over and cut her
off. Ryan seemed very angry, moving his arms a lot as he talked,
and then Christina started talking and Ryan had his arms crossed
in front of his chest. Jake had no idea why they would have so
much to say to each other.

Finally Christina left Ryan standing there, looking like a
pathetic loser, and came over to Jake.

'Ready?' Jake asked.

'How're we gonna leave?'

'Out the back.'

'What about all your fans outside?'

'Fuck 'em.'

Jake took Christina by the hand and led her toward the kitchen. Jake had to have short conversations along the way, but they kept moving; then Jake pushed open the swinging door. Shit, there were people packed into the kitchen too. What did his mother do, invite all of Brooklyn to this party? People shook Jake's hand and Jake smiled, not stopping, continuing to lead Christina along toward the back door.

Finally they made it outside. Jake led Christina down the porch steps, across the patio.

'Where're we going?' Christina asked.

'Just come on.'

They went across the lawn to a row of thick bushes.

Jake parted the bushes and said, 'Cool, it's still there.'

'What's still there?'

'Secret passageway. When I was a kid we used to make it all the way to Avenue J, going through backyards.' He stood aside to let Christina pass, then said, 'Go ahead.'

'Why do we—'

'Just go – quick. Before anybody sees us.'

Christina hesitated, looking back toward the house, then bent down and went through the bushes. Jake followed her through the hole in the fence into the backyard of the house behind Jake's parents'. As Christina brushed dirt off the bottoms of her jeans, Jake said, 'Come on,' and led her toward the fence at the end of the lawn, adjacent to the next backyard.

'I can't climb fences,' Christina said.

'I'll help you.' Jake crouched. 'Get on my back.'

Christina climbed on. She was heavier than Jake expected, and he realized this wasn't such a bright idea – if he pulled a muscle or something it could throw him out of whack for next season, his contract year, and it could wind up costing him millions. She managed to hoist herself up, and Jake stood to help her over, noticing her ass again.

'I can't make it,' she said.

'Yes, you can.'

She struggled, getting the top of her body over, and then Jake helped with her legs and ass, finally getting her all the way over and on the other side. Jake climbed it easily.

'I'm not climbing or crawling anywhere else,' Christina said.

'We only have to go through a few more backyards,' Jake said, and then decided that right here, behind these bushes, would be a great spot for a quickie. He kissed Christina hard, running his fingers through her unconditioned hair.

With his lips pressed against hers, Christina managed to say, 'What're you doing?'

Jake kissed her even harder. He pushed her back against the fence and undid the button and zipper to his pants, freeing willy.

'Stop it,' Christina said, trying to push him away.

'All right, chill, chill,' Jake said.

'What's the matter with you?' Christina was fixing her hair. 'You're like an animal.'

'It's been so long, baby,' Jake said. 'I just thought it would be nice to—'

'Nice? You were attacking me.'

'God, you look beautiful.' Jake reached out and held her cheeks, as if about to kiss her, then guided her head downward.

Christina pushed him back again, then said, 'Are you out of your fucking mind?'

'Wait, I get it – you don't feel comfortable doing it outside.' Jake reached into his jacket pocket and took out a little pill container. 'How about some E? It's great shit – I guarantee it'll loosen you up.'

Christina started to walk away, and Jake reached out and grabbed her hand. She tried to yank her arm free, but Jake wouldn't let go.

'Sorry, baby, sorry,' Jake said. 'It's just you're so beautiful, and I haven't been with you in so long, I just wanted to, like, be close with you. Is that so wrong?'

'I have to tell you something.'

'Me, too.'

'I think we should—'

'Let's go for it.'

Christina seemed confused for a few seconds, and then said, 'Go for what?'

'We've been engaged for what, six years now?' Jake said. 'That's way too long, baby. I mean, before, I had my career to think about, and I knew it wouldn't be fair to you if I couldn't, you know, devote myself to you. But now that we're older and more mature and whatever, I'm ready to do it. So let's do it.'

'Do what?'

'Set a date, baby. And trust me – it's gonna be the best wedding in the world. We'll spend a hundred grand, two hundred grand – whatever. Maybe we'll have it on an island somewhere, by the water. How about Hawaii? Rick Reynolds – maybe you heard of him – he's a pitcher for us, used to play for the Cubs? Really cool dude. Anyway, Rick got married last year out on Maui, said it was fuckin' spectacular. You'll spend fifty grand just on your dress and you'll invite anybody you want to, all your family and friends, and then the exclusive photos will come out. We'll get my PR guy to leak them; then they'll be in every newspaper in the country.'

Christina stayed deadpan for a while, then finally said, 'This is a joke, right? I mean, we barely see each other anymore. When was the last time I spoke to you on the phone, two months ago?'

'What're you talking about? I called you last week.'

'Yeah, for two minutes – to tell me you were coming home.'

'Come on, baby, try to understand – I'm not just a baseball player; I'm a *celebrity*. I'd love to spend an hour on the phone with you every day, but I've got people on my back twenty-four, seven.' Jake's cell phone started making a farting sound, the ring tone he'd set for calls from his agent. 'See what I mean?'

He clicked on and said to Stu Fox, 'What's the good news?'

'Don't got any good news,' Stu Fox said. 'I got bad and I got very bad.'

'Gimme the bad.'

'Ken won't budge. Nixed the limo, nixed the private trainer.'

'You tell him I'm not reporting to spring training?'

'No, I didn't tell him that.'

'Call him back and tell him that now. Tell him I'll sit out the whole season if I have to.'

'I don't think that's a good idea, Jake. Think about it – next year's your contract year.'

'So?'

'So don't you think it's best to make like a model citizen, not rock the boat?'

'Just take care of it,' Jake said, and clicked off. Then he said to Christina, 'Sorry 'bout that, baby – what was I saying? Right, the wedding ... Look, I know we haven't seen a lot of each other lately, but that's why people get married, right? I mean, we'll have our whole lives to sit around looking at each other.'

'Why do you think I'd want to marry you?' Christina asked.

'What do you mean?' Jake said. 'Because we're in love.'

'Oh, really? You love me? That's why you never talk to me, why you've been cheating on me for years?'

'Whoa, I've never cheated on you, baby.'

'You think I'm an idiot? I know what's been going on – I even knew in high school. You screwed my own cousin behind my back!'

'Cousin? What cousin?' Jake was truly lost.

'Sophia,' Christina said. 'Sophia Scarramuchia.'

'Sophia Scarra-who-chia?' Jake said. 'Who the hell is ...' Then it clicked as Jake remembered Sophia – tall, skinny, good-looking. 'Oh, *that* Sophia. Nothing happened with us – I swear.'

'What about all the other women? Every day, it seems like, I open the papers and see a picture of you with this model or that actress.'

'That's trick photography. Everybody knows that. They splice and dice – do crazy shit just to sell papers. What, you think when you see those two-headed freaks on Mars they really *exist*?' Jake's cell phone started farting again. 'Shit.' He clicked on and said, 'Look, I'm in the middle of something.'

Jake was about to hang up again when Stu said, 'Want to hear the very bad now?'

Jake braced himself. 'What is it?'

Christina had her arms crossed in front of her chest. Jake held up two fingers and mouthed, *Wait*.

'Got a call from Ronald,' Stu said.

Ronald Lufkowitz was Jake's lawyer.

'What did Fuckowitz say?' Jake asked.

'He spoke to Mr Fernandez's lawyer today about your offer. Bottom line – they won't make the deal. Now Fernandez wants two hundred grand wired into his bank account by midnight tonight or he's going public with the story.'

Christina, looking away, didn't seem to be listening in, but Jake cupped his hand over the earpiece just in case.

'How did this happen?' Jake said, trying to disguise his panic.

70

'Don't know all the details,' Stu said. 'Ronald suggested we conference later to strategize, but I think you see my point about the SUV and trainer issues. Hopefully we'll be able to resolve the Fernandez mess with no harm done. Who knows? Maybe he's bluffing.'

'Did Jimmy find out anything?' Jimmy Mulligan was the detective Jake had hired.

'Spoke to him before too,' Stu said. 'Unfortunately, he hasn't been able to dig up any dirt so far. The girl's never been arrested, and no one else in the family has a record either. I really think you're gonna have to play ball with this guy and make some kind of payment.'

Jake looked back over his shoulder and smiled at Christina. Then he said, 'I won't do that.'

'Look, I can tell this is probably a bad time to discuss all this,' Stu said. 'Wanna gimme a shout later on? I'll be home or you can get me on my cell.'

'Righto,' Jake said, and ended the call.

'I wanna go home,' Christina said.

'Yeah, sure,' Jake said, distracted.

As Jake helped Christina over the next fence and into the next backyard, he realized how serious his situation was. Now that it looked like the Fernandezes were going to go public with the rape claim, Jake had to announce his wedding date to his high school sweetheart ASAP – ideally in tomorrow morning's papers – to get some positive PR going.

At the bottom of the fence Jake said, 'So how 'bout next December?'

'How about what next December?'

'The wedding. That'll give us over a year to plan it. And you're gonna need time to pick out a dress and—'

'If you think I'm marrying you, you're out of your mind. I came out here to break up with you.'

'Baby . . .' Jake tried to put his arms around her but she shifted away.

'Don't touch me.'

'All right, just chill, just chill.'

He led her over another fence and through another backyard, and then they emerged onto Avenue J.

'Bye,' Christina said, and she started walking away.

'Wait up, where're you going?' Jake was next to her, trying to keep up.

'Home.'

'I'll walk you.'

'It's okay, I—'

'Come on, you can get killed out here at night. I promise – I'll be a gentleman.'

They continued along Avenue J. Jake tried to break the ice, cracking jokes, but Christina wouldn't even look at him.

When they got to the corner of Christina's block, she said, 'I can walk home from here.'

'No way,' Jake said. 'I'm walkin' you to the door.' Then, when they reached her house, he said, 'Hey, can I use your bathroom?'

Christina deep-breathed and looked away.

'Come on,' Jake said, 'you don't want me to have to piss in the bushes, do you? I'm just gonna use the bathroom, then I'll go – I swear.'

Christina continued to look away, shaking her head; then she turned back to him, with her arms crossed in front of her chest, and said, 'Fine, but you're just gonna use the bathroom and then you're leaving.'

The house looked the same as it always did – dark, dingy, and dirty – and it smelled like a dog lived there, even though Christina and her father didn't own a dog. It had the same old wall-to-wall carpeting, stained in places, and the furniture had to be fifty years old. Jake decided this would be great, like a real Cinderella story. Jake Thomas rescues the beautiful girl from her dirty, ugly house, and they ride away together on a white horse.

Jake followed Christina, wincing as he noticed her ass, which seemed even bigger than it had before. The TV was blaring in the living room – it sounded like horse racing, which meant Christina's degenerate father was home.

Passing the living room ahead of Jake, Christina said, 'Daddy, Jake's with me.'

The TV immediately went off, and when Jake reached the living room, Al Mercado had already stood up from the couch. His thin gray hair was a mess, and he was tucking a wrinkled pin-striped button-down shirt into gray sweatpants.

'Hey, Jake, what a surprise ... Wow, this is really great.'

Al came around the coffee table to greet Jake. He wiped his palm on the seat of his pants a couple of times before shaking hands with Jake, but his hand was still sweaty. Jake noticed about a quarter of the *Racing Form* sticking out from underneath a couch cushion.

'So what're you up to?' Jake asked.

'What? Oh, nothing, just watching a little TV. So how're you doing? You look great, really great, and you had another big year, huh?'

'I did all right.'

'Look how modest he is. The best baseball player in the world and he says, "I did all right." That's why you're such a great guy, Jake – that's why everybody always tells me how lucky I am to have you as my future son-in-law.'

'Thanks, man,' Jake said. 'That's really nice of you to say. And I'd be lucky to have you as a father-in-law too.'

Christina looked away, shaking her head.

'Hey, that's really something – wow,' Al said. 'Well, I don't want to get in your way. I mean, I know you haven't seen each other in a long time and probably have a lot of catching up to do, so I guess I'll—'

'Jake's just coming in to use the bathroom,' Christina said.

'Oh,' Al said. 'Well, that's too bad. You should stay – have something to eat. I don't have anything to offer you right now, but I can go out and, um, pick up some stuff, or—'

'You know, that sounds like a great idea,' Jake said.

'No, it doesn't,' Christina said.

'Why not?' Jake said. 'I'd love to hang for a while.'

'Great,' Al said. 'I'll just run to the store and pick up some—'

'Jake isn't staying,' Christina said firmly. 'He's using the bathroom, then he's going home.' She turned to Jake and said, 'Go ahead,' stepping aside to let him continue onto the staircase.

'Be back in a sec,' Jake said, smiling.

Jake went upstairs, along the wall-to-wall-carpeted hallway, and then right into Christina's room and turned on the light. The room smelled like Christina, like Eternity – Jake made a mental note to buy her a classier perfume – and it looked pink and girlie in a Marcia Brady, Barbie-doll kind of way. The wallpaper, carpeting, and bedsheets were all pink, and she had the same pink dresser opposite her bed that she'd had since high school, with a large pink-framed mirror hanging over it. In the corner near the window there was a vanity, also pink, with all of her makeup, perfume bottles, and combs and brushes spread out.

Jake turned on the stereo and Enrique Iglesias started crooning. *Perfecto*, he thought. He dimmed the light to the level of candlelight, then undressed and got into bed.

A few minutes later Jake heard Christina in the hallway, outside the bathroom, say, 'Jake?'

'In here, baby,' Jake called out.

Christina entered the room and saw Jake in bed, then looked away quickly.

'Get dressed right now,' she said, turning on the light to its full brightness.

'Come on,' Jake said.

Christina shut off the stereo. As she was walking away, Jake said, 'Whoa, hold up,' and got out of bed.

Christina stopped near the door with her back to Jake.

'Look, I know I've been an asshole,' Jake said, 'and I should've called you more. But the past is the past. I grew up – I matured.'

'Come on, Jake—'

'I know you don't want to break up with me. If you did, you wouldn't've kissed me the way you did before.'

'I was surprised—'

'You liked it. Besides, if you really wanted to break up with me, you would've dumped me years ago. But you didn't, because you know we were meant to be together.'

Christina didn't say anything.

'I mean, come on,' Jake went on. 'We were what, eighteen when we got engaged? We were kids. But now things're different. You know how much money I'm gonna be making after next year? I know you don't wanna be stuck in Brooklyn forever. After we're married, we'll move to LA, into a fuckin' mansion – you'll be set up for life, baby. And what about your father? You want him to stay in this house and rot for the rest of his life?'

'You'd help my father?'

' 'Course I would,' Jake said, thinking he'd never give that degenerate a cent. 'I'd help him like I'd help my own father. I'll

74

buy him some condo somewhere out in Florida or Arizona. Your father play golf?'

'He used to.'

'I'll get him a condo on a golf course in Tucson. He'll look out his kitchen window and see the fuckin' eighteenth hole.'

Christina remained with her back to Jake.

'Come on,' Jake said, 'why don't you dim the lights again and put my man Enrique back on?'

Christina let several seconds pass, then said, 'You hate Enrique.'

'What do you mean?' Jake said. 'I love his shit, and I hang with the dude all the time.'

Christina turned and faced Jake, forgetting that she'd been trying to avoid looking at his naked body.

'You know Enrique Iglesias?'

'Yeah, of course. He stops by the clubhouse sometimes when I'm in LA and we hang and shit. I just saw him last month at the Lounge. Yeah, we had a great time. It was me, Enrique, Leo, Tobey—'

'You know Leonardo DiCaprio?'

' 'Course I know him – and his whole posse. Yeah, Leo's got some spread out there in Malibu, right on the water. When you come out to the coast I'll introduce you to everybody.'

Jake went past Christina, toward the wall, and dimmed the lights again.

'What are you doing?' she asked.

'Sshh.' Jake turned on the stereo and 'Be With You' started playing. 'How 'bout a dance, baby?'

Christina turned back toward the door to avoid looking at him.

'One dance,' Jake said. 'What's the big deal?'

Jake went up to her and put his arms around her waist from behind. She tried to move away, but Jake held on to her tightly and she stopped resisting. For several seconds he didn't say anything. Resting his chin on her shoulder, he held her, breathing in that cheap perfume, then said, 'God, this song is beautiful, isn't it?'

'Did you mean that about my father?' Christina said. 'You'll really buy a condo for him?'

'Of course I will,' Jake said. 'I love your dad. He's a great guy.'

They continued dancing. Christina sniffled, and Jake realized she was crying. He started kissing the back of her neck, then continued around to under her jaw.

'Stop,' she said, but didn't move away.

'You know, when I saw you out there on the street before, I felt like I was home, back where I belong.' Jake kissed her neck some more, then said, 'I missed you so much this season. Sometimes, when I was in the outfield, in the middle of a game, I'd start thinking about you. One game against the Cubs, I missed an easy fly ball, let in two runs, because I was thinking about your beautiful face. . . . Lemme see your face, baby.'

Jake turned Christina around. She was crying harder than he'd thought – her cheeks were wet. Using his thumb, he wiped some of the tears, and then he licked his thumb and said, 'Mmm, delicious.'

Keeping his hands tightly around her waist, he started dancing with her, rocking slowly from side to side. He tried to kiss her lips, but she turned her head.

Then she pushed him back and said, 'You better not be bullshitting me about any of this. Because if you are, I swear to God I'll—'

Jake went to kiss her again, and this time she kissed him back.

He made out with her for a while, telling her how beautiful she was and how he'd love her forever, and then he steered her toward the bed. As he undid her bra he noticed she was still crying, but he didn't let that stop him.

PART TWO

Seven

Saiquan Harrington went up to the information desk at Brookdale Hospital and said to the skinny, light-skinned girl with Venus Williams-style braids, 'Where Desmond Johnson's room at?'

Without looking at him, the girl said, 'I'm on the phone.'

The girl was wearing a headset, but she didn't seem to be on the phone. She was looking at the copy of the *Post* that was lying open on the desk in front of her.

After about a few seconds of looking down at the paper, chewing on gum, she pushed a button on the phone and said, 'Brookdale, hold on,' and then started looking at the paper again, turning to the horoscopes. After several more seconds she looked at the computer monitor and tapped a few keys on the keyboard, then said into the phone, 'Brookdale, hold on,' and started reading the newspaper again.

Saiquan said, 'Can't you just tell me where Desmond—'

'Wait,' the girl said.

She looked up more shit on the computer, read more horoscopes, and said 'Brookdale, hold on,' into the phone a few more times. Then, finally, she said to Saiquan, 'What you want?'

'I wanna know where Desmond Johnson's room's at,' Saiquan said.

'He a patient?' The girl couldn't give a shit.

'Yeah.'

'How you spell the last name?'

'Johnson. You don't know how to spell Johnson?'

'Yeah, I know how to spell Johnson. You didn't tell me his name was Johnson, did you?'

'I told you I wanna see Desmond Johnson.'

The girl punched some more keys, then looked over at the monitor and said, 'Lucy Johnson's in room seven-oh-two.'

'I don't want no Lucy Johnson,' Saiquan said. 'I want Desmond Johnson.'

'There ain't no Desmond Johnson in the hospital.'

'Come on, yo, just look it up.'

'I am lookin' it up, and there ain't no Desmond Johnson. All we got's Lucy Johnson.' Then, looking back the monitor, she said, 'Wait. Desmond Johnson – room three fourteen.'

'See, what the fuck I tell you?'

But the girl, not listening, said into the phone, 'Brookdale, hold on.'

Saiquan headed toward the elevators, wondering why everybody always had to give him so much bullshit.

A white cop with a mustache sitting in front of room three fourteen said to Saiquan as he was about to go inside, 'Can I help you?'

'This Desmond Johnson's room?' Saiquan asked.

'Who are you?' the cop said in a normal white-cop kind of way, talking down to him and shit.

'His brother.'

'You don't look like his brother.'

'Just tell him his brother's here, man.'

'What's your name?'

'Saiquan.'

'Saigon?'

'*Saiquan.*'

The cop went into the room, then came out, frisked Saiquan, and said, 'Okay.'

Saiquan entered the room, hit by that usual odor of shit that hospital rooms had. A TV up high on the wall was blasting CNN. A nurse was sitting watching TV, and didn't even look at Saiquan as he passed by.

The bed near the door had the curtains drawn, and Saiquan peeked in and saw an old guy sleeping with his mouth hanging open. He went farther into the room and saw Desmond on the other bed, lying on his back, staring at the ceiling. A big tube was coming out of the middle of his neck, and he had one of them metal things screwed into his head with scabbed blood all around the screws. Saiquan had seen other brothers from his neighbor-hood wind up this same way, paralyzed and shit. Motherfucking sixteen-year-olds got shot in the neck and got sent away to nursing homes like old people.

Saiquan had never believed in God. Even when he was away he didn't get into it. All that Jesus/Allah bullshit was just for people in lockup to make themselves happy about something and believe their lives were less fucked-up than they were. If God was really around, the Man would've made sure that bullet went right into Desmond's heart or his brain – ended his life quick.

Desmond was looking up toward the ceiling, so Saiquan couldn't tell if he saw him, or if he even knew he was in the room.

Saiquan went right next to the bed and leaned over Desmond's face and said, 'D. D, yo, it's me, man – Saiquan.'

Desmond used to joke around and shit all the time, but now he looked like he'd never laughed or even smiled, his whole life. His eyes opened slowly, they looked all bloodshot and watery, and he didn't seem to know where he was.

'What up, D, man?' Saiquan said. 'How you feelin', yo?'

Desmond didn't say anything; he just looked at Saiquan without blinking. Seeing his best friend looking so fucked-up made Saiquan sick inside, but he wasn't going to cry, especially around another man, no matter what.

'Don't worry, man, you're gonna be a'ight,' Saiquan said. 'Hear me, man? You're gonna beat this shit. They gonna do some rehab on you, get you back on your feet walkin' and shit. You trust me on that shit.'

Of course, Saiquan knew Desmond would probably never walk again. Shit, he'd probably never eat or breathe on his own, but he had to say something to make the dude feel better.

Saiquan stood there, listening to the air going in and out of the tubes of that machine he was hooked up to. Again, he had to try hard not to cry.

'I told that cop I was your brother,' Saiquan said. 'Shit's funny, right? But, yo, I'm gonna talk to them 'bout all that shit. You need a real brother outside your door, know what I'm sayin'? That white nigga didn't even frisk me. I coulda come up here to cap yo' ass, but he don't give a shit – just cost him some OT, that's all, know what I'm sayin'?'

Desmond was trying to cough, his face turning red.

'What up, man?' Saiquan said. 'Yo, want me to get you some water or get the nurse?'

Desmond stopped coughing and mouthed, *No.*

'So what up, man?' Saiquan said. 'You can't talk none at all?'

Again Desmond mouthed, *No.*

'That's cool, that's cool, man,' Saiquan said. 'I'll do all the talkin' then, that's all. I ain't got no problem with that.'

Saiquan checked over his shoulder to make sure the nurse wasn't listening, and then he leaned closer to Desmond and said, 'Who got you, man?'

Desmond didn't try to say anything. He just gave Saiquan a look that Saiquan knew meant, *Stay out of it.*

'Naw, naw, this my business now, man, know what I'm sayin'?' Saiquan was talking low, almost whispering. 'Just tell me who it was, man, and I'll take care of all that shit.'

Desmond gave him more of that same look.

'I don't care what you say, man, I'm involved now,' Saiquan said. 'They cap my boy, niggas better know they gonna get some payback.'

Desmond's lips said, *Don't.*

'Naw, fuck that shit, man,' Saiquan said. 'I ain't forgettin' all them times you got my back, yo. Like that time I got cut in the stomach by that punk Damon up by Seaview Estates – lost all that blood, almost died – what'd you do? You took care of that shit, that's what you did. So who was it, man? Was it Karl? 'Cause that's who I'm figurin'. Nigga loves to shoot people in the back when they ain't lookin'.'

Desmond mouthed some words.

'What?' Saiquan said.

Desmond repeated what he'd tried to say, and Saiquan made out, *It wasn't Karl.*

'Then who was it, man?'

Desmond's eyes looked angry, and he didn't try to say anything.

'You don't tell me I'm gonna find out on my own, know what I'm sayin'?' Saiquan said. 'So who was it? Was it Tariq? One of 'em Glenwood Road boys? The DIS crew? Chrome Warriors?

Spanish niggas from Queens? Kevin? Eduardo? Or was it Jamaicans – fuckin' Bloodstains?'

Desmond mouthed something.

'What?' Saiquan said.

Desmond's lips moved again, slower, and Saiquan made out the word *parole*.

'Forget that shit, man,' Saiquan said. 'This is about you and me, man – I don't care 'bout nothin' else. 'Sides, yo, I be careful – you can count on that. So who was it, man? Just say the name, yo.'

Desmond's eyes shifted away, toward the window. It was cloudy outside and the window was dirty, making it look even darker out there.

After about twenty seconds Desmond's eyes shifted back toward Saiquan, then he mouthed, *Jermaine.*

'*Jermaine?* You mean Jermaine, Jermaine? *Your* boy Jermaine?'

Yeah, Desmond mouthed.

'I don't get that shit, man. *Jermaine.* J's with y'all in the Crips. Why'd your own boy cap you?'

Desmond stared at Saiquan, tears coming to his eyes, then mouthed something Saiquan couldn't make out.

'What?'

Desmond's lips said it again.

'Mona?'

Desmond tried again, slower.

'Oh, Ramona who the fu … Wait, you mean that ho he's always with? The one wears 'em short leather shits all the time? Always got 'em big-ass titties showin'?'

Desmond mouthed, *Yeah.*

'So what's she gotta do with it, man?'

Desmond looked at Saiquan and Saiquan knew.

'Wait. You was bonin' her?'

Yeah.

'So just 'cause you been hittin' it with his ho he capped you?'

Yeah.

'Sick-ass motherfucka. That ho, man, she been bonin' every nigga in the 'hood since she was twelve years old. I heard she takin' it up the ass, she takin' it everywhere. So what'd he do, just jump out and cap you when you ain't lookin'?'

Drive-by.

'Fuck it, man. You and him in the same crew. We used to hang with that motherfucka when we was kids and shit. Yo, you tell the cops it was J?'

Fuck, no.

'Cool, man – yo, that's cool. Then you just forget about the whole thing, know what I'm sayin'? It's gonna be all taken care of, you don't gotta worry 'bout nothin'.'

Desmond tried to talk, making some fucked-up gurgling sounds, spit coming out of his mouth. Then he started making some kind of bird noise with his tongue and the nurse came over and said, 'I gotta suction.' When the nurse was done she went back to watching CNN, and Desmond's lips started moving again. Saiquan didn't know what the fuck he was saying and had to make him repeat it three times. Finally he made out, *Watch yo' back.*

'I will, man, I will. You don't gotta worry 'bout that shit. I always be watchin' my back.'

Saiquan raised his hand to do a high five, but then he remembered that Desmond couldn't move.

Resting his hand on Desmond's arm instead, Saiquan said, 'You just rest up man, hear? You gonna be walkin' outta here next month. You gonna see.'

Desmond's eyes, looking watery again, shifted away toward the dark.

'Later on, D.' Saiquan left the room.

Outside, the white cop didn't even look up as Saiquan headed fast toward the elevator.

As Saiquan drove home along Linden Boulevard, thick smoke started coming out of the hood of his ride – a Pontiac Sunbird with a million miles on it.

'Damn,' Saiquan said.

He waited for the smoke to go down and then he went outside and opened the hood. He didn't know why he was bothering to look under there because he didn't know shit about fixing cars. After a few more seconds of looking, he closed the hood and got back into the car. He turned the key but the shit wouldn't start. He knew it wasn't the battery this time, not with all that fucking smoke. It was something worse – the engine, carburetor, whatever. He knew if he got somebody to tow the car home they'd charge him a hundred dollars, and he didn't have no hundred dollars to tow no broken-down car. He'd bought the car for three hundred and fifty bucks at a lot on Utica Avenue, and he could probably buy another one for how much they'd charge to fix this one.

Fuck it, man, Saiquan decided.

After checking the glove compartment and the backseat – there was no personal shit, just a lot of garbage – he ditched the car and started walking toward Rockaway Avenue with his hands deep inside the pockets of his old, black, ripped-up North Face winter jacket.

Waiting for the bus, feeling like a chump, Saiquan started thinking about capping Jermaine, wondering if he could go through with it. He'd killed three people before – two from the Bloods, one from another gang – and he saw their ghosts all the time, especially at night; the last thing he needed was the ghost of Jermaine following him around too. He knew he had to do it, for Desmond, but he didn't like killing people like some other brothers he knew did. It didn't do nothing for him – it didn't give him no high. He didn't like seeing the blood and fucking up people's lives just for the hell of it.

But Saiquan told himself that Jermaine was different – Jermaine was a punk, a sick-ass motherfucker who deserved to die anyway, so there was no use feeling bad about it. He thought about all the people Jermaine had killed – some who didn't do nothing. Like those dudes who were playing basketball that time and Jermaine went up to them and said, 'Lemme play.' The dudes said no, so Jermaine popped both of them and walked away. Jermaine was like that – he didn't give a shit.

Saiquan wanted to pop Jermaine right now, get the shit over with while he was all pumped up to do it – problem was, he didn't have a piece. It was no real problem, though, because he knew his boy Marcus would hook him up with that shit.

After about twenty minutes a bus pulled up. Saiquan got on and put all the change he had, a dollar twenty-five, into the change slot and continued onto the bus.

'Where you goin'?' the driver asked. He was a big, fat, hard-assed brother with a beard – reminded Saiquan of a *harder*-assed brother, Lawrence, a guard upstate who always gave him shit.

'What?' Saiquan asked.

'You need seventy-five more cent,' the driver said.

'My car broke down, man.'

'You still seventy-five cent short.'

'I ain't lyin', man. I just left my car out the street. Shit broke and I gotta get home to my kids.'

'Put in seventy-five more cent or get off my damn bus.'

'Yo, anybody got change for a dollar?' Saiquan said to the passengers.

Nobody even bothered to check.

'You don't got the money you gotta get off my bus,' the driver said.

'Come on, man. Gimme a break one time. What the fuck you care anyway?'

'Get off the bus if you don't have any money,' said an old white-head church lady sitting in one of the handicapped seats.

Saiquan hated when people didn't know how to shut their damn mouths and mind their own damn business.

'Why don't you shut up and mind your own damn business?' he said.

'Who you sayin' shut up to?' the old woman said, pointing her cane at him. 'I'll shut *yo'* ass up with this cane 'cross yo' head, boy.'

Other people on the bus started yelling shit at Saiquan.

'You gonna get off my bus or you want me to call the cops?' the driver said, acting even more like that motherfucker Lawrence.

Saiquan wanted to grab the bus driver around his neck and squeeze till the man shut up for good, but instead he said, 'Fuck you, man,' and turned and went down the steps.

He went to a bodega up the block and got change for two dollars. Back at the bus stop he had to wait another twenty motherfucking minutes till another bus came. He got on and walked right to the back and sat down with his legs spread far apart, taking up three seats, and stared blankly out the window.

At the One Hundred Third Street stop, he got off and headed toward his building in the Breukelen Houses. Except for the six and a half years he'd been away, he'd lived at Breukelen his whole life. Growing up he lived with his mother, father, and two sisters in a two-bedroom apartment. When he was nine, his old man tried to rob a liquor store for crack money and shot the owner's wife in the head. He got sent away for life but got killed two years later by some brother at Attica. The same year his father died something went wrong with his mama's diabetes and she died too. He and his sisters went to live with his grandma in another apartment at Breukelen, and then Saiquan went away to juvie for dealing when he was sixteen and his grandma died. His sister Shanella met a guy and moved to South Carolina, and his sister Latisha moved to Philly. Saiquan came back to Brooklyn and lived in his grandma's apartment alone for a while, and then his girl, Desiree, moved in with him. They had a kid, then Saiquan got busted for dealing rock and got sent away to Riker's. He got fucked in the ass a bunch of times and joined up with the Crips for protection. When he got out two years later, he and Desiree had another kid. He was dealing for the Crips, making sick-ass money, but he blew most of it on rock and clothes and other bullshit. Then he got picked up for dealing again, and this time they sent him way the fuck upstate to Southport. When he got out he was twenty-seven and decided he was sick of this going-to-jail-all-the-time bullshit and was gonna go straight. So he quit the Crips and started looking for work. He had a job for a few months working off the books on a construction site, but then he got laid off and he couldn't find any other work since. Desiree had another kid, and they were packed into a one-bedroom apartment. They were behind on all their bills, and the bitches at Cablevision and Con Ed said they were gonna turn off the cable and electric if they didn't get paid soon. Desiree got a four-hundred-and-fifty dollar welfare check every month, but the rent was four hundred ninety-five bucks alone. They hadn't paid rent in three months, and just last week the man came and told them if they didn't pay it soon they were gonna get evicted.

Saiquan knew he could take care of all his money problems easy if he started dealing again. Before he got busted that last time he was taking in a thousand a week, sometimes double or triple that shit, and the niggas in the Crips were always asking him to get back with them. If he didn't have to worry about bullshit jail, he would've gone back to dealing in no time. But them parole board motherfuckers warned him that the next time he went away it was gonna be for some serious time, and that white judge downtown told him that same shit at his sentencing. And his PO, Tony Italian-something, was always reminding him how strict the judge would be the next time, how he could go away for ten years just for getting caught selling a bag of pot. And now, with three kids and his dawg depending on him to provide and shit, he couldn't take a chance of going away again, especially for no ten years.

So after Saiquan got fired from the construction job, he'd tried to find a job on another site, but most of them had all that white, union shit going on. Then he heard about people getting jobs in customer service – just sitting by the phone all day, waiting for it to ring – and that shit sounded good to him – beat the fuck outta working his ass off in ninety-degree weather, carrying cinder blocks and pouring cement, working like a damn slave for them damn white, racist, motherfucking foremen from Staten Island anyway. So he went to an interview at an agency in Manhattan. He knew he was in trouble when they handed him some papers to fill out. Saiquan had dropped out of high school in tenth grade, but by that time he'd already been left back four times and he didn't know how to read or write. He could make out most of the sounds and words, but when he tried to put them into sentences he always got messed up. He could read most of the form they gave him, and he filled in his name and address and that shit, but there was a lot of shit in the middle and the bottom he had to leave blank.

They made him sit around for a long time, like he was at the damn Medicaid clinic. Finally they called his name and he went inside. An uppity-looking white bitch wearing a lot of jewelry and a diamond ring – shit probably cost ten thousand bucks – shook his hand and told him to sit down.

Then, looking at Saiquan's form, the white bitch said, 'You didn't answer all of the questions.'

'Yeah,' Saiquan said, looking away.

'Why didn't you answer all of the questions?'

'Didn't see it there.' Saiquan wished the lady would just shut the fuck up and give him the damn job.

White Bitch made a face, then started asking Saiquan a bunch of questions like: 'What was your highest year of completed education?' 'Who were your last three employers?' 'What is your desired salary?' 'How many words a minute do you type?' Lot of shit like that. Saiquan answered the questions the best he could, but White Bitch didn't seem to like that the construction job was the only real job he'd ever had, or that he wanted to make fifty dollars an hour, or that he could type one hundred words a minute. The only question Saiquan lied about was the typing one. The truth was, he didn't know how to use a typewriter, or one of them computer Internet shits neither. He figured one hundred words a minute would be enough, but she must've wanted to hear more than that.

Saiquan hoped White Bitch was through asking questions, but she had one more.

'There seems to be a big gap between the time you finished – I mean stopped going to high school, and the time you had the construction job. What were you doing during that period?'

'I was away,' Saiquan said.

'Away? What do you mean, away?'

White Bitch looked at him for a few more seconds, then said, 'You mean you were in prison?'

'Yeah.'

White people were so damn stupid sometimes.

White Bitch shook her head, looking at the form again, then said, 'I'm sorry, Mr Harrington. I wish I could help you, but I can't.'

'What?' Saiquan said. 'You don't got no jobs for no ex-cons? That shit's discrimination.'

'Your prison record isn't the issue,' White Bitch said. 'Actually, we would never discriminate against you for your time in prison. But without a high school diploma or any prior office experience we just can't place you with any of our clients.'

'How'm I supposed to get office experience, you won't give me no job?'

'I'm really very sorry,' White Bitch said, then stood up and gave him a look like she was thinking, *Get the fuck out my office right now, nigger.*

Saiquan remained seated and said, 'Yo, so why'd you axe me all 'em questions, bustin' my ass, when you know you ain't even gonna give me no job?'

'Excuse me?' White Bitch said, like he'd just grabbed her ass.
'Yo, you heard me. Why you gotta do that shit? You know you
got no job for me soon as you see my black ass walk in here.'
'You're not qualified,' White Bitch said. 'Without a GED I
can't—'
'You knew I didn't have no motherfuckin' GED, man. You seen
my damn paper, so don't gimme no more that damn bullshit.'
Now White Bitch looked scared, like she thought Blacky was
gonna rape her or some shit. She told him to leave her office or
she was gonna call security.
Saiquan left the office, slamming doors and cursing at all the
white people he saw.
Riding the L train home, Saiquan decided, *Fuck it*. He was sick
of white people always telling him there ain't no jobs for brothers
who ain't got no GEDs. Meanwhile, how the fuck was he
supposed to get a GED when he didn't know how to read? And
even if he learned how to read better, how was he supposed to
start spending his time going to damn GED classes when he had a
wife and kids and all them bills? Naw, he couldn't waste his time
forever. He'd look for a job for another couple weeks, but if he
didn't find one he'd just have to get back with his boys in the
Crips, that was all.
Saiquan passed the playground and the basketball court, where
kids were still playing even though it was dark out, with only
lamppost light, and you could hardly see the rim. When the kids
saw Saiquan some said, 'Yo, Saiquan!' 'Saiquan!' 'What up,
Saiquan?' and others just nodded at him silently, giving props to
an ex-gangsta who'd spent time away. Saiquan nodded back at
them without smiling or stopping.
Since Saiquan got out of lockup, he was used to getting respect
from the kids in the projects. He knew he was their role model
and shit and they wanted to grow up to be just like him, just like
when he was a kid he used to want to grow up to be like the
dealers and the gang kids, especially the ones who had done a lot
of time. When Saiquan was a kid, dreaming of playing in the
NBA, his real hero wasn't Shaq or M.J. – it was Tyrone, the head
of a local gang called the Breukelen Boyz. Tyrone had been away
five times, the first time for murder when he was eleven years old,
and he wore the finest leather coat, a big Run-DMC-style gold

necklace, diamond earrings. He had motherfucking guns too – Kel-Tecs, Tec-9s, Hi-Points, everything. He even had an Uzi he sometimes brought out and let kids hold. Tyrone liked Saiquan, talking to him all the time, making the other kids jealous. One time Tyrone took Saiquan up on the roof of the building – taught him how to smoke crack, then let Saiquan play with his Hi-Point, taking shots into the air with real bullets. Saiquan knew right then that all that fucking school, getting educated, being like Mike bullshit wasn't for him; he wanted to be like his man Tyrone.

Saiquan entered his building and waited for the elevator. It wasn't coming, so he headed up the stairs, stepping around crack vials and mouse shit. As he got higher, near the third floor, he heard a woman screaming for help, trapped in the elevator. He went up to the doors, recognizing the voice. It was Nadera Wallace.

Nadera was old now, like thirty, and had two kids, but ten years ago, damn, she was the flyest honey in the whole Breukelen Houses. She used to wear them real tight jeans, like the ones the Spanish girls wore, and them little shirts with her big titties all pushed up, and she did her makeup good too, putting on lots of shiny pink ho lipstick and straightening her hair Brandy style. Saiquan never boned Nadera, never even got close, but he always wanted to.

Nadera was pushing the alarm button, screaming, 'Get me outta here! Get me the fuck outta here! Help! Help!'

'Chill, y'all, chill. It's me – Saiquan. I got ya, baby. I got ya.'

'Saiquan, you gotta get me the fuck outta here right now! I been trapped in here an hour already and I got my kids home alone waitin'!'

'Why don't you call up the Chinks? Order some fried dumplings in there.'

'Stop playin' 'round and help me. My kids is alone – big one can't watch the little one all night!'

'A'ight, just chill. I'm goin' home right now. I'll call the company and they get you out.'

'Don't call the damn company. They won't do nothin' till mornin', and I ain't waitin' here all motherfuckin' night. Call nine-one-one.'

'All right. Just stay cool.'

'You get yo' ass locked in some damn elevator, see how fuckin' cool you stay. You better call nine-one-one right now, Saiquan. I got my kids home alone, waitin' for dinner. Please, Saiquan, check on my kids. Tell 'em what's goin' on.'

'A'ight. I'll call right now and they'll get you out. Don't worry 'bout nothin'.'

'Thank you, Saiquan. Thank you so much, baby.'

Saiquan continued up the stairs, taking them two at a time, hoping Nadera was making herself nice and comfy in there. The firemen would come to the projects quicker than the elevator company, but they'd still take their sweet time.

On the seventh floor Saiquan, breathing hard and sweating in his winter coat, opened the door to his apartment. The TV was blasting, Trey was chasing Felicia around with a cap gun near the bunk beds where they slept, and the whole place was hot and smelled like burned fish. Desiree was trying to feed Tanya in the high chair, trying to force the spoon into the baby's mouth.

With the TV noise and the kids screaming, Desiree didn't hear Saiquan when he came in, but she turned around when the door slammed and said, 'Where the fuck you been?'

'I told you I was goin' to the hospital, visit D.'

'You didn't tell me nothin'. You said you was out job huntin' and be home at five.'

The baby wasn't opening her mouth, and the apple sauce, or whatever, was going all over her face.

'I told you I had to visit D. You just don't listen, that's all.'

Saiquan took off his jacket and tossed it onto a chair, wondering how shit with Desiree had gotten so fucked-up.

'Walk in the door, can't even hang up your coat. And where the hell's the milk and diapers at?'

Saiquan remembered Desiree telling him to stop at the store on his way home.

'Ah, shit.'

'I told you you gonna forget. Now the kids ain't got no milk to drink and we only got one diaper left. Why you always gotta be so stupid?'

Trey and Felicia ran past the high chair. Desiree slapped Trey on top of her head as he ran past, chasing his little sister, and screamed, 'I told you to sit yo' asses down and watch the damn TV!'

Trey dropped his cap gun and started crying.

'Don't hit him like that,' Saiquan said.

'Now you tellin' me how to mother my kids? Gone all day, ain't makin' no money, can't even get no diapers or milk like you suppose to.'

'I forgot.'

'Why you forgot? Ain't got nothin' else on yo' damn unemployed mind to think about.'

Turning away, going into the kitchen, Saiquan said, 'I ain't in the mood for yo' bullshit tonight, girl. Walk in the door, bitchin' at me, don't even ask me how D's doin' and shit.'

'How is he?'

'Paralyzed. Can't move nothin', neck down. Nigga can't even talk.'

'That's too bad.'

'Yeah, it is too bad. Shit's fucked-up, what it is.'

Looking down, feeding the baby, Desiree said under her breath, 'He only gettin' what he deserve.'

'What you just say?'

'I said he's gettin' what he deserve.'

'You crazy?'

'That's what he get, dealin' drugs for them gangs. You think Desmond never paralyzed nobody else?'

'The man can't move. Probably gonna put his ass in a home. You still gotta talk that shit?'

'I'm just sayin' I ain't gonna feel sorry for no gangsta thug goes shootin' other people, then winds up gettin' shot himself and put in a chair, that's all.'

Saiquan picked up the lid on the frying pan and saw nothing there except the burned bottom. He said, 'Damn, bitch, can't you save me one piece of fish to eat?'

'Wasn't even enough to feed the kids.' Then she said to the baby, 'Eat it, come on, eat it.' Then back to Saiquan, 'So just 'cause you at the hospital you can't stop at the store and pick up no milk and diapers?'

'Car broke down,' Saiquan said, 'had to take the motherfuckin' bus home, a'ight?'

The baby started crying as Desiree forced the food into her mouth.

'What you mean, the car broke down?' Desiree said.

'Shit broke,' Saiquan said. 'Stopped workin' right on Linden Boulevard. Coulda got my ass killed, didn't pull over in time.'

'We can't afford to get no car fixed.'

'I know that – that's why I left the shit there in the street.'

'What you mean, left it?'

'Ain't you listenin'? Shit broke.'

'But you coulda got it fixed – sold it for two, three hundred bucks. Coulda paid some bills with it or part the rent. Now we don't pay the rent they gonna put our asses in a shelter.'

'Don't worry,' Saiquan said. 'I got a plan.'

'Oh, you got a plan? Hear that, kids? Daddy's got a plan. So now we don't gotta worry no more that the building man was here again today, sayin' we got two more days to get up the rent for the last three months, or he's evictin' our asses onto the street. We don't gotta worry 'bout none of that shit 'cause yo' hardworkin' daddy say he got a plan.' Then she said to the baby, 'Swallow it – swallow the damn food,' and then back to Saiquan, 'So tell me – what's yo' big plan? What you gonna do, join back up with the Crips, start sellin' to them junkies and crack hos again, carryin' guns 'round the house, shootin' people—'

'I'm gonna find a job,' Saiquan said.

'A job? Where you gonna find a job? In the refrigerator? Under the stove? You think the job's just gonna come flyin' in the damn window? How you gonna find a job, all you do sit home all day, watchin' Maury Povich?'

'I don't watch no Maury Povich.'

'Then how come I see Maury Povich on that damn TV every day?'

'I ain't watchin' it.'

'It go on by itself?'

'I don't know how it get on but I don't watch no fuckin' Maury Povich. I watch Jerry and Montel, but I don't watch no Maury.'

'What kinda man are you?' Desiree said. 'Loungin' 'round all day on your lazy ass with three kids dependin' on you. Might as well stayed in jail.'

'Better off in jail. Least I don't gotta take yo' bullshit every damn day.'

'Hear that, kids? Yo' daddy's plannin' to go back to jail.'

'Don't tell 'em that.'

'Why not? It's the truth. They should know their daddy's just a good-for-nothin', drug-dealin', crack-pimpin', money-stealin' gangsta, gonna wind up dead, in jail, or a motherfuckin' vegetable like his boy Desmond.'

Saiquan came at Desiree with his fist cocked.

'Go 'head – hit me front of the kids,' Desiree said. 'Show 'em what a great man they daddy is.'

Saiquan looked away and saw Trey and Felicia staring at him, and even the baby's eyes were wide open. He lowered his fist and went to the sink and drank lukewarm water straight from the faucet, trying to calm down.

When he finished drinking Desiree said, 'What you gonna do to go away this time? You gonna sell more crack to ten-year-old boys? You gonna kill somebody?' Then Saiquan picked up the first thing he saw, a glass quarter-filled with Hawaiian Punch, and flung it against the wall, glass and red liquid going everywhere. The kids ran into Saiquan and Desiree's room and the baby starting screaming. Desiree was yelling too, but Saiquan didn't give a shit.

Saiquan picked up the phone on the kitchen wall, but didn't hear a dial tone. He pressed TALK a couple of times, still hearing nothing, and then he said to Desiree, 'How come the damn phone don't work?'

Desiree had the screaming baby out of the high chair, holding her in one arm like a running back holding a football.

'Why you think?' she said.

Saiquan put the phone down hard on the countertop.

'Go 'head,' Desiree said, 'break more shit, scare the kids, make 'em think their daddy's a monster. And they'll be thinkin' right, 'cause that shit's the truth – you a monster! A motherfuckin' monster!'

Saiquan went past Desiree, toward the front door, and grabbed his jacket.

'Where the fuck you think you goin' now?' Desiree said. 'You gotta take care of the damn baby!'

95

Saiquan left the apartment, slamming the door, hearing Desiree still screaming at him. He took the stairs up to the ninth floor and rang the bell to Nadera's apartment. It opened, with the chain on, and Willie, Nadera's ten-year-old son, looked through at Saiquan. Willie was a quiet kid, read books all the time, stayed out of trouble.

'Yo, what up?' Saiquan said. 'Yo' ma's stuck in the elevator. I gotta use your phone.'

'I ain't s'posed to let strangers in.'

Saiquan had known Willie since Willie was a baby.

'I ain't no stranger, man,' Saiquan said.

'How I know you ain't gonna rob us?'

'Yo' mama's stuck in the elevator. Come on outside, you can hear her screaming. You wanna make her stay stuck in there all night?'

Willie thought about it for a few more seconds, then let Saiquan inside.

'Where the phone at?' Saiquan asked.

'Bedroom,' Willie said. Then, as Saiquan headed down the hallway, Willie called after him, 'Better not steal nothin'!'

Saiquan glared back at him and went into the bedroom. Lisa, Nadera's daughter, kindergarten age, was on the floor doing a puzzle. When she saw Saiquan come in she got up and ran out of the room.

Saiquan sat on the bed and looked around. Shit was nice – clean blanket and sheets, pictures hung up. Whole apartment was nicer than Saiquan's – all cleaned up, a new TV, rugs – and Nadera didn't even have a man. She worked in downtown Brooklyn somewhere, doing something with computers.

After calling 911, Saiquan closed the bedroom door and made another call. The phone rang five times, then Marcus picked up and said, 'Yeah.'

'Saw D,' Saiquan said, looking back to make sure the bedroom door was still closed and the kids weren't listening in. Then he whispered, 'He said it was Jermaine.'

'What?' Marcus said, like he couldn't hear. There was noise in the background – a TV or stereo.

'It was J,' Saiquan said louder. 'He fuckin' paralyzed D, man. Motherfucker got screws in his head.'

'Got what in his head?'

'Screws.'

'Shoes?'

'Why don't you turn down that fuckin' noise so you can hear what my ass is sayin'?'

'Why don't you just talk louder?'

''Cause I can't. I'm at my neighbor's crib.'

'You eatin' ribs?'

'Just shut the damn noise!'

A few seconds went by, then the noise went away. Marcus came back on and said, 'The fuck you sayin', man?'

'Jermaine capped D,' Saiquan said.

'Jermaine?' Marcus said. '*My* Jermaine?'

'D was bonin' his bitch or some shit, and J found out and capped his ass. D's got screws in his head. Can't even talk.'

'Yo, that ain't what I heard,' Marcus said. 'They sayin' one of 'em Bloods niggas popped him.'

'That's just what they spreadin' 'round so it don't look like Crips be poppin' they own and shit, but it was Jermaine, man. D told me it was J, and I wanna give that motherfucka some payback *tonight*.'

'Hold up, yo – *Jermaine?* That's Crips-on-Crips shit, yo.'

'So? I ain't in the Crips no more.'

'But I am.'

'So you don't gotta come. Just gimme the piece, that's it.'

'But what about you? What you think they gonna do, go "Saiquan capped J. That's cool, what we havin' for dinner"?'

'I don't give a shit they come after me. D's my boy and I gotta get his back like he always got mine.'

Saiquan heard Marcus breathing. Then Marcus said, 'How you know this shit's true?'

'Why'd D lie, man?'

'Dunno. Maybe when they put those screws in his head they hit his brain, man ain't thinkin' straight.'

'J popped D, man,' Saiquan said. 'I don't give a shit what crew he in – I'm gonna give his punk ass some payback.'

'But shit don't make sense,' Marcus said. 'Why'd J smoke D over some ho?'

' 'Cause fuckin' nigga's crazy, that's why. How the fuck should I know why? But listen up, yo – you don't want nothin' to do with it, that's cool. I just need a piece – somethin' clean, man, know what I'm sayin'? I ain't gonna fuck up my parole with this shit, that's for damn sure. I just wanna get this one thing done, then I be on my way.'

'I'll hook you up,' Marcus said, 'but I'm goin' too.'

Saiquan didn't want Marcus to come along. Marcus had a rep around the hood for being a sick-ass, especially when he was high on rock. Saiquan just wanted the piece and that was it.

'Naw, you don't gotta come,' Saiquan said.

'Yo, D's my boy too,' Marcus said. 'If J capped him I wanna be there to see him feel some pain, know what I'm sayin'?'

Saiquan didn't know how to keep Marcus out of it. Desmond and Marcus were tight too, and besides, Marcus had the guns.

'Whatever,' Saiquan said. 'You wanna come, that's cool.'

Saiquan told Marcus he'd meet him at his crib in fifteen minutes, then he left the bedroom and went back through the apartment. Willie and Lisa were standing near the front door, Lisa hiding behind her brother's back.

'Is our mama gonna get rescued or not?' Willie asked.

'Fireman's comin',' Saiquan said. 'But that shit might not happen too fast, know what I'm sayin'? Y'all be a'ight here alone?'

'Yeah,' Willie said.

'Cool,' Saiquan said. 'But if you wanna go hang out at my place, that's okay too – my girl's home right now with the kids, and you can just knock on the door and chill there. I gotta go take care of some shit right now, but I'll come back later and look in on y'all if yo' mama ain't out by then, a'ight?' He was about to leave when he turned back to Willie and said, 'I never see you outside, hangin' with them niggas on the corner. That's cool, man, that's cool. You stay in school, do all that readin' and writin' shit – get yo' degree, know what I'm sayin'? Most important thing is you get yo' degree so you can get the fuck outta here.'

Willie looked confused, like he didn't understand why Saiquan was telling him all of this.

'Whatever, man,' Saiquan said, and left the apartment.

Heading downstairs, Saiquan heard Nadera screaming in the elevator.

On the fourth floor Saiquan yelled to her, 'Nadera, baby, don't worry, yo – I called nine-one-one. They gonna get you out!'

'You check on my kids?'

'Yeah, don't worry 'bout nothin'. Kids're cool – everybody cool.'

'Thank you, Saiquan. You a good man, baby. God bless you!'

Eight

Standing in front of his bathroom mirror, Ryan went into a set position, checked the runner at first, then lifted his right leg and started his delivery. As he cocked his left arm back to fire toward the plate he caught himself, cursed under his breath, and continued washing his face.

A couple of minutes later he went down the hallway into his bedroom. He turned on his stereo, blasting Jay-Z's '99 Problems' so loud that his eardrums ached, and then sat on the single bed with the springy mattress he'd had since he was a kid and looked at the clock on his night table. It was 9:36, eight minutes since the last time he'd checked, and now it was three hours and twenty minutes since Christina had left the party with Jake. Ryan had thought they'd just gone into the backyard to talk, but then he looked back there, through the kitchen window, a few minutes after they left and they were gone. Since there was no way out of the backyard to Eighty-first Street, Ryan figured that Jake must have taken the old secret passageway out to Avenue J. Jake was such an asshole, making Christina climb fences, and Ryan couldn't understand why Christina even went with him. Why didn't she just break up with him in the backyard and come back inside?

After Jake and Christina had been gone for half an hour or so the crowd outside started to get impatient and chanted, 'Jake, Jake, Jake. . . .' Mrs Thomas asked Ryan if he knew where Jake and Christina went and Ryan said he had no idea.

'Oh, they probably just went somewhere to be alone,' she said. 'I guess you can't really blame them, can you?'

After it became clear that Jake wasn't returning anytime soon, Mrs Thomas made an announcement to the crowd that Jake wasn't feeling well and that he wouldn't be able to sign any more autographs. The crowd groaned and some people booed, which made Ryan feel a little better, but he couldn't stop making up stories to himself. He imagined that Jake had sweet-talked Christina into staying with him and they'd checked into a hotel somewhere. He pictured Jake kissing Christina and them in bed together, fucking.

Ryan turned off Jay-Z and started listening to Nelly. Nelly wasn't Ryan's favorite rapper – that honor went to Nas – but nothing beat 'Oh Nelly' when he was pissed off. Sitting on his bed, slapping his fist hard against his knee in synch with the throbbing beat, Ryan couldn't stop thinking about Christina with Jake. He took out his cell phone and called Christina's cell for what must've been the twentieth time. Like the other times, her voice mail picked up before the first ring, meaning that, for some reason, she'd turned her phone off. This time, instead of hanging up, Ryan decided to leave a message.

'Chrissy, Ry. Call me.'

He listened to the rest of the CD, then went downstairs to get something to eat. He hadn't heard his father come home, but Rocco Rossetti was sitting at the kitchen table, eating leftover lasagna, a copy of the *Canarsie Courier* spread out next to the dish. Rocco was dark, overweight, with streaks of gray in his messy hair. He worked for a plumbing contractor, and, as usual, he was sweaty and dirty, in a white wife-beater and jeans after a long day's work.

'What's up?' Ryan asked.

Rocco grunted but didn't answer.

Ryan opened the fridge, stared for a while, still thinking about Jake and Christina, then snapped out of it and realized he was looking for something to eat. He took out a package of bologna and then stood at the counter near the sink, making a sandwich with rye bread.

'What'd the Knicks do?' Rocco asked.

'Dunno,' Ryan said.

'Were up four in the third but probably fuckin' blew it.' Rocco shook his head miserably.

Ryan finished making the sandwich, then started eating, standing up.

About a minute went by, then Rocco said, 'Jesus, you read this?

A sixteen-year-old nigger breaks into a house, shoots a woman in the face, steals sixty dollars. Happened right up on Hundred and Third near Farragut. I used to play stickball on that block with my friend Joey Mantello and his brother Tommy. Fuckin' spook bastards fuckin' up the neighborhood. Now you need fuckin' assault weapons to go up there.'

Rocco was slurring, and Ryan realized that he'd been drinking. Although Rocco had been in AA for years, he still drank beer, claiming that beer didn't count – it was only the hard stuff he had to avoid.

Rocco took a big bite of lasagna, shaking his head. Ryan checked his cell phone to see if he had any messages, then put the phone back in his pocket.

'Every week you read the same shit in the paper,' Rocco went on. 'Rapes, murders, all that fucking crack. When I was growing up you could stay out on the street all night, you could leave your door open. I remember when the Thomases moved on the block. Your mother said' – Rocco's voice got whiny, imitating Rose-Marie – ' "Don't worry, Rocco, it's one black guy – what's the difference?" Now look what happened. It's like when you see the first cockroach in your house. You don't do anything about it, then boom – you're infested.'

Rocco took hard, angry bites of his lasagna, as if he were trying to gnaw into a tough steak.

'So you go to the party?' Rocco asked.

'Yeah,' Ryan mumbled.

'What?' Rocco said, although Ryan knew he'd heard him.

'Yeah,' Ryan said louder.

'They still had the fucking street closed off when I came home,' Rocco said. 'Had to park around the corner, but those people don't give a shit.'

Ryan knew that this was true, but he didn't like hearing it, especially from his asshole father.

'I remember back in Little League,' Rocco went on, 'you were the big star, not Jake. Yeah, he could hit, but you could pitch. That's why people came to the games – to see you throw those curveballs. A twelve-year-old kid, lettin' it fall off the table like that. Anybody who saw the two of you play back then would've thought you were gonna be the superstar someday, not that fuckin' monkey.'

'So what's your point?' Ryan asked.

'Nothing. I'm just saying you had the talent, and talent like that doesn't just go away. . . . Hey, I heard the Cyclones have tryouts out in Coney Island sometimes. Why don't you go down there and show your stuff? They got big-league scouts can sign you up.'

'Why would they sign me?'

'What do you mean? To pitch.'

'I can't pitch anymore.'

'How do you know?'

Shaking his head, Ryan stuffed the rest of the sandwich into his mouth and wiped the crumbs off the counter into his hand.

'What do they always say?' Rocco said. 'You gotta be in it to win it. How do you know you can't pitch till you try? Those injuries heal. You can come back if you want to, if you put your head into it.'

'Okay, let's drop it.'

'You're better than that fucking Jake Thomas. The only thing he ever had on you is he's half-spook. You got the black blood in you, you're gonna make it in sports. Look at his father. The guy's built like a gorilla. It's in their fuckin' blood, I'm telling ya. They lived in the jungles, running around, throwing fuckin' spears; of course they can throw fuckin' baseballs. But they can't throw footballs. That's how come you never seen a black quarterback win the Super Bowl.'

'How many beers you have tonight?' Ryan asked.

'What?'

'You think you're hiding it? You think I can't tell?'

'I had one – with dinner.'

'Yeah, more like ten with no dinner.'

Ryan took out a pack of cigarettes from his back pocket. He put one in his mouth and lit it with the burner on the stove.

'So you gonna go to those fuckin' Coney Island tryouts or what?' Rocco said.

'My baseball career's over,' Ryan said. 'Just get that into your fuckin' head, all right?'

'You never used to be a quitter. You used to have fight.'

Ryan finished a long drag on the cigarette, looking away.

'Look at you,' Rocco went on. 'Smoking like a fuckin' chimney, listening to that goddamn rap music all the time. Can't you just dress normal, tie the laces on your goddamn sneakers? Who woulda thought my own son would turn nigger?'

'Watch it.'

'Look in the mirror. You're fuckin' white!'

Rose-Marie entered the kitchen.

'What're you two fighting about now?'

'Nothing,' Ryan said.

'Your son's a quitter,' Rocco said.

'Shut up,' Ryan said.

'He could pitch for the Mets if he wanted to, but he just wants to paint houses and pretend he's a nigger. The kid's a fuckin' loser.'

'Look who's calling me a loser,' Ryan said, 'a fucking fifty-seven-year-old plumber who gets drunk every night like a bum.'

'Hey!' Rocco stood up, like he was about to go after Ryan.

'Were you drinking?' Rose-Marie asked Rocco, sounding concerned.

Rocco pointed his index finger at Ryan. 'You better fuckin' watch it, you little piece of shit!'

'Both of you, stop it,' Rose-Marie said. 'Just stop it!'

'Kid's got no fuckin' respect,' Rocco said.

'You said you were gonna stop drinking,' Rose-Marie said.

'I wasn't fuckin' drinking,' Rocco said. 'You gonna listen to him?'

Ryan put his cigarette out in the sink and left the kitchen, hearing his father screaming, 'Who you callin' a liar, huh? Who you callin' a fuckin' liar?'

Ryan went to his room, locked the door, and cranked Mobb Deep's 'Bitch Ass Nigga,' just to piss his father off.

Lying on his back, staring at the ceiling, Ryan took out his cell phone. He changed the ringer setting to vibrate and kept the phone in his hand so he wouldn't miss Christina's call.

After about fifteen minutes, Ryan lowered the music and called Christina, again getting her voice mail. He clicked off without leaving a message and decided enough was enough. Christina had left the party with Jake over four hours ago, and that was plenty of time to break up. Either they were fucking or something else had gone wrong. Maybe she walked home alone and got mugged or raped.

He dialed her home number, not realizing that he'd done it until her father answered.

'What?' Al Mercado said.

'Hey, it's Ryan. Is Christina there?'

'She's upstairs with Jake.'

A sharp pain ripped through Ryan's stomach.

After a couple of seconds Al said, 'Hello?'

'Can I talk to her?' Ryan asked.

'Wait till tomorrow, will ya?'

'D'you know what they're doing up there?'

'What?'

'I really need to talk to her. It's important.'

'I'm sure it's not that important. Call tomorrow.'

'But—'

Al hung up.

'Damn it,' Ryan said, clicking off.

Ryan pressed TALK again, redialing, but when Al barked, 'What?' Ryan disconnected.

Ryan closed his eyes and took deep breaths, trying to control himself. He wanted to call again and keep calling, but he didn't want to do anything stupid. She was probably in her room breaking up with Jake and nothing had gone wrong. At least she was safe – she hadn't been attacked or anything.

Ryan turned the stereo back up and sat at the edge of his bed, his legs bopping up and down hyperactively, out of synch with the beat of Cam'ron's 'Lord You Know.'

Someone started banging on his door.

'Hey!' Rocco said. 'Turn that shit down! Hey, you hear me?'

Ryan made the music even louder, drowning out his father's voice and the banging.

For the next hour or so Ryan killed time listening to gangsta rap, smoking cigarettes, and surfing the Net. He went onto rapboard.com and skimmed a thread a poster caller 'Flava4U' had started, accusing Eminen of being a racist. Flava had been posting the same crap for months, and Ryan didn't even bother responding. On the AOL rap and hip-hop board, there was a very long thread about the latest rumors about the 50 cent/Ja Rule rivalry.

Ryan typed a long post about how the rivalry was a lot of commercial BS, that the two guys were probably best friends, and people should forget about it already and move on. He read part of another thread – somebody was dissing Usher and Beyoncé for selling out to white suburbia – and then he checked out the BET message board where people were posting lists of the best lyricists of all time. The usuals – Tupac, Jay-Z, Eminem, Nas – were mentioned, but Ryan typed in, 'What about Canibus? What about Murs?' Then he skimmed another long thread discussing the latest rumor about who'd killed Jam Master Jay, including some nonsense about how the CIA had done it. Every few minutes, as Ryan mindlessly read more posts, he checked his cell phone for messages in case the ringer wasn't working or something, but Christina wasn't getting in touch.

At 11:41 Ryan got offline and took a shower. He scrubbed himself hard, trying to get all the paint off his body. As he massaged soap into his balls, he remembered how he'd come prematurely with Christina – again. Although she'd said she understood, maybe she thought the problem would go on forever, that they'd never be able to have good sex, and this drove her back to Jake.

Or maybe it was all about money.

Ryan remembered Christina in the car, suggesting that she sell her engagement ring so that Ryan could use the money to start his painting business. Christina always seemed concerned about Ryan's future, and didn't seem to believe in him. If she married Jake she'd have millions of dollars, fancy houses, cars, expensive clothes, jewelry, and everything else she wanted. But with Ryan, especially if his business didn't work out, life would always be a struggle. They'd have to scrounge for money for rent and bills, and they might never be able to afford a house or take vacations or buy the things she wanted. Maybe she thought that a guy like Jake Thomas was too good a thing to give up.

With soap still covering most of his body, Ryan got out of the shower. He wrapped a towel around his waist, then went to his bedroom. To hell with it – he'd just go over to her place and see what was going on. Then, pulling on his jeans, he changed his mind. If he barged into her house like a psycho she'd never forgive him.

Ryan took off the jeans and put on sweats and a T-shirt and lay in bed with his eyes closed. He wasn't tired at all, and his mind was still spinning. He went downstairs to the living room and watched TV. His parents had gone to bed, and the house was dark except for the TV light. He channel-surfed mindlessly for a while, then stopped on Jay Leno. He felt like somebody was playing a sick joke on him, because Jake was sitting there next to Jay in some expensive suit and shiny shoes. It must've been a repeat, but what were the odds of this show playing tonight?

Jake was telling Jay some long story about something that had happened on his flight to LA. Ryan didn't think it was funny, but Jay and the audience were cracking up. Jake's fake smile and cockiness, the way he was acting like he was Jay's best friend, made Ryan nauseous, and he had to change the channel.

It was past midnight now – too late to call Christina again. Somehow seeing Jake acting like a jerk on TV had made Ryan feel better about everything. Jake was an asshole, and Christina knew it. She complained about him all the time, talking about how she felt like an idiot for getting engaged to him, and there was no way she'd ever stay with him. Sure, the thought of being married to a multimillionaire famous baseball player had to be tempting, but she wouldn't have fallen in love with Ryan in the first place if money were so important to her.

Ryan was glad that he'd restrained himself, that he'd left only one message on Christina's cell, and that he hadn't gone over there. He was also glad that her cell phone had been off so she wouldn't see any missed calls on her display and know how many times he'd tried to contact her. In the morning she'd probably call him and apologize for not getting in touch. She'd explain how Jake had broken down crying when she dumped him and how she felt like she had to stay with him until he was in shape to go home. And she'd say that she'd shut her phone off only because she didn't want to cause any big scene. Christina was always like that – caring about other people's feelings. Then Christina would say that Jake was officially out of the picture, and she was ready to spend the rest of her life with Ryan. Ryan would make a reservation for next Friday night at her favorite restaurant – Luna in Little Italy. He'd hold her hands and lean over the table, then look into her eyes and say, 'There's something I have to ask you.'

She'd say, 'What?' and then he'd get on one knee, in the middle of the restaurant with everybody looking at them, and she'd start trembling. Then he'd pop the question and she'd say, 'Yes, yes, of course!' and she'd be smiling, the happiest girl alive.

Ryan flicked off the TV and went back up to his room. He stirred for a long time, unable to get comfortable.

Around two in the morning, he fell asleep.

Nine

Ryan was jolted awake by his alarm clock at the usual time – 8:25.
After putting on basketball pants and an old Ronnie Lott jersey,
he went downstairs. His mother was in the kitchen, having coffee,
watching *Good Day New York* on the little set on the table.

'Morning,' Ryan said.

Rose-Marie didn't answer right away, then said, 'Oh, good
morning,' distracted, her gaze focused away from the TV, toward
her mug of coffee, or at something near it.

'So what happened last night?'

'What?' Rose-Marie said, lost.

'With Dad . . . after I went upstairs. Did he calm down?'

'Oh, everything's fine. Don't worry about it.'

Ryan could tell that Rose-Marie was lying.

'Did he hit you?' he asked.

'No,' she said.

'Tell me the truth, Ma.'

'He didn't hit me – I swear. Why don't you take some leftover
lasagna for lunch? There's a whole tray of it in the fridge.'

'I'm gonna call his sponsor today,' Ryan said.

'What good's that gonna do?'

'What's his name . . . Joe? No, Jim . . .'

'Don't call anybody.'

'I'm not gonna let him hurt you again.'

'Promise me you won't call anybody. That'll only make things
worse.'

'All right, whatever . . . but I'm not gonna let him hurt you
again – I promise you that.'

Ryan kissed his mother on the forehead, then said, 'See ya,' and
left the kitchen.

It was a perfect morning – probably fifty degrees, without a cloud in the sky. Ryan walked up the block toward where he'd parked his car yesterday evening, around the corner on Flatlands. There was a small crowd of about twenty people in front of Jake's house. Passing the WELCOME HOME JAKE, OUR HERO banner, Ryan didn't feel the slightest pang of bitterness or jealousy. Who cared if Jake Thomas had a great baseball career and was loved by everybody? Ryan had Christina, and that was all that really mattered.

In his car, before he pulled out, Ryan put his cell phone earpiece in, and then, as he drove, he called Christina. A few seconds later her voice mail answered, but this wasn't unusual. She usually had her phone off in the morning, and she and Ryan talked to each other at some point later on, after she arrived at work.

Ryan clicked off without leaving a message. He double-parked in front of the deli on Flatlands, then went inside and ordered his black coffee with four sugars and ham-and-egg on a roll.

At the counter, Andre said to him, 'You were at the party yesterday, man?'

'Yeah,' Ryan said.

'I got Jake Thomas's autograph,' Andre bragged, 'right on the barrel of my bat – Louisville Slugger. Gonna put that shit away in a case – shit's gonna be worth money someday, yo.' He gave Ryan his change from a five. 'But, you know, man, he wasn't like what I thought.'

'Yeah?' Ryan said. 'Why's that?'

'Dunno, man. I mean, you'd think some big-time baseball player's gonna be all into himself and shit, but he was like a normal, regular guy, know what I'm sayin'? I mean, you can talk to him and shit.'

Ryan didn't want to tell Andre that he had the totally wrong impression of Jake, that Jake was a big time dick and nothing like the great guy he pretended to be in public. If Andre wanted to go through his life thinking Jake was some big hero, why bust his bubble?

'Yeah, I know exactly what you mean,' Ryan said.

Driving toward Mill Basin, with the front windows open all the way, letting in the cool ocean air, Ryan's phone started ringing. The display read, CHRISSY.

'Hey,' Ryan said into the phone, but there was no one there. Figuring the call had been lost, Ryan called her back but got her voice mail. He tried a few more times, continuing to get her voice mail, and he figured she was probably on the bus, in an area where she couldn't get service. He figured she'd call him again when she got to work, probably in another ten minutes or so.

In a parking space on Whitman Drive, Ryan ate his breakfast, imagining seeing Christina later. It would be so different with Jake out of the picture. All the tension would be gone, and Ryan could make love to her, *really* make love to her for the first time. They could do it slow and relaxed, looking into each other's eyes, with no pressure, knowing that they were in love and would be together forever, and that nothing could ever tear them apart.

'What you doin' in outer space, man?' Carlos said.

Ryan turned and saw Carlos looking into the car, smiling.

'How's it goin'?' Ryan asked.

'All right, man. Yo, I brought that ball in my trunk for you to get signed. You're gonna hook me up, right?'

Ryan doubted that Jake would want to do him any favors, but he didn't want to let Carlos and the other guys down. He figured he could get his mother to ask Jake's mother to have Jake sign the stuff. As long as Jake didn't think it had anything to do with Ryan he'd do it.

'No problem, man,' Ryan said.

'That's cool, yo,' Carlos said. 'I'm gonna owe you one now. Gettin' Jake Thomas's autograph on a baseball – my little cousin's gonna think I'm a superhero.'

Carlos went into the house. Before Ryan left the car, he called Christina at work.

'Hi, Allison, how's it going? Is Christina there?'

'Oh, hi, Ryan,' Allison, the receptionist, said. 'Nope, she's not here yet.'

'Oh, okay,' Ryan said. 'Can you tell her to call me when she gets in?'

'Yeah, okay.'

As Ryan went into the house, he was getting the feeling that something wasn't right, but he tried not to pay any attention to it.

He changed into his painting clothes upstairs, then joined Carlos and Franky in the kitchen.

'Hey, so how was it?' Franky asked.

'Pretty good,' Ryan said.

'I read in the paper they had a lot of people there, huh?'

'Yeah,' Ryan said.

'I shoulda gone,' Franky said, 'but I don't like that crowd shit. I get claustrophobic, you know?'

'So you hang out with Jake Thomas last night or what?' Carlos asked.

'Little bit,' Ryan said.

'He say he gonna come play for the Yanks next year?'

'I don't know.'

'Hey, you see him on Leno last night?' Franky asked.

'Yeah, I did catch some of that,' Ryan said.

'Shit cracked me up,' Franky said. 'You know, he had a good personality on TV. I bet he could make it in movies if he wanted to. He ever talk about doing anything like that?'

'Not to me,' Ryan said.

'Yeah, I could see him up there on the screen,' Franky said. 'He's a good actor, you know? Ever see him in that Pizza Hut commercial?'

'Where the girl orders the pizza and J.T. is standin' there behind the counter,' Carlos said.

'And that girl gets that look on her face, like, "Holy shit." '

'And J.T. is just standing there, actin' like it's no big deal.'

'He's good,' Franky said. 'I mean, in a Pizza Hut commercial you can't tell if the guy's gonna be the next Bobby De Niro, know what I mean, but you can tell he knows how to act. He's got that whatchamacallit, too. Star quality. The guy's definitely got star quality.'

'Hey, you hear he's gettin' married?' Carlos asked.

Ryan had climbed to the top of a stepladder, and now he stumbled, nearly falling off it.

'Whoa, you okay?' Franky said.

'Yeah, man,' Carlos said. 'You all right?'

'The fuck're you talking about?' Ryan said to Carlos.

'What?' Carlos said.

'Who's getting married?' Ryan said.

'J.T.,' Carlos said. 'It said so in the paper. He's marrying his high school sweetheart or some shit.'

Ryan's legs buckled, and he felt light-headed. He started losing his balance again, and Franky had to rush over and grab him by the waist to keep him from falling.

'Whoa, what's wrong with you, man?' Franky said.

'Where?' Ryan said to Carlos. 'What paper?'

'*Daily News*,' Carlos said. 'Hold up – I'll show you.'

Carlos went into the dining room and returned with a folded newspaper. Ryan got off the stepladder and took the paper from him. First he looked at the picture of Jake picking up Christina and kissing her, taken when Christina arrived at the party last night, and then he saw the headline: 'J.T. to Wed!'

He stared at the short article for several seconds, unable to think or see clearly. He felt like he'd just left the eye doctor's office with his eyes dilated and then someone sneaked up behind him and hit him on the head with a sledgehammer. Finally he was able to read random portions of the article – 'a sad day for single girls,' 'bachelor days behind him,' 'announced he will wed his high school sweetheart, Christina Mercado, next winter,' – and portions of quotes from Jake – 'both very excited about this,' 'our wedding is going to be magical,' 'we hope the public respects our privacy.'

Ryan was outside, calling Christina at work. He was so frazzled and dazed that he didn't remember anything about the ten or so seconds it must have taken him to leave the house and make the call. He kept telling himself that there had to be some mistake; the article couldn't be true. Even if something had happened between Jake and Christina last night, if they had decided to stay engaged, the news about their wedding plans couldn't have made it into the papers so quickly.

'Hey, it's Ryan. Is Christina there?'

'Um, no,' Allison said, 'not yet.'

Ryan knew she was lying.

'Just put her the fuck on.'

'But she's not here.'

'Put her on the fucking phone,' Ryan said, nearly screaming. 'It's a fucking emergency, all right?'

After a pause Allison said, 'Hold on.'

Ryan started pacing back and forth along the sidewalk. He kept telling himself, *Stay calm*, but he couldn't.

Allison came back and said, 'I just checked. She's not here yet.'

'Did she tell you to screen my calls?'

'What?'

Ryan clicked off and headed toward his car. He reached into the pockets of his painting pants, so angry and distracted that it took him a few seconds to realize that his car keys were in his jeans, inside the house.

He returned to the house, going right upstairs and changing back into his jeans and Lott jersey.

Franky came into the room and said, 'What's the matter?'

Ryan pushed past him, heading toward the stairs.

'Hey, where the hell you goin'?'

Ryan left the house, got in his car, and sped away.

He ran a red on Avenue U, just missing a laundry truck. Tears were streaming down his cheeks, and his heart was pounding.

He zipped along the Belt Parkway, weaving in and out of traffic, almost crashing into the railing and into other cars several times. He excited at Bay Parkway. Several minutes later he arrived at McDonald Avenue and left the car double-parked in front of the dental office where Christina worked.

The office was on the second floor, above a pizza place. He took the stairs two at a time, then pressed the button on the intercom. When he was buzzed in he bypassed the waiting area and the desk where Allison was seated. 'Hey, wait, where're you going?' she said, but he ignored her and went down toward the short hallway, toward the examination rooms.

He opened the door to one room where Dr Hoffman, the dentist, and Lisa, another hygienist, were working on a patient. They were wearing surgical masks and Dr Hoffman had goggles on.

Dr Hoffman, who knew Ryan, said, 'Yes?' looking surprised and sounding angry.

'Where's Christina?' Ryan asked.

'Look, I'm busy here,' Dr Hoffman said. 'You can't just come in here and—'

'Ryan.'

Ryan turned around and saw Christina standing there. He knew, just looking at her, that it was all true.

Dr Hoffman said, 'Christina, you're gonna have to take this outside.'

'Sorry,' Christina said.

'What's going on with this shit?' Ryan said.

'Ryan, please—'

'What the fuck happened last night? Did you fuck him? Is that what happened? Did you fuck that asshole?'

The patient, a middle-aged woman who seemed out of it, was looking over.

'Christina,' Dr Hoffman said angrily.

Christina pulled Ryan away by the arm, and then Ryan jerked free.

'I want you to say it to my face,' Ryan said. 'Say it's all true.'

'Let's go outside.'

'Say it. Say it right here.'

Christina stared at Ryan. She was crying.

'I can't believe you did this to me,' Ryan said. 'Why? What the hell is wrong with you?'

'I'm sorry.'

'You're sorry?' He was yelling. 'You lie to me, you tell me all this bullshit, saying you love me, saying we're gonna be together—'

'I do love you.'

'Bullshit! You lied to me! You lied to my fucking face!'

Dr Hoffman poked his head out of the office and said, 'I want this outside – right now.'

'You're gonna get me fired,' Christina said.

'What do you care? You got Jake's money now. What do you need this stupid job for?'

'Let's go,' Christina said, then walked ahead of Ryan toward the waiting room. She left the office and started toward the stairs that led to the street, when Ryan grabbed her arm from behind at the top of the landing.

'What did he say to you?' Ryan said. 'What fuckin' lies did he tell you?'

'He didn't tell me any lies.'

'Something must've happened last night. He must've laid it on real good, but you can't believe anything he tells you. You know how full of shit he is. I know you wouldn't fall for that. You're way too smart for that shit.'

'It's complicated.' More tears dripped down her cheeks.

'What's complicated? You were supposed to break up with him and stay with me. Is it money? Because if you're worried about money, I'm telling you I'm gonna make it someday. I don't know how I'm gonna do it, if it'll be my painting business or something else, but I know I'll have money someday. I won't have as much as Jake, but I'll have enough to—'

'It's not about money.'

'Then what is it? I know you don't love him.'

'That's not true, I . . . I mean, we've been together for a long time and it's not easy to . . . I mean, I feel like I have to give it a chance to—'

'You're so full of shit.' Ryan was raising his voice again. 'You know he's a scumbag, that he treats you like shit, but you just wanna stay with him for the money. That's all you care about – his goddamn bank account!'

'That's not true.'

'What the hell were you doing with me for ten fuckin' months, huh? Were you just using me, trying to get him to get off the pot to marry you?'

'Come on,' she said, touching his arm. 'You know it wasn't like that.'

Ryan pulled his arm away, said, 'Then what was it like? I mean, I know what you've been telling me, but I guess I was an idiot for believing any of that.'

Christina was crying harder now, her lips trembling.

'I really didn't want to hurt you,' she said slowly, struggling to get the words out.

'Bullshit. You couldn't even tell me to my face. I had to read about it in the fucking newspaper.'

'I have no idea how it got into the papers – I swear to God. I just got here, and Dr Hoffman said congratulations, and I was like, "What're you talking about?" I called you, but I hung up – I didn't know what to say. Please – please don't hate me. I still love you. I know that's hard for you to believe, but I really do love you. I'm just in a really complicated situation right now. I mean, you knew that all along – you knew I was engaged, and I really did want to be with you, but I also feel like I have to give me and Jake a chance. It might not work out, but I just have to see. And I'm really, really sorry you had to read about it in the newspaper. Jake must've called them last night or something and told them – I honestly had no idea. . . . But, look, we should talk about this. Maybe we could, like, meet for coffee later, or maybe we could have dinner or . . . Why won't you look at me?'

Ryan, who'd been staring at the floor, looked up at Christina standing there, crying, with her back to the stairs, and imagined pushing her. It would be so easy – just one little push and she'd go tumbling backward.

He stood there for a few more seconds, staring into her eyes, hating her.

Then he said, 'Just stay the fuck away from me,' and he went by her and headed down the stairs.

He was hoping she'd say, 'Wait, come back,' or, 'Don't go,' or something to show she gave a shit. But she said nothing – zippo. She just let him walk out to the street as if she didn't care whether she saw him again or not.

A meter maid was standing in front of Ryan's car, writing a ticket. She handed it to him, explaining that he was parked illegally. Without an argument, Ryan snatched it and drove away.

A few minutes later, as he drove along Bay Parkway, it hit him. Christina was gone, really gone – they might never even talk to each other again. How could everything have turned to shit so quickly? Just yesterday, at her place, she was saying all those things about how great it would be when Jake was out of the picture, about how much she loved Ryan and wanted to be with him forever, and now she was back with Jake. How could she have done this to him? How could she be so sick and heartless?

Ryan managed to drive a few more blocks, but then he couldn't take it anymore. He pulled over, sobbing, with his head resting against the steering wheel. After his baseball career ended he had cried on and off for weeks, but this pain was much worse. Christina had meant everything to him. When he was down and out and had nothing left, she had given him hope, a reason to live. But now she was gone, and that hope was gone too. He wanted to take pills, slit his wrists, jump in front of a subway, end his stupid fucking life.

He continued to sob, occasionally pounding the dashboard with his fists. His beeper started vibrating. He wasn't going to check it, but then he realized it could be Christina.

He looked at the display, angry to see Franky's number flashing. How could she not call him? How could she not give a shit? What the hell was wrong with her?

He stopped crying, wiping the tears off his cheeks with his forearms. He was angry at himself for losing control, for being weak. He remembered standing in front of Christina on the landing, listening to her 'explain' why she'd treated him like total dogshit and feeling like he wanted to push her down the stairs.

Franky beeped him again and he turned the beeper off. He didn't give a shit about work – he didn't give a shit about anything.

He started the car, made a sharp U-turn, and headed back toward the dental office. He was imagining going in there, grabbing her, taking her someplace, and beating the living hell out of her.

He pulled over again. With his eyes closed he took slow, deep breaths, trying to calm down.

After a couple of minutes he made another U-turn and drove away. He put on 50 Cent with the volume all the way up and kept going. He had no idea where he was going – he just wanted to keep moving. He took Flatbush to downtown Brooklyn, and then he drove through the streets of Williamsburg and Bed-Stuy. He drove through parts of Brooklyn he'd never been to before, slums where white boys got killed if their cars broke down, and then wound up in Queens, and on Long Island. Eventually, after he'd been riding around for about two hours, he returned to Brooklyn and drove through East New York back toward Canarsie.

He was tired, empty, numb, and nauseous, and he wanted to go home, get into bed, and sleep for a very long time, maybe forever. Then he turned onto East Eighty-first Street and saw the crowd in front of Jake's house, and that huge banner still hanging over the street, and he felt the blood rushing to his head again.

Without realizing what he was doing, he screeched to a stop, backed out onto Flatlands Avenue, and started speeding toward Christina's office. Then, after going about ten blocks, he decided he had to get a grip and he pulled into a spot near Cousin's, a sports bar his father used to take him to on Sundays to watch football games. It had just opened for the day, and there was only one old drunk at the far end of the bar. Ryan sat at the other end and the bartender came over.

'What can I get you?' the bartender asked.

Ryan recognized him. His name was Mike and he'd been working there for years.

'Rum and Coke – heavy on the rum,' Ryan said. Then he handed Mike a MasterCard and said, 'Start a tab.'

'You got it,' Mike said.

Mike brought the drink, and Ryan sucked it down like there was no rum in it and ordered another. After he chugged the second drink, Mike said to him, 'You feeling okay, guy?'

'Just get me another,' Ryan said, already slurring.

Mike stared at him for a couple of seconds, then went and made the third drink.

Ryan finished it in several gulps and immediately held up the empty glass and shook it, signaling for number four.

'Let's take it easy now,' Mike said. 'Maybe you want to wait ten, fifteen minutes and—'

'Just make it,' Ryan said.

'I want you to slow down, buddy. You're drinking way too . . . Wait a sec – I know you, don't I? You're Rocco Rossetti's kid.'

'Wrong,' Ryan said.

'No, come on, you're Ryan Rossetti – the baseball player.'

'Okay, that's me, but I'm not a baseball player anymore; I'm a house painter. Can I just get that drink?'

'I thought you looked familiar when you walked in here. I just couldn't place the face. You haven't been by here in a long time, huh?'

Ryan was getting drunk, but the rum wasn't lessening his rage. He needed another drink fast.

'Few years,' Ryan said. 'Can you just—'

'You used to be buddies with Jake Thomas, right?' Mike said. 'I remember your old man coming in here, talking about you two all the time, and he'd show me all the articles about you guys in the papers. You got drafted by who? St Louis?'

'Cleveland,' Ryan said.

'Right, the Cleveland Indians. Yeah, your old man was real

proud of you – never shut up about you, matter of fact. Hey, your old buddy Jake's in town, ain't he? Read about it in the paper – they had some big party for him yesterday, right?'

'Right,' Ryan said, 'but—'

'Guy's some ballplayer,' Mike said. 'Can do it all – hits, runs, and the ladies love him. The guy's got a charmed life, don't he?'

Ryan stared at his drink.

'So what's up with you, anyway?' Mike asked. 'Why're you sucking down the rum and Cokes like you're going to the chair?'

'I'm just thirsty.'

'Come on, I been tendin' bar long enough to know when a guy's got something on his mind, and you definitely got something on your mind. You can tell me all about it – I'm a real good listener.'

Ryan didn't feel like talking, then decided maybe it was a good idea. Maybe it would help get all of the sick ideas out of his head.

'Okay, you really want to know,' Ryan said, 'my girlfriend just dumped my ass, all right? She swore we were gonna be together forever; then she just flat-out dumped me.'

This didn't come out the way Ryan meant it to. It didn't sound serious enough. It sounded like he was some brokenhearted high school kid.

'Look, I'm sure this girl was real special and everything,' Mike said, 'but trust me when I say this – no woman is worth it.'

Ryan was going to go on, explain that this wasn't any woman; this was Christina Mercado, Jake Thomas's fiancée. He was going to tell him how he'd been in love with her since kindergarten, and how they'd planned to spend the rest of their lives together until he read in the newspaper this morning that she and Jake had set a wedding date. But he knew he'd just be wasting his time, that Mike would never understand. Everybody loved Jake. Jake was a hero – he could do no wrong. If anything Mike would feel sorry for Jake for almost losing his fiancée to some other guy.

'Never mind,' Ryan said. 'How 'bout just bringing me that refill?'

'Drinking's not gonna get your girl back,' Mike said.

'I just need one more. I'm not driving, and I know how to handle my liquor. It's not a big deal.'

Mike thought it over for a few seconds, then said, 'All right, but you better nurse this one or I'm cutting you off.'

Mike made the new drink and brought it over. Ryan took a sip, then rested the glass on the bar and looked around. The guy at the end of the bar had left, so now Ryan was the only customer. Old-fart music, maybe Tony Bennett, was playing at a low volume, and the air was musty, making it hard to breathe. Ryan looked in the mirror behind the bar and saw himself sitting with his shoulders slumped, looking bitter and depressed.

After he took another small sip of the drink, resisting the impulse to chug it, he wondered if it all had to do with sex. Maybe Christina thought that she and Ryan would never do it for longer than thirty seconds and that she'd never be able to come with him. Maybe last night Jake seduced her and lasted a long time. Maybe she made her decision right then – *To hell with Ryan, I'm staying with Jake*. Sex and money. That was what it always came down to, wasn't it?

Ryan lifted the drink angrily, ready to swallow it in one tip of the glass, and then he looked over at Mike, watching him at the other end of the bar. Ryan took a big sip, leaving the glass half-full; then he swished the alcohol around like mouthwash before swallowing.

Fuck Christina, that little whore. All that crap, promising how great the sex would be when Jake was out of the picture and laying on all that bullshit about what a relief it would be not to have to sneak around anymore. And how about all those times they talked about what their kids would look like – whose eyes, nose, and hair they would have? They'd even named their kids – Justin and Amber – and decided that they'd have a golden retriever named Max.

Fucking whore. Fucking lying little tramp.

The alcohol wasn't working, or at least he hadn't had enough yet. Ryan was afraid that if he left the bar right now, he'd drive right to Christina's office and kill that lying, cheating little bitch.

He had to take a leak. When he stood up he realized he was drunker than he'd thought. He was wobbling, bumping into bar stools. In the bathroom, standing over the toilet bowl, he decided it was all his dick's fault. His dick had let him down big-time. If his dick just worked the way it supposed to, maybe Christina would still be with him right now. He hated his dick. He couldn't stand looking at it anymore.

Then he started staring at his left elbow, at the surgery scars. He hated his elbow as much as he hated his dick. If his elbow worked the way *it* was supposed to, his whole life would've been different. Instead of getting drunk in a Brooklyn bar, trying not to want to go kill his girlfriend, he'd have been in his ten-million-dollar mansion somewhere outside Cleveland. He'd have a wife and kids and would've forgotten about Christina a long time ago.

He finished peeing, then flexed his left arm. He didn't have any pain in his elbow. He remembered what his father had told him about trying out for the Brooklyn Cyclones. Maybe that wasn't such a bad idea. He hadn't even tried to throw a baseball in over three years – how did he know he couldn't pitch? There'd been stories before about miracle recoveries, guys defying the odds. Maybe his elbow had healed. Maybe he could do it.

After he finished peeing he stood in front of the mirror and went into a windup. He was so drunk it was hard to keep his balance on his right leg, and then, as he cocked his left arm as if about to throw, he felt the familiar sharp twinge. Maybe it was nothing, just some stiffness, but he knew he was kidding himself. His arm even hurt sometimes while he was painting, using the roller, so how would it feel when he tried to throw a ninety-mile-per-hour heater? Miracle comebacks were for movies. In real life, when things got fucked-up they stayed that way.

Ryan walked unsteadily back toward the bar. As he settled on the stool, he realized he hadn't had a smoke all day. He took out a cigarette from the pack in his jacket pocket, lit up, and took a drag.

Mike came right over and said, 'Sorry, can't smoke in here.'

Ryan inhaled again, exhaling the smoke through his nostrils, then looked around and said, 'But nobody's here.'

'Sorry, you still gotta put it out,' Mike said.

Ryan brought the cigarette to his lips again and took another drag.

Mike took out an ashtray from behind the bar, placed it in front of Ryan, and said, 'I'm serious.'

'What's the big deal?' Ryan said.

'The big deal is you can't smoke in here,' Mike said.

'I don't think you understand,' Ryan said. 'I need to smoke this cigarette, and I'm gonna smoke this cigarette.'

'Not in here you're not,' Mike said.

Ryan continued smoking.

Mike watched him, shaking his head slowly, then went to the register, charged Ryan's drinks to the credit card, and put the card and receipts in front of Ryan.

'I'm cutting you off,' Mike said, 'so you can just take it outside right now.'

Ryan blew smoke at Mike's face, then said, 'Fuck off.'

'Big shot,' Mike said. 'Got a few drinks in you – think you're Superman now, huh?'

Ryan didn't know what the fuck Mike was talking about.

'Yeah, that's me, fucking Superman,' Ryan said, feeling very drunk.

'Guess it don't fall far from the tree,' Mike said. 'Your old man used to get the same way. Nice guy till the drinks set in. Then he'd turn into a fucking asshole. Used to start fights; had to call the cops on him. Remember one time he started grabbing this girl's tits. Girl's boyfriend dragged him out to the street, beat the fuckin' crap out of him.'

Puffing on the cigarette, Ryan remembered the times his father would come home bloodied after a night of drinking, telling Rose-Marie stories of how he'd been mugged again.

'Looks like you're heading in the same direction,' Mike went on. 'Things don't go right in your life you start hitting the bottle, acting like a prick, taking it out on the world.'

'Fuck you,' Ryan said.

Mike shook his head, then walked toward the other end of the bar. Without looking back at Ryan he said, 'Just get the hell outta here.'

Ryan muttered to himself for a while, then realized Mike was right – he *was* acting like his father, sitting at a bar and getting drunk in the middle of the day, thinking about going to beat up his ex-girlfriend.

Ryan put out the cigarette in the ashtray and said, 'Hey, lemme get a ginger ale, will ya?'

Mike, looking at a newspaper, didn't answer.

'Look, I'm sorry,' Ryan said. 'You're right, I've been acting like an asshole. I just wanna sober up, then I'll go home. I swear.'

Mike hesitated, then went and filled a glass with ginger ale and brought it to Ryan.

'It's on the house,' he said.

'Thanks,' Ryan said, 'and I'm really sorry.'

Ryan sipped the ginger ale, proud of himself for being stronger than his father. He figured he'd stay at the bar for about an hour, then drive home and sleep it off. Maybe, after some time went by, he'd start to realize that losing Christina wasn't the worst thing in the world. Maybe he'd find someone else, someone he had more in common with, maybe someone who loved hip-hop and who didn't mind being married to a housepainter. He and this new girl could raise a family in Brooklyn, and his son would play Little League. Maybe Ryan would coach the team and make sure his kid didn't throw curveballs until he finished growing. His son would listen and get drafted in the first round. He'd play for the Mets, become their number one starter, and he'd pitch a shutout in game seven of the World Series.

For a while Ryan felt better, but then, as he finished the ginger ale, he started thinking about Jake.

He remembered how Jake had talked down to him and tried to set him up with one of his groupies, like he was a loser who couldn't get a date. Ryan had wanted to tell Jake to go fuck himself or, better yet, belt him in the mouth, break those fake choppers, but he'd held back, not wanting to make a big scene in front of Chrissy and all those people. Then, when Jake started making those disgusting comments about Christina, obviously not giving a shit about her, Ryan really wanted to beat the hell out of him, but he didn't because he figured Christina was going to dump Jake anyway, so why do something that might piss her off?

Sitting at the bar, squeezing the empty glass, Ryan decided it was all Jake's fault. Jake had done this – not because he wanted Christina or cared about her – no, those were the last things on that prick's mind. He wanted Christina for only one reason – to keep Ryan from having her. Jake had always been that way – trying his hardest to beat Ryan at everything. When they were kids it didn't matter if they were playing stickball, pickup basketball, or Monopoly; when Jake won, he would taunt Ryan, loving it, but when Ryan won Jake would sulk for days. After Ryan blew out his elbow and had to quit baseball, he had a feeling that Jake got off on it. Jake loved being the big winner, especially when Ryan was the big loser, and to him Christina was just another prize.

The more Ryan thought about it, the more convinced he became that Christina hadn't left him – Jake had stolen her away. Last night, when Jake and Christina left the party, Christina had probably told him about her and Ryan, which made Jake want her more than he ever had before. He probably poured on that fake charm and told her how much money he'd give her. Jake knew she was vulnerable, stuck in a run-down house with her loser father, and that he could sway her if he tried hard enough. He'd probably made her promises, told her about all the things he'd buy her, places they'd go, and after a while Christina started to cave. It made a lot of sense – when Jake wanted something bad enough nothing stopped him from getting it, and getting something that Ryan wanted only made the victory sweeter.

Mike came over and said, 'Another ginger ale?'

Ryan ignored him, signed for the drinks, and stormed out of the bar.

Moments later he was in his car, speeding, swerving toward Canarsie, his hands squeezing the steering wheel as hard as they would soon be squeezing Jake's neck.

Ten

Marcus Fitts lived in a one-bedroom apartment in the Bay View Houses on Seaview Avenue. His crib was small, maybe even tighter than Saiquan and Desiree's, but it had all the shit that Saiquan had always dreamed of getting but could never afford – black leather furniture, a big-ass rectangle-shaped plasma HDTV on the wall, and everything that went with it – DVD, surround sound, PlayStation, motherfucking TiVo. And his bedroom – damn, it had a king-size bed with one of those flat stereo-speaker combo shits, and his bathroom had one of those showerheads where the water came at you from every side, like you were standing in the middle of a waterfall.

Whenever Saiquan went over to Marcus's, he thought, *Why don't I got all this shit?* Like Saiquan, Marcus had started dealing in junior high and hooked up with the Crips in the joint, but Marcus spent more time away than Saiquan, finishing up a stretch upstate just last year. On top of that, the man used to be a sick-ass crackhead, almost killing himself a couple times on that shit. But now, while Saiquan was spending his time trying to fit into society, Marcus went on dealing and stealing, and he'd filled up his crib with all this cool shit.

It made Saiquan wonder. It made him wonder a lot.

In the hallway outside Marcus's, Saiquan heard some movie or video game playing – shit exploding. He rang the doorbell a few times, waited, then rang it a few more times. He smelled crack, and he hoped it wasn't coming from Marcus's – maybe somebody was just basing in the stairwell or some other crib.

After ringing the bell a couple more times, Saiquan had to start banging on the door with his fists because he didn't think Marcus could hear him over all of that noise. Finally Marcus opened the door, looking whacked – his eyes open so wide Saiquan could see white all around the brown.

'Yo, yo, yo, what up?' Marcus said, talking crackhead fast, like he'd been sitting home basing all motherfucking day.

Marcus was wearing baggy jeans with patches all over them, and a triple-X T-shirt hanging down to his knees, prison-style. He used to have tight cornrows like Saiquan, but he'd let his hair grow out when he was away and now he had long, Sprewell-style braids. He wore beige Timbs, a solid-gold chain with a big gold peace sign hanging over his shirt, and a big gold earring that spelled CASH.

'Shit,' Saiquan said. 'How long you been gettin' fucked up?'

'I ain't fucked up, man,' Marcus said. 'You comin' in or what?'

Saiquan noticed the braces on Marcus's teeth – thick, shiny silver on the tops and bottoms.

'Yo, I don't need this shit right now, man,' Saiquan said. 'Basin' all day, then goin' out to the street, gettin' wild and shit. Just gimme a clean piece and I be on my way.'

'You comin'?' Marcus said.

Saiquan stood there for a few seconds, deciding what to do. He remembered how crazy Marcus used to get when he was high on crack, shooting and cutting brothers just for looking at him the wrong way or stepping on his Jordans. There was no way Saiquan was gonna bring Marcus along with him to smoke Jermaine. He just had to get a piece off him and that was it.

Saiquan went into the apartment, and Marcus said, 'Rest your ass down, take a seat. Watch some Jackie Chan.'

Saiquan glanced at the TV on the wall, at the paused scene of Jackie Chan in midair, doing a karate move.

Then Saiquan looked over at the glass coffee table with the two Baggies of rock – one full, one half-empty – and the crack pipe, the joint paper, and a Baggie of what looked like H. There were also a few empty bottles of Bud Light.

'That Chinese nigga Jackie Chan knows some *moves*, man,' Marcus said. 'Before, yo, he did this fuckin' split in the air and shit, kicked both these niggas' teeth out. He comes up to these niggas, right, smiles in that Chinese-man way, all polite and shit; then he goes *whack*, takes the nigga's piece, and nigga's just got this dumb-ass look on his face, like, *What the fuck just happened?*

Then you see my man Jackie leave his feet, go in midair, and kick both motherfuckin' niggas in the mouth at the same time. I slow-mo'd that shit, man.'

'Talkin' 'bout teeth,' Saiquan said. 'What up with all that shit?'

'They cool, right?' Marcus said, smiling, showing the braces off.

Saiquan did think they looked cool.

'They a'ight,' Saiquan said. 'Why'd you get 'em, man?'

'To fix my teeth – why the fuck you think? I wish I could keep 'em on forever, man. Bitches love 'em. Serious. I be walkin' down the street, they be lookin' me up and down, smilin' and shit. They never did that 'fore I got my braces.'

'Don't that shit cost money?'

'Hell, yeah. Had to pay one of 'em ortho-dentists two grand, and that's just the first payment. Muthafuckas make you pay four times. Shit hurts too. They use this wrench and shit, start twisting and pulling, but shit's worth it. I was sick of lookin' all bucktooth, teeth overlappin' all the time. Wanna smoke, man?'

Wondering where Marcus got two fucking grand to get his teeth fixed, Saiquan said, 'Naw, just gimme a fuckin' piece, man, and I be on my way.'

Marcus stared at Saiquan with his big glassy eyes, then said, 'The fuck you talkin' about, man? I'm comin' with you.'

'You think I'm takin' yo' fucked-up ass with me, you crazy,' Saiquan said. 'I don't need this shit, yo – my parole getting all fucked-up 'cause you sittin', doin' rock all day, then gettin' wild. Nuh-uh, man. Nuh-uh.'

'I told you, I ain't on no motherfuckin' rock, yo.'

'Man, you think I ain't on to yo' bullshit? You got all this shit out on the fuckin' coffee table, probably been basin' all mother-fuckin' day. You think I'm stupid?'

'I just had to test my product, man, know what I'm sayin'? Had to make sure I ain't holdin' no bad shit.'

'Who you lyin' to, man?'

'I smoked one pipe, yo – just one pipe, that's it. Why don't you shut up and do one too? Help relax yo' pussy ass.'

'Naw, man,' Saiquan said. 'You can keep on basin', watchin' Jackie Chan on your stolen motherfuckin' TV set. Just gimme my fuckin' piece and I be on my way.'

'Yo, yo, hold up.' Marcus was smiling. 'Lemme get this shit straight, yo. So what you gonna do, just go up to J on the street, cap the man, and walk away? And what you think his boys is gonna do? Just say, "There goes the man capped our cuz," and let you cruise?'

'I'll do a drive-by,' Saiquan said.

'Drive-by?' Marcus laughed. 'Shit, yo' bitch ride can't even get twenty mile an hour. You mi'se well be ridin' a motherfuckin' Big Wheel.' He laughed again.

Saiquan wondered how hard he'd laugh if he knew Saiquan's car was probably being towed to the junkyard right now.

'But now if you take *my* ride, yo, you'll be all hooked up,' Marcus said. 'My seven hundred goes zero to sixty in four-point-three. That's what you need when you got bullets comin' at your back, know what I'm sayin'?'

'Where'd you get a BMW?' Saiquan asked.

'Bought the shit last week,' Marcus said with a straight face.

Saiquan looked at Marcus, then said, 'Man, you must think I'm stupid. Go with you, get pulled over for grand theft auto and shit. Get five to ten for just sittin' there, doin' nothin'.'

'I don't go with you, you'll wish yo' ass was doing five to ten,' Marcus said. 'Shit, they'll give yo' ass life when you start shootin' wild into them crowds, hittin' people you ain't suppose to. Maybe you'll get a lady with a baby carriage and shit. When's the last time you shot a gun? You was away, what, three years, and I bet you ain't held a piece since you got out. You think that shit's like ridin' a bike?' Marcus held out his hand, his thumb and forefinger like a gun. 'You'll be like, "Fuh, fuh, fuh, fuh. Where them bullets at? I don't know, you see 'em?" ' Marcus laughed, then said, 'Yo, but if you got me, you got aim, know what I'm sayin'? Last week, two weeks ago, whatever, I shot this high school nigga in the Bloods. Shit made the paper – you can go read about it. Motherfucka was tryin' to play my customer, know what I'm sayin', so I capped his ass. Punk was standing in front of Mickey D's on Flatlands eatin' a Big Mac, and I came by, got five off with my nine. First shot went into the Big Mac. Nigga looked at his hand like, "What the fuck just happened to my burger?" Next two shots went right into his chest. Didn't hit nobody else neither. That's 'cause I know how to aim.'

Saiquan knew Marcus was full of shit – he didn't hear anything on the news last week about no bullet hitting no Big Mac. Besides, if Marcus really popped somebody he would've called Saiquan to brag about it right after it happened.

'So you wanna go yourself, go on,' Marcus said. 'But someday you're gonna be in your cell, some bitch greasin' yo ass, sayin' to yourself, "Maybe I made a mistake. Maybe I shoulda had Marcus come along."'

Saiquan still wanted to take a piece off Marcus and get on his way, but Marcus was making some sense. Thing made the most sense – you can't do a drive-by when you don't got a car. And if he tried to cap Jermaine on a street corner or in a schoolyard or wherever, a cop could catch him, or one of J's boys could smoke him in the back while he was running away, and he'd wind up dead or in a chair like D.

'Whatever,' Saiquan said. 'But you only gonna drive. I ain't havin' yo cracked-up ass shootin' no motherfuckin' guns.'

Saiquan followed Marcus down the short hallway into the bedroom. Marcus opened the closet, dug under a pile of clothes, and took out a big box of guns and dumped them onto the bed.

'Shit, what you got, a fuckin' store here?' Saiquan asked.

'I didn't tell you?' Marcus said. 'I been dealin' chrome to kids. You know, junior high, that kinda shit. There a lot of new gangs comin' up, kids and shit, know what I'm sayin', and they all need weapons. They money to be made, my man. Take one you want.'

'They all clean?'

'Shit, yeah.'

'I ain't playin', man. I ain't takin' a piece from yo' ass, get picked up, they take me down to the station and go, "How come you shot up that cop last week?"'

'The guns're clean, man, they clean. They imported from South Carolina.'

'So how you know they ain't shot nobody down there?'

'Just take a piece, man and shut the fuck up.'

Saiquan started looking through the pistols and handguns – picking some up and checking them out. It was true what Marcus had said – Saiquan hadn't held a gun since before he went away last time, three and a half years ago. He played with a few more, then picked up a white-and-gold one.

'Figures you'd take the bitchiest-ass piece I got,' Marcus said. 'You hit somebody with that ho gun the bullets bounce off, know what I'm sayin'? Gotta take something has some power, yo – make sure when you hit a man he go down way he suppose to.' He grabbed a shotgun. 'Check out this shit. Now that's gonna do some damage. Yo, or how 'bout this?' He held up a black semi. 'SIG two twenty-six. Got ten shots, and shit fires hard. Or maybe you likes my man the Tauras? Got ten plus one and got a spot for your pinkie to rest on. Or, wait, wanna do some serious damage, here we go.' He had a MAC-11. 'Now we gettin' there, yo. That shit, you put a hole in a man you could stick yo' fist through.'

Saiquan checked out a few more, then picked up a Glock nine-mill.

'Hope you remember how to aim that shit, man,' Marcus said, smiling with his shiny braces. 'Yo' hand don't look too steady.'

'It's cool,' Saiquan said, pressing the trigger again. 'You got a clip?'

Marcus reached into another box and gave Saiquan the ammo.

As Saiquan loaded the gun, Marcus said, 'Yo, better take more, case you need some backup, know what I'm sayin'? You ain't shot a gun in a long time, so you prolly gonna be doin' some serious missin'.'

Saiquan took another clip and tucked the gun under his belt.

'Yo, hold the piece like that, better make sure you keep the safety on that shit,' Marcus said. 'That shit go off you gonna have a big damn pussy to piss outta.'

'Let's just get the fuck outta here,' Saiquan said.

'Wait, what you gonna cover up with?'

'What you mean?'

'Shit, you been upstate too damn long, nigga. You forget they got somethin' called witnesses? What happens somebody sees yo' nigga ass smokin' J? Some little old lady ID's you and shit, goes, "Yeah, that's him. My glasses don't work too good, but that's him."' Marcus laughed. 'And I don't want none of them Crips niggas seein' my ass neither. They know I'm doin' this shit, they gonna be diggin' a grave for my ass real quick, know what I'm sayin'?'

Saiquan realized Marcus was right.

'So what you got?' Saiquan asked.

'See, you lucky you got me comin' 'long,' Marcus said. ' 'Cause you need my brains, that's why. I'm like the fuckin' Wizard and you the fuckin' Scarecrow. I think of shit you never think of. You don't got me, witness ID's yo' ass, and 'fore you know it some nigga at Riker's got you up against the wall, you feelin' his dick jammin' all the way up to yo' stomach like the shit's gonna pop a hole out yo' belly button.'

Knowing exactly what that felt like, Saiquan said, 'So what you got, stockin', ski masks . . . ?'

'Naw, I got somethin' better 'an 'at shit.'

Saiquan followed Marcus out toward the front door. Standing on a chair, Marcus reached up to the top shelf of the hallway closet, saying, 'Remember when we was, like, twelve years old and shit, we used to go trick-o'-treatin', except when they answered the bell, we took out blades and robbed their asses?'

'Yeah,' Saiquan said, wondering if he was making a big mistake getting in with Marcus.

'Lucky I saved up all my old costumes, man – come in handy tonight.' Marcus held out two masks. 'So who you wanna be, Batman or my man Casper the Friendly Ghost?'

Marcus's ride was a lot hotter than Saiquan expected. Shit looked brand-new – shiny silver on the outside, fine suede seats inside.

'You likes, right?' Marcus said when Saiquan got in next to him.

'It's a'ight,' Saiquan said, playing it down, not wanting to make the man's head any bigger than it already was.

'A'ight?' Marcus said. 'Shit's *fine*, yo, and you know that's the truth. I seen this shit double-parked on Canarsie Road, no Club, key in the ignition, like the muthafucka be sayin', "Take my car – please take it." And I'm goin' to myself, "*This shit gots to be mines.*" So I went, stepped on the gas, and drove that shit away. Check out the leather steering wheel. It also got ten speakers, six-speed active transmission, LCD, cruise control, and a whole lotta other cool shit.'

Marcus turned on the engine and started blowing AC out the vents even though it was a cool night outside and they didn't need it.

'Cops better not have this shit in their computers,' Saiquan said.

Marcus laughed. 'Computers – that shit's funny. The fuck you know about computers, man?' He turned on the stereo and reggae started blasting.

'I know they can bust your ass – that's what I know,' Saiquan said over the music.

'Chill, mon,' Marcus said, with a stupid Jamaican accent. 'You gots to learn to chill, mon.'

Saiquan turned the music down, then said, 'I ain't playin' around, yo. Them computers can bust yo' ass hard, yo. Nigga Leon on my block – he got busted that way. They caught his punk ass on radar, ridin' around the Bronx and shit.'

'Radar?' Marcus said. 'What the fuck you think we on, *Star Wars*?'

'That's what they usin' now. Got the LoJack shit built into the car. Shit comes up on the screen and they know where you at.'

'LoJack,' Marcus said. 'Man, I think you the one been smokin' some crack today.'

'How you know this car don't got no LoJack in it?'

' 'Cause I had the car a week already. Shit. They had LoJack in it don't you think they woulda busted my ass already?'

This was probably true, Saiquan realized, but he still had a bad feeling. Shit was gonna get fucked-up. He didn't know how, but it would.

They drove out of the lot onto Seaview Avenue. Marcus had the pedal down, getting to the intersection at One Hundred Second Street, then jammed the brakes.

'Maybe J be hangin' at the playground on Hundred Third tonight,' Marcus said. 'Maybe we pop him quick and I be back home to see the rest of *The Tuxedo*.'

They drove to Avenue K and stopped around the corner from the playground. Marcus put on his Batman mask and Saiquan put on Casper the Friendly Ghost.

'Let's do it,' Marcus said.

As they drove up the block, Saiquan saw a group of Crips brothers in blue do-rags standing on the sidewalk in front of the playground. Marcus slowed down, maybe going fifteen miles per hour. The brothers were still too far away for Saiquan to see their faces.

'You see J?' Saiquan asked, surprised that his voice sounded shaky.

Marcus squinted, leaning over the steering wheel. 'Can't tell. That might be him there in the back.'

Saiquan opened his window, realizing his hand holding the gun was shaking.

The Crips brothers saw the BMW coming down the block and some of their hands went under their shirts.

'I don't see him,' Saiquan said.

'Me neither,' Marcus said.

Marcus and Saiquan took off their masks, then Marcus sped up, honking the horn five times fast, a signal of respect to his fellow gang members. Saiquan showed his respect, nodding once as the BMW passed by.

'Nigga prolly be home right now,' Marcus said. 'We could go by his crib and check it out.'

'What we gonna do,' Saiquan said, 'knock and he come to the door and say, "Oh, good, people here to kill me, come inside"?'

'Naw, naw, it ain't like that, man. I was just by his crib last week. Motherfucka never know nothin's up when he sees my ass. And you're with me – so what? He don't think you gonna pop him neither.'

'I don't like it, man. I wanna do it drive-by.'

'Yo, thought you wanted to take care this shit *tonight*.'

'I do.'

'Then fuck's yo' problem? We drive around all night lookin', maybe we find him, maybe we don't. But we go to his crib, he be there, we take care this shit right now, yo, know what I'm sayin'? Drive-by, smoke him in his crib – long as we get him dead, what difference it make? And we do it in his crib – nobody sees nothin'. No witnesses rat on yo' ass, no nothin' goin' wrong.'

'Yeah,' Saiquan said, 'but what if he got niggas there with him?'

'Then we get him in the car with us,' Marcus said. 'Say, "Kemar and Manny need to see you, told me to come get you," some shit like that. He get in the car with us, you plug him, we drop his ass on the street someplace or in some landfill, and we on our way.'

Marcus's plan made sense, but Saiquan didn't feel like giving him props.

'Whatever, man, whatever,' Saiquan said, staring out the window.

Marcus turned the reggae back up, singing along. When they got to Flatlands Second Street, Marcus turned the stereo off and pulled over, double-parking near the corner.

'This it?' Saiquan asked.

Marcus didn't answer. He took out a Baggie filled with crack.

'The fuck you doin'?' Saiquan asked.

Marcus put the rock into the pipe and lit up.

'Yo, put that shit out.'

Marcus held the flame under the pipe and the crack started sizzling.

'I told you, I ain't gettin' into no crazy crackhead bullshit tonight.' Saiquan tried to grab the pipe, but Marcus turned quickly toward the driver-side door, blocking Saiquan with his right elbow as he took a hit from the pipe.

'Motherfucka,' Saiquan said, and he pressed the barrel of the Glock hard against the side of Marcus's head and had his finger on the trigger.

Acting like he didn't even feel the gun – or if he did he didn't give a shit – Marcus held the flame under the pipe again and took another hit.

'I'm countin' to three,' Saiquan said.

Marcus closed his eyes, smiling, getting high.

Saiquan clicked the safety off. 'One . . . two . . . You think I'm playin'? Driving around with rock in a stolen car – I must be crazy. . . . Two and a half . . .'

Marcus kept smiling, saying, 'Ah,' a few times under his breath. Then he opened the door, tapped the pipe against the side of the car a couple times to clean it out, then said to Saiquan, 'A'ight, let's do it.'

Keeping the gun against Marcus's head, Saiquan said, 'Do what? You takin' my ass home.'

'We at J's crib, man. That's it right over there.'

'You think I'm goin' in with you now?'

'Come on, yo – you wanna get this shit over, right? Man could be dead already, we ain't sittin' here bullshittin'.'

Saiquan didn't move the gun.

'I know you want me to go in that house with you,' Marcus

went on. 'I go in there all shaky, I might fuck shit up, but now I'm cool, I'm real cool, and we can go get this shit done, know what I'm sayin'?'

'You ain't shootin' nobody,' Saiquan said. 'Why it matter if you shaky?'

'A'ight,' Marcus said, and then he licked his lips a few times. 'But what if I smash up the car and shit? See, you didn't think about that. I be needin' rock I be drivin' swervy and shit, might crash into a lamppost or a tree or whatever; then the cops come and everything gets fucked-up. You don't want that shit happenin', right?'

'Whatever.' Saiquan lowered the gun. 'But I'm tellin' you – you fuck this shit up, I poppin' yo' ass too.'

Saiquan put on his Casper mask and opened the door.

'What you doin',' Marcus said, 'goin' trick-o'-treatin'?'

'What?'

'Leave the fuckin' mask in the car, yo. You think J gonna open the door, he see us with masks?'

Saiquan tossed the mask onto the backseat.

'See, you lucky you got me here,' Marcus said. 'I ain't here I bet you be doin' a lot a stupid shit tonight.'

Shaking his head, Saiquan got out of the car, and then he and Marcus headed along the sidewalk toward Jermaine's with their hands deep inside their jacket pockets.

Saiquan followed Marcus up the stoop. The house wasn't too fancy – it was skinny and looked kind of run-down – but it was still a house, and Saiquan felt the same way he did when he was in Marcus's crib, thinking, *This shit just ain't right. Why don't I got no house? Why don't I got none of this shit?* Saiquan didn't know Jermaine too good because J was just coming up when Saiquan went away last time, but he knew J was just a punk-ass street hustler, five years younger than Saiquan, and it was totally fucked-up that the man had this big motherfucking house all to himself and Saiquan had nothing.

'Stay back there, till he open up,' Marcus whispered.

Saiquan stood with his back against the house. He had his piece out in his hand. It was quiet except for some dog barking somewhere.

Marcus rang the bell. Nothing happened. He rang it again.

136

'Yeah,' somebody inside said.

'Yo, it's Marcus.'

'Who?'

'Marcus, man.'

Locks turned. The door opened. A second later Marcus was pressing his SIG into Jermaine's upper lip and mustache.

'The fuck you doin', man?' Jermaine said.

'Get the fuck inside,' Marcus said, forcing Jermaine back into the house.

Saiquan went inside too and said to Marcus, 'Yo, put that shit away, man.'

Marcus had the piece in Jermaine's mouth now, and Jermaine was biting on the barrel with his gold front teeth. Marcus pushed Jermaine up against a wall in the living room.

'Yo,' Saiquan said, 'you hear what I say?'

Jermaine was a tall dude – not b-ball tall, but still tall, like six-two. He had braids like Marcus's, but shorter.

'Why you pop D?' Marcus was saying to Jermaine. 'Huh? Why the fuck you pop him, bitch?'

Jermaine tried to speak, but he couldn't with the gun in his mouth. Saiquan was aiming his Glock toward the back of the house, maybe toward where the kitchen or staircase was, in case some of Jermaine's boys were home. Now Saiquan's arm was shaking badly, and it was hard to keep the gun steady.

Marcus was going, 'Why you pop him, man? Why you fuckin' pop him?'

'Maybe you take the gun out of his mouth he can tell you,' Saiquan said.

Jermaine's upper lip was bleeding. Marcus removed the gun and said, 'Talk, nigga.'

'Fuck you,' Jermaine said, spraying blood and spit. 'Punk-ass bitch.'

Marcus whacked Jermaine across the face with the gun, and Saiquan heard bone crack. Blood gushed from Jermaine's nose.

'Fuck you, man,' Jermaine said. 'I'm gonna fuck yo' punk asses up.'

'Shit's funny, man,' Marcus said, smiling. Then he said to Saiquan, 'You hear that shit, man? He gonna fuck our asses up.'

Then, back to Jermaine, 'How you gonna fuck anybody up when you gonna be six feet underground?'

Jermaine tried to grab Marcus's piece, but Marcus yanked his hand out of the way, then came down hard with the gun against the side of Jermaine's head.

'You best answer my motherfuckin' question,' Marcus said. 'Why you pop D?'

'Yo, you gonna *pay* for this shit,' Jermaine said.

Marcus whacked Jermaine again, this time in the mouth. A gold tooth popped out and more blood sprayed.

Marcus laughed. 'That shit's funny. Maybe I should do that again.'

'The fuck's wrong with you, man?' Jermaine said, spitting blood. 'I told you – I didn't do shit.'

Marcus came with the gun again against Jermaine's mouth. More blood splattered, but no more teeth came out.

'You gonna have to have a closed casket, man,' Marcus said. 'Mama ain't gonna be able to kiss you good-bye.'

'Don't talk about my fuckin' mother, bitch.'

'I can talk about whatever the fuck I wanna talk about, *pussy*. Know why? 'Cause I got the chrome in my hand and you just the sorry-ass sucka 'bout to get popped, that's why.'

'Fuck you.'

This got Jermaine another whack across the face. He screamed, putting his bloody hands over his eyes.

'You got two fuckin' seconds to answer my question, bitch, or I'm gonna pump ten into you real quick.'

'I didn't do shit.'

Marcus shot Jermaine in the left foot. Jermaine yelled even louder and keeled over. Saiquan couldn't stand looking at Jermaine anymore; instead he looked toward the back of the house, the direction he was still aiming his gun, in case Jermaine's boys were hiding somewhere and came out shooting.

'Tell me that lyin' shit one more time, your other foot gonna go,' Marcus said.

Jermaine continued screaming and cursing for a while, making sounds that didn't sound like a man making them. It sounded like they were coming from a dog – a dog that was about to die. Then he said, 'Bloods did that shit. Axe anybody you want – they tell you same shit. Why'd I pop a nigga in my own fuckin' crew?'

Marcus pulled the trigger again. Saiquan wasn't looking, but he could tell by the way J was screaming that foot number two got shot up.

'Say it, nigga!' Marcus screamed. 'Say you did it! Just fuckin' say it!'

Saiquan looked over at Jermaine, who was sitting down in a puddle of blood, making more animal noises.

'I saw D at Brookdale,' Saiquan said. 'He's paralyzed, can't move shit, got one of them metal shits screwed into his head. He said you did it. He said it was 'cause he was bonin' Ramona.'

'Bullshit,' Jermaine said, crying, his face covered in blood. 'Nigga's fuckin' lyin', man.'

Marcus put the gun up to J's messed-up face.

'A'ight,' Jermaine said. 'I smoked him, man – I fuckin' smoked him. But it wasn't 'cause a' no ho. I did it 'cause the nigga was jackin' supply, playin' us like punks. Caught his nigga ass, cold – selling rock on Cozine and Alabama. That ain't even his corner. I go, "Fuck you doin'?" and he go, "Fuck you," and pull a motherfuckin' piece on me. So I fuckin' capped the bitch. Shit's the motherfuckin' truth, man. Why'd I lie? Why the fuck I'd—'

Marcus shot Jermaine in the neck. Blood splattered all over Marcus's face and jacket and onto the white wall behind Jermaine. Jermaine was still squirming, blood coming from his mouth.

'Ah, shit,' Marcus said. Then he screamed at Jermaine. 'Look what the fuck you did! You fuckin' stupid-ass piece of shit!'

Marcus shot Jermaine again – this time in the middle of his forehead. Jermaine's body fell over into the blood puddle and was still.

Saiquan was staring at the body, at the spilled-out brains, thinking about so much shit at once that all he heard in his head was a lot of loud, crazy noise.

'Shit better come out,' Marcus said as he brushed past Saiquan and headed toward the kitchen.

Starting to feel sick, Saiquan turned and followed Marcus, and then he keeled over, gagging.

Marcus, at the kitchen sink, splashing water over his face and the top of his head, said, 'The shit better not be on my Timbs.'

A few seconds later he said, 'Damn, yo, and I just stole them shits last week.'

Saiquan couldn't hold back any longer, and he chucked up the slice of pepperoni pizza he'd had before he went to visit D at the hospital.

'Fuck you doin'?' Marcus said, looking over.

Saiquan continued gagging; his throat burned, but nothing else came up.

'See? You lucky you got me here, yo. A little blood get you sick, how you gonna shoot a man?'

As Saiquan tried to get the sick taste out of his mouth, Marcus continued washing up at the sink.

'Yo, so what you wanna do now?' Marcus said. 'You gotta go home to yo' dawg or you wanna go out ho-in'?'

With his throat still burning, Saiquan said, 'We gotta get the fuck outta here.'

'Wait, I still gotta get blood out my coat.'

'Now, nigga. People mighta heard them shots. Cops could be here any second.'

'Yeah? And how 'bout nobody heard the shots and I walk outta here with blood all over me? Some old lady sees me, calls nine-one-one, or I gotta pop her so she don't. Then somebody see me pop the old lady and we get caught for that shit.'

'Why you gotta shoot him?' Saiquan said. 'Why you gotta do that shit?'

'Fuck you talkin' about? That's what we came here for.'

'But he sounded like he was talkin' the truth, man. Maybe D was jackin' supply.'

'Naw, J was just talkin' shit, tryin' to save his black ass; that's all he was doin'.'

'How you know that? You don't know nothin'.'

'D told you at the hospital. He said it was over J's ho, right?'

'Maybe D was lyin'.'

'You told me he wasn't lyin'.'

'Couple weeks go, I saw D out on Cozine,' Saiquan said. 'Same corner. Maybe J was tellin' the truth and D was playin' me like a punk.'

'Yeah, well, maybe you shoulda thought of all this smart-ass, who-lyin'-to-who shit 'fore you called me to come down here and pop a nigga in my own crew. If this shit's fucked-up, *you* the one got it that way, not me.'

Sick of looking at Marcus's face, Saiquan turned and took a few steps back toward the living room. He heard a sound coming from the staircase; then he looked over and saw J's girl, Ramona, trying to sneak down the stairs.

'Yo!' Saiquan shouted.

Ramona screamed and ran back up. Marcus came past Saiquan with his piece out and ran after her.

'The fuck you doin'?!' Saiquan yelled. 'Yo, get back here!'

Now, upstairs, Ramona was yelling like crazy. There were a lot of bangs, things getting knocked over. Ramona was shouting, 'Stop it! No! No! No! Get off!' and Saiquan thought, *Shit, don't be hittin' it now, yo. Don't be doin' that wild shit now.*

'Marcus, yo, get the fuck down here!' Saiquan yelled.

Saiquan stood there in the kitchen, listening to more screaming and banging upstairs. He wanted to run, but Marcus had the car keys.

'Marcus!'

Ramona was yelling, 'Stop it! No! Stop!' and Saiquan wondered what the hell he was thinking, bringing crackhead Marcus in on this shit.

Then Marcus started screaming in pain, making sounds like Jermaine did when Marcus was fucking him up.

And then Saiquan heard a shot.

'Marcus, the fuck you doin'? Get yo' ass the fuck down here! Marcus? Yo, Marcus!'

There was another shot.

'Marcus! Fuck you, man! What the fuck you doin'?'

The house was quiet. Saiquan couldn't hear anything, and he didn't know what the fuck happened. He didn't know if Marcus got shot, if Ramona got shot, or if they both got shot.

'Marcus!' Saiquan called upstairs. 'Marcus!'

Saiquan heard a creak above him – somebody was coming downstairs. He thought, *Shit, it's Ramona.*

Saiquan took out his Glock and started shooting. He got two shots off, maybe three, and then heard Marcus screaming, 'Yo, the fuck you doin', man? The fuck you doin'?'

Marcus waited to make sure Saiquan had stopped, and then he came down the stairs, holding his right hand over his right eye.

'What happened?' Saiquan asked.

'Ho jumped out the window,' Marcus said. 'Landed on her feet like motherfuckin' Catwoman. C'mon.'

Saiquan followed Marcus through the house, past Jermaine's fucked-up body, outside. Marcus went around the house toward the driveway. A few people were on their porches or on the sidewalk, trying to see what was going on. One brother across the street was looking right at Saiquan, and Saiquan knew the guy could ID him, no problem. Saiquan pulled out his Glock and fired a shot in the guy's direction – not trying to hit him, just trying to scare his ass. The bullet came a lot closer to the guy than Saiquan wanted it to – smashing a window about five feet away from the dude. But at least the shot did what it was supposed to do, because the guy ran back into his house.

Marcus came back from the driveway and said, 'Bitch got away.'

'We gotta get outta here, man,' Saiquan said.

'Wait, maybe she—'

'Now, yo.' Saiquan grabbed Marcus and pulled him toward the BMW.

'Get the fuck off my jacket, man,' Marcus said. 'Better not be stretching that shit out.'

When they got to the car, Saiquan heard cops' sirens; they sounded far away, but they were getting louder.

Marcus was checking out his jacket, making sure there was no damage.

'Drive, nigga,' Saiquan said.

Marcus sped away.

'Chill, yo,' Saiquan said. 'Just go slow and shit, like we be mindin' our own.'

'Naw,' Marcus said. 'First we gotta get the fuck outta here; then we go slow.'

Marcus made a sharp right onto One Hundred Eighth, turning so fast, the car almost spun out and hit a parked Jeep.

'Chill!' Saiquan shouted. 'Chill that shit! Chill!'

Marcus kept on the gas for a few more blocks and didn't slow till they got onto Avenue M.

'There,' Marcus said. 'Now we safe.'

'Safe?' Saiquan said. 'The fuck you talkin' about? The bitch seen both of us.'

'She ain't gonna tell nobody.'

'Why not?'

' 'Cause she wanna stay alive, that's why.'

A cop car sped past, probably heading toward Jermaine's. Saiquan looked at Marcus, noticing the scratches, still bleeding, on his right cheek, going right up to his eyes.

'So what the fuck happened up there, man?' Saiquan asked.

'Nothin',' Marcus said. 'I was just trying to pin the bitch down, tryin' to poke her, know what I'm sayin', but she was fightin' me hard and shit. Then I finally get her down, get her panties off and shit, when the bitch grabs my hand and bites it.'

Marcus showed Saiquan his right hand, with the teeth marks and the blood.

'Damn,' Saiquan said.

'Shoulda popped her right then,' Marcus said. 'But bitch gets loose and comes at me with these big-ass nails. Shits was gold and shit, like two inches long, and motherfuckas was sharp too. Bitch scratched me in the face, man. Then I look up and she's jumpin' out the window. I shot at her but fuckin' missed. I look out the window and she starts runnin' up the driveway. I shot again but she was gone.'

'So how you know she ain't goin' to the cops now?'

' 'Cause she ain't.'

'How you know?'

'Just shut the fuck up, man.'

Saiquan turned away, shaking his head.

They cut over to Seaview Avenue. Marcus pulled into a parking lot next to a Shell station.

'The fuck you doin'?' Saiquan asked.

Marcus parked near a red Saturn.

'Gotta switch rides, man.'

Marcus went to the trunk of the BMW and took out a tire jack. Then he went up to the Saturn and smashed open the driverside window. The alarm went off, and Marcus leaned inside the car and started hot-wiring the shit.

Getting a new ride might help them get home safe, but Saiquan knew they were still fucked. Ramona saw both of them, and people on the street could probably ID them too. It was only a matter of time before the cops tracked their asses down. Or, if the cops didn't, Crips niggas would; that was for damn sure.

The Saturn's engine caught. Marcus gave Saiquan the thumbs-up sign and then got busy wiping away all the broken glass.

Eleven

Jake opened his eyes, bummed out to see Christina in bed next to him and not Penélope Cruz. Jake had been having an intense dream where he and Penélope – whom he'd partied with last month at Light in Vegas – were on a beach, screwing on a lounge chair. Penélope was loud and wild, digging her nails into his back, screaming, 'Harder, Jake! Harder!' with that hot Spanish accent.

Jake closed his eyes, trying to get back into the dream, but he couldn't fall back asleep. Pissed off, he looked at Christina again. She was good-looking, yeah, but she just wasn't Jake Thomas wife material. Her face was too plain-looking, not exotic enough, but the biggest problem was her ass. It looked even bigger naked than in jeans, and it wasn't one of those muscular, dancer asses either; there was actual fat on it. Her ass was such a turnoff that, at one point last night, while they were doing it from behind, Jake had started losing his hard-on. To keep himself going, he imagined that Christina was Kelly, the Hooters waitress from Philly. The fantasy worked for a while, because he had his eyes closed, but when he opened his eyes and saw Christina it was a major buzz kill.

Afterward, as Christina cuddled next to him, Jake wanted to take off, and he wondered if he was making a big mistake with all this marriage bullshit after all.

Then he reminded himself that he had to at least make the wedding announcement. For all he knew, the Marianna Fernandez story was going to break in the morning's papers, and he needed the wedding story to overshadow it, but that didn't mean he had to get married. Maybe, after a few months, the Fernandez story would fade and he and Christina could quietly split. Or maybe he'd have to marry Christina, but, if after a year or two the Fernandez story cooled, they could get divorced. If he had to get married, Jake was going to make sure he had an airtight prenup. Christina would get a mil or two tops and no property.

Lost in thought, Jake realized Christina had asked him a question.

'What?' he asked.

'I said, Did you mean everything you told me tonight?'

'Of course I meant it.' He looked in her eyes for a long time, then said, 'I promise I'll never hurt you again.' He kissed her. 'Gotta take a leak.'

He put his pants and shirt on, making sure he had his cell phone, and went down the hallway into the bathroom.

He dialed a number, and then, talking low, almost whispering, he said, 'Robby?'

'Jake?' Robert Henderson asked.

Jake heard background noise – people talking.

'I can't talk any louder,' Jake said. 'I need you to take care of something for me – it's very important.'

'I'm actually at a restaurant right now with my wife—'

'You don't do this for me right now, you're fired.'

'If this is about *GQ*, I talked to the editor there, but I really can't control what they—'

'Fuck *GQ*. This is something big – very big. I need you to break a story for me.'

'What story?'

'I just set a wedding date with my fiancée.'

'You have a fiancée?'

'Of course I have a fiancée. She's my high school sweetheart. We've been engaged for six years.'

'I had no idea.'

'Just listen to me.' He wanted to add *you dumb fuck*, but didn't. 'You have to call the *Daily News* right now and give 'em the scoop on my wedding. There's still time to get it into the early edition.'

'Why can't it wait till—'

'Because it can't. Call Mike Kelly, a *News* reporter – I just saw him today at this big party my parents threw for me. Tell him it's an exclusive but that we want the story out nationally too. Then you start working the phones. Make sure the Internet picks it up – make sure the whole world finds out about it ASAP.'

'My sushi just arrived.'

'Are you kiddin' me?'

'All right, look. I'll call that guy, Mark . . . ?'

'Mike,' Jake said, raising his voice slightly. 'Mike Kelly.'

'Right,' Robert said. 'But I can't make any guarantees about tomorrow morning. I mean, it's getting kinda late and—'

'Just tell them to wrap the fuckin' sushi up, because you're gonna be busy for the rest of the night.'

Jake gave Robert more details about the story – how the wedding date was set for next December, how excited he and Christina were, and a few quotes to use.

When Jake returned to bed, Christina said, 'You okay?'

Jake had been gone for about ten minutes and needed a good excuse.

'Ryan's mother's lasagna,' he said, wincing.

Jake got out of bed quietly, trying not to wake Christina. He got dressed, then opened the top drawer of her dresser and found a notepad. He was fumbling around, looking for a pen, when Christina said, 'Hey, there, sexy.'

Jake looked over and saw her lying in bed, propped up on one elbow, smiling.

'Hey, morning, beautiful,' he said smoothly. 'How'd you sleep?'

'Great,' Christina said. Then she squinted, suddenly looking serious, and said, 'Going somewhere?'

'Nope,' Jake said. 'I was just, uh, looking for a comb.'

'A comb?'

Jake realized this didn't make any sense, with his close-cropped 'do.

'I mean gum. Did I say comb?'

'Why don't you come back to bed? Just for a few minutes.'

'I was getting hungry. Why don't we go out and grab a bite?'

'I have to go to work in an hour.'

'Really?' Jake said, acting disappointed.

'I would've taken off, but I thought we were gonna . . . I mean, I could call in sick. It wouldn't be a big deal.'

'No, no, it's all right. I should probably spend some time with my parents anyway. Go to work – it's fine.'

'I'll be home at five thirty,' Christina said. 'We can go out, if you want to, maybe to the city, Little Italy or the Village?'

'Sounds like a plan,' Jake said.

Christina sat up. She had a nice set; he had to give her that much. They were small, yeah, but they were perky and round. Then she stood up and bent over to pick up her panties from the floor. In daylight the cellulite was totally noticeable. If the paparazzi ever took a picture of her in a bikini and published it in the *Star* or the *Enquirer*, it would be a major fucking embarrassment.

After pulling on her panties, Christina turned back toward Jake and he cringed, noticing some flab on her stomach.

'I'm so excited,' Christina said. 'I was up in the middle of the night and I couldn't fall back asleep. I mean, I know the wedding's more than a year away, but that's not so long when you think about it. There's so much to do. We have to pick a place, and a band, and the flowers, and I have to get a dress. But I really don't want to use a wedding planner. I mean, I know it'll be a lot of work, but I've always dreamed of planning my own wedding. Is that okay with you?'

'No,' Jake said, thinking about how all the guys on the team would get on him for having a fat-assed wife.

'It's not okay?' Christina said.

'What?'

'What's not okay?'

'Nothing.' Then Jake realized what they were talking about. 'Plan the wedding yourself. Why not?'

'Thank you,' Christina said. 'So how much you wanna spend?'

'Whatever. Couple hundred grand, half a mil.'

'You want to spend half a million dollars on our wedding?'

'Why not?'

'Wow, I can't believe this is happening. I might have to take some time off work to start planning everything. First we have to decide where to get married. You said you want to do it in December, right? So if we do it in New York, we'll have to do it indoors.'

'Right.' Jake was distracted again, remembering how great Penélope Cruz had looked in his dream.

'I was also thinking about something else,' Christina said. 'Maybe I should move in with you in Pittsburgh.'

Jake began to sweat.

'Why would you want to do that?'

'Why not? I mean, I'm gonna have to quit my job anyway after we get married, and it would be easier to plan everything if we're together.'

'I don't think it's a good idea.'

'Why not?'

'Because I'm not gonna be around a lot. I mean, I start working out in Florida in December, then I have spring training in February.'

'You're always gonna be busy with baseball. But I'll see you a lot more in Pittsburgh than I will if I stay in Brooklyn.'

Looking in her eyes, trying not to look at her ass, Jake said, 'But I thought you said you didn't want to live with anybody before you got married.'

'Yeah, but now that we have a date set – or at least we have a month set – I don't see the point in being apart. I mean, we're gonna be spending the rest of our lives together anyway, so we might as well get started. . . . Why? You don't want me to move in with you?'

'No, of course I want you to move in with me,' Jake said. 'But I don't want you to have to leave your job and your father—'

'I don't care about my job, and my father'll be okay here until he moves into the condo. . . . You know, maybe we should move up the wedding date. I want to get pregnant right away and start a family. Wouldn't that be great?'

Jake pictured her pregnant, ballooning up to one hundred and eighty pounds.

'I gotta talk to you about something,' he said. 'Something very important.'

'What is it?' Christina asked, concerned.

'Don't take this the wrong way,' Jake said. 'I mean, I don't mean anything personal by this or anything. I mean, you can do whatever you want to do, but how about you go on a diet?'

'Excuse me?'

'Just to drop, like, five, ten pounds. I mean, I'm not saying you *need* to lose weight or anything. I'm just saying maybe if you want to, you know, firm up a little – I mean for the wedding and everything – maybe that wouldn't be such a bad idea, you know? If you want, I can hire a trainer for you. It wouldn't be a big deal –

just, like, five days a week till you get in shape. I mean, get in better shape.'

Christina turned away from Jake and stood there with her arms crossed in front of her chest. Again Jake noticed the cellulite and dimples on the sides of her thighs, and he was glad he'd had the balls to say something about it. Honesty was always the best policy, and it was better to nip a problem in the bud before it blew up into something big.

In this case, something really big.

After several seconds Christina went to the closet and put on a robe, standing with her back to him. He realized she was crying.

'What's wrong, baby?'

'Just stay the hell away from me.'

'I don't get it. Why're you freaking?'

'You're such an asshole. I can't believe I was so stupid.'

'Whoa, baby, I think you're getting the wrong idea here. I just thought you wanted to look your best for the wedding, that's all. I mean, lots of players' wives have PTs and if you're gonna have paparazzi following you wherever you go, I just thought you might want to lose some weight off your ass, that's all.'

'My ass?'

'Not your ass.'

'You just said ass.'

'I didn't mean ass. I meant everywhere. I mean—'

'Why don't you just get out?'

'Whoa—'

'I'm serious.'

'This is crazy, baby. You know I love your ass. Your ass is the best thing about you.'

'Just leave!'

'Whoa, whoa, come on, relax, okay? Just take it easy.' Jake was panicking, imagining the big headlines – 'J.T. Accused of Sexual Assault,' 'J.T. Rapes Teenager,' 'Wedding Canceled' – and how his whole career would be shot to hell.

'Come on, baby, you know I think you're the most beautiful woman in the world. If I didn't, why would I want to marry you? Think about that for a second. You know how many marriage proposals I get in the mail every day? I get so many letters guys on the team call me Santa.'

Christina almost smiled.

'Look, I don't know why I said those stupid things,' Jake went on. 'It must be stress, you know? All this weekend, party, coming-home shit. I think you're the greatest thing that ever happened to me. I mean it – I couldn't live without you.' Quoting Enrique Iglesias, he, said, 'I will stand by you forever. You can take my breath away.' He held her from behind and rested his chin on her shoulder. 'You drive me so crazy – you're so perfect in every way. Let's start over, pretend we just woke up. How'd you sleep, baby?'

Christina waited a few seconds, then said, 'Good.'

'Me too,' Jake said. 'Know why? Because I had the most beautiful woman in the world in bed next to me, that's why.'

He kissed her neck softly; then he turned her around and started kissing her lips.

When he could tell he was getting her all worked up he pulled back and said, 'I better let you get dressed, but I'll see you tonight, okay? We'll go out to some hot restaurant in the city, Nobu, Balthazar, Bobby Flay's joint – you name it. Then we'll go uptown and take a horse-and-buggy ride in Central Park. We'll talk about the wedding, and where we're gonna live, our whole future. Sound cool?'

'I guess,' Christina said.

Jake kissed her again, then called a limo. Christina showered and dressed for work, then the limo arrived.

'You go,' Christina said. 'I still have to put on my makeup.'

'Sure, baby? I mean, I can have the guy stick around till you're ready.'

'No, it's okay, you go. I can take a bus.'

He kissed her good-bye at the front door, then asked her if she was okay with everything. She said she was, and he said, 'Cool,' and took off.

In the back of the limo Jake stretched out, glad to be alone. He knew he'd smoothed things over, but he figured he'd do more damage control later, just in case, telling her how sorry he was, and then eventually he'd have to figure out some way to get her to drop that poundage. Maybe he'd stick her in a Pilates class, or better yet, just cut to the chase and take her in for some lipo.

Jake asked the driver to swing over to Flatlands and stop at a newsstand. Jake went out and picked up a copy of the *Daily News*, then handed the bearded Pakistani dude a dollar.

'Hey, how are you?' the guy said to him, smiling widely.

Jake didn't mind being recognized, but he hated it when total strangers talked to him like they were old friends.

'Great,' Jake said, waiting for the guy to take the buck.

'No charge for you, buddy,' the guy said. 'But how about you give me autograph?'

He held out a notepad and a Bic for Jake to sign with. Jake took the pen and scribbled his name.

'Hey, thank you, buddy,' the guy said, 'I keep this forever. And wait . . .' He took out a disposable camera and said, 'For to hang up in store, okay? I take your picture?'

'Go ahead,' Jake said, rolling his eyes slightly, and then he managed a smile as the shutter snapped.

'Thank you, buddy,' the guy said. 'I put this in frame and keep forever. And congratulations – may you have a beautiful baby boy.'

Jake had started out of the store, but now he turned back excitedly and started turning pages of the newspaper. 'Where is it?'

'Right here, buddy. I show you.'

The guy took the newspaper, folded it open to a page, and handed it back to Jake.

At first Jake was disappointed. He'd expected to see a big story with a booming headline, but it got only a sidebar, as part of the article about the block party last night. But at least the headline was there, 'J.T. to Wed', and there was a picture, taken last night, of him kissing Christina. Thank God the picture caught her only from the waist up.

Jake read the story, glad that most of his quotes had made it in, but he was still pissed off that the paper didn't make a bigger deal about it. The front page headline was 'Horror in the Bronx', about a guy who'd shot his wife and three kids while they were asleep, then blown his brains out. Fathers were always doing things like that to their families, but how often did Jake Thomas announce a wedding date?

Then Jake turned back to the story about himself, deciding that at least he'd one-upped Marianna Fernandez. Now if she took her story public, the press would be so psyched about the wedding that no one would care about some statutory-rape claim by a fourteen-year-old Mexican girl from San Diego. Her story might not even make it into the papers at all.

The limo turned onto Eighty-first Street, and Jake was happy to see, among the crowd in front of his house, camera crews and guys with mikes. When the groupies and reporters noticed the limo they rushed into the street.

'Do you have a location picked out for the wedding?'

'Not yet.'

'Where're you going for your honeymoon?'

'We're keeping that private.'

'You gonna have kids right away?'

'You bet.'

'Does this mean your partying days are behind you?'

'Absolutely. I'm a family man now.'

There were more questions, and Jake answered them all patiently and politely, smiling the whole time as he signed autographs. A girl in the back yelled, 'Dump her, Jake!' and a very good-looking redhead up front begged, 'Marry me instead – please!'

After a while Jake made his way to the stoop leading to his parents' house. His mother had opened the door, waiting for him, and Jake waved good-bye to the cheering crowd.

'Oh, my God, I'm so happy for you!' Donna Thomas said, hugging Jake tightly.

Jake was lost for a few seconds, then realized she was talking about the wedding news.

'Oh, thanks,' he said. 'Yeah, I'm really happy too.'

'So is it true? It's really going to be next December?'

'That's the plan,' he said.

'This is so wonderful. Reporters have been calling all morning. It's been so crazy, I just started letting the machine pick up.'

Jake's cell started ringing.

'We should celebrate tonight – have a special dinner.'

'Sorry,' Jake said. 'Christina and I want to have a romantic thing tonight.'

'Oh,' Donna said, sounding disappointed. 'Well, I guess I can understand that. How about breakfast tomorrow? Or brunch? Michelle and Roger want to see you again.'

'Yeah, sounds great.' Jake headed up the stairs, flipping open his cell. 'J.T.'

'Good, didn't wake you,' Robert Henderson said. 'So you see the paper yet?'

'Didn't make the front page, but gotta hand it to you – nice job, bro.'

'That's just the tip of the iceberg. Reuters and AP picked up the story and it's all over the Net. It's what, eight-something your time, and chat rooms are buzzing about it, and you have a record number of posts on the "J.T. Talk" message board. I got dozens of interview requests – we're talking *USA Today, Extra, ET.* Everybody wants to know details. Can you give me some more info on Christina? What does she do for a living? When did you meet her? How did you meet? Can you get me some pics?'

Jake, now upstairs in the guest bedroom, put his phone's hands-free earpiece in and said, 'I don't think that's the right way to go.'

'What's not the right way to go?'

'I mean, we got them coming after us now, right?'

'You kiddin' me? My phone's ringing off the friggin' hook. I got e-mails up the wazoo.'

'That's what I'm talking about,' Jake said, opening his garment bag, deciding what shirt to wear, the black linen Dolce & Gabbana or the rust silk Versace. 'If a girl puts out on the first date, the guy never calls her again, right?'

'I'm not following,' Robert said.

'We gotta play hard to get.' Jake decided on the Dolce & Gabbana because he remembered he got laid the last time he wore it. 'Tell them I'm spending some alone time with Christina and won't be available for public comment until next week. It'll make them wonder, What's going on? Where's the wedding gonna be? Who's Christina Mercado? All that shit. Then we start leaking the info slowly, not giving them too much to chew on, you know? That way we keep the story in the news – it stays big.'

'I hear what you're saying,' Robert said, 'but I think that's a mistake. The media's fickle – they get on one story, then get on another. Something happens in the Middle East or Britney gets married again and it's sayonara.'

'I told you how I want to do it,' Jake said, laying out the Dolce & Gabbana on the bed with beige Valentino slacks, loving the way they went together. 'I'm not shooting my load with this baby today – no way.'

Robert didn't say anything for a few seconds – Jake just heard deep breathing – then Robert said, 'Throw me a bone, at least. What does she do for a living? What do her parents do?'

'She's a dental hygienist, her mother's dead, and her father's a degenerate gambler. Whoops, there's my other line.' Jake cut Robert off and took the other call. 'J.T.'

'Jake, Stu,' Jake's agent said.

'You calling to congratulate me?' Jake said.

'I just saw it scroll across the bottom of the screen on E!,' Stu said. 'So when did this happen?'

'Last night.'

'Spur-of-the-moment thing?'

'Kinda.' Unbuttoning his shirt, Jake caught a glimpse of himself in the mirror on the back of the door and immediately furrowed his eyebrows.

'Christina Mercado, huh?' Stu said. 'I don't think I've heard you mention that name before.'

'We've been engaged six years.'

'That's what it said – high school sweetheart. I didn't know you were engaged, though.'

'So what's up?' Jake took off his pants, still looking at himself.

'I just wanted to congratulate you,' Stu said, 'and I wanted to give you some more good news. Spoke to Ken again late yesterday, and he okayed the PT in the clubhouse.'

'What about the SUV limo?'

'That's gonna be a tough nut,' Stu said, 'and I really advise you to back off on that. Just play it cool, have a killer year next year; then the ball's back in our court. We can go in there with whatever team we negotiate with, whether it's the Dodgers or the Yankees or whoever, and ask for the world.'

'I got a better idea,' Jake said. 'Call him back and tell him, "No limo, no Jake-O."'

'Jake, I really—'

Jake ended the call and went down the hallway to the bathroom. He took a long shower, then was tweezing a few nearly microscopic hairs around his eyebrows when his cell rang. The display showed it was Christina, so he let his voice mail pick up. About ten minutes later, when he was finished tweezing, he listened to her message:

'Jake, I don't know why you're not picking up. I just got to work and saw the article – I can't believe you did this to me. I mean, we didn't even discuss it. I'm so pissed off at you right now. I just can't understand why—'

Jake deleted the message without listening to the rest of it. He had no idea what was going on in that chick's head, why she was freaking so much about everything. This should've been the happiest day of her life. Her plans to marry Jake Thomas were announced in the *Daily News*, and the story was spreading across the country like the fucking West Nile virus. Other girls would've killed to be in her place right now, and here she was, finding something to bitch about.

Suddenly feeling a little down, Jake returned to the guest room and decided on the Ritmo Mvndo watch instead of the Charriol. After spending a few minutes putting on his Crème de la Mer face cream and styling his hair with Fréderic Fekkai Texturizing Balm, he dabbed himself with some Acqua di Parma cologne and went downstairs.

Donna Thomas was in the kitchen, mixing batter in a bowl.

'I'm making you pancakes.'

'I don't eat carbs,' Jake said. 'How about some scrambled egg whites?'

'Oh . . . okay. Why don't you sit down and relax? You've been home almost a whole day and we've hardly spent any time together.'

She started cracking eggs, and Jake sat at the kitchen table. Outside, fans were chanting his name.

'There they go again,' Donna said. 'You know a few of them were here all night?'

'Really?'

'Yeah, these three girls. They rang the bell after midnight, asking if you came home yet; then they were still here in the morning. So many people love you, Jake.'

Donna made the egg whites, and Jake was eating them with a

glass of skim milk when Antowain entered and said, 'There he is – my son the party animal.'

'Here we go again,' Jake said.

'I'm surprised you're awake,' Antowain said. 'I thought you'd be sleeping in till at least noon today.'

'Come on,' Donna said to her husband.

But Antowain continued, 'So where'd you go? Clubbing? Hit the town hard? Get your picture on Page Six of the *Post?*'

'I was with Christina.'

'Oh, yeah, your bride to be. Funny, but I never heard you talk about her too much the past few years. Actually I didn't know you two were engaged anymore.'

'Please, Antowain,' Donna said.

'What, I'm just telling the truth,' Antowain said. 'How many times has he even seen her lately, and now he's marrying her?'

'You have no idea what you're talking about,' Jake said.

'So why don't you tell me the way it is?' Antowain said. 'You gonna tell me you're in love with this girl? You're Romeo and Juliet?'

'Antowain,' Donna said.

'Actually, I am in love with her,' Jake said.

Antowain smiled. 'Who do you think you talkin' to? You know nobody knows you better than me. You know I can see right through you. I don't know why you're marryin' this girl, what you think it's gonna get you, but it has to have something to do with you, because that's all you ever think about.'

Jake got up and said, 'I don't gotta take this shit.'

'That's enough,' Donna said. 'Both of you just stop it.'

'No, it's okay, Mom, I'm used to it. He never gives me any respect.'

'Want respect, earn some,' Antowain said. 'Take your damn life seriously for a change.'

Shaking his head, Jake went upstairs to the guest room and locked the door. His father was such an asshole. Jake didn't know if Antowain was jealous because he couldn't make it as a pro athlete and his son was living out his dream, but nothing was ever good enough for that prick. Even when Jake was a kid, in Little League, Antowain gave him hell. If Jake got a double, Antowain would ask, 'How come you didn't hit a home run?' Jake thought

Antowain would lay off in high school, when it was obvious Jake was on his way to becoming a superstar, but the badgering continued. In a game against Tilden, Jake hit a monstrous walk-off home run and hammed it up a little, taking his time rounding the bases, and Antowain gave him hell for it. He told Jake that he had no respect for the game and warned him that he'd never make it to the majors with that attitude. Now here it was, seven years later, and Antowain was still criticizing Jake every chance he got. But Jake was long past feeling bad, or even caring about anything his old man said to him. He knew there was nothing he could ever do to impress the old bastard, so what was the point in trying?

Jake sat on the edge of the bed and turned on the bullshit twenty-inch TV to ESPN. Tony Gwynn was giving his analysis about the latest National League Championship series game. Bored because the commentary had nothing to do with himself, Jake fell asleep. When he woke up he checked his watch, surprised to see he'd been out for a couple of hours. He started channel-surfing, stopping on some dumb cop movie on Showtime. After a couple of minutes, he realized he'd had sex with one of the actresses – Lara – no, Laura . . . yes Laura. He wondered if she still lived in New York and, if so, if she was in town this weekend.

A couple of minutes later his cell started ringing. He checked the caller ID and saw it was Christina. Figuring that if he didn't pick up she'd keep calling, he clicked on and said, 'Hey, baby, I was just thinking about you.'

'Didn't you get my message?' Christina said, all bitchy.

Remembering the message, Jake wished he hadn't picked up.

'Yeah, just got it,' Jake said, staring at the TV, at Laura's bee-stung lips. 'I was just about to call you back.'

'Why couldn't you at least tell me first?' Christina said.

Man, Laura looked hot. Maybe he shouldn't have stopped calling her.

'Are you there?' Christina asked.

'Yeah, I'm here, I'm here.'

'So?'

Staring at Laura's breasts as she leaned over to interrogate a prisoner, Jake said, 'I'm sorry, baby. I promise I'll never let anything like that happen again.'

'That's not good enough. How could you do this to me?'

'Holy shit.'

'What?'

'Nothing.'

'Are you even paying attention to me?'

'Yeah, I'm paying attention, I'm paying attention. Look, I don't know what you want me to say. Besides, I don't see what the big deal is anyway. So it's in the papers – so what? This is gonna be a high-profile wedding, baby. And you better get used to it, because this is what the rest of your life is gonna be like. You'll always have the press on your back, following you around. You're not gonna be Christina Mer . . . Mer . . . Mer . . .—' He forgot her last name for a couple of seconds, then said, 'Mercado. You're not gonna be Christina Mercado anymore; you're gonna be Mrs Jake fucking Thomas. The spotlight's gonna be on you twenty-four seven.'

Jake heard sniffling. He had no idea what the hell she was crying about now.

'You don't understand,' she said. 'Just this one time I wanted it to be something *I* announced, not that people had to read about in the papers.'

'It doesn't matter, baby.'

'Yes, it does matter. You have no idea how much it matters.'

Jake wondered if there was something wrong with Christina mentally. Her father was a nutcase, so maybe she had screws loose too.

'There's nothing I can do about it now, baby,' Jake said. He tapped the phone against the bed's box spring then said, 'Whoops, there's the call waiting.'

'Don't hang up on me.'

'I have to take it – it must be my agent calling me back.'

'When did you call the papers anyway? I was with you all night.'

'I gotta take this.'

'Don't go—'

'It's an important call—'

'Jake—'

'I'll pick you up at seven, baby.'

Jake clicked off, relieved. He lay in bed with his eyes closed, trying to chill. He didn't know how much longer he could take this getting-married bullshit. Christina had way too much baggage, and he wasn't just talking about her ass. He was starting to think about Patti, the United stewardess, wishing there was some way he could go hang with her, when his cell phone started bocking like a crazy chicken.

'Yeah,' he said to his lawyer, Ronald Lufkowitz.

'I wake you?' Lufkowitz asked.

'Yeah,' Jake said.

'Sorry. Just wanted to give you an update on the Marianna Fernandez sitch.'

'Stu told me last night – they want two hundred grand.'

'Yeah, well, things have gotten worse. Just got a fax from his lawyer. He says because you missed the first deadline now he wants one million by midnight tomorrow.'

'Is he high?'

'I know his lawyer and the way he deals – honestly, I think it's all a ploy. I think if we go back and say two hundred grand and that's our final offer, this all goes away.'

'No,' Jake said.

'Well, we have to come back with some kind of counter or—'

'Didn't you see the papers?'

'The papers? . . . Oh, yeah, Stu mentioned it. Your wedding. Congrats.'

'You see what kind of PR I'm getting? The whole country loves me. Who cares what the Fernandez girl says now?'

'I'm not sure I follow.'

'No deals,' Jake said. 'Let 'em go public – nobody gives a shit. People'll just think it's some blackmailers, some scammers trying to bring me down. It might not even make the papers.'

'Right . . .' Lufkowitz said, sounding confused, as if waiting for Jake to go on.

'Right,' Jake said confidently, as if Lufkowitz were a stupid jerk idiot lawyer who just didn't get it.

'Look, I think I know what you're getting at,' Lufkowitz said. 'You think one thing outweighs another or something like that, right?'

'You're catching on.'

'I'm not sure I agree with that, Jake. Statutory rape is a serious allegation – I'm not sure the public will just ignore this.'

'Whoa, I never touched that girl.'

'I'm not saying you did, but the right thing to do in a negotiation—'

'I'm not negotiating anything. The offer's off the table. End of story.'

'I think that's a mistake, Jake. My opinion, from a legal standpoint, is we should make some kind of deal with them. Maybe we can get them down to two, three hundred thou. It's a bite to take for you, I know, but it makes the problem disappear.'

'The answer's no.'

'Maybe you want to think about it and get back to—'

Jake ended the call, deciding that he was going to fire Lufkowitz ASAP. He didn't care what that asshole said; there was no way in hell he was going to play ball with the Fernandezes. If he made any payoff now, and the press got wind of it, it would make him look guilty as hell, like he was trying to cover something up before his wedding. No, those greedy Mexicans had had their window to make a deal, and now the window was shut. If they wanted to go public with the rape story, nobody would believe them, and if it caused any flak at all, Jake would just do a smear job on the girl – have his people make shit up if they had to – and she and her family would wish they never set foot in the US of A.

Jake left the guest room, confident that he had the whole situation under control, when he saw Ryan standing in the hallway.

'Hey,' Jake said, surprised, his smile fading quickly when he saw how demented Ryan looked. His face was sweaty, and he had a dazed, lost expression, as if someone had just hit him over the head with a brick.

'You feeling okay, dude?' Jake asked.

Ryan continued staring stupidly.

'I didn't hear the bell ring,' Jake said. 'You sure you're okay, man?' Then Jake smelled alcohol. 'Dude, you been drinkin'? Isn't it a little early in the day for—'

And that was when Ryan attacked him. It happened so fast that Jake didn't realize what was going on until he was on his back and that little faggot was on top of him, squeezing his throat. Jake was gagging, barely able to breathe as he looked up at Ryan's crazed, beet-red face. Finally Jake managed to pry Ryan's fingers away long enough to get out the gargled words, 'What the fuck—' but then Ryan pushed down and squeezed with more force.

At six-three, two-twenty, Jake had five inches and maybe forty pounds on Ryan, but Ryan was so bonkers that Jake had a tough time fighting him off. He couldn't get Ryan's hands off his neck, so he pushed up against Ryan's chest, trying to bench-press the nut away. Still, he couldn't free himself, and Ryan was squeezing even harder. Panic set in as it hit Jake that this was it – he was going to fucking die – and then he was holding his throat, gasping for air. He realized that Ryan wasn't strangling him anymore, and he looked up and saw Antowain holding Ryan back.

'She fuckin' loves me!' Ryan was shouting. 'She doesn't love you, you fuckin' asshole! She fuckin' loves me! You're never gonna get her! Never!'

Jake had no idea what Ryan was talking about. The guy was totally whacked out of his mind.

'Fuck you,' Jake said hoarsely, and then he started coughing.

Ryan tried to break free, to go after Jake again.

Still holding Ryan back, Antowain said, 'Son of a bitch.'

'What did you say to her?!' Ryan screamed at Jake. 'What kinda fuckin' bullshit lies did you tell her?! Huh?! What fuckin' bullshit?!'

Jake realized Ryan was talking about Christina, and he remembered how Ryan had gotten all psycho over her yesterday. He obviously still had a crush on her and had flipped when he heard the wedding news, going out and getting ripped, then coming here. Jake had always known Ryan was pathetic, but he had no idea the guy was this far gone.

Jake coughed some more, catching his breath. He was okay; maybe he hadn't been as close to dying as he'd thought.

'Just get the hell out of here,' Jake said, pretending it was difficult to speak, 'before I call the cops.'

Donna Thomas called from the bottom of the stairs, 'What's going on up there? Jake? Antowain?'

'She doesn't want you!' Ryan yelled at Jake. 'She never wanted you! She thinks you're an asshole – a cheating, lying, fuckin' asshole! You think you won her back? You didn't win shit back! She hates you! She couldn't give a flying fuck about you!'

Feeling sorry for Ryan because he was such a loser, Jake said, 'You need some serious help, dude. Maybe you should go on Prozac, or lithium, or check yourself into fucking Bellevue.'

Ryan broke away from Antowain and went after Jake again. This time Jake was ready and stuck an arm out, easily knocking Ryan back against the wall. Antowain grabbed Ryan again, and Ryan took a wild swing at him, his fist just missing Antowain's jaw. This set Antowain off, and he grabbed Ryan by the shoulders and pushed him back hard. With his face maybe two inches in front of Ryan's, Antowain said, 'I want you outta this house now. Hear what I'm sayin' to you? You come in here again I'm callin' the cops on your sorry ass.'

Donna, who'd come halfway up the stairs, said, 'Stop this fighting – all of you! Just stop it right now!'

Ryan was screaming at Jake: 'I'm marrying her – not you! She loves me – she loves me, damn it! All year we've been together. You didn't know, did you? You had no fuckin' clue, huh? You know why you had no fuckin' clue? Because you don't give a shit, that's why. You were too busy fucking everything that moved to give a shit what your fiancée was doing. Now you want her because I want her. It's all a fuckin' game to you – a stupid fuckin' game! But I love her and I'm marrying her, and I don't give a shit what I read in the paper. I don't give a shit!'

Antowain was still holding Ryan's arms, restraining him from going after Jake.

'This what your father taught you?' Antowain said to Ryan. 'Get drunk in the middle of the afternoon? Act like a fool?'

'Fuck you,' Ryan said.

'I don't need none of this bullshit in my house,' Antowain said, and he pushed Ryan ahead of him toward the stairs.

As Ryan went down he screamed up at Jake, 'You're not fuckin' marrying her! There's no fuckin' way! I'll kill you first! I swear, I'll fuckin' kill you!'

Jake remained on the second-floor landing, hearing Antowain warn Ryan to 'Stay the hell out of my damn house' before the door slammed.

Donna stood at the bottom of the stairwell and called up to Jake, 'Are you okay?'

Jake didn't answer. He went into the bathroom and locked the door.

Staring in the mirror, he noticed that his neck looked a little red, but he didn't think he was seriously hurt. If he wanted to, he could probably call the cops and press charges against Ryan – aggravated assault . . . hell, maybe even attempted murder. But he knew Ryan was just drunk and he didn't want to get him into that kind of trouble.

As Jake restyled his hair, he thought about what Ryan had said, about how he'd been screwing Christina. He didn't know if Ryan was lying, but he had a hunch he wasn't. It explained why Christina had been acting so weird last night, hitting him with all that wanting-to-break-up bullshit, and why she'd gotten so bitchy on the phone about the wedding announcement in the *Daily News*. Christina had probably told Ryan she was going to break off the engagement, and then Ryan had to read all about the wedding in the morning paper.

Jake didn't care about Ryan fucking Christina. Actually, he thought it was kind of funny. Poor Ryan – the guy just couldn't catch a break. He probably went after Christina only because she was Jake Thomas's fiancée, because he was jealous of Jake Thomas's career, and he figured that if he started banging Jake Thomas's girl it would be the next best thing to making the show. Poor fucking Ryan. Didn't he know the deck was stacked against him, that there was no way he could ever come out on top?

Then Jake smiled widely, looking in the mirror, realizing that finding out about Ryan and Christina was probably the best thing that could have happened. Now the pressure was off; a huge door had been opened. After all, if Christina was getting some on the side, why the hell couldn't he? Quid pro quo, tit for tat, and all that shit.

Jake took out his cell, wondering who he should call first – Patti the stewardess, or Jasmine the light-skinned chick from last night? Or maybe he could swing some way to get them both into a hotel room somewhere.

Nah, Jasmine was a dumb idea. She was way too young, and he definitely didn't need another Marianna Fernandez in his life. So, from his wallet, he slid out the card with Patti's number.

He dialed, ready to leave a message, when a sexy-sounding chick came on.

'Hello?'

'Patti?'

'Yeah.'

'It's your lucky day, baby.'

Twelve

Saiquan sat shotgun, staring at his lap as Marcus backed the Saturn out of the lot. They drove down Seaview Avenue, past the park. Saiquan could still hear sirens, probably heading toward Jermaine's house.

'Can't believe I gotta give up my motherfuckin' BMW for this bitch ride,' Marcus said. 'Shit's fucked-up.'

He turned right onto Rockaway Parkway.

'Shit ain't gonna work, man,' Saiquan said, shaking his head. 'Ain't gonna work.'

'What ain't gonna work?'

'All this switchin' cars, thinkin'-we-so-smart-when-we-ain't shit, that's what. That bitch seen you, man. The cops prolly already makin' a cartoon of yo' ass right now. They gonna have the shit posted all over Brooklyn. I open the paper tomorrow – I'm gonna see yo' ugly motherfuckin' face lookin' back at me.'

Marcus was shaking his head, not paying attention. 'I tellin' you, yo – we pass another BMW, Jeep, anything looks cool, I'm takin' that shit. I feel like a pussy drivin' this shit-ass ride.'

'Yo, you hear what I'm sayin'?' Saiquan said. 'They gonna have a cartoon of you. That bitch is gonna pick you out in a lineup.'

'She ain't pickin' out shit,' Marcus said. 'Ho's prolly home right now, happy she ain't dead. She ain't goin' to no po-lice.' He looked at the dashboard. 'Damn, look at this bullshit – don't even got a motherfuckin' CD player. Shit smells too. Nigga be eatin' tuna fish in this car.'

Saiquan looked away, rolling his eyes. J's girl Ramona was probably talking to the cops right now – why wouldn't she after somebody killed her man and tried to rape her ass? Shit, the cops would probably show up at Marcus's crib tonight to bust his ass hard, if they weren't waiting there already. After that, how long would it take Marcus to say the name Saiquan? Once them cops took him into the back room and started Louima-ing his ass with a motherfucking plunger he'd cop a plea real quick. Then the cops would be busting into Saiquan's joint, slapping the damn cuffs on him, telling him all that you-got-the-right-to-remain-silent bullshit. Saiquan never understood why they said that shit for. What kind of fucking right was it to shut up?

Wiping sweat off his forehead with the back of his hand, Saiquan started thinking about how it was gonna go down. While the cops were cuffing him, his kids would be standing there screaming and crying, just like *he* used to scream and cry every time the cops came to take his old man away. And Desiree . . . Damn, Saiquan couldn't even imagine the shit that'd be flying out of her mouth. Then the cops would take him out of the building, and the kids from the projects would be out there, looking at Saiquan like he was a hero. Saiquan would have to play it up, acting like getting picked up for murder was cool, and no big deal, and that he was down with all that shit. The cops would push him into the backseat, cracking his head against the top of the car while they were doing it, because cops always cracked niggas' heads against the top of the squad car – must've been some bullshit they taught them all in the police academy. He'd probably need five stitches in his head to sew that shit up, but the cops wouldn't care. They'd stop off for some Mickey D's or White Castle and start talking shit about how good the food tasted – *Ain't these fries great? I love these little cheeseburgers.* Then they'd book him and stick his ass in jail. First night in the pen he'd have to put on more of that cool, I'll-fuck-you-up-if-you-look-my-way shit so he wouldn't get his ass greased. But then, when the lights went out and he was alone on his cot, he'd start crying like a bitch into his pillow, wondering how his life got fucked-up all over again.

'It's only, like, nine o'clock, man,' Marcus said. 'Let's go party.'

Saiquan felt a tear drip over his upper lip. He licked it up quickly and looked away, out the window.

'Come on, man,' Marcus said. 'They got this new ho house open on Argyle Road. Only been there one time, but they got some tasties there, yo. West Indian bitches like to swing low, know what I'm sayin'? And they got drinks there too, so you sip

on a margarita while you watchin' yo' dick get sucked. . . . Yo,
'less you gotta get back home. Yo' bitch got a curfew on yo' ass?'

Saiquan remembered the way Jermaine had screamed when
Marcus shot his feet off. The man wasn't lying. Nobody goes
through that kind of pain and starts making shit up.

'Whatever,' Saiquan said.

'You serious?' Marcus said. 'You comin'?'

Saiquan knew he was going away for thirty to life. When he got
out he'd be a stupid old man, if he got out at all. Why not go to
the ho house with Marcus? It was gonna be the last night of his
life anyway.

'Whatever, man,' he said.

'Shit, I can't believe it,' Marcus said. 'Maybe you ain't such a
pussy after all.'

At a red light Marcus took out his crack pipe. He put some
more rock in, lit up, and took a hit. When the light turned green
he handed the pipe to Saiquan.

'Want some?'

Thinking, *What fuckin' difference does it make?* Saiquan took the
pipe. He lit up and inhaled as long as he could. A few seconds
later everything went away. There was no more jail, no more
being poor – no more nothing except that good, fucked-up-on-
crack, not-giving-a-shit-about-nothing feeling taking over his
whole body.

Then the good high faded as fast as it came, and he wanted
more.

As Saiquan lit up again, Marcus said, 'See? You based with me
before, maybe you wouldn't be freakin' so much.'

'Where the fuck's that ho house at?' Saiquan asked.

'Chill, man, chill. Gotta get some money for the honeys first,
know what I'm sayin'?'

'What you mean? Where's all yo' money at?'

Marcus turned right onto Glenwood Road and started driving
slowly. A couple of brothers were hanging out in front of a candy
store on the corner, but no one else was around.

Picking up the empty Baggie, Saiquan said, 'Where's the rest?'

'Ain't no more.'

'What about all that shit you had at your crib?'

'Don't worry, you'll get all the rock and all the hos you want.'
Marcus pulled over and stopped the car. 'C'mon.'

'What you—'

'Just c'mon.'

Marcus took out his piece and got out of the car. Saiquan
waited, then followed him.

Marcus stopped in front of a parked van and held out his hand
to block Saiquan. After a few seconds, an old dude carrying two
shopping bags came by. Marcus let him pass, then went up behind
him and put the piece up to his head.

'Give it up,' Marcus said.

'Hey,' the dude said, 'what the hell're you—'

'I said give that shit up, yo, 'less you wanna die right now.'

'C'mon,' the dude said, 'I don't got nothin' on me. Lemme
alone.'

Still holding the gun up to the guy's head, Marcus let go of him
with his other arm and reached into the dude's front pocket and
took out his wallet. The guy wasn't as old as Saiquan thought.
Maybe he was forty.

'C'mon, man,' the dude said. 'I ain't lookin' for no trouble with
y'all. What'd I do to you?'

Marcus handed the wallet to Saiquan and said, 'What he got?'

Saiquan opened the wallet and took out the bills. 'Twelve,
thirteen, fourteen dollars.'

'Where the fuck's the rest?' Marcus said to the dude. 'In your
shoe? In your damn Fruit Of The Looms? Maybe I should pop a
hole in yo' head and look there.'

The dude shoved Marcus backward with his elbow and ran
down the sidewalk.

'Stupid motherfucker,' Marcus said, and he shot the guy in the
back. The guy made it a few more steps, then went down, falling
on his face.

'Shit,' Marcus said.

Saiquan was staring at the man who was lying on the sidewalk,
blood leaking out of his back through his coat.

'Let's get the fuck outta here,' Marcus said, walking fast back to
the car.

Saiquan stood there for a few more seconds, staring at the man on the ground. Then Marcus shouted, 'Yo, c'mon, man!' and Saiquan went back to the car too.

Driving away, back onto Rockaway Parkway, Marcus started laughing, saying, 'See that shit, man? I shot that nigga in the back, right up where the heart is, but he was still runnin' – was probably already dead 'fore he hit the ground.' He laughed harder. 'They should put that shit in one of 'em Jackie Chan movies. Shit was fucked up.'

Life. Saiquan thought. *I'm goin' away for life now for damn sure.*

'Don't worry, yo, don't worry,' Marcus said. 'We'll find more cash. Next nigga we see we gonna bust hard, gonna get enough money for some titty for both of us.' He looked over and saw that Saiquan was still holding the dead dude's wallet. 'Yo, you crazy, nigga? Chuck that shit.'

Saiquan just sat there, dazed. Marcus grabbed the wallet from him and tossed it out of his own window.

Marcus was driving slowly again.

'Life,' Saiquan mumbled.

'What?' Marcus said.

Saiquan didn't answer.

Life. Motherfuckin' life.

'Yo, check out my man Eminem,' Marcus said.

Saiquan saw the white guy in a Ronnie Lott jersey, new LeBrons, and a backward Spurs cap, stumbling along the sidewalk.

'Man's so fucked-up he can't even walk straight,' Marcus said. 'It's like my man be *tryin'* to get his wallet jacked. He might as well have a sign hangin' off his ass sayin, "Take my money. Please take my money".'

Marcus pulled over and took out his piece.

'Wait,' Saiquan said.

Marcus looked at him. 'What?'

Saiquan wanted to say, *Fuck it, man; let's go home,* but he needed to get high again.

'Nothing,' Saiquan said.

Marcus and Saiquan got out of the car.

'Shit,' Marcus said.

The drunk white dude stumbled into the Canarsie Bar and Grill.

'Fuck it, man,' Saiquan said. 'We'll find somebody else.'

'Naw, naw, man,' Marcus said. 'White boy's so fucked-up, shit'll be easy. Prolly got money on him too – get us some rock *and* some booty. C'mon.'

Ryan was waving, trying to get the bartender's attention, when somebody grabbed his forearm. He turned his head slowly to his left and saw Aretha Franklin. At least, she looked like Aretha. She must've weighed three hundred pounds, and her eyes looked as glazed over as Ryan's must've.

'Hey, baby, wanna buy me a drink too?'

'Sorrrry,' Ryan slurred. A few seconds later he realized the woman was still holding his arm, and he yanked it away.

'Don't be like that, baby.'

Now the woman was squeezing his right ass cheek, rubbing her huge tits up against his back. He moved closer to the bar and shouted, 'Hey, hey!' to the bartender, over the loud Missy Elliott song.

The bartender was having a conversation with a guy at the other end of the bar. He glanced at Ryan, then ignored him.

Ryan headed toward the end of the bar where the bartender was when his foot caught on something – maybe the leg of a bar stool – and he stumbled and fell onto his side. It didn't hurt as much as he knew it should.

He made it back onto his feet and stood next to the guy the bartender was talking to.

'Rum and Coke,' Ryan said. His lips felt numb, and he wasn't sure he was talking clearly.

The bartender ignored Ryan and said to the guy, 'That's what I tell her. I tell her that all the time.'

'Excuse me,' Ryan said, talking extra slowly, just in case the bartender couldn't understand him. 'I want a rum and Coke.'

'I saw you,' the bartender said without looking at Ryan. Then he said to the guy, 'But that's just the way she is, know what I'm sayin'? She don't listen. . . . Hey, you know who I saw yesterday? You remember that brother with his dog who used to come 'round here?'

'Dog?' the guy said.

'Yeah. One of 'em rottweilers.'

'Oh, yeah.'

'Well he come in here and—'

'Can I just get my drink?' Ryan asked.

'Wait,' the bartender said. Then he said to his friend, 'What was I sayin'? Right, the brother with the rottweiler. So he come in here yesterday and . . .'

Ryan stood there, staring at the bartender, who was going on, bullshitting to his friend. After a few seconds Ryan realized he was swaying, and he stumbled over to an empty bar stool. He sat down, feeling some pain in his hip from the fall he'd taken. Then he looked around, noticing for the first time that everyone in the bar was black. He tried to remember how he'd gotten there, but, like just about everything else about the day, it was a blur. He remembered having his hands around Jake's throat and drinking at Vinny's Bar on Ralph Avenue and then not being able to find his car, but that was about it.

He figured he was probably on Rockaway Avenue, maybe near Avenue D? It was definitely a shitty part of Canarsie, a place he would've avoided, especially at night, if he were sober; but right now, as long as there was alcohol to drink he really didn't give a shit.

Ryan was about to scream for his rum and Coke again when he saw the bartender coming over with it.

The bartender put the glass down in front of Ryan, but before he let go of it he said, 'Five bucks.'

Five bucks sounded like a rip-off, expecially in a dive like this, but Ryan didn't feel like arguing. He opened his wallet and stared at it, forgetting what he was looking for, and then he thought, *Oh, yeah, money*. He took out a single, stared at it for a couple of seconds, then took out another bill. He was pretty sure it was a ten – yep, there was a one *and* a zero – and handed it to the bartender.

The bartender released the glass and brought Ryan his change. As Ryan guzzled the drink he could barely feel his lips. He couldn't taste much either – he could've been drinking piss on the rocks, for all he knew. But the alcohol was giving him a nice buzz, and at least he wasn't thinking about *them* anymore, which was all that really mattered.

As Ryan was finishing the drink, he felt a hand touch his arm.

Expecting to see Aretha Franklin again, he turned his head as quickly as he could, and it took him a few extra seconds to realize that the woman wasn't standing there. There was just a skinny guy with long braids, smiling, showing a mouthful of braces. He had a few long scratches on his face.

'What up, money?' the guy said.

The guy wasn't alone. Another guy – bigger, with cornrows – was with him, but hanging back.

Even ripped out of his mind, Ryan knew he was in deep shit. He looked away, hoping the guys would leave; then the skinny guy grabbed his arm again, harder this time, and said, 'You should look at a man when he talkin' to you.'

Ryan looked at the skinny guy, but the skinny guy didn't let go of his arm.

'That's better, man. What, yo' mama don't teach you no manners?'

Ryan felt his body swaying. He suddenly had to piss.

'I'm not lookin' for any trouble,' he slurred.

'Yo, you hear that?' the skinny guy said to the big guy. 'My man Eminem ain't lookin' for no trouble.' Then to Ryan, 'If you ain't lookin' for no trouble you came into the wrong fuckin' place.'

Ryan looked away from the skinny guy, at the mirror behind the bar. In the reflection he saw the door to the outside. He thought about making a run for it, but decided that would be the stupidest thing to do. The guys would have a much easier time mugging him outside the bar than inside.

The skinny guy grabbed Ryan's San Antonio Spurs cap off his head and flung it away.

'We in New York. You should be wearin' Knicks shit.'

The bartender had seen the skinny guy toss Ryan's cap, but he and his friend were talking again, obviously not giving a shit. Some old guy at the other end of the bar was slumped over, probably asleep. The fat woman who'd approached Ryan before was at a table, talking to some guy. The few other people in the bar weren't paying attention either, and Ryan knew none of them would help.

'Look, man, you got it all wrong,' Ryan said, trying to keep it real. 'I just came in here to chill and have a drink, know what I'm sayin'? I ain't tryin' to start nothin', know what I'm sayin'?'

The skinny guy started laughing. Then he said to the big guy, 'Check out my man Eminem talkin' with his "ain'ts" and "know what I'm sayin's" and shit.' He looked back at Ryan, said, 'You be gottin' all you ebonics down real good, huh? What you gonna do, start rappin' now?'

'I love rap, man,' Ryan said.

'Ooh, you be lovin' rap too?' the skinny guy said. 'Next you be tellin' me how you be lovin' fried chicken and watermelon, 'cause then I definitely ain't gonna fuck with yo' grits-and-collard-greens ass.' The skinny guy backed away a couple of steps and opened his coat, showing the handle of a gun sticking out of his jeans. 'Give it up, yo.'

Ryan's gaze shifted slowly from the gun back up to the skinny guy's face.

'Come on,' Ryan said. 'Why you gotta—'

'I said give it up, yo, or I'm gonna pop you in the head – give you a third motherfuckin' eye to see outta. 'Cept you won't be able to see outta it 'cause you be dead.'

Ryan reached down and patted the side of his pants a few times. Finally he found the opening to his pocket and he reached in and pulled out his wallet. He opened it and took out six dollars. He was surprised he had so little; he thought he'd left his house with sixty or seventy bucks this morning.

Holding the bills out toward the skinny guy, Ryan said, 'There, six bucks, that's all I got. Take it – it's yours.'

The skinny guy didn't take the money.

'What about yo' ATM?'

'What about it?'

'There a bodega right 'cross the street – got a money machine inside. How 'bout we go take a walk?'

Even ripped, Ryan realized that if he went to the cash machine with these guys they'd probably kill him afterward, just for the hell of it.

'I don't have any money in my account,' Ryan said.

'Bullshit you don't,' the skinny guy said, 'wearing 'em new LeBrons an' shit. Prolly got a million dollars in the bank.'

'All right, I'll give you my code. It's NOLAN. You know, like Nolan Ryan. Go 'head – take out the pennies I got in there.'

NOLAN was actually Ryan's old code; he'd changed it to TUPAC after his baseball career fell apart.

'Yo, you think I'm a stupid motherfucka, don't you?' the skinny guy said. 'Givin' me bullshit digits and shit. Naw, naw, man, you comin' with us. You gonna type that Nolan Ryan shit in yo' self. And you better hope motherfuckin' pennies don't come out.'

Ryan looked away from the skinny guy, toward the big guy. Suddenly the big guy looked familiar. Ryan didn't know where he knew him from – high school? junior high? – but he knew he knew him from somewhere.

'Wait,' Ryan said. 'I know you, man.'

'No, you don't,' the skinny guy said.

'Yeah – yeah, I do.' Ryan wasn't sure anymore. He was just stalling, praying he could find some way out of this mess. 'Your hair was different, but your face is the same. I went to South Shore. Where'd you go?'

'No place,' the big guy said. It was the first word he'd spoken, and his deep voice sounded familiar to Ryan; he didn't think he was just making all this up.

'Wait, what do you mean, no place?' Ryan said. 'You from Canarsie?'

'Yeah.'

'Then what—'

'I didn't go to school.'

'Stop with all this bullshit, a'ight,' the skinny guy said, 'and get me my money.'

'I know I know him,' Ryan said, although he was feeling more like he didn't.

'You know bullshit,' the skinny guy said. 'You better get yo' ass to that ATM real quick, or tomorrow mornin' yo' mama's gonna be plannin' yo' funeral.'

Ryan knew the skinny guy meant it. The skinny guy would kill him tonight whether he gave him the money or not. There was no way out – he was officially fucked.

Then it hit him.

'Basketball,' Ryan said to the big guy. 'Yeah, that's it – basketball. We played ball a few times together – Canarsie Park. Right?'

'I didn't play no ball with you, man,' the big guy said.

'Yeah, you did. Seven, eight years ago, the summer after my junior year of high school. You played point; I was shooting.' It was all coming back now. 'Your name's Sa ... So ... Sen ... Saiquan. Saiquan. That's it, right?'

The skinny guy looked at the big guy. The big guy was looking at Ryan, squinting, trying to remember. Then it clicked for him too.

'Oh, shit. Yo' name's Ryan, right?'

'See, I knew it, man!' Ryan was truly excited, feeling like he'd just saved his life.

'Shit was a long time ago,' Saiquan said.

'You had a great crossover, man,' Ryan said. 'You were quick too.'

'Yeah, and you knew how to shoot, yo. Used to hit that J from the top of the key every time.'

'I was all right.'

'Hold up. You a baseball player, right?'

'Was. I paint houses now.'

'But you was suppose to go to the major leagues, man.'

'Shit didn't work out. So what're you up to?'

'Not much. I just been—'

'Yo, yo, how 'bout both y'all shut the fuck up with the gettin'-to-know-each-other-again bullshit,' the skinny guy said. Then he turned to Saiquan. 'The fuck you doin', man?'

'I know this dude,' Saiquan said.

'I don't give a shit he yo' long-lost motherfuckin' cousin. White boy's gonna take us to the ATM.'

'Gimme a break, man,' Ryan said. 'I'm a fuckin' house painter, all right? I make ten bucks an hour.' He took off his jacket and rolled up the left sleeve of his sweatshirt, showing the guys the scar on his elbow. 'Had Tommy John surgery and it didn't do shit. I had to quit baseball, man. I live with my fuckin' parents.'

Ryan hoped this would convince the guys he was broke. Even if it didn't, they couldn't be dumb enough to try to mug someone who knew one of their names.

Saiquan said to the skinny guy, 'C'mon, Marcus – he don't got no money, man.'

Make that both of their names.

Marcus glared at Ryan. Ryan thought he was off the hook; then

Marcus said, 'Naw, naw, man – I think he's bullshittin' us. Check out 'em sneakers – shits cost hundred forty bucks at Foot Locker. Nigga was playin' baseball – he prolly got money in the bank.'

'I'm telling you the truth,' Ryan said. 'I'm poor as shit.' He stood up and pulled the insides out of his pockets. Then he sat back down on the bar stool, nearly falling off it. After he regained his balance, he said, 'See? I don't have no money, man.'

'Yeah?' Marcus said, grabbing Ryan's arm. 'Let's see you punch 'em digits in, then we see 'bout that.'

'Come on, gimme a break, man,' Ryan said. 'I had a shitty fuckin' day, all right? Jake Thomas stole my girl away from me today. That's right – he fuckin' stole her. He doesn't give a shit about her – he doesn't give a shit about anything.'

Marcus caught a whiff of Ryan's breath and said, 'Yo, how much you drunk tonight? Damn.'

'He could get any girl on the planet,' Ryan went on, 'but he went after my girl, *my* girl, and you know why? Because he's the biggest asshole in the world, that's why. He was always an asshole and he'll always be an asshole, and I don't give a shit what Jay Leno or anybody else in the world thinks. I almost killed him, you know. It's true. Today I had my hands around that asshole's throat. I almost fuckin' killed him. Jay Leno laughing like that. I know the real Jake Thomas. Me, I'm the only one who knows it.'

'Let's just get the fuck outta here,' Saiquan said.

'Hold up,' Marcus said to Ryan. 'You ain't bullshittin', man? You really know that rich Oreo motherfucka Jake Thomas?'

'Yeah, I know him,' Ryan said. 'We used to play baseball together in high school. We were the Dynamic fuckin' Duo – Ryan and Jake. Sorry, Jake and Ryan. That asshole's name always had to go first. Alphabetical order, he always said. That's what he always said – alphabetical order. Yeah, that was us – Jake and Ryan. Buddies.' Ryan laughed bitterly. 'We were supposed to go to the big leagues together.'

'It's the truth,' Saiquan said to Marcus. 'I remember all that shit.'

'You bet your ass he's rich,' Ryan said. 'He wears diamonds, gold, fuckin' Rolex watches. You know how much the guy made last year with his fuckin' commercials and shit? The asshole's got all the money *and* he got my girl.'

'So where's J.T. at right now?' Marcus asked.

'He's staying with his parents three houses down from me on Eighty-first Street off Flatlands. You can't miss the house. It's got this big banner hanging out right in front of it.' Ryan held out his arms, as if measuring a fish he caught. ' "Welcome Home Jake, Our Hero." That's what that fuckin' banner says. I have to drive right under it every fuckin' day. Fuckin' makes me sick.'

'But nigga's prolly got bodyguards, right?'

'Not this weekend. He's just got my fuckin' girlfriend.'

'C'mon,' Saiquan said to Marcus. 'He ain't got no money, man. Let's just be on our way.'

Marcus glared at Ryan for several seconds, then said, 'Man, I hope you know what a lucky little motherfucka you is,' and headed toward the door. Saiquan started following him, and then he turned back to Ryan and said, 'Yo, man, if you wanna play some ball sometime—' Marcus grabbed him by the arm and pulled him out of the bar.

Ryan stared at the door for a few seconds, amazed that he'd actually gotten rid of the guys and not really sure how he'd done it. He knew he should leave too, get the hell out while he had the chance, but he also wanted another drink badly.

Ryan waved the bartender over and said, 'Refill.'

Expressionless, the bartender took all the money off the bar – six bucks, even though the last drink had cost five – and then brought Ryan his new rum and Coke.

Ryan started guzzling it when he realized someone was sitting next to him. He turned his head slowly and his eyes focused on Aretha Franklin.

With her hand sliding down over his ass, she said, 'Hey, baby, how you doin'?'

'Not bad,' Ryan said.

'Yeah? Them boys was givin' you a hard time, huh?'

'Who, those guys? Nah, not at all. I used to know one of 'em. Yeah, used to shoot hoops with him.'

'That's cool, baby,' the woman said, moving closer to Ryan, rubbing up against him. 'I was worried 'bout you for a while there, suga'. I thought them boys was tryin'a give my new boyfriend some trouble.'

Ryan took a closer look at the woman and decided she wasn't so bad.

'I can't afford to buy you a drink,' Ryan said.

'That's all right, baby. I ain't thirsty no more – I'm just hungry now.' She moved even closer to him, looking into his eyes. She smelled weird, like Pampers or baby powder, but he liked it. 'Look how cute you is.'

The woman leaned in and started nibbling on Ryan's earlobe.

'I got an idea, baby,' the woman said, close enough that Ryan could smell her hot whiskey breath and feel it against his face. 'How about you gimme a walk home? It's scary out there at night, and I need somebody big and strong to protect me.'

A few minutes later Ryan had his arm halfway around Aretha Franklin's waist, trying to keep his balance, as he steered her toward the door.

Thirteen

Christina stuck the periodontal probe into Mrs Jacobson's lower lip, and the old woman groaned.

'Sorry,' Christina said. 'Go ahead – rinse.'

Mrs Jacobson rinsed and spit a few times, then said, 'What's wrong with you? That's the second time you stuck me with that thing.'

'You have to sit still,' Christina said, covering for herself. She knew she'd been careless with a few patients since that whole scene with Ryan earlier today.

'Sure, sit still.' Mrs Jacobson spit out more bloody water. 'What happened to the other girl who works here? Sharon or Karen – you know, the nice blond one. She never used to hurt me the way you do.'

'I'm almost finished.'

'Oh, no, you don't. I'm not letting you touch me with that thing again. It's like a torture chamber in here.'

'I just have to clean one more quadrant—'

'Get away from me. There's no way I'm letting you touch my mouth again!'

Dr Hoffman heard Mrs Jacobson's loud, piercing voice and came into the room.

'Something wrong in here?'

'Your girl's stabbing me to death, that's what's wrong in here.'

'I nicked her lips,' Christina explained.

'She's stabbed me twice with that thing.'

'Christina, can I have a word with you?'

As Christina followed Dr Hoffman to his office, she heard Mrs Jacobson shout, 'I should sue!'

In his office, with the door closed, Dr Hoffman said, 'What happened in there?'

'Nothing,' Christina said. 'I just pricked her a little. You know how she gets. She complains about something every time she's here.'

'Look, I think you have a lot of personal things on your mind today, Christina. Why don't you take the rest of the day off?'

Now Christina couldn't hold back. She started crying, tears streaming down her cheeks.

'Hey, come on.' Dr Hoffman handed her a couple of tissues. 'Everything's gonna be okay.'

Christina didn't take the tissues. She was looking away, embarrassed to be crying in front of her boss.

'It's okay. I'm all right.'

'Look, I really think you should take the rest of the day—'

'No, I can—'

'I insist. I'll see you Monday morning.'

Christina didn't bother arguing. She couldn't focus at all today, and she knew she was better off going home.

She left the office and went down the steep stairs. In the vestibule she sobbed for a while, then composed herself. She went out to McDonald Avenue. Afternoon shoppers crowded the sidewalk, and a sliver of bright sunshine shone through the subway el. It felt good to be outside, and she was glad Dr Hoffman had sent her home.

Then panic set in.

She remembered the way Ryan had acted earlier, how enraged he'd been. She'd never seen him act that way before. It was terrifying, as if he were possessed. There was a moment when he was looking at her with venom in his eyes, and she felt like he wanted to kill her. She'd seen him looking toward the bottom of the stairwell, and she wondered if he was thinking about pushing her. Later, after he left, she'd tried to rationalize it, telling herself that it was all her imagination, that he would never really do anything to hurt her.

But now she wasn't so sure.

Although Ryan had never gotten violent toward her – he'd always been the perfect gentlemen; a truly sweet, considerate guy – she'd never dumped him before either. Rejection brought out the worst in people. Besides, Ryan had all that pent-up anger about his failed baseball career, and that jealousy toward Jake that he never really expressed, and then, of course, there was his obsession with gangsta rap. Somebody who was so into all that violent, misogynistic music had to have a lot of hidden rage – especially toward women.

Christina walked quickly along the sidewalk, looking back every few seconds. When she bumped into someone accidentally, she almost screamed.

She had to calm down. Ryan wasn't here. She was just making up stories to scare herself. Ryan didn't want to hurt her. Nobody wanted to hurt her.

She stopped looking back, but noticed that her hands were shaking.

The bus was crowded, mainly with loud, laughing Catholic-school kids. Christina had to stand near the back door, holding on to the pole with one of her sweaty hands.

She'd called Jake earlier from the office and left a message, but he hadn't gotten back to her. She called again and this time he picked up.

'Hey, baby, I was just thinking about you.'

'Didn't you get my message?'

'Yeah, just got it. I was just about to call you back.'

'Why couldn't you at least tell me first?'

Jake didn't answer, so Christina said, 'Are you there?'

'Yeah, I'm here, I'm here.'

'So?'

'I'm sorry, baby. I promise I'll never let anything like that happen again.'

He sounded distracted and Christina wondered if he was even paying attention.

'That's not good enough,' she said. 'How could you do this to me?'

'Holy shit.'

'What?'

'Nothing.'

'Are you even paying attention to me?'

'Yeah, I'm paying attention, I'm paying attention. Look, I don't know what you want me to say. Besides, I don't know what the big deal is anyway. So it's in the papers – so what? This is gonna be a high-profile wedding, baby. And you better get used to it, because this is what the rest of your life is gonna be like. You'll always have the press on your back, following you around. You're not gonna be Christina Mer . . . Mer . . . Mer . . .—'

Christina couldn't believe it – he couldn't even remember her last name. He really didn't care about her at all. Everything he'd ever said to her was total bullshit.

'Mercado,' he finally said. 'You're not gonna be Christina Mercado anymore; you're gonna be Mrs Jake fucking Thomas. The spotlight's gonna be on you twenty-four, seven.'

Christina had started crying.

'You don't understand,' she said. 'Just this one time I wanted it to be something *I* announced, not that people had to read about in the papers.'

'It doesn't matter, baby.'

'Yes, it does matter. You have no idea how much it matters.'

Jake deep-breathed, then said, 'There's nothing I can do about it now, baby.' Christina heard a loud noise; it sounded like Jake had banged the phone against something. 'Whoops, there's the call waiting.'

'Don't hang up on me.'

'I have to take it – it must be my agent calling me back.'

'When did you call the papers anyway? I was with you all night.'

'I gotta take this.'

'Don't go—'

'It's an important call—'

'Jake—'

'I'll pick you up at seven, baby.'

'Jake? . . . Jake? . . . Jake?'

He'd hung up.

Christina continued crying, realizing that staying with Jake was probably the stupidest thing she'd ever done. Yeah, Ryan had seemed like he wanted to kill her before, but at least he had passion; at least he cared about her.

An old woman sitting next to Christina said, 'Here you go, sweetie,' and handed her a few Burger King napkins.

'Thanks,' Christina said, taking the napkins and wiping her tears with one of them.

'Whoever he is, trust me, he's not worth it,' the woman said.
'Yeah,' Christina said. 'You're probably right.'

A couple of stops later the woman told Christina that everything would be okay and got off the bus. Staring out the window, still dabbing tears, Christina decided that she needed to be alone for a while, without any guy in her life. She hadn't been single since junior high school, and she needed some space to try to figure out what she really wanted.

Then, at the Brooklyn College stop, *he* got on. Christina didn't know his name, but she'd seen him dozens of times on the B6 bus over the last couple of years. He was a light-skinned black guy, skinny but muscular, with an adorable bald head. He looked like Taye Diggs or Tyson with a little Will Smith mixed in. He had great teeth and wore trendy rectangular rimless glasses, like the ones she'd seen in the latest circular from Lenscrafters. She knew he was a student because she'd seen him highlighting biology textbooks. She had never said a word to him, but sometimes, when the bus was crowded, they stood cramped next to each other, holding the same pole. Other times they'd sat across from each other and made brief eye contact. A few times Christina had wanted to say hi to him, but she was too shy, and she could tell he was shy too.

Today when he got on he didn't see her, and sat in a seat near the front, with his back to her. She was about to get up to sit next to him when a woman got on at Flatbush Avenue and took the seat.

When the bus approached the Kings Highway stop, the guy got up. He had his back to Christina, still not seeing her. Then the bus pulled to the curb and the door opened and he got out. As he headed along the sidewalk, past Christina, he looked over at her and smiled. Christina was smiling back at him as the bus pulled away.

Christina was about to turn up the walkway leading to her house when two men – one fat with a mustache, holding a notepad, the other bald and thin, with a camera – got out of a parked car. The fat man said, 'Christina?'

Caught off guard, Christina said, 'Yeah.'

The bald man snapped a photo of her as the fat man said, 'Tom Pavano, *Newsday*. Mind if I ask you a few questions?'

'Yes, I mind, and get that freakin' camera away from me.'

The bald man snapped another photo.

'Bastards,' Christina muttered.

She went up the stoop and opened the front door, ignoring the reporter's questions.

When she entered, her father came out of the kitchen to meet her by the front door. He looked better than he had in years. He'd gotten a haircut and a close shave and was wearing clothes – a navy button-down shirt tucked into beige slacks – that she hadn't seen him wear since he'd left his teaching job.

'There's my little princess,' Al said, and he came over and kissed Christina on the cheek. 'Congratulations.'

'There's nothing to congratulate me for.'

'What're you talking about? I heard the news. It's official – you finally have a wedding date. I tried to call you at work, but the girl said you were busy; then when I called again she said you went home early. So Jake wised up and got off the pot, huh? I knew he'd do it eventually. He'd be crazy to keep you waiting any longer.'

'Daddy, I—'

'Hey, you talk to Tom from *Newsday*? Nice guy – they took pictures of me and everything. Guy from the *Post* was here before – forget his name. Anyway, he said he'd be back later.'

'Dad—'

'I want to take you out to dinner tonight – you and Jake. How 'bout Nino's? I'll make a reservation for three.'

'I don't think I'm gonna go through with it, Daddy.'

A few seconds went by, then Al said, 'Through with what?'

'The wedding,' Christina said. 'I mean, I'm just not sure Jake's the one for me.'

'Is this some kind of joke?'

'Why would I joke about this?'

'You've been with Jake for years, since high school. Of course he's the one for you.'

'I don't think I love him.'

'You're just nervous. That's understandable.'

'Listen to me, Daddy.'

'I am listening, and I know it's just nerves.'

'It's not nerves.'

'Yes, it is,' Al snapped. Suddenly his face was pink and his forehead glistened with sweat. 'I mean, you have to sit back, honey, and look at the big picture. Opportunities like this don't come around very often.'

'So you think I should marry him for his money?'

'No. Of course not – no. No, no, don't be crazy. I want what's best for you, honey—' He hugged her tightly, then said, 'I mean, try to imagine how great your life would be if you never had to worry about money again. And it's not like Jake's some disgusting old man. He's a great-looking guy, a matinee idol. I think once you get married to him you'll be very happy – as happy as a girl could be.'

Christina couldn't take listening to this crap anymore.

'Never mind,' she said, and went upstairs.

She was pissed off for a while, then the guilt set in. She knew her father only wanted her to be happy, and besides, this wasn't only about her future; it was about her father's too. She decided she had to at least give Jake a second chance. After all, what exactly did he do that was so awful? He made some insensitive comments and jumped the gun on the wedding announcement. Maybe she was being too hard on him, making a big deal about nothing. Maybe she'd have a great time with him tonight and realize that staying with him was the smartest thing she'd ever done.

She wasn't used to being home on a weekday afternoon and didn't know what to do with her time. She listened to some music and watched TV – *One Life to Live*, *General Hospital*, *Oprah*. At around five thirty she showered. When she came out and started getting dressed to go out with Jake, she noticed she had a message on her cell phone. She hesitated before listening to it, expecting it to be Ryan, but it was Jake saying:

'Hey, sunshine. Just wanted to let you know I won't be around tonight. I have to go out with my parents and my cousins – they want to have a little family time; you know how it is. I'll definitely throw you a call later, and maybe we can hang tomorrow or something. All right, babe? Cool. I'll be thinking about you.'

Fourteen

Jake couldn't decide which outfit to wear – the Valentino shirt with the John Varvatos suit, the lace-up Burberry shoes, and the Movado watch, or the Prada shirt, the Brioni suit, different Burberrys, and the Baume & Mercier watch. He modeled both outfits for half an hour and finally decided on the first one because he thought it made him look the sexiest. After doing some last-minute forehead tweezing, he splashed on more Acqua di Parma cologne all over his body, including his balls, and he was ready to rock 'n' roll.

At eight o'clock, he peeked out of the guest room window and saw the limo waiting, with the driver standing next to it. The reporters and fans had finally taken off, so he'd be able to make a clean break. It would be great to get away for a while, to take a break from being Mr Happy Fiancé, and to let some of the old Jake Thomas loose.

He tiptoed down the stairs, hearing his parents talking in the kitchen – perfect. He slipped out the front door and went down the steps toward the limo.

The driver, holding the back door open for him, said, 'Good evening, Mr Thomas.'

'How's it going?' Jake said. 'Can we just get the hell out of here?'

As the limo pulled away, Jake opened the bar and fixed himself a Grey Goose on the rocks, thinking about his prospects for an orgy. Earlier, when he'd called Patti, he'd thought his chances were slim to none when she mentioned that three of her five stewardess roommates were out of town this weekend.

'Do you think you might be able to get some other friends to come by?' Jake asked.

'Why?' Patti said.

'Just to, you know, hang out. I love meeting new people.'

'That's so cool. Okay, well, I'll see if anybody's around.'

'Just make sure they're as pretty as you are.'

'What?'

'I'm just kidding. I'm sure all your friends are beautiful.'

Jake was confident that Patti would come through. She was a player, so her friends were probably players too, and he knew if he got at least five players in the room everything else would take care of itself.

Jake's cell rang – ROBBY flashing.

'Yeah,' Jake said.

'I've got one word for you,' his publicist said. 'Actually, two letters – *GQ.*'

'I got the cover?'

'You got the cover.'

'Baby!'

The limo driver was looking back at Jake in the rearview. Jake, sick of drivers listening in on his conversations, shut the partition.

'Just got the call,' Robert said. 'They were on the fence between you and Ben, and I talked them into you. I told them, "Ben Affleck is so two years ago. Jake Thomas is the future. You gotta go with J.T."'

'Way to go,' Jake said. 'Now if you score me cover stories in *Time, Newsweek,* and *People* you can keep your job.' He let the silence linger, then said, 'Kidding, kidding.'

'I knew that,' Robert said.

'Seriously, you don't have to worry. As long as you get me on *Oprah, Biography,* and *60 Minutes* you'll keep your job.' Jake paused again, then said, 'It's a joke. Come on, bro.'

'I'm also still getting a lot of calls about you and Christina,' Robert said. 'Who knows? If I could set up a sit-down for you two with this Kathleen Graham at *People,* maybe they *would* put you on the cover.'

'Still too early,' Jake said. 'Let's see how the next few days play out and we'll make a decision about that next week.'

'If you don't mind my asking, what exactly are you trying to accomplish by trickling out information about the wedding?'

'Actually, I do mind you asking. Remember, if you don't want to do your job, it's not like I can't find a hundred other PR guys who'd love to have it.'

Several seconds of silence went by, then Robert said, 'You're kidding, right?'

'Wrong,' Jake said, and flipped the phone shut.

Kicking back, sipping his drink, Jake was confident everything would continue to go his way. News about the wedding would keep leaking out, and rumors would start flying about where the wedding would take place, how much it would cost, and which celebrities would attend. And then the *GQ* cover story would hit the stands, giving Jake more awesome PR. Jake remembered telling the *GQ* reporter that he loved getting involved with the community and interacting with the Pittsburgh fans, and a lot of other stuff guaranteed to make him sound like a saint.

The limo went along the Belt Parkway, making the big loop around Brooklyn. After passing Bensonhurst and the Verrazano Bridge, Jake finally saw part of the downtown Manhattan skyline.

Manhattan. Ah, Manhattan. Beautiful fucking Manhattan.

Until now, Jake didn't realize how much of his energy Brooklyn had sapped. Brooklyn was such a wasteland, such a downer, such a total buzz kill. That was why there were so many people in the world *from* Brooklyn – because anybody with half a brain got the hell out as fast as they could, or at least moved to the Slope or the Heights, which were really parts of the city. *The city.* That was what they called Manhattan, because Manhattan *was* New York. Brooklyn was bullshit.

Patti lived all the way up on the Upper East Side, near Harlem. Bumper-to-bumper traffic in the East Fifties slowed them down awhile, and it was about nine thirty when the limo pulled into the circular drive of Patti's apartment complex on Ninety-fifth Street. Jake instructed the driver to pick him up in two hours sharp and then got out and strutted toward the building's entrance, noticing people noticing him.

The black guy swinging the revolving doors gave Jake the usual J.T. double take. It went like this – guy looked at Jake like he was a nobody, guy looked away; guy realized that the nobody looked like J.T.; guy looked at the nobody again; guy realized that the nobody *was* J.T.; guy's eyes widened like he just stuck his finger in an electric socket.

Jake went to the concierge's desk and told the Puerto Rican girl to ring Patti's apartment.

'Your name?'

Jake got this a lot too – people who obviously recognized him but pretended to be one of those I'm-so-cool-because-I-don't-like-to-intrude-on-celebrities'-space types.

'J.T.'

The girl called upstairs and said, 'J.T.'s here to see you,' her face turning pink. Then she said to Jake, 'Go right up.'

Jake took the elevator up to the twenty-sixth floor. After putting a breath strip on his tongue and adjusting his balls a few times, he rang the bell.

A plain blond girl opened the door and said, 'Hey.'

'Hey,' Jake said, looking past her into the dingy apartment. 'Is Patti here?'

'I am Patti.'

Jake squinted. Out of the stewardess outfit, with less makeup, she looked a lot different. He remembered a low-budg Cameron Diaz, but she was just an okay-looking blonde. But then he looked her up and down – she was in jeans and a pink scoop-neck thing – glad to see that her body was still as Cameron Diaz-like as he remembered.

'I was just messing with you,' he said. 'How's it goin', baby?'

As he gave her a tight hug hello – happy to feel that she was very thin and tone – he looked over her shoulder, through the pass-through kitchen into the tiny living room area. He was bummed to see only two girls there, and one guy. He hoped there were more girls in another room or something.

'Hey, so I see you have a few friends here.'

'Yeah,' Patti said, 'lemme introduce you.'

Jake followed her into the living room area and found out why the place was such a dungeon. A wall had been put up in the middle of the original living room, probably to make another bedroom, so the new living room had no windows. The two girls in the room were sitting on a cheap purple couch – probably from IKEA – and the guy was sitting on one of the three chrome stools at the breakfast bar. One girl – the dark-haired Italian- or Greek-looking one in black boots, a short black skirt, and a black top – was definitely hot. She was smiling at Jake in an I-want-you-so-

bad way, and Jake knew he had her in the bag. The other girl –
with curly red hair and designer glasses, in a plain gray pin-striped
business suit – was eye-fucking him too. She wasn't Jake's type –
too conservative-looking, hips a little too wide, a double chin –
but she'd do for an orgy.

The guy – squat, receding hairline, in a wrinkled navy suit,
probably from fucking Sears – got up from the stool and rushed
over to Jake, sticking a hand out to shake.

'Wow, it's really great to meet you. I'm Mark. Mark Gottlieb.'

Jake shook Mark's sweaty hand, getting germ vibes. He wished
he'd brought some Purell.

'This is like a dream come true for me, man,' Mark went on.
'I'm a big, big fan of yours.'

Jake knew he was just kissing up.

'Yeah?' Jake said. 'You like the Pirates?'

'No. I mean, I'm a Yankees fan, but I've always been a big
baseball fan, and I've been following your career since you started
out. I have the first All-Star Game you played in on videotape.'

'Great,' Jake said, 'that's really flattering.' Then he said to the
girls, 'And who are these lovely ladies?'

He enjoyed watching the girls blush.

'Diane,' the hot, dark one said.

'Little ditty about Jake and Diane,' Jake said smiling.

Everybody laughed.

'Great to meet you, Diane.' Jake shook her hand, holding it for
a couple of seconds longer than necessary. Then he looked at the
redhead and said, 'And you are . . . ?'

'Susan.'

She had a raspy, sexy voice that moved her up a few notches in
Jake's mind.

'Great to meet you, Susan.'

He held her hand for a few seconds, looking intensely into her
light brown eyes.

'Sorry we don't have a lot of places to sit,' Patti said to Jake.
'Why don't you sit on the couch?'

'Thanks,' Jake said, and he sat between Susan and Diane,
smiling at both of them. He noticed that Susan was wearing a
wedding ring, but he didn't care.

'You want something to drink?' Patti asked. 'A beer, soda?'

'That's all right,' Jake said. 'So when are the other girls gonna get here?'

'There aren't any other girls.'

Shit, this is why he drove an hour and a half into Manhattan – for three girls and a guy?

'Come on,' he said, forcing a smile. 'You can make a few calls, find some friends to invite over, right?'

'These are my friends.'

'Don't you know any other girls in the building or in the neighborhood? I mean, I love meeting people. I mean, people's friends.'

'Isn't he so cool?' Patti said to the girls. Then she said to Jake, 'I called everyone I knew, but no one could make it.'

'What about your roommates?' Jake asked. 'I mean, you said three were out of town, so where are the other two?'

'I live here,' Diane said.

'Oh,' Jake said. 'So you're a stewardess too?'

'Flight attendant.'

'Cool,' Jake said, hoping she wasn't some kind of feminist. 'Do you know any other flight attendants in the neighborhood?'

'No, not really,' Diane said.

Jake didn't want to press too hard. He didn't get the right numbers, but he had to look on the bright side – at least he had a great shot of getting into a five-way. He had the three girls, plus him and Mark. Orgies with guys usually weren't Jake's thing – they were a little too porno for him – but once in a while he didn't mind.

'Well, this is great,' Jake said. 'I'm just glad I had the chance to meet all of you.'

'How long're you in New York?' Mark asked.

'Just the weekend,' Jake said.

'I bet you've had a blast so far, huh? I read about that party in the newspaper.'

'Yeah, I've had a great time,' Jake said, smiling at Susan, then at Diane. 'But I think the best is yet to come.'

Jake winked at Patti, who had sat down on a stool next to Mark, and she smiled. Jake knew he had Patti all locked up. His strategy was to make a move on Diane first, then get Susan to join in. Patti would come right over and get in on the action, and Mark would either take off or stick around to get some himself.

This was going to be easy.

Jake leaned back, spreading his arms over the back of the sofa, around Susan and Diane.

He said to Susan, 'So are you a stewardess too?'

'No, I work in advertising. I'm an account exec for BBDO Worldwide. We do a lot of work with professional athletes.'

'Yeah, I think I've done some stuff with BBDO.'

'You have.'

'Cool,' Jake said, trying to figure out if she was being bitchy.

'I work in advertising too,' Mark said. 'Creative at Omnicom.'

'Yeah?' Jake didn't care.

'I can't believe you're really here,' Diane said to Jake, making goo-goo eyes at him.

'I know, isn't it, like, so surreal?' Patti said.

'It's cool, man,' Mark said.

Jake sensed the time was right to get this party rolling. He reached into the inside pocket of his Varvatos jacket and took out his pillbox.

'E, anybody?'

The girls and Mark exchanged looks, everyone waiting for the first person to say yes so they could too.

'I'll have one,' Diane said.

'All right,' Patti said.

'Why not?' Mark said. It was obvious he'd never taken a drug in his life, but he didn't want to seem like a faggot in front of Jake and the girls.

Jake gave them the pills, then offered one to Susan.

'No, thanks,' she said.

'Sure?' Jake asked. 'This is great shit. It really helps you kick back.'

'It's okay – thank you.'

Jake didn't want to push it. Susan seemed kind of stuck-up, but maybe it was all a front. He had to hope, anyway.

Jake took a pill himself – swallowing it dry. Then he had to listen as Mark went on about how he'd grown up dreaming of playing in the major leagues and how he once hit three home runs in a game in Little League. Finally, after about ten minutes, Jake felt the E kicking in, and he moved his left arm closer to Diane's shoulders until he practically had his arm around her. Then he started to gently massage her left shoulder with his fingers, and he could tell she was getting into it because she started leaning into him. Patti seemed ready too, and Jake decided the time was right to make his move. He started kissing Diane's neck. She pulled back at first, but then she let him continue, and he knew she was into it. Meanwhile he lowered his right arm around Susan's shoulders. Susan was the key; if she let loose, Jake was home free.

Jake pulled her closer, hoping she was a player, but he knew he was in trouble when she jerked away and said, all bitchy, 'What're you doing?'

Shit, Jake thought. *If she just took one fucking pill.*

Jake stopped kissing Diane and said to Susan, 'Something wrong?'

Susan went over to Mark. Mark put his arm around her.

'Susan's my wife, dude,' Mark said.

'Oh,' Jake said.

'What're you doing?' Patti said. 'I thought you came here to see *me*?'

Hoping he could at least salvage a three-way with Patti and Diane, Jake said, 'I did come here to see you, baby. But I thought you wanted to . . .' He held out his hand toward the empty seat on the couch. 'Come on, why don't you join us?'

'God, the rumors about you really are true,' Patti said.

'What rumors?' Jake said, worried. Had the Marianna Fernandez story leaked somewhere?

'Didn't I read in the paper that you and your fiancée set a wedding date yesterday?' Mark asked.

'You have a *fiancée*?' Patti said.

'No, that was just bullshit in the papers,' Jake said, smiling, hoping he could win them over with his great choppers. 'I don't even know that girl they said I'm engaged to. I'm gonna sue over that – was talking to my lawyer on the way over here. So why don't you come over and join us?'

'Maybe you should just leave,' Patti said.

Jake looked at Diane, hoping at least she'd be on his side, but she was looking away, obviously not into it anymore, and said, 'Yeah, you should go.'

'Look, guys, you all have the wrong idea,' Jake said. 'I don't know what you think was going on here, but that wasn't what was going on at all. It was just the E, that's all. I took it on an empty stomach – I haven't had anything to eat all day. I apologize if I offended anybody.'

'God,' Susan said. 'You know, you really epitomize what's wrong with professional sports today. You athletes think you can just do whatever you want and there're no consequences, ever. You're supposed to be role models – you're supposed to set an example for the rest of society.'

'Hey, you guys took those pills too,' Jake said. 'So if you're thinking about telling anybody about this, don't think that's not getting out. Your bosses'll find out you were taking drugs. You'll all lose your jobs.'

'Just get out of here,' Patti said, starting to cry.

'I have an idea,' Jake said to Patti. 'How about we start over? We can go out to dinner, just me and you. We'll—'

'Get out!'

Jake left the apartment, wondering how everything had gotten so fucked-up.

In the lobby people recognized him – nudging their friends, saying, 'Hey, look over there,' and 'Oh, my God,' or just staring at him. Jake pulled his Varvatos jacket up over his head and left the building.

Outside, Jake remembered telling the limo driver to pick him up in two hours. He took out his cell to call the limo company, then realized that he didn't have the number, and he couldn't even remember the company's name. He could've called for another car, but there were a lot of people around, and he didn't want to hang out, getting recognized and being hounded for autographs.

Jake walked to the corner of Third and Ninety-fifth and tried to hail a cab. It took about five minutes before one stopped for him. He opened the door, brushed a couple of Starburst wrappers off the seat onto the floor, then slid in and said, 'East Eighty-first Street, Brooklyn.'

'I don't go to Brooklyn,' the driver said in his foreign accent.

'Why not?' Jake asked.

'No Brooklyn. Just get out of my cab, okay?'

'Come on,' Jake said, 'don't you know who I am?'

Jake saw the driver's tired, swollen eyes in the rearview.

'No.'

'I'm Jake Thomas.'

'Who?'

'Jake Thomas. The baseball player, Jake Thomas?'

'Look, man, I'm not going to Brooklyn – forget about this, okay? You want to go to Manhattan somewhere, I take you, okay? But I don't go to Brooklyn.'

'You don't understand – I'm famous baseball player. You know, baseball – batty, bally . . . '

'Just get out, man, or I call police.'

'Look' – Jake glanced at the driver's ID – 'Salojin. I'm having a really shitty night, okay? How 'bout I give you an extra fifty bucks? Here.' Jake took out a fifty-dollar bill and held it up. 'Come on, what do you say?'

The driver thought it over, then said, 'A hundred.'

Jake didn't feel like arguing. An extra hundred to get this night over with seemed like a bargain.

'Just get me the fuck out of here,' he said.

About forty-five minutes later they exited the Belt Parkway at the Rockaway Parkway exit. Jake gave Salojin directions to his parents' block, and then, as they passed some slummy housing project, Salojin said, 'If you famous, why don't you live in Westchester, or New Jersey, or Park Avenue? You not really famous basketball player, right?'

'Right,' Jake said.

'See? I knew it.'

The cab pulled in front of Jake's parents' house. Jake paid the fare plus the extra hundred. He was exhausted and just wanted to get into bed and crash and put this whole stupid night behind him.

He was heading along the walkway toward his parents' house when someone said, 'Yo.'

At first Jake thought it was another asshole reporter, but it didn't sound like a reporter. It sounded like some homeboy hanging out, hoping to get an autograph from Jake Thomas to sell for twenty bucks on the Internet.

Yeah, right.

Jake looked over his shoulder, ready to tell the guy to come back tomorrow, when he saw two guys there on the sidewalk. They looked like gang kids, except they weren't kids – they were in their mid-twenties or older. One guy had his hands in the pockets of his big red leather jacket and had long braids. The other, taller guy was hanging back, and had his hands in the pockets of his North Face winter jacket. He had on baggy jeans, bunched up at the ankles, and wore ratty cornrows.

Jake had a feeling these guys were bad news, but he hoped he was wrong. Maybe they were actually guys he went to school with, or old friends, or relatives.

'Do I know you?'

'Naw, you don't know nobody,' the guy with braids said.

Jake still sensed he was in trouble. He turned away and took another step toward the stoop.

'Yo, give it up.'

Jake stopped again, instinctively moving his right arm closer to his rib cage. When he was home in Pittsburgh, or traveling during the season, he usually carried a .44 Magnum around with him for protection. Since he'd broken into the big leagues, he'd had a few psychos threaten him, and he'd had to have bodyguards from time to time, but he still felt safest when he was carrying. He even took a gun with him on road trips, bringing it into the stadiums and keeping it in his locker during games. But now, because he'd flown to New York this weekend on a fucking commercial flight, he was unarmed.

Figuring he'd play dumb, Jake said, 'Give what up?'

The guy with the braids took out a black-and-silver handgun and aimed it at Jake's face.

'Your wallet. Give that shit up, man.'

Jake shifted his eyes back and forth, hoping to see somebody who could help him or call the cops, but the block was empty. All day yesterday and this morning, fans, photographers, and reporters were hounding the hell out of him; now, when he needed them, they were gone.

'Come on, move it, man – gimme your fuckin' wallet 'fore I shoot your motherfuckin' head off.'

'Hey, you guys know who I am, right?'

'Yeah, we know who the fuck you are. Why you think we here?

Now give up your fuckin' wallet, man, or I'm gonna start
shootin'.'

As Jake reached into his pocket he said, 'You guys are making a
big mistake.'

'Gimme that shit,' the guy with the braids said, grabbing the
wallet. He looked inside it, then said to Jake, 'Yo, where the fuck's
the rest?'

'I don't have any more.'

'Bullshit. There only, like, two hundred somethin' dollars here.'

'That's all I have.'

'Don't fuck around, bitch. I *know* you got money.'

'Yo, maybe we should go,' the guy with the cornrows said.

'Shut the fuck up,' Braids said to him.

Jake wondered if they were both high on crack.

Then Braids said to Jake, 'Gimme the gold, yo – chain, watch,
rings, all that shit.'

Moving slowly, hoping someone would come by and scare the
guys off, Jake removed his Movado watch and handed it to the
guy.

'Faster, yo,' Braids said.

Jake took off his nameplate necklace and rings.

'Diamond earring too, bitch.'

As Jake handed Braids the jewelry, a car came down the block.
Braids moved the gun closer to his body so it was concealed by his
jacket, but he kept it aimed at Jake.

The car didn't stop.

'Now where's your fuckin' money at, bitch?' Braids asked.

'What,' Jake said, 'that's not enough for you?'

'Yo, give it up, 'fore I shoot you in yo' pretty-ass face.'

'You saw my wallet. That's all I got.'

'Maybe you got another wallet. Or maybe you got money in yo'
shoe, or in yo' Fruit Of The Looms. Maybe I should pop a hole in
yo' head and look there.'

'Come on,' Jake said. 'Why do you think I have money?'

''Cause you J.T.'

'So? What, you think I walk around with wads of cash in my
pockets?'

'He said you do.'

'Who said?'

'The fuck cares who?'

'Who said that? Who told you I have cash?'

'I don't know his fuckin' name, man.'

'Wait. You're saying somebody *sent* you here?'

'Just give it up.'

'I wanna know his name.'

'Ryan,' Cornrows said, speaking his first word. He seemed calmer, less whacked-out than Braids.

'Yeah, Ryan, that's right,' Braids said. 'Nolan motherfuckin' Ryan.'

Jake remembered how Ryan had attacked him before. That sick fuck must've sent a couple of his gangsta friends over here.

'Ryan lied to you, all right?' Jake said. 'I gave you all I got.'

'Let's just get the fuck outta here, man,' Cornrows said.

'Shut up,' Braids said. Then he said to Jake, 'What about inside? You must got money there, right?'

'I got nothing inside.'

'Let's go check it out.'

'My parents're home.'

'So?'

There was no way Jake was letting these guys inside the house. He knew they'd kill him *and* his parents without giving a shit about it.

'The fuck you waitin' for?' Braids said.

'You know anything about guns?' Jake asked.

'What?'

'You know about guns?'

'Yeah, I know about guns.'

'You know what a Barrett is?'

'A Beretta?'

'No, a Barrett. It's a sniper's rifle. Fifty-caliber. Can take down a fucking airplane.'

'So? Who gives a shit?' Braids said. 'You don't got one.'

'Yeah,' Jake said, 'but my old man does. He was a sniper in the Gulf War. Used to shoot guys between the eyes from a thousand yards away.'

'Who gives a shit 'bout yo' damn father?'

'You should. He has his Barrett aimed at you right now through the living room window and he's about to blow your fucking brains out.'

When Braids's eyes shifted toward the house, Jake went for the gun and quickly had both his hands around the asshole's wrist.

'Shoot him,' Braids said to Cornrows.

Cornrows was aiming a gun at Jake. His hand was shaking.

Jake was struggling, trying to get Braids's gun.

'Just shoot him, man,' Braids said. 'The fuck you waitin' for?'

Then a shot was fired. The backfire forced Jake backward; he almost lost his balance. Then he realized he had Braids's gun in his hand. He aimed at Braids, ready to fire, when he realized that Braids was groaning, holding his chest. Braids stared at Jake, his eyes widening for a moment, before he collapsed onto his side.

Jake looked over at Cornrows. Cornrows still had his gun aimed at Jake. Jake aimed Braids's gun at Cornrows, ready to blow the asshole away, when Cornrows took off, sprinting up the block.

Jake ran too, up the stoop. He fumbled, searching for his parents' house keys on his chain; then he thought, *Fuck, the jewelry*. He went back to Braids, dug into his jacket pocket with his free hand, but there was nothing there. Then he checked the other pocket and found his watch, necklace, and rings, but couldn't find the diamond stud. Cursing, he continued to feel around the lining. He heard voices; they seemed far away. He was about to leave without the earring; then he felt a prick and pried it loose out of the lining. He went back up the stoop, fumbled again with the keys, finally found the right one, and opened both locks and went into the house. A light was on in the living room, but the kitchen was dark. He went into the kitchen, now hearing footsteps upstairs. His mother's muffled voice said, 'Call the police,' and his father – his voice a little clearer, probably at the top of the staircase – said, 'Wait right here.'

Jake looked down at his hand, saw he was still holding Braids's gun. He thought about stuffing it into the garbage can. No, that was stupid. How about under the sink? No, that was even worse. It had to be someplace where no one would find it. He put the gun in the inside pocket of his Varvatos jacket, figuring he'd get rid of it later.

Then Jake realized he was screwed. If Braids lived he could make up a story, say that Jake shot him; then the police might find the gun with Jake's prints on it and Cornrows could back the story up.

Jake considered going back out there, waiting for the cops and the ambulance to show up. He'd tell the truth about everything, say he'd been mugged and the gun went off by accident.

He took a few steps back toward the living room, then stopped, realizing that telling the truth would be the dumbest thing he could do. Jake Thomas's being involved in a shooting would make headlines all over the country; if it came out that he'd fired the gun – forget about it. He could say it was self-defense, but there would be all kinds of questions: Did he have to kill him? Did the gun really go off by accident? No matter what the evidence showed, people would assume he was guilty because he was half-black, and of course young black men were always shooting people. And if Braids and Cornrows were drug dealers, it would be even worse. People would assume Jake was mixed up with drugs, and by tomorrow morning he'd lose all of his endorsement deals and he could kiss his Hollywood career good-bye.

Jake decided to deny everything. Who gave a shit what those guys said? He was Jake Thomas; they were nobodies. Who would people believe?

Then, listening at the kitchen door, Jake got some good news.

'He's dead?' Antowain asked.

'Yeah,' a man said – it sounded like Jim from next door.

'Damn,' Antowain said. 'You call the cops yet?'

'My wife's callin'.'

'You see anything?'

'Naw. Just heard the shot.'

'Us too.'

Then Jake heard his mother's footsteps coming down the stairs. He went out of the kitchen and said to her, 'What happened?'

'Thank God, you're okay,' Donna said. 'When did you get home?'

'About ten minutes ago,' Jake said. 'I was in the kitchen, grabbin' something to eat, when I heard some loud noise. It sounded like a firecracker.'

'It wasn't a firecracker.'

Antowain came back into the house and said to Jake and Donna, 'Guy's dead.'

'Oh, my God,' Donna said.

'Who is he?' Jake asked.

'Dunno,' Antowain said.

'Shot right in front of our house?' Donna said. 'That's it – we have to get out of this neighborhood. I can't live here anymore. I can't!'

Jake made an excuse that he had to go to the bathroom and slipped upstairs. He went into the guest room and searched for a good place to hide the gun. His suitcase? No. Under the mattress? Yes.

He felt relieved until he checked himself out in the mirror and noticed something funny about the left sleeve of his jacket. It took him several seconds to realize he was staring at Braids's blood.

He rushed into the bathroom and scrubbed the sleeve in the sink until the water wasn't pink anymore. It was a good thing that the jacket was dark or his parents might have noticed the blood. He didn't see any redness or stains anywhere else on his clothes or on his body, and he knew he'd lucked out big-time; if Braids had gotten shot in the head or the neck, blood would've splattered everywhere.

Jake hid the jacket in the bottom of one of his suitcases and went back downstairs. His parents were outside now, talking to neighbors. Jake rehearsed his story in his head. It was easy – he saw nothing. He was in the kitchen eating when he heard the shot. What was he eating? What the fuck difference did that make? The cops wouldn't give a shit what he was eating. A sandwich – he was having a fucking turkey sandwich. And if Cornrows got caught and started talking shit, Jake would just deny everything. The cops would take Jake's word over some crackhead's.

Jake couldn't wait for this weekend from hell to end, so he could go back to Pittsburgh for some peace and fucking quiet. Then he realized how close he had come to dying tonight and how, for the second time today, Ryan had tried to kill him. Before Jake went anywhere he was going to figure out a way to give that slimy little scumbag some payback.

PART THREE

Fifteen

Moments after opening his eyes, Ryan realized he had no feeling in his left arm. It took several more seconds for his still-half-drunk mind to realize that something very heavy was lying on it, and several more seconds to realize that the very heavy thing was an enormous naked black woman.

With his other hand Ryan nudged the woman, but she was fast asleep, gurgling-snoring, and wouldn't budge. He pushed her harder and she still wouldn't move or wake up. Using all his strength he tried to yank his arm free, but couldn't tell if he was getting anywhere because he had zero feeling below his left shoulder. Continuing to pull, he saw he was making some progress, and then he grabbed the top of the trapped arm with his right hand – it felt like he was gripping a piece of cold rubber – and finally was able to work the entire arm free.

The arm flopped at his side uselessly. He'd never had a limb fall asleep this badly, and he tried to stay calm, telling himself that it wasn't possible to get paralyzed or have any permanent damage from an arm falling asleep. He slapped his arm and rubbed it, and after a long time – maybe a minute – he started feeling pins and needles, and then the pain set in. After awhile he was able to move it normally, and then he took his first good look around the bedroom, realizing that he had no idea where the hell he was. He had a hazy memory of walking with someone – this woman? He didn't think so – up a steep staircase, but he couldn't remember where the staircase led, and this room didn't look at all familiar. There was pink-and-yellow floral wallpaper, a dresser, two night tables, a pale green carpet on the wooden floor. On the dresser there was a picture of a woman and a guy wearing a Yankees cap. Next to it was a picture of a number of people, including the woman, dressed up for a wedding or something. A window was open and there was a fire escape, and Ryan could see the back of another building with another fire escape, but the view didn't ring any bells either.

Not much light was coming into the room, so Ryan had no idea what time it was. He checked his watch, pushing the little button to turn on the light, and saw it was past eight thirty.

The woman snorted loudly, then turned onto her side toward Ryan, her tremendous breasts and rolls of stomach fat jiggling and settling for several seconds after she finished the turn. Ryan stayed perfectly still, not wanting to wake her. Then, for the first time, he realized that he was naked too and that he'd probably had sex with this woman. He touched his pubic hair, and sure enough there was stickiness there. He brought his fingers to his mouth and smelled a pungent odor, and then he realized he had the same odor around his mouth.

He managed to sit in an upright position at the side of the bed. Now that his arm was feeling better, he became aware of the intense pain in his head and neck. He felt nauseous too, and when he swallowed he winced because of the sour aftertaste in his mouth, mingling with his morning breath and the odor around his lips. He figured he'd probably yacked at some point during the night.

He tried to concentrate, doing his best to think through all of the pain in his head and piece together yesterday. He remembered his arguments with Christina and Jake, and drinking at Cousin's and Vinny's and winding up at some other bar, but after that he couldn't remember shit.

Finally a memory came to him – sitting at the bar trying to get the bartender's attention. He was pretty sure that had happened last night. The bartender – a thin black guy with graying hair and maybe a mustache – was talking to somebody, and there was a rottweiler there. Okay, this was progress, Ryan thought. And didn't someone steal his Spurs cap? He remembered someone grabbing the cap off his head and tossing it away. He looked around the room – which was spinning badly now – and saw his jeans and Ronnie Lott jersey on the floor, but no cap. It hurt keeping his eyes open, so he closed them again.

Saiquan.

Who the hell was Saiquan? The name sounded vaguely

familiar, but Ryan didn't know why he— Wait, wasn't that the name of one of the guys he used to play basketball with at Canarsie Park? Yeah, it definitely was, but what did he have to do with anything? Was Saiquan at the bar last night? Did Saiquan steal his Spurs cap?

And wasn't there a woman at the bar? Was it this woman? Ryan remembered telling someone – definitely not Saiquan – that the code for his ATM card was NOLAN. Why would he have given someone a fake code for his ATM card? Why would he give someone *any* code for his ATM card? Was it possible he had been mugged?

Trying not to let the bed creak or the mattress move too much, Ryan made it to his feet. He had to steady himself a couple of times, but he managed to get to where his pants lay. He crouched and felt his right front pocket – his wallet was still there. There was no money inside, but going by how he felt, he figured it was very likely he'd blown all his cash on booze. His ATM card was there, as well as the couple of credit cards he carried, and nothing seemed to be missing.

He looked around but couldn't find his boxers. When the woman stirred he thought, *Fuck it*, and grabbed his jeans, jersey, sneakers, and socks and went out into the living room. He dressed quickly, noticing an almost empty bottle of JD on the coffee table and the biggest bra he'd ever seen on the floor. He went into the kitchen – it was a railroad-style apartment – and then into the vestibule. He bolted and unbolted the three locks until he found the right combination, and then he exited, closing the door quietly behind him.

With his head throbbing, he went down the three flights of steep stairs. When he made it outside, the building and the entire block looked totally unfamiliar. He walked along the sidewalk with his head down to avoid the eye-stinging sunshine, and saw the street sign on the corner – Snediker Avenue. Ryan had no idea where he was, but he knew he was someplace he didn't want to be.

He wasn't sure which direction to head in. He waited on the corner until a woman walking her German shepherd came by, and he asked her how to get to Flatlands Avenue. The woman pointed to the right, so Ryan went that way.

His head was splitting and he was thirsty as hell. He wished he'd drunk some water before he left the woman's apartment. He didn't have any money to buy anything, and he didn't have a MetroCard to take the bus. He figured it was about a thirty-block walk to his house, but the way he felt, he knew it would seem like a hundred.

On the next block he took a leak between two cars, and then continued walking, trying to piece together more of last night. So far all he knew was that after Jake's he went drinking, lost his car, and wound up in a bar, maybe around this neighborhood. A bartender with a rottweiler gave him a hard time, and then that guy Saiquan stole his hat, and he met some woman there, maybe the same woman he woke up with. It all seemed hazy, like a dream.

Then, as he continued walking, the name Elly came to him. *Elly likes that . . . Do that to Elly again . . . Mmm-mm . . . Oh, yeah.*

He remembered the smell of Pampers, and a huge black body. He remembered, at the bar, thinking that she looked like Aretha Franklin. Except for her weight, she actually looked nothing like Aretha, but this proved that the woman he woke up with was the same woman he'd met last night.

Now he remembered being in the apartment with the woman, sitting in the living room, doing shots of JD. The woman was naked and Ryan was sucking on something thick and rubbery – probably one of her huge nipples. He remembered being pulled into the bedroom, being pinned against the wall, and being undressed. *Elly wants it so, so bad, baby.* They were doing it doggie-style, and the woman was screaming, *Gimme that big boy! Gimme that big boy!*

Ryan couldn't remember anything else, and he still had no idea what had possessed him to go home with that woman. It was hard to tell exactly what she looked like when she was sleeping, but she seemed very unattractive, even ugly, and must have been at least fifty years old. But while the idea that he'd had sex with the woman pretty much disgusted Ryan, he was proud of himself too. She wouldn't have been screaming, 'Gimme that big boy!' if he wasn't satisfying her. He must've been good last night – really good. Now there was no doubt in his mind that all of his 'sex problems' with Christina were from tension and anxiety.

Then, for the first time this morning, it hit Ryan that Christina was gone, that he'd lost her forever. The idea seemed half-unreal, like one of the foggy memories from his hangover. How did all this happen? How could she have gone back to Jake? She hated Jake; she complained about him all the time. It couldn't've just been about money and sex. Christina wasn't that superficial. She was a romantic – she wanted to be in love. And Ryan knew that she loved him. He remembered the way she always looked at him. That wasn't faking.

Jake must've lied to her, somehow convinced her that he loved her. Then Ryan remembered having his hands around Jake's throat.

Ryan knew it was the alcohol that had made him lose control like that, but when Jake told Christina he'd spin it into something else. He'd tell her that Ryan was crazy and dangerous and belonged in a mental institution. After the scene Ryan had caused at the office, she'd believe him. Why wouldn't she?

Ryan had to talk to Christina. If she'd changed her mind so quickly to go back to Jake, she could easily change her mind again. All he had to do was reason with her, find the right words. He'd say to her, *Look into my eyes and tell me you love Jake. Just say you love him and I'll leave you alone forever.* If that didn't work, he'd kidnap her. He'd take her to a motel somewhere and keep her mouth taped until she listened to what he had to say. He'd tell her again and again how much he loved her and what a lying jerk Jake was, and eventually she'd believe him.

Ryan walked for about ten minutes, past projects and other shitty apartment buildings, and still didn't recognize anything. Then, after he passed some train tracks, he reached Linden Boulevard and realized he was heading toward East New York. He asked a sanitation worker hanging off the side of a garbage truck where Flatlands Avenue was, and the guy pointed in the direction from which Ryan had just come.

Ryan cursed, heading back. That fucking woman on the street had probably sent him the wrong way on purpose. It was probably a big joke to her – tell the stumbling white guy with a hangover to head toward one of the worst neighborhoods in Brooklyn.

Approaching a project he'd passed a few minutes earlier, Ryan noticed some threatening looks from a group of angry gang kids hanging out near the entrance to a building, but he doubted anyone would give him a hard time. The way he looked, it could've been his first day in the prison yard, and he could've had a sign around his neck that read, FRESH MEAT – COME GET SOME, and the inmates would've left him alone.

Ryan felt very weak and out of it and had pains practically everywhere. His mouth was so dry he doubted he could produce spit, and his lips were badly cracked. He didn't know how he'd make it home without passing out, but one thing was for sure – he wasn't going to have another sip of alcohol for as long as he lived.

At about ten o'clock, after walking for nearly an hour, Ryan turned onto his block. He couldn't wait to have some ice-cold water, to get that sour, sickening taste out of his mouth.

He was so dazed and focused on thoughts of water that he didn't notice all the commotion near his house until he was about twenty yards away. There were several police cars and news trucks and a crowd of maybe fifty people on the street and sidewalk. Most of the crowd was right under the WELCOME HOME JAKE, OUR HERO banner, and Ryan wondered if Donna Thomas was throwing another party.

Then, as Ryan got closer, he realized that there were too many cops and news crews in front of the house for this to be a party. He also noticed the yellow police tape surrounding the stoop and part of the front of Jake's parents' house.

Ryan went over to Jamal, the high school kid who'd deejayed Jake's party the other day, who was among the onlookers.

Ryan said to Jamal, 'What's going on?'

Jamal turned to Ryan and did a double take because of how messed-up Ryan looked.

'Shit,' Jamal said. 'The fuck happened to you?'

Ignoring that, Ryan said, 'What happened here?'

'Guy got shot last night.'

'Really? Who?'

'Some dude from the Crips. That's what they sayin' anyway.'

'And he was shot right here?'

'Yeah, they got the chalk outline right in front of the stoop.'

'You mean the guy died?'

'Yeah.'

'Shit.'

Ryan noticed a gray-haired man in a wrinkled sport jacket, probably a detective, talking to a guy who lived across the street.

'So who shot him?' Ryan asked.

'Nobody knows nothin' yet,' Jamal said.

'Right in front of Jake's parents' house. That's pretty weird, isn't it?'

'It's damn weird.'

Ryan walked around the crowd toward his house, overhearing one woman saying, 'It had to be over drugs – it always is,' and another woman saying, 'Yeah.'

In his house Ryan made a beeline for the refrigerator. He started drinking Pepsi straight from the bottle when he heard his mother's shrill voice behind him: 'Ryan – oh, thank God!'

Before he could turn around, Rose-Marie came up behind him and hugged him tightly and wouldn't let go.

'I was so worried. I thought something terrible happened to you.'

Ryan stopped drinking and said, 'It's all right. Everything's cool, Ma.'

Rose-Marie still had her arms around him. 'Where have you been?'

'I was just out . . . with some guys from work.'

'Why didn't you call?'

'I forgot. Why're you freaking?'

Now Rose-Marie let go of him, and he turned around to face her.

'God, you look awful,' she said.

'I'm fine,' Ryan said.

'You smell like alcohol. Were you drinking all night?'

Ryan knew what was going through her mind – her son was developing a drinking problem, turning into her husband. Her biggest nightmare was coming true.

'I just had a few beers with the guys – it was no big deal.' He was trying to be casual, reassuring, but he didn't think his mother was buying it. Then, changing the subject, he said, 'What're you so freaked out about, anyway?'

'Didn't you see all the commotion outside?'

'Yeah. So?'

'I thought it was you. You didn't come home from work yesterday. You didn't call, and you *always* call, and then I heard the shot. When I went outside people were in front of the Thomases' house, looking down at a body. You can imagine what went through my head.'

'But why'd you think it was me?'

'Because I didn't know where you were. You weren't answering your phone, and I called everyone I could think of and no one had heard anything from you.'

'Why were you checking up on me?'

'Because I was scared. Thank God you're okay.'

Rose-Marie tried to hug Ryan again, but he backed away, not letting her.

'I don't get it,' he said. 'I don't come home for dinner one night and you fly into a fuckin' panic?'

'When you live in my house I have a right to know where you are.'

'That's bullshit.'

Ryan started to leave the kitchen when Rose-Marie said, 'I heard what happened with you and Jake.'

Ryan stopped, turned back, and said, 'Yeah? What'd you hear?'

'I called the Thomases, to see if you were over there. Antowain said you were there yesterday afternoon. He said you were drunk and you attacked Jake. Is that true?'

'No ... I mean, it's true I was over there, but Antowain's blowing it way out of proportion. Jake and me, we just had a little confrontation, that's all.'

'The police wanted to talk to you before.'

'To me? What for?'

'I don't know ... Maybe Antowain told them something.'

'What did he tell them?'

'I have no idea. But why were you—'

'Man, that pisses me off. It's all because of fuckin' Dad, you know.'

'What is?'

'That's why Antowain's talking shit about me. Because of all of that old bullshit between him and Dad. He's just putting that on me now.'

Rose-Marie started to cry.

'Look, I know what you're thinking, but it's not true. I'm not turning into Dad.'

'You're acting like him.'

'Because I had a few beers?'

'That's how it starts.'

'I don't have a drinking problem. I swear on my life, I'll never let that happen to me.'

'Antowain said something else. He said you've been . . . having some relationship with Christina. Is that true?'

Ryan waited, then said, 'Yeah. Actually, it is.'

'With Jake's fiancée? Why, Ryan? Of all the girls in Brooklyn.'

'Because I love her.'

'How did this happen? Why her?'

'Didn't you hear what I said? I'm in love with her.'

'That's why she just announced a wedding date with Jake?'

'She didn't announce that, okay? Jake announced it.'

'I really don't understand what's going on with you lately,' Rose-Marie said. 'Where were you last night anyway? Were you drinking all night or did you sleep someplace?'

Ryan was thinking fast, trying to come up with some lie – maybe say he was at Christina's or had crashed someplace else – but he was sick of having to defend himself.

'I gotta take a shower,' he said, and left the kitchen.

Following him through the living room, Rose-Marie said, 'You don't tell me anything anymore. I don't even know where you're sleeping or who you're sleeping with.'

'You could be happy for me, you know.'

'Happy! What do I have to be happy about?'

'I tell you about Christina and all you do is take Jake's side. And you wonder why I don't tell you anything?'

Ryan was heading upstairs.

'You're an alcoholic,' his mother called after him. 'You need help – before it's too late. Your father never thought he had a problem, either – now look at him!'

In his room Ryan lay in bed with his eyes closed, feeling shittier than when he woke up in bed next to that woman – Elly, or whatever the hell her name was. The long walk home had taken more out of him than he'd thought, and then having to hear all that crap from his mother had been the kicker. He didn't care what she thought – he was nothing like his father, and he was pissed at her for even comparing him to that wife-beating son of a bitch.

Then Ryan realized that today was Saturday – a workday for him. The idea of inhaling paint fumes all day sickened him, and he didn't feel like he had the energy to get out of bed, no less paint a house. But then he remembered how he'd left yesterday, and that if he didn't show up today he'd probably get fired.

He took his cell phone out of his jacket pocket and saw that it was off. He didn't remember turning it off yesterday, but he must've at some point. He had eleven messages.

Several were from his mother – he deleted those without listening to them. The rest were from Franky and Tim. He listened to the first couple, getting the gist about how pissed off they were at him for not coming back to work yesterday, then deleted the rest.

Ryan went to voice dial and said, 'Tim,' then closed his eyes again, feeling like he might blow chunks.

'What happened to you yesterday?'

Tim's voice was too loud for Ryan's brain.

'Sorry,' Ryan said, wincing.

'What?'

'Sorry,' Ryan said, louder. 'I had a rough night.'

'Night? What about all day? Franky said you took off at nine fifteen.'

'My friend Stevie was in a car accident. I was at the hospital with him all night.'

'Oh,' Tim said. 'That sucks.'

'Yeah, it does suck.'

Ryan couldn't tell if Tim knew he was bullshitting.

'So why didn't you call and tell somebody?'

'Sorry, I just forgot to,' Ryan said. 'It was a really fucked-up situation. He was in a coma.'

'Jesus.'

'He came out of it . . . this morning. The doctor said he'll make it, but it didn't look good for a while.'

'That's cool,' Tim said. 'So you're coming in today, right?'

Fuck, Ryan thought. *Why did I have to say he came out of the coma?*

214

'Yeah,' Ryan said. 'Course. I'm just gonna be a little late. I only got a couple hours' sleep last night.'

'I appreciate that,' Tim said. 'As you can imagine, the guys're behind on the job now. I need you to finish by Monday so you can start that Midwood job.'

It was about ten fifteen now, so Ryan told Tim he could be at work by eleven. Tim said that would be fine.

Ryan clicked off and started dozing, with the phone still in his hand. He forced himself to open his eyes and get out of bed, knowing that if he fell asleep he wouldn't be able to get up for work.

In the bathroom he drank some water from the faucet, then showered. He felt a little better – more awake, but still very weak.

He got dressed quickly, putting on sweats, a Kevin Garnett jersey, and a white do-rag covered by an Oakland Raiders cap. Heading downstairs, he wanted to get something to eat, but he heard the TV going in the kitchen and he couldn't deal with another lecture from his mother, so he shouted, 'Goin' to work, Ma!' and left the house quickly.

There was still a crowd with all of the news crews and cops in front of the Thomases' house. Ryan remembered Rose-Marie telling him that a detective wanted to ask him some questions, and since he still had plenty of time to make it to work before eleven, he figured he'd get it over with.

Ryan went over to a cop who was standing alone in front of a squad car and said, 'Hey, I'm Ryan Rossetti – I live over there.' He motioned with his jaw back toward his house. 'My mother said a detective wanted to talk to me.'

The cop pointed toward the gray-haired guy Ryan had seen before; now the guy was talking to a couple of cops near the yellow tape in front of the Thomases'.

Ryan went over to the guy, waiting until there was a break in his conversation, then said, 'Yeah, I'm Ryan Rossetti. My mother said you wanted to talk to me.'

'Gimme a couple,' the guy said to the cops. Then to Ryan, 'I'm Detective Noll, Sixty-ninth Precinct, I did wanna talk to you. Got a few minutes?'

'Yeah, but I don't think I can tell you anything.'

'Why's that?'

' 'Cause I don't know anything. I wasn't here last night.'

'Yeah, your mother said you didn't come home. Where were you?'

'I was out,' Ryan said. 'At a bar.'

'Yeah? What bar?'

'I don't know the name of it,' Ryan said, feeling accused.

'Do you know where it was?'

'Look, I had a little too much to drink last night, all right?'

'So I heard.'

'I don't know what Antowain Thomas said, but he's lying. Me and Jake – we had a little issue, that's all.'

'He said you had your hands around his son's throat.'

'That's bullshit.'

'He also said you threatened to come back and kill his son.'

'*What?*'

'But Jake Thomas wouldn't confirm the story. He said it was just an argument.'

Wondering why Jake had covered for him, Ryan said, 'What does this have to do with anything anyway?'

'Maybe nothing,' Noll said. 'We're just talking to everybody, seeing if we can put a picture together of what was going on around here yesterday. So you say you don't remember where you were last night, huh?'

'I didn't say that,' Ryan said. 'It was up near Rockaway Avenue somewhere.'

'What time did you get home?'

'I came home this morning.'

'Where'd you sleep?'

Ryan hesitated. 'With . . . somebody.'

'Christina Mercado?'

'How do you know about me and Christina?'

'Antowain Thomas said you two had gotten together while Jake was out of town.'

'I wasn't with Christina . . . I was with somebody else.'

'What's her name?'

'Elly . . . I think.'

'Is "Elly I Think" a girlfriend?'

'I met her last night – at the bar I was at.'

'Congratulations, you scored. You have a number where I can contact the lucky lady?'

'Look I gotta go, all right?' Ryan said. 'I wish I could help you, but I wasn't here last night – I came home about a half hour ago.'

'Do you have Elly's address?'

'Snediker Avenue,' Ryan said. 'I don't know the number.'

'Does the name Marcus Fitts mean anything to you?'

'Should it?'

'He was the guy who was shot last night.'

Ryan shook his head. 'Sorry, never heard of him.'

'Did you happen to hear or see anything suspicious around here yesterday? Maybe hear about a drug deal going down?'

'No,' Ryan said, 'but I hope you catch the guy.'

Ryan turned and started back toward where he usually parked his car, then remembered that he'd lost it last night. He could've borrowed his mother's, but he didn't want to bother explaining everything to her. The house in Mill Basin wasn't very far away, and if he jogged he could still make it in time.

Sixteen

Ryan arrived at work at a little before eleven o'clock. Franky was in the living room, painting a windowsill.

'Hey, there's the man,' Franky said.

'What's going on?' Ryan asked.

'Not much, shy one guy on the job.'

'Didn't Tim tell you about my friend?'

'Yeah. Sounds fucked-up.'

Ryan could tell Franky didn't buy the story.

'It was pretty rough,' Ryan said. 'But he'll pull through.'

'That's what Tim said. So where'd this accident happen anyway?'

'Ralph Avenue.'

'Ralph and what?'

'J.'

'Huh? I drive by there all the time – doesn't seem like a dangerous intersection. Who hit him?'

'I'm not sure.'

'Didn't he tell you?'

'He was in a coma.'

'Right, I forgot.'

Wanting to change the subject, Ryan said, 'Where's Carlos?'

'Upstairs,' Franky said, 'laying on the primer in the master bedroom. We *should* be puttin' on the final coat upstairs today, but we didn't even finish the downstairs yet.'

Not wanting to get into it with Franky, Ryan went into the kitchen. Jogging to work had taken more out of him than he'd thought it had. He drank some water, but he needed something to eat. In one of the cupboards he found a box of Ritz crackers. He took out a handful and started eating them as quickly as he could.

Franky came into the kitchen and said, 'Come on, jeez. Can't you eat before you come in here?'

With his mouth stuffed Ryan couldn't answer.

'And you're eatin' the client's food, too,' Franky went on. 'You know you're not allowed to do that – we could get fired for that shit.'

Ryan swallowed, then said, 'It's just a few crackers.'

'Still. Can't you order in if you're gonna eat?'

Carlos came into the kitchen and said, 'Hey, man, what's up?'

'Hey,' Ryan said.

'Look at him,' Franky said, 'stuffin' his fuckin' face.'

'Gimme a break, all right?' Ryan said.

'You give us a break,' Franky said. 'Stop doin' shit that's gonna cost us money, get us fuckin' fired.'

''Cause I'm eating a few crackers?'

'I'm not talkin' about the fuckin' crackers. I'm talkin' about runnin' out of here yesterday, not tellin' anybody where you're goin'.'

'What're you talking about? My friend was in a coma.'

'You expect us to believe that shit?'

'Fuck this.' Ryan picked up his painting clothes to go change in the bathroom upstairs.

'We saw the way you took off here yesterday,' Franky said to Ryan. 'It was right after you saw that article in the paper about Jake Thomas getting married.'

'I got a call about my friend Stevie, you fuckin' idiot.'

'You almost fell off the ladder when Carlos showed it to you.'

'You're such an asshole, man.'

'Yo, maybe he's tellin' the truth,' Carlos said.

'He's full of shit,' Franky said. 'It hit me this morning, driving in. That chick J.T.'s gonna marry – Christina somethin'. That's the chick Ryan talks to on the phone.'

'So what's that gotta do with it?' Carlos asked.

'It's got nothing to do with it,' Ryan said.

He tried to leave the kitchen, but Franky moved over, blocking him, and said, 'When I remembered the name Christina from the paper it all made sense. The article said Christina was Thomas's high school sweetheart. Well, Ryan went to the same school – South Shore – so I started thinking, maybe Ryan had something goin' with this Christina chick too. Maybe that's why Ryan freaked when he read that article about Jake getting married, and why he always acts so weird when we start talking about J.T. He probably took off here to try to get his girlfriend back. Then, when he got busted, he made up that bullshit story to Tim about his friend in the car accident.'

Ryan was amazed how accurately Franky had put everything together.

'Nice try,' Ryan said, 'but you have no idea what you're talking about.'

He pushed past Franky and went into the living room.

Following him, Franky said, 'You better get your fuckin' act together, Rossetti – stop slackin' off. You already cost us a shot of gettin' that bonus on this job. When your shit starts fucking with my paycheck I got a problem with that.'

Ryan went upstairs. He changed into his painting clothes and got to work, putting on a first coat in the bathroom. The crackers he'd wolfed down hadn't made him feel much better, and inhaling paint fumes wasn't helping. Rolling on the paint, feeling queasy, he realized he had to talk to Christina as soon as possible. She'd probably already heard about how he'd attacked Jake yesterday, and he was worried what she'd think if that detective talked to her.

He called her cell and got her voice mail, so he tried her at home.

Al answered: 'Yeah.'

'Is Christina there?' Ryan was talking low, almost whispering, so Franky or Carlos couldn't overhear.

'I can't hear you,' Al said.

'Is Christina there?' Ryan said, not much louder.

'Who's this?'

'Ryan.'

Al grunted in a pissed-off way. 'Call back some other time, will ya?'

'Is Christina there or not?'

'Yeah, she's here.'

'I gotta talk to her.'

'She locked herself in her room. She won't talk to anybody.'

'What happened?'

'Nothing. Look, she just can't talk to you right now, all right?'

'Put her on.'

'I'm hanging up.'

'Wait, don't—'

The line was dead.

Ryan started to call back, then clicked off, knowing Al was screening calls.

Working through his hangover pains, Ryan put in a solid hour of painting. Then, at around twelve thirty, he washed up, changed back into his street clothes, and went downstairs.

'You gotta be kidding me,' Franky said.

Ryan said to Carlos, 'I need a favor – can I borrow your car for, like, a half hour?'

'What for?'

'I just gotta do some errands, go to the bank. I wrote a bad check – it's gonna bounce if I don't cover it.'

'What happened to your car?' Franky asked.

'Battery trouble.' Ryan looked at Carlos. 'Come on, what do you say?'

Ryan had once loaned Carlos his car when Carlos had to pick up his cousin from somewhere, and Ryan knew he would have a tough time saying no.

'I don't got a problem you borrowing my car, man,' Carlos said. 'I just don't know if my insurance covers that shit.'

'I'll be gone a half hour, forty-five minutes tops. I'll be extra careful – don't worry.'

'Don't lend him the car if you don't want to,' Franky said.

'How about you shut up?' Ryan said.

'How about you make me?'

'Chill, yo, chill,' Carlos said. Then he said to Ryan, 'It's cool, man.'

'Thanks,' Ryan said.

As Carlos gave Ryan the keys, Ryan and Franky exchanged glares.

'Just be careful at them intersections, yo,' Carlos said. 'I don't want you gettin' into no accident like your homeboy.'

'What homeboy?' Franky said, smirking.

The muffler of Carlos's Oldsmobile was noisy, but the car was a smooth ride – smoother than Ryan's Impala, which wasn't saying much.

One cool thing about Carlos's car – it had a new CD player with kick-ass Dolby speakers, which was the main reason why Ryan had asked to borrow it. Ryan's plan was simple: Christina's all-time favorite movie was *Say Anything* with John Cusack. She always talked about how romantic the scene was when Cusack holds the boom box up above his head in front of the girl's house, blasting Peter Gabriel's nauseating 'In Your Eyes.' It worked for Cusack – he got the girl back in the end – and Ryan knew that if he did it, Christina would be so touched that she'd have to forgive him.

Ryan went to Sam Goody at the Kings Plaza shopping mall and looked for the Peter Gabriel CD with 'In Your Eyes' on it, but they didn't have it in stock. He hit a couple of smaller stores on Flatbush, then found it in a store on Kings Highway and headed to Christina's.

He double-parked in front of her house, opened all the car's windows, and cranked the song. Then he stood in front of the car waiting, feeling like an idiot, but trying to look as intense and sincere as John Cusack did.

The whole song played; nothing happened, so he played it again. A couple of neighbors came out, wondering what was going on, but there was no sign of Christina. He put the track on repeat play, figuring that she'd have to come out eventually.

Finally, when the song was playing for the fourth or fifth time, Al came out. Ryan smiled at him and waved, but Al remained deadpan. Then Al came over to the car.

'The fuck're you doing?' Al said. He was talking loudly, nearly shouting, to be heard over Peter Gabriel.

'Waiting for Chrissy to come down,' Ryan said.

'Didn't I tell you on the phone – this isn't a good time.'

'And I told you I have to talk to her.'

'Turn that shit off.'

'Not till she comes out.'

'What the hell you think you're doing anyway? Why're you here?'

'I'm in love with your daughter.'

Al glared at Ryan.

'What do you mean, "in love"?'

'I mean I want to marry her.'

'Son of a bitch,' Al said. 'So that's how everything got all fucked-up. It's 'cause of you.'

Ryan said, 'I'm sorry that you—' then had to duck to avoid Al's right hook. It was a feeble old man's right hook that wouldn't've hurt if it had connected.

'Whoa,' Ryan said. 'What the—'

Ryan dodged another lame punch – a kind of right jab – and then grabbed Al, holding him.

'I knew it had to be you, you son of a bitch,' Al said. 'You're over here all the time, trying to get into Chrissy's pants. I should've kicked your ass a long time ago.'

Al struggled to break free.

'Hey, come on,' Ryan said. 'I don't want you to get hurt.'

'Hurt, my ass – I'm gonna fuckin' kill you!'

Al was still trying to get loose, but Ryan held him tightly. Then Al stumbled backward and banged his back against the side of the car with Ryan still holding on to him.

Christina came out of the house and rushed over and tried to pull Ryan and Al apart.

'Stop it,' she said. 'Just stop it.'

Ryan let go of Al.

'What the fuck is wrong with you?' Christina said.

Al was trying to catch his breath, staring at Ryan like he wanted to murder him. Peter Gabriel was still going on about the light and the heat in the girl's eyes.

'Why're you smiling?' Christina said to Ryan. 'You think this is a big joke?'

'No,' Ryan said. 'I'm just happy to see you.'

'So it's because of him, huh?' Al said. 'The fucking house-painter? That's why you're suddenly so confused?'

'Is that true?' Ryan said hopefully. 'You're confused?'

'I'm not gonna get into this now,' Christina said, and then she looked at Ryan. 'You shouldn't be doing this. Just go home, all right?'

'Not before I get a chance to talk to you.'

'You heard her,' Al said, 'get the fuck outta here.'

'That's enough, Daddy. Just go inside.'

'You don't need this loser, this fuckin' bum,' Al said. 'He'll ruin your life.'

'I said go.'

Al stared at Ryan for a few more seconds; then he walked away, mumbling to himself, looking back at Ryan a few times as he went toward the house.

When Al was inside, Christina said to Ryan, 'I want you to leave too.'

'In Your Eyes' started again.

'I want you back,' Ryan said.

Christina reached into the car and shut off the music.

'I had to figure out some way to get your attention,' Ryan said. 'You look beautiful, by the way.'

'Please – just go.'

'I love you.'

'Don't say that.'

'Why not?'

'Bec . . . Just go – please.'

'First tell me – is it true? You and Jake aren't together?'

'Who said that?'

'You said you're confused.'

'I never said that.'

'Your father said you did.'

'I'm just taking some time to be alone . . . to think.'

'So you have something to think about. It means you're not happy.'

'It doesn't mean that.'

'Then why aren't you with Jake right now?'

'Because . . . Just stop it, all right?'

Now Ryan knew the timing was right to unleash his killer line, the one he knew would win her back for sure.

'Look in my eyes and tell me you don't love me,' he said. 'Say it and I'll leave you alone forever.'

Ryan looked at Christina like a sad puppy.

'I'm going inside,' Christina said, and headed away.

'Wait,' Ryan said, sidestepping to block her. 'Is it because of what I did yesterday? Because if it is I'm really sorry, all right? I shouldn't've come to your office – that was stupid. I was just so pissed off when I read all that shit in the paper that I—'

'Get out of my way, please.'

'I know,' Ryan said. 'It's because you heard what happened at Jake's. Just so you know, I had nothing to do with any of that shit – I swear.'

'What're you talking about?' Christina said. 'I just heard that a guy was shot in front of Jake's house – a drug dealer. What does it have to do with you?'

'Nothing.' Ryan realized he should've kept his mouth shut. 'I'm just trying to figure out what I did that was so wrong.'

'Look, it's cold out here and I'm going inside, so please let me, okay?'

Christina sidestepped past Ryan and continued toward the house.

'Christina—'

'We'll talk soon, okay?'

Ryan watched her go inside. He stood there for a while, staring at the house, and then he got in the car and drove away.

When Ryan pulled up to the house in Mill Basin he saw Tim's pickup in the driveway. Ryan knew something was up, because Tim almost never came to job sites on weekends.

Then Ryan remembered how Tim had asked him to get that baseball card autographed by Jake, and Ryan quickly concocted a story in his head about how Jake had to leave town earlier than expected and wouldn't be able to sign anything.

After Ryan parked Carlos's car, he ejected and removed the Peter Gabriel CD. When he got out he saw Carlos walking toward him, fast.

'Where the fuck you been?' Carlos demanded.

'What?' Ryan said.

'You said you'd be gone a half hour.'

'What time's it now?'

'Past two o'clock.'

Ryan realized he must have spent more time than he'd thought driving around looking for that CD, because he'd been gone about an hour and a half.

'Sorry,' Ryan said. 'There was a long line at the bank. I lost track of time.'

Carlos was circling the car, as if inspecting it for damage.

'The car's fine,' Ryan said.

Looking in the window, Carlos saw the wrapping from the CD.

'That's where you was at? Damn CD shoppin'?'

Ryan wanted to give a good explanation for this, but all he could come up with on the spot was, 'No.'

'Hey, Ryan.'

Ryan turned and saw Tim walking toward him. Franky was trailing a few feet behind.

'Hey,' Ryan said, knowing right away, by the look on Franky's face, that Franky had ratted him out.

'Had a nice long lunch, eh?' Tim asked Ryan.

'I was at the bank,' Ryan said.

Tim looked almost as unconvinced as Franky.

'The guys said you left at twelve thirty,' Tim said.

'So I ran a little late,' Ryan said. 'That's why you came down here?'

'There also seems to be an issue about what happened yesterday . . . about the accident your friend was in.'

'What about it?'

'Franky and Carlos say you left because of some girl. That true?'

Ryan looked at Franky, who was looking away. Then he said to Tim, 'No, it's not true.'

'Fuckin' liar,' Franky said.

'Fuck you,' Ryan said.

'Hey, cool it,' Tim said to both of them. Then to Ryan, 'Look, I'm not here to point fingers, all right? I only care about one thing – getting a job done on time. If we go over on this job, I can't use the Fiorellas as a reference for the next job and I'll lose out on word-of-mouth. You see what I'm saying?'

'Yep,' Ryan said.

'You think this is a joke?'

'Nope.'

'Good. Now, back to yesterday. Just so we can clear this up so you guys can get back to work, what's the name of your friend who was in a coma?'

'Stevie.'

'Stevie who?'

'Stevie Marks.'

Stevie Marks had been the first baseman on the South Shore team, but Ryan hadn't seen him since high school graduation.

'What hospital is he in?'

'What difference does it make?'

'I just want to give them a call,' Tim said. 'If they say your friend is a patient there, Franky gives you a big sorry and we put this behind us.'

Ryan knew he was fucked.

'This is bullshit. Why do you have to check up on me?'

'See?' Franky said. 'What'd I tell you?'

'Just give us the name of the hospital,' Tim said. 'We'll make one call and put this all to rest.'

'So what's this?' Ryan said. 'You don't trust me?'

'I don't like to be lied to,' Tim said. 'I'm not *saying* you're lying, but if you're not how about just clearing it up?'

Ryan glared at Tim as if disgusted by him. Then he gave Carlos a similar look. He didn't bother looking at Franky.

'You know what? Fuck all of you,' Ryan said, and stormed away. He expected Tim to call after him, try to get him to come back, but Tim didn't say anything.

Ryan was pissed off about it for a while, but then he decided that if Tim was willing to let him quit over something like this, who needed him? It wasn't exactly like Pay-Less Painting was the best job on the planet. Ryan didn't have a lot in savings, about two thousand bucks, but hell, he could probably even start his own painting business. After he got a few jobs under his belt, he could do a little advertising, get some word-of-mouth going, and before he knew it he'd have steady business. Then he could start hiring other crews, buy a truck, and expand to other neighborhoods in Brooklyn. In a year or two his business would be bigger than Pay-Less, and Tim O'Brien could kiss Ryan Rossetti's Italian ass.

As Ryan turned up his block he noticed that the crowd in front of the Thomases' house was gone, and he hoped that meant Jake had gone back to Pittsburgh. Then maybe Christina would realize that she'd made a huge mistake, and Ryan would get her a ring and start his painting business, and everything would work out the way it was supposed to.

Ryan reached his house and headed toward the stoop. He was planning to go straight up to his room and pass out and not wake up till tomorrow morning when he heard the two loud pops. He didn't realize somebody had shot at him until a couple of seconds later when his knees buckled and he was lying on the ground.

A car screeched away up the block. Everything went black.

Seventeen

'So you sure you're okay?' Ken Jarvis, the Pittsburgh Pirates owner, asked Jake for what seemed like the gazillionth time.

'Fine,' Jake said. 'It's all cool. Really – you don't gotta stress.'

'Well, this is a huge relief,' Ken said. 'When I heard this morning that there was a shooting at your parents' house and that you were *there*, I naturally started thinking the worst. But you say you're okay.'

'Yes,' Jake said, rolling his eyes, wanting to get off the fucking phone already.

'Great,' Ken said, 'that's really wonderful – fantastic. Actually, I'm on vacation right now – Santorini. If I couldn't reach you I was going to get on the next plane to the States. You're the most important member of this franchise, by far, and we hope you'll be an important member of it for years to come.'

Ken's bullshit was so strong Jake could practically smell it all the way from Greece. Yeah, Ken was calling to make sure his superstar was okay, but he also knew that if Jake Thomas left the Pirates after next season the franchise would be toast, so he was trying to show Jake how much he meant to the team by calling him from Santorini during his vacation.

The truth was, there was no way in hell Jake was going to re-sign with the Pirates, but to keep his market value as high as possible Jake and his agent had been dicking Ken around for months, making out as if Jake loved the city of Pittsburgh, and playing for the Pirates, and wanted to remain with the team for the rest of his career.

'It's always great to hear how much respect you have for me,' Jake said. 'And I think you already know how much respect I have for you and for the whole Pirates organization.'

'Well, that's wonderful to hear,' Ken said, soaking all that shit up. 'So when do you leave New York?'

'I'm supposed to leave Monday morning.'

'Can't you get out any sooner? Maybe I'm being paranoid, but until the police resolve this it sounds like it could be a dangerous situation there.'

'I'll see what I can do. But there're a few things I need to take care of first.'

'Maybe you should get a bodyguard then. Should I send one over?'

Thinking about how he had to get rid of that gun at some point today and how having some goon bodyguard hovering over him would make that next to impossible, Jake said, 'Nah, it's all right – really.'

After assuring Ken again that he was fine and there was nothing to worry about, he finally got off the phone and went downstairs. It was eight A.M. and he could still hear the commotion outside. He peeked through the curtains in the living room and saw cops, reporters, and fans standing around the yellow police tape. Jake was sick of this shit. He would've loved to take Ken's advice, say sayonara to Brooklyn, and get on the next flight out, but he didn't want any negative PR. Although he was pretty sure the cops had believed his story that he was in the kitchen, grabbing a bite to eat at the time of the shooting, he knew that if Cornrows got caught that could fuck everything up, and he wanted to be in town to deny everything in person.

Then, of course, there was also a chance that Marianna Fernandez would go public with her rape charge at midnight tonight. If that shit hit the fan, Jake wanted to be in Brooklyn, to catch a photo op with Christina so the public could see right away what a happy fiancé he was and how Marianna's story had to be bullshit.

Jake went into the kitchen and opened the fridge. There was still nothing to fucking eat in the house – just leftovers from the party the other night. Even the cabinets were filled with shit he couldn't eat – cereal, bread, pasta, rice, crackers, cookies. Searching in the back of the fridge, behind the trays of lasagna, he finally found some protein – a chunk of cheddar cheese and an unopened log of Hebrew National salami. He wolfed down the cheese and took the salami up to his room.

Sitting on his bed, he took a few bites of salami and then called Christina.

'Hello,' Al said, sounding half-asleep.

'I wake you?' Jake asked, not really caring if he did.

'Who's this?'

'J.T.'

Suddenly upbeat, like he was happy to have a ringing phone startle him out of a deep sleep, Al said, 'No, no, hey, I'm wide-awake. How're you doing?'

'I'm fine. Chrissy there?'

'Yeah, but, hey, I just wanted to congratulate you about setting the wedding date. That's really terrific. I called yesterday, but you weren't home.'

'Thanks,' Jake said. 'So is Chrissy—'

'It's gonna be great having you as part of the family,' Al went on. 'I wanted to take you out to Nino's last night to celebrate, but Christina didn't think it was a good time. I'd love to take you out some other time, though. How long you in town?'

Tired of listening to Al kiss up to him, Jake said, 'Sorry, I'm kind of in a rush. Is she there or not?'

'Sure, Jake, I'll get her. Congrats again. Hold on.'

Al was gone for a long time, maybe a few minutes, and Jake wondered if the old man had fallen back asleep. He was about to hang up and try Christina's cell when Al picked up and, sounding pissed off, said, 'She's still sleeping.'

'Tell her it's me.'

'Could you just call back a little later?'

Jake rolled his eyes, said, 'Do me a favor, when she wakes up, make sure she calls me right away. There's something on the news about me, and I don't want her to get all freaked out about it.'

Al wanted to know what was going on.

'No big deal,' Jake said. 'Just a guy in front of my house got shot.'

'Shot?'

'Yeah.'

'Is he okay?'

'He's dead.'

'Dead?'

'I had nothing to do with it,' Jake said quickly. 'I mean, the only reason my name got in the news at all was because it happened in front of my house. It's not like I was there or anything. So anyway, just tell Chrissy it's all cool, okay?'

'Sure, Jake. No problem. It's really nice of you to call. And I'll be sure to—'

Jake hung up. He did some push-ups and isometrics; then he remembered that he had a weight bench and some barbells in the basement. At least, he used to have them – he hadn't used them since he was in high school, and his parents might have gotten rid of them.

He tossed on Calvin Klein sweats and an Honro T-shirt and went down to the basement. Although there was paneling on the walls and indoor-outdoor carpet, it was a mess with boxes and other shit everywhere. In the back room, near the boiler, Jake spotted the weight bench. He had to move boxes out of the way to reach it, and then he dragged the bench to an open space.

After hunting around awhile, he finally found the weight bar and some plates. He brushed off the bench the best he could, then put on the weight – a fifty and a twenty on one side, and seventy pounds in tens and fives stacked up on the other. The bench was so rickety that when he lay back on it he thought it might collapse. He imagined how stupid he'd feel, breaking his neck while benching in his parents' basement in Brooklyn.

He did a couple of sets and was in the middle of his third when his mother shouted, 'Jake, you down there?'

Jake didn't answer.

'Jake!'

'What?'

He couldn't hear what the hell she was saying.

'What?' he said louder.

'A detective's here – he wants to talk to you!'

Jake almost lost control of the bar.

'Fuck.'

'What?'

'Tell him to come back later!'

'He says he has to talk to you now. It'll only take a few minutes.'

Jake knew he had no choice.

'All right, one sec.'

Trying to keep his cool, he went upstairs. He entered the kitchen and saw a gray-haired white guy in a cheap suit sitting at the table with a mug of coffee in front of him.

When the detective saw Jake he stood up quickly and said, 'Hey, how are you?'

'What's up?' Jake asked.

'Sorry to bother you. Just had a couple of things to ask you and clear up – if you have a few minutes, I'd really appreciate it.'

'Shoot,' Jake said.

The detective took out a business card and a pen and handed them to Jake.

'First off, my son's a big fan. You think you could . . . ?'

'No *problema*,' Jake said. 'What's your son's name?'

'Trevor . . . But he calls himself Trev. *T-R-E-V.*'

'How old's he?'

'Gonna be seven next week.'

'You should've brought him over to meet me.'

'I don't bring him on police work.'

'Yeah, guess that makes sense. You don't want the kid to get shot, right?'

Jake scribbled his name illegibly on the card and handed it back to the detective.

'Thanks,' the detective said, beaming, like he really did think that getting Jake Thomas's scribbling on the back of a business card was the greatest thing that had ever happened to him.

'Yeah,' the detective said, still smiling stupidly, 'he'll get a big kick out of this.'

'So,' Jake said, 'how can I help you?'

'Oh, right,' the detective said, putting the card away in his wallet. 'By the way, my name's Noll – Edward Noll, Sixty-ninth Precinct. I know you already talked to Detective Jennings last night, but the investigation's proceeding, and there're a few things I just wanted to run by you. This'll take a couple minutes, tops.'

'I'd like to help any way I can,' Jake said, smiling politely.

'First off,' Noll said, 'I was talking to your father just before. . . . He was telling me how Ryan Rossetti stopped by here yesterday.'

'Yeah . . . So?'

'Your father said Rossetti'd been drinking and attacked you. Then, when he left, he threatened your life. Is that how you recall it?'

'Why do you want to know about me and Ryan?'

'We're just checking out every possibility,' Noll said. 'I mean, Rossetti attacked you yesterday, right? It's conceivable he came back here later with Marcus Fitts to try to attack you again.'

'But Fitts is the guy who got shot, right?'

'Maybe they had a dispute. Rossetti shot him and fled the scene.'

Jake thought it all through quickly. He would've loved to pin the shooting on Ryan – exaggerate the story, say, *Yeah, he said he was gonna kill me – go arrest the fucking prick.* But he knew Ryan was friends with Marcus and Cornrows, and if Ryan got arrested, Cornrows would get arrested, and then Jake would be totally fucked.

'You got it all wrong,' Jake said. 'Ryan and me, we just exchanged a few words. It was nothing.'

'So he didn't have his hands around your throat?'

Jake laughed. 'That's what my father told you? That guy . . . Man. Nah, it was no big deal – really.'

'You sure about that?'

'Swear to God, nothing happened.'

'What about when Rossetti left here?' Noll asked. 'Didn't he threaten to kill you?'

Jake laughed again, like this was the biggest joke of all. 'No, of course not. Something you gotta understand – my father and Ryan's father . . . there's been bad blood between them for years. And as far as my father's concerned a Rossetti's a Rossetti, if you know what I mean. Don't listen to anything my father says about any of this. Did you talk to Ryan?'

'Not yet. He didn't return home last night, and his mother doesn't know where he is.'

'I'm telling you, there's no way Ryan had anything to do with any of this. It's obvious this was just some kind of gang-related thing.'

'Why is that obvious?'

'The guy was dressed like he was in a gang, wasn't he? I mean, wasn't he?'

'He had associations with the Crips, but that doesn't mean the shooting was necessarily gang-related.'

'I'm just saying . . .'

'We're gonna check out every possibility,' Noll said, 'but if you say nothing happened here between you and Ryan yesterday, you're right – Ryan probably isn't involved. I just had one more question for you.'

'About Ryan?'

'No, about you. I know you told Detective Jennings last night that you were in the kitchen eating when you heard the shot.'

'I was.'

'But we spoke to a woman across the street – Renee Gardner. When she heard the shot last night she looked out her window. She said she saw you going into the house right afterward.'

Mrs Gardner had been living across the street from the Thomases for years. She was old when Jake was a kid. She had to be eighty now.

'She made a mistake,' Jake said. 'I wasn't there.'

'She sounded pretty sure—'

'You're saying I'm lying?'

'No, but—'

'Come on, you can't trust anything that old lady tells you. I mean, what's she, a thousand years old?'

'She's in her sixties.'

'Still. She's probably senile.'

'She's a civil court judge downtown. I don't think there's anything wrong with her mentally.'

'Oh,' Jake said. 'Look, I don't know what . . . Wait, I know – she probably saw my father, not me. Yeah, that must've been it. My dad was out there first, right after the guy got shot, to see what was going on. She probably saw him going back into the house and figured it was me.'

'You don't really look like your father.'

'Look, I wasn't out there. I don't know what else you want me to say.'

'I guess you've said enough. You'll be around the rest of the weekend anyway, so if I have any more questions I can run them by you later. Oh, and thanks for the card. I know Trev's gonna love it.'

When Noll was gone, Jake opened the refrigerator and took a swig of milk from the carton. Then he closed the refrigerator and punched the door as hard as he could. Pain ripped through his fist. He screamed and opened the freezer and started searching for an ice pack. He couldn't find one, so he took out some ice cubes, wrapped them in a dish towel, and put it on his sore, aching hand.

'Was that you screaming?'

Donna had just entered the kitchen.

'Oh,' Jake said, as if he'd forgotten, 'yeah.'

'What happened to your hand?'

'Nothing.'

'Then what's with the ice?'

'The refrigerator door closed on it.'

'How did that happen?'

'No idea.'

'Poor thing. I hope you're okay.'

'I'm fine.'

'If you're feeling well enough. I was just outside – the reporters wanted to know if you'd answer some questions.'

'Jesus H . . . .'

'I'm sorry,' Donna said. 'I wanted you to have a relaxing time here this weekend. It's so awful that this had to happen.'

Figuring the reporters would be here all day if he didn't give them some kind of statement, Jake said, 'Do me a favor – tell them that I'm very concerned about the situation, and that my heart goes out to the victim's family.' Jake tried to think of some more bullshit. 'Oh, and tell them that I'm trying to spend some time with my family and my beautiful fiancée this weekend and that I hope they respect my privacy.'

'You sure you don't want to tell them all that yourself?'

'Positive.'

Jake had some breakfast – an egg-white omelette and skim milk. He replayed Noll's questions over and over in his head. There were still a few answers he wished he could take back, but overall he thought he'd done pretty well. The thing that freaked him out was the whole Mrs Gardner thing. He was afraid that she wasn't the only one, that someone else had seen him run into the house or even shoot Marcus. He wanted to get the gun out of the house as fast as possible, but he didn't want to do anything stupid. He had to go about his routine – pretend everything was normal, that he had nothing to hide.

His hand was okay, so after breakfast he went back down to the basement to continue his workout. He did more chest, then did back, shoulders, and abs. After over two hours he felt nice and pumped and went back up to the guest room.

He immediately checked under the mattress to make sure the gun was still there, and panicked when he didn't see it. He was convinced that the cops must've searched the room while he was working out. Then he lifted the mattress higher and saw it right where he'd left it last night. He didn't want to dick around any longer, but there were still a lot of people outside. He had to wait for things to calm down; the last thing he needed was some paparazzi snapping a picture of him dumping the gun somewhere.

After a long shower he threw Christina another call, but Al said she still wouldn't come to the phone. Jake didn't know what the hell was wrong with her, and he was wondering if it had something to do with Ryan. He remembered Ryan saying that shit about how he was in love with Christina. Maybe Ryan wasn't lying. Maybe it was more than just a fling and they really were in love. Maybe that little scumbag had tried to kill him twice *and* was trying to steal his fiancée.

Jake kicked the night table and the lamp on top of it fell over, crashing onto the floor. Several seconds later the guest room door opened – Jake's mother was there. She turned around quickly when she saw that Jake was naked.

'You should learn to knock,' Jake said.

'Sorry,' Donna said. 'What was that crash?'

'Oh, the lamp just fell.'

Without looking at Jake, Donna turned and saw the lamp on the floor.

'Get dressed and come downstairs,' Donna said. 'Michelle and Roger just got here.'

Jake had no idea his sister and brother-in-law were coming over.

'Oh, man, why'd you have to do that?'

'They want to see you. How often do you get a chance to spend time with your family?'

'Whatever, I'll be right down.'

Donna left. Jake threw on some clothes – Armani jeans, a black Moschino T-shirt, a tan Evisu sport jacket – and went downstairs.

Donna, Michelle, and Roger were sitting in the living room, talking about the shooting, and didn't even notice Jake arrive.

Then Roger, the dork accountant, saw him and said, 'Hey, Jake!'

Roger shook Jake's hand with a dead-fish grip, and Jake and Michelle said hi the way they always did, air-kissing each other's cheeks.

'So this has been an eventful weekend, huh?' Roger said.

'Yeah,' Jake said. 'But everything's cool now.'

'Michelle was saying she thinks the shooting has something to do with you,' Donna said.

Michelle was looking at Jake in a proud, know-it-all way. Because she had been good in school and got a scholarship to Cornell and was teaching whatever at Butt Fuck U, she acted like she was Miss Expert about everything, and his parents totally bought into it. Ever since Jake could remember, even when Michelle was six years old, his parents always asked for her opinion about every little thing. But if Jake had an idea about something his parents never listened.

'Really,' Jake said, fake-smiling. 'And why's that?'

'Think about it,' Michelle said. 'You're in one weekend of the year – and then someone just happens to be shot in front of Mom and Dad's house? Doesn't that sound a teensy bit coincidental?'

'I think she's right,' Donna said.

'Well, I don't,' Jake said.

'This is what *I* think happened,' Michelle said. 'I think two guys came over to mug Jake, or break into the house, or do something, and then something went wrong. Maybe one guy had a fight with the other guy and shot him, but they definitely weren't here by accident.'

'It's so frightening,' Donna said to Jake. 'You could've been killed. *We* could've been killed.'

'Why're you listening to her?' Jake said. 'She has no idea what she's talking about.'

'It sounds logical,' Donna said.

'You're just saying that because Michelle said it.'

'I think she's making a good point.'

'It's a stupid point.'

'It was just a theory,' Michelle said to Jake.

Jake, glaring at his sister, didn't say anything.

'It doesn't matter why it happened,' Donna said. 'It's just scary – someone getting killed right in front of the house.'

'Let's look on the bright side,' Roger said. 'It sounds like they're gonna get the guy soon anyway.'

'What do you mean?' Jake said.

'Oh, I didn't tell you?' Donna said. 'The police have a suspect.'

'Really?' Jake said as calmly as possible. 'Who's that?'

'They didn't tell me much, but they said they have a description of the guy.'

'Why didn't you tell me this before?'

'I didn't have a chance to, with you coming down here, screaming at your sister.'

'But I talked to Noll. He didn't say they had a suspect.'

'I'm telling you, I just heard while you were in the shower. They also said something about some other shootings last night.'

'What other shootings?'

'I don't know, but they say they think it's related to what happened here.'

Donna continued talking but her voice faded to white noise. Jake knew that as soon as Cornrows got caught he'd tell the cops that Jake had shot Braids, and he'd probably try to pin these other shootings on him. Jake could deny everything, but how would that look if the cops found the gun under his mattress?

'Can I borrow your car?' Jake blurted out.

Whoever was talking stopped, and Donna said, 'What for?'

'I need to go to Christina's. I forgot, I told her I was gonna pick her up and bring her back here today.'

'Oh, wouldn't that be nice?' Donna said.

Jake got the car keys from his mother, then said he needed to use the bathroom but headed upstairs to the guest room. He reached under the mattress and took out the gun. Then, in a dresser drawer, he found an old T-shirt and he began wiping down the gun ultracarefully, as if he were polishing silver. When he was convinced there couldn't be a print anywhere, he wrapped it in the T-shirt and put it in the inside pocket of his jacket. It looked kind of bulky. He patted it down as flat as he could get it and decided it was good enough.

Downstairs, he announced he'd be back in about an hour, figuring that would give him plenty of time to dump the gun, and then he went outside.

The crowd had mostly cleared. The news trucks and cameras were gone and there were only a few people hanging around. Jake figured they were just neighbors or fans, but then two of them rushed him as he headed down the stoop, shoving mikes in his face.

'How 'bout a comment about the shooting, Jake?' a thin blonde asked.

'I already gave my comment,' Jake said, not stopping.

'Are you relieved the police have a suspect now?' said a black guy, maybe Jake's age.

'Very relieved,' Jake said.

There were more questions, but Jake stopped answering. He kept saying, 'Excuse me,' and 'Sorry,' as he continued toward his mother's Explorer, parked a few spots away, up the block. But the reporters had probably been waiting all night to get their Jake Thomas sound bites and wouldn't let up. They walked alongside him, the black guy rubbing up against him right where the gun was. Jake was afraid the guy would feel the gun, get all nosy, and say, 'What's that in your pocket?' Or what if, the way Jake was getting all jostled, the gun fell out?

But Jake made it into the car and closed the door. He worried that he'd been acting suspicious, hurrying to the car, and if any trouble came up later the reporters would remember and tell the police. Trying to do some preemptive damage control, just in case, he smiled and waved at the reporters in an it's-all-cool way as he drove up the block, going at an easy ten-mile-per-hour clip.

Now he had to figure out what the hell to do with the gun. His first idea was to bury it somewhere, but he knew that was stupid. What would he do, start digging a hole in the ground in broad daylight? Besides, he didn't have a shovel or anything to dig with. He could drive to a bridge, throw the gun in the river, but someone might spot him.

Heading along Avenue J, trying to decide where to get rid of the gun and coming up with no new ideas, Jake wondered if the red car behind him was paparazzi. There was glare on the car's windshield, so Jake couldn't see the driver, but he thought the car had followed him from his parents' block. Jake started driving through the intersection at Remsen Avenue, then made a sharp right, and sure enough the red car turned with him. *Goddamn sons of bitches.* He made a right at the Canarsie Cemetery and stepped on the gas, figuring he'd try to lose the fucker, but he realized that getting caught for speeding right now probably wasn't such a great idea, so he hit the brakes. The red car braked hard behind, almost rear-ending him.

Jake marched toward the car, ready to give the guy hell, when he saw it wasn't a guy driving; it was a girl – a teenage girl. Not bad-looking – dark skin, long, straightened hair, maybe sixteen. Jake could tell she recognized him because she covered her mouth with her hand, obviously surprised to see Jake Thomas storming toward her like he wanted to kill her.

Jake smiled widely, trying to cover for the mistake, then got back in the Explorer and drove away.

Staying on Church Lane, he veered right and, in the rearview, watched the girl turn onto Avenue J.

He still didn't know what to do with the gun. He considered driving over to East New York and dumping it at a project somewhere when he realized that he didn't have to go anyplace special to get rid of it – hell, he didn't even have to try to hide it. As long as the gun didn't have his prints on it, let the cops find it – what the hell did he care? They'd just figure Cornrows dumped it last night, after he shot Marcus whoever. Then if Cornrows got caught and told his bullshit story about Jake shooting Marcus, there was no way in hell the cops would believe it, especially when they had the gun connected to two other shootings.

Jake went around the block and drove past the cemetery again. He cut over onto a quieter side street, trying to find a spot where there weren't any people around. On Stillwell Place he pulled up as close as he could to the space between two parked cars. He removed the gun from his jacket pocket and unwrapped it, careful not to touch it. Then he opened his window and looked around in every direction to make sure the coast was clear. When he was convinced no one was watching, he quickly tossed the gun out the window into the gutter between the cars. He looked around again, seeing no one, and then rolled the window back up and drove away.

As he headed back toward his parents' house, Jake ran everything through his head a few times, to make sure there wasn't something major he was forgetting or not considering, but it all seemed perfect – he was in the clear.

A few minutes later he turned onto Eighty-first Street and saw Ryan coming toward him along the sidewalk.

The little bastard turned up the walkway leading toward his house, and Jake pulled up to the curb, maybe fifty yards away. Jake was ready to bolt out of the car when he saw the car that had been going down the street ahead of him slow down near the Rossettis' house. The driver pointed a gun out the window and started shooting at Ryan. Ryan stood there, wobbling for a second or two, and then collapsed onto his side. The car – dark blue, maybe a Subaru – sped away.

Jake's first clear thought was, *Run like hell*, but he did nothing – just sat in the car, watching Ryan lying still on the ground. Rose-Marie Rossetti was the first to Ryan's side. She started wailing, screaming for help. A guy from up the block came running over and, when he saw Ryan lying there, made a call on his cell – probably to 911. Then other neighbors came out and rushed over to see what was going on. Jake's mother, sister, and brother-in-law came out and went toward the Rossetti house without seeing Jake.

Watching the scene unfold through the windshield, Jake felt like he was watching TV, like what was happening had nothing to do with him. Then he realized that Cornrows, or one of his gangsta friends, must've shot Ryan. Jake had no idea why Cornrows would want Ryan dead, but he couldn't think of any other idea that made any sense.

Now there must've been thirty, forty people in front of the Rossetti house. Jake decided he couldn't just sit in the car – being at the scene and not going over there would look as bad as running. So, casually, he got out, flipped down his Ray•Bans, and strutted toward the crowd.

Eighteen

Lying on a bench in Canarsie Park, staring at the black sky, Saiquan wondered how everything had gotten so fucked-up.

It was supposed to be easy – get a piece, smoke J, and then he could get a job, make some clean money, and go on with his life. But along the way, everything got stupid. First stupid thing was getting in with Marcus. He knew that sick-ass crackhead was bad news – he just didn't know how bad. Second stupid thing was smoking rock himself. Hadn't touched that shit in years – why'd he have to start again? Third stupid thing was stupidest of all: not shooting Jake Thomas when he had the chance.

When he had the gun pointed at Thomas and Marcus was saying all that, 'Shoot him. What you waitin' for? Shoot him,' shit, Saiquan was saying to himself, *Why should I listen to Marcus? I been listening to that stupid-ass motherfucker all night, and what it get me 'cept a chance to go away for life?*

Then, after J.T. shot Marcus, Saiquan had another chance to smoke the man. He had the gun aimed right at J.T.'s head. All he had to do was pull the trigger and he would've had a chance to live a life outside of jail. Maybe Marcus was dead and maybe the cops wouldn't figure out what happened at the house. Maybe if he capped J.T. he would've been a free man.

But he didn't pull the trigger – he ran like a pussy, and he knew Thomas probably got right on the phone, gave the cops a description of the dude that ran away. The cops probably had that shit going out on their radios all night – black man, six-two, cornrows, wearing a black North Face jacket, armed and dangerous.

Saiquan went into Canarsie Park, figuring he'd hang out there till he came up with a plan. *A plan* . . . Like he had any plans for his life that didn't get fucked-up. He wondered how long it would take the cops to find him in the park. Not too long, if they were looking hard enough. He couldn't go home – that was for damn sure. If Marcus was alive, Saiquan knew that motherfucker would say anything to save his own ass. He'd tell the cops Saiquan's name, where he lived, anything the cops wanted to know, if it cut down his own time. Shit, Marcus would probably try to pin the other shootings on Saiquan too – say Saiquan shot Jermaine and that dude with the shopping bags and he had nothing to do with none of it.

And if the cops didn't catch Saiquan, the Crips would, after Ramona started talking.

Thinking, *Fuck it*, Saiquan took the Glock out. He looked at it for a while, playing with the safety, and then he stuck the shit deep in his mouth. He wanted to get it over quick – get to heaven or hell or wherever the fuck dead people went. Shit, even hell had to be better than where he was right now.

His finger started to move and he was screaming at himself, *Do it, bitch! Just do it! Do it, man! Do it!* and he was all ready to die.

Then he started thinking about when he was eighteen years old, when Desiree told him she was pregnant. He felt like his whole life was about to get fucked-up, although, truth was, it was fucked-up already – he was just too young and stupid to know it. So he left her on her own for a few months, then came back to her a week before she was gonna have it, because it hit him one day that it was the right thing to do. He was in the hospital room with her when she was all screaming and shit and he was scared as hell. He didn't know nothing about being a father, and he was afraid he was gonna be like his old man – beating his kids, smoking crack. Then the nurses started yelling, 'Push! Push!' and Saiquan saw the baby's head coming, and he knew he wasn't gonna be like his old man. Because Saiquan loved that kid, even before he held him or looked at him, and his father never loved him, ever.

Saiquan put the gun down. There had to be some way out of this – some way out besides putting a bullet in his brain – and after thinking about it a long time he had an idea.

He could leave the park right now, stop at the first bodega he saw, and put the gun up to the Spanish motherfucker's head and take all the cash. Maybe he'd make four, five hundred bucks. Then he'd jack the first car he saw and book the fuck out of

Brooklyn. He'd go to Mexico. Naw, that was too far – Canada. Go up someplace far up there, Bigfoot land, where there was ice and snow even in the summer, and just chill out. Maybe he'd hit stores along the way to get some more cash, and then he'd go straight – find a job, place to live. After a while, maybe a year or two, he'd call Desiree and tell her where he was at. She'd give him hell for sure, for disappearing and shit, but once she calmed down she'd understand why he did it. She'd put the kids in a car, drive up north, and they could all be together again, living happily ever after.

The idea sounded good, for a couple minutes anyway. Then Saiquan realized there was no fucking way that shit was gonna work. With all the heat on him now, how the hell was he gonna make it up to Canada? Shit, he wouldn't even make it out of Brooklyn. Maybe if he and Marcus didn't try to rob Jake Thomas, if they just went after somebody else, somebody nobody gave a shit about, he would've had a chance. But with Jake Thomas, man, there was no fucking way.

So Saiquan just lay on the bench, staring at the night sky, feeling the way he did some nights in jail. He fell asleep crying like a damn baby.

When he woke up it was raining – at least, that's what he thought. He heard water hitting the ground, and then he looked over and saw it was just a dog pissing next to him.

The dog, one of them pit bulls, was on a leash – some old man holding it.

'Yo,' Saiquan said.

'C'mon,' the man said, pulling the damn dog away.

Saiquan sat up. He was still wearing his North Face jacket, but he was freezing his ass off anyway. He was hungry too, and his head . . . shit, felt like somebody was hammering nails into it.

Then Saiquan thought, *This shit's bullshit.*

If the cops or the Crips were gonna get him, they were gonna get him, and hiding in the park like a pussy wasn't gonna help. Far as he saw it he had two choices – shoot himself or go out into the world and see what happened. Thinking about his kids, about how he couldn't do them any good if he was dead, he picked choice number two.

Leaving the park, Saiquan passed the basketball courts where he used to play ball with Ryan, that white dude from last night. Nobody was out there now, but he remembered how it used to be on all them hot summer days, playing full-court for five hours straight, never getting tired. He saw himself grabbing a rebound and bringing the ball up court with Ryan. He gave a head fake and went around the dude defending him and drove to the hoop. He got closed off and spun around, not losing the dribble, and no-looked a pass to Ryan in the corner. Ryan nailed the jumper with a man in his face.

He and Ryan made up some backcourt, all right. Ryan always seemed like a cool dude too – not like other white people Saiquan knew. But last night, something about the dude seemed different. He never used to dress the way he did now, all trying to be hip-hop and shit, and he looked like a drunk old man, slumped over by himself at that bar. Maybe it was his baseball career getting fucked-up, or what he said about losing his girl, but something went wrong somewhere.

Saiquan left the park. Walking with his hands in his pockets, he kept his head down, staring at the sidewalk. He looked over his shoulder a lot too, checking for cops or Crips, but nobody was around.

Saiquan didn't like the idea of walking around with Marcus's piece. He didn't need the shit now, and even though Marcus said the shit was clean, that was probably bullshit. A motherfucking serial killer probably used that gun, shot forty people with it. Saiquan wiped his prints off the handle and dropped the gun into the first sewer grating he saw and kept walking.

He was heading up Flatlands, near Ninetieth Street, when he spotted a cop hanging out on the corner a block ahead, across the street, in front of a funeral home. He was going to turn around, go a different way, and then he thought, *Fuck it, man.* He couldn't go around the rest of his life running. If they were gonna catch him he might as well get it over with and get caught.

He jaywalked across the street, right past where the cop was standing. Maybe he should've been scared, but he wasn't. He was sick of being scared. He'd been scared his whole damn life, since he was a kid and had to hide in the closet at night, afraid his father would come home high on crack and beat the fuck out of him. He was sick of all that shit. He wasn't gonna be afraid of nothing no more.

Saiquan looked right at the motherfucking cop as he passed, his eyes saying, *Here I am. You want me? You got me. I don't give a shit no more.* He thought the cop would pull a gun on him, cuff him, and that would be it – he'd start a new stretch upstate, twenty-five to life, whatever – but the cop didn't do shit. He just let Saiquan walk right on by.

Marcus must be dead, Saiquan decided. And J.T. must not've described Saiquan to the cops right either. Those were the only reasons Saiquan could think of why the cops didn't catch on to him by now.

Saiquan kept walking, deciding that if the cops didn't catch him yet, maybe they never would.

After going a few more blocks, he realized he was starving. He stopped at a Korean place and bought a couple of muffins, a big thing of peach Snapple, and a little pack of aspirin. He took the aspirin and sucked down the food. He was heading home to be with Desiree and his kids, where he belonged, when he decided there was one thing he had to take care of first.

'Yeah, I wanna see Desmond Johnson.'

The sister at the desk – a different one from yesterday, but with the same attitude – said, 'He a patient?'

Wondering why the hospital hired only nasty, something-stuck-up-their-ass bitches to work at the front desk, Saiquan said, 'I just saw him last night.'

The girl looked at the screen.

'How you spell his name?'

'Yo, I don't got time for this shit,' Saiquan said. 'I went through all this same shit yesterday.'

'How you spell the name?'

Saiquan shook his head, then spelled Johnson. He messed up the first time, leaving out the *h*, and then spelled it with an *e*. Finally he got it right.

'First name?' the girl asked.

'Desmond.'

'What?'

'Desmond.'

The girl looked at the screen a long time, hitting keys, using the mouse, then said, 'You sure he a patient here?'

'I just saw him,' Saiquan said. 'Don't y'all hear what I'm sayin'?'

'Just 'cause he was here yesterday don't mean he's here today.'

'He's here today. He can't move. He didn't go anywhere.'

'Wait,' the girl said. 'There he is.'

'Thank you,' Saiquan said.

'But you can't see him now.'

'Why not?'

'Visiting hours don't start till eleven o'clock.'

Saiquan looked up at the clock behind the desk. It was only twenty past eight.

'Shit,' he said.

Saiquan fell asleep in the hospital's coffee shop. He woke up when a security guard tapped him on the back and said, 'No sleeping.'

Saiquan forced himself to stay awake, drinking coffee, till eleven o'clock finally came. Now, of course, somebody else was on duty at the desk, an older brother, and Saiquan had to go through the same 'Desmond Johnson, Desmond who?' bullshit before the dude gave him the pass to go upstairs.

A different cop from yesterday was at Desmond's door – a black dude who kind of reminded Saiquan of Marcus. He didn't have Marcus's braids, but the face and skin tone were the same, like he could've been Marcus's cousin or something.

The cop said to Saiquan, 'Can I help you?'

'I'm here to see my brother – Desmond.'

The cop stared at him, and Saiquan knew it was a big mistake to come here. The cops probably figured that Jermaine's getting shot last night had something to do with Desmond, and they were probably watching D extra close today, just in case there was retaliation.

'What's your name?' the cop asked.

Saiquan felt the muffins he'd eaten sinking though his stomach.

'Saiquan,' he managed to say.

He expected the cop to throw him up against the wall, slap the cuffs on him, tell him he had the right to shut the fuck up.

But instead the cop frisked Saiquan quickly, then said, 'Wait,' and went into the room for a few seconds. Then he came out and said, 'Go 'head.'

Saiquan went into the room, which was as dark as it was yesterday, and it smelled like somebody had taken a shit in the middle of the floor. The curtains were up around the bed near the door, and Saiquan wondered if the old dude had died and shit up his pants. A nurse was sitting in a chair, reading some book, and the TV was playing CNN crazy loud, like the doctors thought Desmond was deaf, not paralyzed.

Desmond looked like he did the last time Saiquan had seen him – zoned out, staring at the ceiling. For a second Saiquan felt bad for his old best friend, and then he remembered why he was there.

Saiquan stood next to the bed and waited till Desmond's eyes shifted toward him. Then he said, 'I took care of it.'

Desmond kept looking at Saiquan for a few seconds, then looked away, and Saiquan knew that Jermaine had been telling the truth – Desmond's getting shot had nothing to do with Ramona. That was just bullshit Desmond made up so Saiquan would go ahead and take Jermaine out.

'Why'd you lie to me, man?' Saiquan asked.

Desmond kept looking away.

'Why, man?' Saiquan went on. 'After all we been through, knowing each other since we was little kids and shit. Shit's fucked up, what it is. Why couldn't you tell me the truth? Why'd you do that shit? Look at me, man. I said look at me.'

Now Desmond looked at Saiquan, his eyes filling with tears.

'Yeah, you sad,' Saiquan said. 'I bet you real sad. You got what you wanted. What the fuck you gotta be sad about? I got cops after me, Crips after me. It's my life got fucked-up, not yours. Your life was already fucked-up.'

Desmond mouthed, *Sorry.*

'Fuck you, bitch,' Saiquan said, and grabbed the big tube that was connected to D's neck. He wanted to do it – pull out the plugs and tubes and watch D die – but he knew that would be the stupidest thing out of all the stupid things he'd done in the past twenty-four hours. Alarms and bells would start going off, and with the nurse and the cop right there he was guaranteed to get busted.

So Saiquan let go of the tube and said, 'Naw, I'll let yo' sorry ass live. But I'm tellin' you right now – you better hope they don't teach you how to walk, 'cause if they do I'm paralyzin' yo' ass all over again.'

On his way out, Saiquan reached up and turned off the TV. Bitch didn't deserve no entertainment.

Heading toward the Breukelen Houses along One Hundred Fifth Street, Saiquan walked right by another cop car. The car was at a red light with two cops in it – a black man driving and a Latina sitting shotgun. The Latina looked right over at Saiquan, staring at him for a couple of seconds, then looking away. Then the light changed and the car drove on.

In Saiquan's building the elevator was still broken, so he had to take the stairs. Before he opened the door to his apartment, he took a couple of deep breaths. Whenever he took too long getting milk or toilet paper from the bodega, Desiree gave him all kinds of shit. For going out last night and not coming home Saiquan was ready for all hell to break loose.

But when he opened the door, Desiree wasn't there. Only Trey and Felicia were in the living room – sitting on the bottom of their bunk bed, watching cartoons on TV.

'Hey,' Saiquan said, excited to see his kids. 'What up?'

Trey and Felicia, looking at the TV, didn't seem to notice that Saiquan had just come home.

'I'm talkin' to y'all,' Saiquan said, louder.

Still, the kids didn't look at him.

Saiquan tossed his jacket onto a chair and went over to the bunk and sat down, squeezing between his boy and girl. They moved out of the way to give him room, but didn't stop watching TV.

Saiquan put his arms around their shoulders. Now the kids looked at him for a second, realizing their father was acting funny.

'It's so good to see both y'all,' Saiquan said. 'What y'all watching?'

'Why you wanna know?' Trey asked.

' 'Cause I'm yo' father, that's why,' Saiquan said. 'I wanna know what my kids be doin' all day. I wanna be involved, know what I'm sayin'?'

'*Pokémon*,' Trey said.

'Cool,' Saiquan said. He squeezed his kids into him. 'Yo, how 'bout we get some pizza or somethin'?'

'You smell,' Felicia said.

'Yo, sorry 'bout that,' Saiquan said. 'Guess I do need a shower, huh? That's 'cause I was out late last night, lookin' for a job. I was checkin' out the clubs, seein' if I could find somethin' there, and I think I did get somethin' lined up. So I'm gonna be workin' soon, bringin' home some money to support y'all.'

The kids were staring at the TV, probably not even listening to him.

'Hey, I got an idea,' Saiquan said. 'How 'bout after we get some lunch we all go to Coney Island?'

'We can't afford no Coney Island,' Trey said.

Saiquan knew this was true. It cost, like, two dollars a ride, and he didn't even have enough to pay for the damn subway.

'Whatever,' Saiquan said. 'We could just walk around – go to the beach or something.'

'It's too cold for the beach,' Felicia said.

'We don't gotta go swimming,' Saiquan said. 'We can just walk around, build sand castles. Remember when we used to do that down Jones Beach? We'd go there and build them big-ass castles with moats and shit and the water goin' underneath.'

'No,' Trey said.

Saiquan realized Trey was only two or three then and probably couldn't remember.

'Oh,' Saiquan said. 'Well, you had a good time runnin' around, gettin' wet and shit. I wanna take y'all more places – as a family, know what I'm sayin'? We be doin' too much stayin' at home all the time, doin' nothin'. I wanna get out there more, take y'all fun places. Maybe we'll go to a Knicks game this year. When my money comes in from workin' I'll get us some tickets. We'll go to the circus too – movies, all that.' Saiquan kissed Trey on top of his head, then kissed Felicia on top of hers. 'Where yo' mama at?'

Trey pointed toward the bedroom. Saiquan went down the short hallway and tried to open the door, but it was locked.

'Yo, baby,' he said. 'C'mon, open up.'

He knocked a few times, then banged harder with his fist, but Desiree wouldn't answer. He heard the baby inside, goo-goo, ga-ga'ing, so he knew Desiree was awake; she just wouldn't open up.

'Come on, don't be like that,' he said. 'Sorry I didn't call last night, but I was out with . . .' He almost said *Marcus*, but stopped himself just in time. It would've been stupid to tell Desiree he was with Marcus if she found out that Marcus got shot last night. 'I wasn't out with nobody – I was just out job huntin' at clubs. I think I got a couple things lined up – might be a bouncer or security guard or some shit. C'mon, lemme in.'

He banged on the door a few more times, then heard the baby starting to cry.

'Fine,' he said. 'Don't wanna open up, don't open up. Be like that.'

He was about to walk away when the door opened. Desiree, holding the screaming baby, said, 'Pack up – you movin' out.'

'C'mon,' Saiquan said. 'I—'

'I don't wanna hear no more bullshit,' Desiree said. 'I want you outta here. Go on the street – sleep on the subway. I don't care what you do.'

She carried the baby to the kitchen. The baby's screaming was getting even louder.

Saiquan followed them, said, 'C'mon, don't be like this, baby. I know you mad, but you wrong.'

'Damn right, I was wrong,' Desiree said. 'I was wrong to move in with you; I was wrong to have yo' damn babies. I shoulda just forgot about you when you was away. Everybody was sayin' how stupid I was to stay with you, I should find some other man, some *real* man, and I guess they was right.'

Desiree took a bottle out of the fridge and stuck the nipple in the baby's mouth.

'You got it all wrong, I'm tellin' you, baby,' Saiquan said. 'I was out lookin' for a job last night, and I'm gonna find one real soon.'

'Get outta my face.'

Saiquan didn't move. 'Listen to me,' he went on. 'I made mistakes – I know I made mistakes – but that's all in the past, know what I'm sayin'? It's the future now, and I'm ready to put all that in-the-past shit behind me. I'm gonna work hard and provide, and I'm not gonna get back into no more of that dealin' bullshit, neither. Look at me when I'm talkin' to you, baby. I'm serious with this shit – this is the new Saiquan talking to you now.

I messed up before – I know that – but I ain't gonna mess up again. You got my word 'bout that.'

Desiree glared at him, then said, ' 'Scuse me.'

'Didn't you hear what I'm tellin' you?'

Pushing past him, Desiree said, 'Just pack your bags and get the hell out – I don't wanna see yo' lyin', drug-dealin' ass 'round here no more.'

She went back into the bedroom and slammed the door and locked it.

Saiquan didn't care – he knew everything would work itself out. Desiree had kicked him out before, and it didn't mean shit. Yeah, she'd be mad for a while, maybe wouldn't talk to him for a couple days, but then everything would go back to normal. And then, when he got a job, and she saw he was for real about what he was saying, they'd stop all this fighting and shit. They'd go back to the way they used to be when they first met, when they used to laugh and get busy and not hate each other so much.

Saiquan opened the refrigerator, seeing the bare shelves, and decided that was gonna change too – soon that fridge was always gonna be filled.

After finding some food stamps in one of the kitchen drawers, Saiquan left the apartment. He walked to the C-Town on Pennsylvania Avenue and bought some Wonder bread, bologna, cheese, and Hawaiian Punch. When he came home his kids were still watching TV.

'I'm cooking y'all lunch,' he said.

He made the sandwiches and put them out on the dining table with glasses of Hawaiian Punch. Trey and Felicia came to the table and started eating. Saiquan knocked on the bedroom door and told Desiree he'd bought food, but she wouldn't come out.

After lunch Saiquan sat on the bunk bed and watched cartoons with his kids. Then, around three o'clock, the doorbell rang. Trey and Felicia, staring at the TV, acted like they didn't hear the bell, or if they did, they didn't care. Saiquan went to open the door, then stopped, thinking it might be the cops.

The bell rang again – a long ring, somebody keeping their finger down on the button. Saiquan opened the peephole slowly and saw the bottom of somebody's face.

'Open the door, yo.'

Saiquan recognized the voice – it was Kemar. Saiquan had known him since Kemar was twelve years old, when Saiquan recruited him to sell crack at his junior high school. Kemar was a thin little kid back then, but now the dude was six-four and looked like he could play linebacker for the Jets. He was sick-ass, too. While Saiquan was away, Kemar had worked his way up in the Crips and gotten a rep around the hood as a nigga who liked to give out pain.

'Who's it?' Saiquan said, buying time, trying to figure out what to do.

'You know who the fuck it is,' Kemar said. 'Open this shit right now.'

Saiquan looked back over his shoulder. Felicia was still watching TV, but Trey was looking right at Saiquan, knowing something bad was going on.

Saiquan opened the door a crack; then Kemar pushed it open all the way. Kemar was with Manny, another crazy-ass mother-fucker. They both had pieces out.

'Yo, wait up,' Saiquan said, 'I got my kids here, man, I got my kids. Just chill. Lemme come downstairs and we talk this shit out, a'ight?'

Manny looked over at Kemar. Saiquan knew that if Kemar gave him the right look back, that would be it – they'd shoot him up right in front of his kids. Shit, they might kill all his kids and Desiree too while they were at it.

But Kemar tucked his piece back in his jeans; then Manny put his away too.

'Five minutes, downstairs,' Kemar said.

Saiquan knew it was his past with Kemar that got him the extra time and that was it. If Kemar got the order to go smoke somebody else, anybody else, he wouldn't give a shit if the dude's kids was there looking on or not.

'Cool, five minutes,' Saiquan said. 'I'll be right down, outside. We'll work all this shit out, y'all, a'ight?'

Saiquan knew he was just talking bullshit, wasting his breath. There was nothing to talk about with these sick-asses. Maybe the past got him a few more minutes, but that was all it was gonna get him.

When the door closed Saiquan turned around and saw Desiree standing there with the baby.

'Yeah, you really changed,' she said.

He didn't know if she'd been there the whole time, or if she'd just come out of the bedroom.

'What you talkin' 'bout?' he said. 'They were just comin' by to see if I wanted to shoot some hoops.'

'You must think I'm real stupid. Just 'cause I'm stupid enough to have yo' kids, to stay with you all those years you was away, don't mean I'm so stupid I don't know what's goin' on. Lookin' for a job last night, my ass. Why don't you leave right now? Go out with yo' gangsta friends. We don't want you 'round here no more!'

The pacifier fell out of the baby's mouth and she started crying. Desiree stuffed the pacifier back in and went into the bedroom, slamming the door so hard the mirror on the living room wall shook.

Saiquan went over to Felicia and Trey, who were still watching *Pokémon*, and said, 'Look, y'all, I gotta go. You heard what yo' mama be sayin' – she don't want me 'round here no more, so I think it's best that I leave for a while. Best for you kids anyway, know what I'm sayin'? I don't want you growin' up being 'round a lot of fightin' all the time, know what I'm sayin'? So I'm gonna go away for a while, give yo' mama what she want, so y'all can grow up in peace.'

Saiquan kissed Felicia on top of her head.

'I love you, baby,' he said. 'You do good in school, hear? And stay away from boys till you eighteen. Any boy come at you 'fore then you tell yo' brother about it and he'll take care of it, know what I'm sayin'? And always be carryin' Mace on you, or that pepper-spray shit. Nigga tries to touch you where you don't want, you blind his ass, know what I'm sayin'?'

Felicia was looking at the cartoon on the TV. Saiquan wasn't even sure she heard anything he'd said.

Saiquan turned to Trey. 'Yo, you watch over yo' sister now, hear? And mind yourself too. Do good in school, don't do drugs, all that shit. I want you to grow up good – I want you to be somethin'. I'm countin' on you, a'ight?'

Saiquan couldn't think of anything else to say, and he was afraid he was gonna start to cry.

So he said, 'See y'all later,' and left the apartment quickly.

In the hallway outside the apartment, he couldn't hold back any longer and he started crying, leaning his head against the wall next to the door. Then he told himself to stop being such a bitch and headed down the stairs again almost making it to the next floor, when he stopped, realizing that Manny and Kemar might not smoke him when he walked out the door. They might want to take him to an empty lot someplace, or some abandoned building, and do it there. And they might not do it right away, either. They might drag it out, torture his ass, to get some payback for what Marcus did to Jermaine.

Naw, he just had to be a man about all this shit. His life was over – he might as well get on with it.

Nineteen

When Ryan opened his eyes everything was blurry. Someone was talking to him, a guy with straight blond hair who kind of looked like Lupus from *The Bad News Bears*.

'How many fingers am I holding up?' Lupus asked.

'Two,' Ryan said.

'What's your name?'

'Ryan.'

'What city do you live in?'

'New York ... Brooklyn.'

'You're fine.'

Ryan became aware of more voices around him. Then he remembered the gunshots, the car speeding away, and how he fell to the ground.

'I was shot,' Ryan said weakly.

'No, you weren't,' Lupus said. Ryan realized Lupus was a paramedic.

'But I heard a car,' Ryan said. 'Somebody—'

'You didn't get hit,' Lupus said. 'You just fainted.'

Rose-Marie Rossetti was kneeling next to Ryan, her makeup messed up from crying. She kissed her son's hands a few times, then hugged his head and said, 'Thank God ... Thank God, thank God, thank God.'

Lupus asked him some more questions, making sure Ryan didn't have any internal injuries, and that he didn't bang his head when he fell. Ryan had a bruise on his side, but otherwise he was fine.

'You wanna come with us for observation, you can,' Lupus said.

'I have to go?'

'It's up to you.'

'Then no.'

As the paramedics helped Ryan to his feet, people clapped and cheered. Ryan looked over, realizing that there were more people gathered around than he'd thought. There must've been thirty or forty people, including several cops keeping people away from the crime scene as a couple of officers were busy surrounding the area with yellow tape. Ryan recognized many of his neighbors, and he acknowledged the crowd with a little wave.

Then, as the paramedics started to help Ryan up the stoop, Ryan spotted Jake in the back of the crowd off to the side. Jake was wearing dark sunglasses, so it was hard to read his expression, but he was looking right at Ryan and wasn't smiling.

The paramedics led Ryan into the living room and helped him settle down on the couch. Sitting felt a lot better than standing. Rose-Marie brought him a glass of water.

'Here. Drink this.'

Ryan took a short sip, then handed her back the glass.

Lupus told Ryan that he should contact his doctor and report any unusual symptoms.

'You got real lucky out there, guy,' Lupus said. 'But you're gonna be okay.'

As the paramedics left a uniformed officer entered.

The cop sat next to Ryan and said, 'How ya doin'? I'm Officer Brisco – Sixty-ninth Precinct.'

Rose-Marie, standing nearby, said to the cop, 'You should let him rest.'

'It's all right, Ma,' Ryan said.

'You got any idea who shot at you?' Brisco asked.

'No idea,' Ryan said. 'But it was a drive-by.'

'You saw the car?'

'Nah.'

'Then how do you—'

'I heard it.'

'Oh. So you weren't looking at the—'

'I was heading up the stoop. I heard the shots behind me.'

Ryan was feeling a little dizzy again.

'It must've been that same lunatic from last night,' Rose-Marie said. 'We're not leaving the house anymore.'

Ryan reached toward his mother for the glass of water, and she gave it to him. As he was drinking, Detective Noll entered. Noll immediately started glaring at Ryan. Brisco went over to Noll and they talked for a couple of minutes – Noll looking over at Ryan every several seconds – and then Brisco left and Noll came over and took Brisco's place on the couch.

'Look, I know what you're gonna say, all right, and it's bullshit,' Ryan said. 'I have no idea what's going on with any of this. I was walking into the house and somebody shot at me.'

'How'd you know what I was gonna say?'

'I don't feel like answering any more questions, all right?'

'Then how about if I arrest you?'

'For what? Almost getting killed?'

'Aiding and abetting . . . obstruction of justice . . .'

'My son doesn't have to talk to you without a lawyer,' Rose-Marie said.

'Somebody just tried to murder your son,' Noll said. 'If he cooperates quickly, maybe we can catch this guy. . . . Unless your son has something to hide . . .'

'Go ahead, ask me your stupid questions,' Ryan said. 'I'll tell you what I don't know about all of it.'

'Who shot at you?' Noll asked.

'I have no idea.'

'Who killed Marcus Fitts?'

'I have no idea.'

'Look, I don't have time for bullshit, all right? Every second you jerk me around a killer gets farther away.'

'What do you mean, killer? I'm not dead.'

'But Marcus Fitts is.'

'What makes you think that has anything to do with what happened to me?'

'You're right – how stupid of me. Maybe two people getting shot at three doors down from each other sixteen hours apart is a big coincidence.'

'It could be.'

'Ryan, I really think you should call a lawyer,' Rose-Marie said.

Ignoring his mother, Ryan said to Noll, 'You know, instead of wasting your time talking to me, maybe you should be out there trying to find this guy.'

'How do you know it's a guy?'

Ryan shook his head in frustration.

'Look,' Noll said, 'we have a good idea who this guy is. If you cooperate we can pick him up faster.'

'You have a suspect?' Rose-Marie asked.

'We have a description of a perp who might be connected to the shooting last night, yes. African-American, about six feet, two hundred pounds, wearing a black winter jacket. Maybe thirty years old.' Noll glared at Ryan. 'Sound like a friend of yours?'

'How many times I gotta tell you?' Ryan said. 'I got no—'

And then it started coming back to him – being at the bar last night and the two black guys coming over, hassling him, calling him Eminem. He remembered Saiquan, the big guy with the cornrows from Canarsie Park, and the skinny, crazier guy with braids, trying to mug him. A lot of the details still seemed foggy, like he was remembering a dream, but he knew it had happened.

'Something wrong?' Noll asked.

'What?' Ryan was barely able to speak. Suddenly he felt light-headed and dazed. 'No. I . . . I just need some more water.'

'This is too much for him,' Rose-Marie said. 'He needs to rest.'

'If you know something,' Noll said, 'you'd better fucking tell me.'

Ryan sipped the water slowly, buying time to get hold of himself. Then he put the glass down and said, 'How many times do I have to tell you? I don't know anything.'

'You're lying,' Noll said.

'Why would I lie?'

'Are you okay?' Rose-Marie asked Ryan.

'No,' Ryan said. 'Actually I feel very shitty suddenly. I think I better lie down.'

'He needs his rest,' Rose-Marie said to Noll.

'If you know who this guy is you'd better fucking tell me right now,' Noll said to Ryan.

'I don't know who he is,' Ryan said, straight-faced.

'What about the car? We didn't get plates, but we have a description from a guy walking his dog of a midsize dark blue car.'

'No idea.'

'Think.'

'I did think.'

'He doesn't know anything,' Rose-Marie said.

'Were you buying drugs from Marcus Fitts?' Noll asked.

'No,' Ryan said, as if offended.

'Were you trying to join the Crips?'

'What?' Ryan and Rose-Marie said.

'Were you out last night with Fitts and whoever else, doing gang initiations? Is that how Jermaine Carter and Kevin Miles were killed?'

'Who're they?' Rose-Marie asked.

'Yeah,' Ryan said. 'Who the fuck are they?'

'Jermaine Carter was a member of the Crips,' Noll explained. 'He was shot to death – brutally shot to death – last night. Kevin Miles was also shot and killed shortly afterward. We believe the shootings are related to the shooting last night in front of the Thomases' house and might be related to the shooting today.'

'I swear to God, I have no idea what you're talking about,' Ryan said.

'Or maybe it went like this,' Noll said. 'Maybe you had nothing to do with the Carter and Miles murders. But you did have a fight with Jake yesterday – you had your hands around his throat. You wanted to get into the Crips anyway, so you called your Crips buddies, who happened to be in the middle of a killing spree, and told them to come along with you to Jake Thomas's house – you'd prove your worth to them. Kill two birds with one stone, so to speak. Then something went wrong. Marcus Fitts was shot and killed – maybe by somebody seeking revenge for the Carter slaying. You and the suspect fled the scene; then the suspect decided you knew too much, so he tried to take you out in a drive-by.'

'Look,' Ryan said, 'you're making absolutely no sense, and I'm really getting sick of this shit.'

'So then how do you explain how you got shot?'

'I have no idea.'

'So somebody shot at you for no reason?'

'That's what it seems like.'

'You're full of shit.'

'That's enough,' Rose-Marie said to Noll. 'Maybe instead of yelling at my son you should go out there and try to find the lunatic who did this.'

Noll looked at Ryan for a few seconds without blinking, then stood up, shaking his head.

'Fine,' he said. 'You wanna be an idiot, be an idiot. But I hope you understand, we're trying to protect you here. You wanna be a stupid son of a bitch and wind up dead, that's up to you. But I'm telling you right now, I find out you lied to me about anything – *anything* – you're in deep shit.'

Noll stormed out of the house.

'What a horrible man,' Rose-Marie said. 'Some maniac shoots at you, you almost get killed, and he starts accusing you?'

Ryan got up, pretending it took more effort than it did.

'I'm gonna go lie down.'

'You sure that's a good idea?'

'What?'

'What if you have a concussion?'

'I'm fine.'

'I want you to call a lawyer.'

'Ma—'

'I didn't like him asking all those questions, threatening you.'

'That's what cops do.'

'I still want to call somebody.'

'Forget it. It's over.'

'Where the hell's Dad anyway?' Rose-Marie was looking at her watch. 'I called him on his cell phone and he didn't pick up . . . . Where're you going?'

'I told you. To lie down.'

'I don't feel safe here alone.'

'Don't worry; there're cops everywhere. Nothing's gonna happen.'

Ryan continued upstairs.

'Don't fall asleep, whatever you do.'

'I'll be fine.'

Ryan went into his room and locked the door and sat on the bed with his head in his hands. Some of it was still foggy, but he remembered sitting at the bar, ripped out of his mind, when Saiquan and Marcus – yeah, that was the name of the skinny guy – came over and started harassing him. It was Marcus who'd tossed away his Spurs cap, and then they started talking about Jake. Ryan wondered if he had told Marcus and Saiquan to go after Jake, or maybe even to kill him. Then, for some reason, Saiquan shot Marcus, and now Saiquan was after Ryan.

Ryan remembered playing ball with Saiquan all those times at

Canarsie Park. Ryan knew that Saiquan was a drug dealer, but he'd always figured that he'd just had a rough life and was doing what he had to do to survive. He'd never imagined him going around killing people.

Lying in bed, Ryan tried to relax, listening to Nas, but the throbbing music was giving him a headache. He shut off the stereo and started pacing, wondering if he'd done the right thing by not telling Noll everything he knew. If he'd told Noll Saiquan's name and what had happened at the bar, they could've caught him quickly, and Ryan wouldn't have to worry about getting killed. Now he'd have to stay in his house, with no police protection, until Saiquan got caught. And it wouldn't accomplish anything either, because eventually Saiquan would tell his story and Ryan would be fucked. He couldn't say he wasn't at the bar last night, because he'd already told Noll he'd picked up Elly there, and other people might remember him. He'd try to explain that he was drunk and was just joking around when he'd told Saiquan and Marcus to go after Jake, or kill him, or whatever the hell he'd told them to do, but Noll would be so pissed off at Ryan for holding back information that he'd press charges against him for something.

Ryan left his room and headed downstairs. There was still a lot of commotion outside – hopefully Noll was still there. Ryan planned on telling him everything; maybe, if he was lucky, Noll would appreciate the cooperation and cut him some slack.

'There he is – my son, the fuckin' spook.'

Rocco Rossetti was in the living room, obviously drunk. Another confrontation with his father was the last thing Ryan needed.

'Leave me the hell alone.'

Ryan headed toward the door.

'Hey.' Rocco grabbed Ryan's arm hard, pulling him back.

'Get the fuck off me,' Ryan said.

'I'm talkin' to you.'

Rocco's breath reeked of booze. It reminded Ryan of his own hangover, disgusting him even more.

Ryan jerked his arm free and said, 'Why'd you even bother coming home?'

'Your mother said you're in some gang now; you're dealin' drugs.'

'I never said that.' Rose-Marie had just entered from the kitchen.

'So that's it, huh?' Rocco said. 'You're a fuckin' drug dealer now? You're a fuckin' nigger drug dealer?'

'Just get away from me,' Ryan said.

'What're you gonna do? Huh? Wanna hit me? Go 'head – try it.' Rocco jutted his jaw toward Ryan. 'Crack me one – gimme your best shot. You better knock me out, 'cause I'm gonna crack you one right back. My own kid turning into a dirty, drug-dealing spook.'

'Stop it!' Rose-Marie shrieked.

She tried to pull Rocco away. He backhanded her in the face, hard enough to knock her into the coffee table and onto the floor.

'Get your fuckin' hands off her,' Ryan said.

'You gonna hit me? Come on, what're you waitin' for?'

Ryan took a swing at his father and missed. Rocco grabbed him from behind.

'My own kid selling fuckin' crack,' Rocco said. 'Fuckin' disgracing me.'

'Motherfucker,' Ryan said, breaking free.

'Come on,' Rocco said, giving Ryan a little come-here motion with his hand. 'You want some too? Huh? You wanna taste?'

'Leave him alone!' Rose-Marie screamed.

'Come on, let's see what you got,' Rocco said.

Ryan charged his father, ramming him back against the bookcase. A hardcover cookbook fell onto Rocco's head, but he didn't seem to notice.

'That's it, huh?' Rocco said, smiling, and gave Ryan an uppercut in the gut.

Ryan keeled over, winded, and then felt harder pain when his father kicked him in the same spot he'd punched him.

Rose-Marie screamed for Rocco to leave Ryan alone. Then Ryan, still bent over, trying to catch his breath, heard a loud smack.

'Stay the hell away from me, bitch,' Rocco said.

Ryan struggled to his feet. Rocco turned, smiling sickly, and Ryan belted him in the mouth. Rocco went down, spraying blood and spit.

'Son of a . . .' Rocco muttered. 'Cocksuckin' . . . mother . . .'

Rocco was trying to get up, wiping blood from his mouth. Ryan had his fist cocked, ready to belt his old man again, when the doorbell rang.

Ryan stood there, swaying.

'Get it,' Rose-Marie said, blood dripping from her nose. 'It's probably the police.'

'Jesus, Ma. Look what he did to you.'

'Just get it.'

Ryan went to the door, then hesitated, realizing how crazy this would look to the cops.

The bell rang again.

'Get it!' Rose-Marie screamed.

Ryan opened the door and saw Jake standing there. He was wearing dark sunglasses.

'We need to talk,' Jake said.

'It's not a good time right now,' Ryan said. 'Maybe—'

'Hey, look who it is,' Rocco said from behind Ryan. 'The man of the hour. Mr Superstar. Mr Pittsburgh fucking Pirate.'

'Shut the fuck up,' Ryan said.

' 'M I talkin' to you?' Rocco slurred. 'I'm talkin' to my buddy, Jake Thomas.' He put his hand on Jake's shoulder. 'Take a good look at this guy. This is what a pro looks like; this is what a guy who made it looks like. This is what you shoulda been, you didn't wimp out. You're a quitter; that's what your problem is. Arm problems, my fuckin' ass. You didn't have what it takes, that's all. You wanted to be a lazy fuckin' nigger drug dealer instead . . . . Oh, sorry there, Jake. Eh, you don't care. You're not a real nigger, anyway – you're just a halfy, right?'

Jake made a movement with his arm, as if he were about to cock it back to hit Rocco.

'He's drunk,' Ryan said to Jake, like this wasn't obvious. 'Look, we have a little family thing going on here, you know? So maybe you should, like, come back some other time.'

Rose-Marie rushed to the door.

'Hey,' Rocco said. 'Where the fuck you think you're goin'?'

'Your mother home?' Rose-Marie asked Jake.

'Yeah,' Jake said.

Rose-Marie went outside and stood next to Jake. Then she turned back to Rocco and said, 'I've had it – I'm divorcing you. This time I mean it.'

'Good,' Rocco said. 'Don't blow me anymore and can't cook for shit. Who the fuck needs you?'

'Bastard,' Rose-Marie said, crying. Then she rushed away toward the Thomases'.

A couple of cops outside were watching the scene curiously, but Ryan didn't see Noll.

Rocco was stumbling around the living room, saying, 'Where the hell's my beer? Where the fuck is it?'

'Let's go somewhere,' Jake said to Ryan.

'Come on,' Ryan said. 'Come back some other—'

'No fuckin' way,' Jake said.

Rocco was in the kitchen now, talking to himself.

'All right, upstairs,' Ryan said.

As they were entering Ryan's room, Ryan said, 'Sorry my father said that shit to you. He's such an ass—'

Jake pushed Ryan into the room, kicking the door closed behind him. Then he grabbed a fistful of Ryan's shirt and lifted him up against the wall.

'Yo,' Ryan said, 'the fuck's your—'

'You fuckin' little piece of shit. I should fuckin' strangle you.'

Ryan tried to free himself, but it was useless.

'Come on, man,' Ryan said. 'Just lemme—'

'Shut the fuck up and listen to me,' Jake said. 'Stay away from Christina. You even touch her again, I'll kill you.'

'I'm in love with her.'

Jake forced Ryan up higher and pushed harder against Ryan's throat. Ryan could barely breathe.

'You're lucky I don't rip your throat out right now,' Jake said. 'You don't know how much I'd love that.'

Ryan tried to talk, but couldn't, so he spit in Jake's face. Jake spit right back, into Ryan's left eye.

'I'm warning you right now, you fucking scumbag,' Jake said. 'You better stay the hell away from me, and you better stay away from Christina too. You hear what I'm fucking saying?'

Jake pushed even harder. Ryan felt like his windpipe was about to get crushed.

Finally Jake let Ryan go, and Ryan crumpled onto the floor, gasping and coughing. Ryan heard the door to his room open and slam shut. He remained on the floor a while, until he was able to breathe normally, and then he got up to his knees. He tried to yell, 'You'll never get her,' but his voice was so weak he barely made a sound.

Twenty

When Saiquan went outside, Manny and Kemar were waiting with their hands in their coat pockets. Saiquan was hoping they'd end this shit quick, smoke him right in front of the building and be on their way, but Manny said, 'Let's get the fuck outta here, man,' and Saiquan knew they had something else in mind.

Saiquan went over there slowly, trying to stay cool. He knew they wanted him to be scared – them niggas got off on that shit – and he didn't want to give them no reason to get off on nothing.

Manny frisked Saiquan quickly, then said, 'He's clean,' and Kemar said, 'Let's go.'

They headed along the walkway toward the street with Saiquan walking between Manny and Kemar. Saiquan didn't want to start begging for his life because begging was a sign of weakness, and he knew these sick-asses didn't have no respect for weakness.

A couple of brothers passed by, going in the other direction, and they looked at Saiquan like they knew something was up, but they were smart – they looked away like they didn't see a damn thing.

Saiquan figured Manny and Kemar were gonna drive him someplace, maybe to tie him up and torture his ass for a while, so he was surprised when Manny said, 'This way,' and they led him around toward the back of the building.

When they got to the Dumpster, where nobody was around, Manny and Kemar took out their pieces, Manny aiming his right at Saiquan's face.

'Why you shot J?' Manny asked.

'I didn't shoot him,' Saiquan said.

'Bullshit, motherfucker.'

'His bitch was there,' Kemar said. 'She said she saw you.'

'She wasn't there; she was upstairs,'Saiquan said, trying to stay cool. 'Marcus capped J, not me.'

'But you was with him,' Manny said.

'That's 'cause Jermaine popped Desmond. He was my boy – the fuck was I gonna do?'

'That Desmond shit came down from up top,' Kemar said.

'What about Marcus?' Manny asked.

'What about him?'

'You got him, right?' Kemar said.

'Naw, that wasn't me,' Saiquan said.

'Then who the fuck was it?' Manny asked.

'Jake Thomas,' Saiquan said.

'Jake Thomas? The fuckin' baseball player?'

'Yeah.'

'Man, you'll say any bullshit to save yo' ass.'

'Naw, that's where Marcus was shot at,' Kemar said. 'Front of Jake Thomas's parents' house.'

'I know that, yo,' Manny said. 'But that don't mean this motherfucka ain't talkin' outta his damn ass.'

'Shit's the truth,' Saiquan said. 'I met him at a bar.'

'You met Jake Thomas at a bar?' Kemar asked.

'Now you say you hangin' with the man?' Manny said. 'Who else you be hangin' with? Stephon Marbury? Jason Kidd?'

'Naw, man, not Jake Thomas,' Saiquan said. 'The white dude – Ryan. Went like this – I was with Marcus Friday night, drivin' around, right, when we seen this dude looked like Eminem and he was all fucked-up.'

'The fuck this gotta do with Jake Thomas?' Manny asked.

'I'm gettin' to it, man,' Saiquan said.

'You gettin' to bullshit,' Manny said, pressing the gun against Saiquan's forehead. 'You just sayin' shit to keep yo' sorry ass alive.'

'No, I ain't,' Saiquan said. 'Just listen up. Marcus was high, man. He wanted money for them West Indian bitches. But Ryan, the Eminem dude, didn't have no money, right, so he was like, "Go get it from Jake Thomas." So we went there, to Jake Thomas's house, but he didn't give it up. He went for Marcus's piece and he shot him, and that's the motherfuckin' truth.'

'Bullshit,' Manny said. 'You capped Marcus and you prolly capped J too.'

'I'm tellin' you straight-up what happened,' Saiquan said. 'Jake Thomas shot Marcus – I saw it. Why'd I make that shit up?'

'I don't think he's bullshittin',' Kemar said.

'It's the truth,' Saiquan said. 'Why you think Marcus got shot at Thomas's house? Think about that shit. Man, you know what a sick-ass Marcus was.'

'What about J?' Manny said. 'I know you was there.'

'I don't wanna do nothin' to J once I found out what was goin' down, but Marcus was crazy, man. J's bitch told you how Marcus was tryin' to rape her ass, right? Marcus was goin' around shootin' everybody that night. He prolly woulda shot more people, he didn't get shot by Jake Thomas.'

'I don't think he's frontin' nobody, man,' Kemar said to Manny. 'Let's just get the fuck outta here.'

Manny was still pressing the gun up to Saiquan's head, looking like he was about to pull the trigger.

'I ain't lyin' to you, man,' Saiquan said to Manny. 'I didn't shoot nobody. Marcus did all the fuckin' shootin', man, not me.'

Manny still looked like he was gonna do it; then Kemar said, 'Oh, shit.'

Saiquan looked over and saw the two cops – the Latina and the black one from before. They both had their guns out, and then the black cop yelled, 'Drop your weapons and get your hands on your heads!'

'Fuck, man,' Kemar said.

Saiquan put his hands on his head.

'Drop the fucking guns!' the Latina cop screamed.

'Now!' the black cop said.

Kemar dropped his gun, but Manny was still holding his.

'Drop the weapon now!' the black cop shouted.

'Just drop it, man,' Saiquan said.

'Yeah, just give it up, yo,' Kemar said.

'I wanna see that weapon on the ground!' the black cop yelled.

Manny didn't move.

'Just do it, man,' Kemar said. 'The fuck you waitin' for?'

Manny turned slowly toward the cops, looking like he was about to drop the gun; then all of a sudden he started shooting. Saiquan saw the Latina cop get hit in the leg, and the black cop was shooting back. Shots were going everywhere and people were screaming. Saiquan, keeping his head down, was trying to go hide behind the Dumpster. He made it a few steps, and then he felt the pain rip through his back and chest. He tried to keep going, but he couldn't, and then he went down hard onto the concrete.

Ryan lifted the window shade, sunshine stinging his eyes. Then he checked the time on his cell phone: 7:58 A.M.

'Shit.'

He got up slowly, his stomach still very sore from where his father had kicked and punched him. His neck hurt too.

After taking a long leak, he headed downstairs. He could hear commotion outside, and he wondered if the cops were still there, investigating the shooting.

He pushed open the swinging door and went into the kitchen and saw his mother sitting at the table, having her usual breakfast of coffee and a bowl of cornflakes with bananas. The area under her left eye was black and blue, and her nose was swollen.

'Jesus,' Ryan said.

'Good morning,' Rose-Marie said as if nothing were wrong.

'I can't believe he did that to you.' Then Ryan remembered how Rose-Marie had stormed out of the house yesterday, threatening to leave for good. 'What're you doing back here?'

Of course, Ryan knew exactly why she was back – because she always came back. For years she'd been talking about leaving Rocco because of his drinking and abuse, but she hadn't gone anywhere and never would.

Rose-Marie continued eating her cereal, ignoring the question.

Ryan went to pour himself a cup of coffee. As he lifted the pot, Rose-Marie said, 'So you heard the news, right?'

'What news?' Ryan said, wondering what else could possibly go wrong in his life.

'Didn't you wonder what all the commotion outside's about?'

'I figured the cops were still here 'cause of yesterday.'

'There's news trucks from all the networks, reporters every-where. It's insanity.'

'What's going on?' It annoyed Ryan the way his mother was dragging this out, keeping him in suspense.

'It's probably gonna be the top story for weeks. I bet it makes the cover of *People* magazine.'

'You gonna tell me what's going on or not?'

'Jake was accused of rape.'

Ryan spilled hot coffee from the pot onto the counter, and some went onto his bare left foot, but he didn't feel any pain.

'Fuckin' son of a bitch – I'll kill him. I'll kill him right now.'

'Look what you did,' Rose-Marie said, getting up.

'When did he rape her?' Ryan asked. 'Last night? After he left here?'

'Are you okay? It's dripping on you.'

'I said when did he fuckin' rape her?'

'I don't know – a few months ago, I think. Why're you cursing at me?'

Ryan was lost. 'A few months ago?'

'Yes. He met some Mexican girl at a nightclub – I think it was in San Diego, they said. She was underage – fourteen. I can't imagine Christina's gonna want to marry him now. Poor Donna. She was so happy when she found out Jake had a wedding date. She thought that's what he needed, to settle down. It's really so terrible.'

The news was starting to set in – Jake was a rapist, a *child* rapist. Finally the whole world would know the truth about that lowlife. No more talk shows and screaming fans and street parties for Jake Thomas – now *he'd* be the big loser. He'd lose his endorsement deals – hell, he could even go to jail. When he got out, he'd probably have to move back in with his parents and become a fucking housepainter.

'What's so funny?' Rose-Marie asked.

'Nothing,' Ryan said. 'Nothing at all.'

'What about your foot? Doesn't it hurt?'

It didn't.

'No, I'm fine, Ma. Thanks.'

He kissed her on her unbruised cheek.

'What's that for?'

'What? I can't kiss my mother?'

'But I didn't even have a chance to tell you the good news yet.'

'The *good* news?'

'Before I left Donna's house, that nasty detective called. You know, Noll. He said the guy they were after, the one they think shot at you and killed that other guy – he's dead.'

'Excuse me?'

270

'He's dead. The police shot him at the project where he lived. Isn't that weird?'

'You sure about this?'

'That's what Donna said Detective Noll told her. Noll thinks he tried to shoot you, then went back to the projects. There was some shoot-out or something and he was killed. It sounds crazy, doesn't it?'

'Yeah, it sounds really crazy. Are they sure that's what happened?'

'Donna said Noll was sure. So at least now we don't have to worry about going outside anymore, right?'

'Yeah,' Ryan said. 'I guess not.'

'You really have no idea why he was shooting at you?'

'Honestly, Ma, I have no clue. Maybe he was just nuts.'

'Noll did say he had a long criminal record.'

'Did Noll tell Donna what the guy's name was?'

'Yeah, it was a funny name. Sackon Harrington or something like that. Why? You know him?'

'Nope,' Ryan said.

He kissed his mother again and left the kitchen.

Rose-Marie called after him, 'Where're you going? Aren't you having breakfast?'

Ryan went upstairs and put on baggy jeans, a DREXLER 22 jersey, and his LeBrons. If he'd gone out and talked to Noll last night he would've been screwed, but finally something had gone his way. He knew Christina would take him back now – there was no way she'd stay with Jake after what he'd done, and she'd have to realize the huge mistake she'd made. He wanted to go over to her house and talk to her, but then he decided to play it cool. Instead of his rushing over there again, acting desperate, it would be better to let her make the first move. He didn't want to make her think he was too obsessed or anything.

He went downstairs and outside. It was an even bigger scene than he'd imagined. Ten news trucks must've been there, and hordes of reporters and other people were jammed in front of the Thomas's house. The WELCOME HOME JAKE, OUR HERO banner was still hanging there, and looking at it, Ryan couldn't help smiling.

Jake's cell started farting, jolting him out of a deep sleep. When he noticed it was still dark outside he knew this couldn't possibly be good news.

'Yeah,' he mumbled.

'Jake?' Stu asked.

'What is it?'

'I wake you?'

'No, I'm always up at four o'clock in the fucking morning. What's going on?'

'Sorry, but I thought you'd want to know . . . . The Fernandez story just broke.'

'What?' Jake heard him perfectly but he was still disoriented from sleep and hoped he'd gotten something wrong.

'Marianna Fernandez,' Stu said. 'Her lawyer did some kind of press release – the DA's office in San Diego is probably going to get involved. I don't know the details, if charges are gonna be filed or what, but I just thought you should know ASAP.'

'You sure you're getting all this right?' Jake asked.

'Positive. Her lawyer just called Ronald, and Ronald'll be in touch with you, I'm sure, as soon as he gets all the facts. What I'm gonna do right now is get on the horn with Ken and try to . . . '

As Stu went on, Jake understood for the first time how serious this situation really was. A fourteen-year-old girl was accusing him of statutory rape. Last night he thought his problems were over when that detective called the house and said that Cornrows was dead, but the media was going to jump all over the rape story, try to ruin him, and he could forget about his big multiyear contract and any career in Hollywood. He didn't know why he didn't see this coming.

'Listen to me,' Jake said, cutting Stu off. 'You have to take care of this. Just do something to make this go away.'

'Look, Jake, I'll try to—'

'Fuck trying. Just do it.'

'I realize how upset you are right now, Jake, but there's a limit to what I can—'

'Just do it, man. And next time you call you better have some fuckin' good news or you're fired.'

Later, as Jake lay in bed, staring at the ceiling, he knew it was his fault, not Stu's. If he'd just stuck to the team's curfew, if he hadn't gone out clubbing that night in San Diego, if he'd thought with his head instead of his dick and realized that Marianna was fourteen, not eighteen, he wouldn't be in this mess. He knew his only way out now was Christina. He needed the PR bump more than ever, and he had to do whatever he had to do to make sure the engagement was solid.

At around five A.M. he heard voices outside, and he knew this was only the beginning. Soon there would be a media frenzy, with reporters from all over the country showing up at the door, and the phone ringing nonstop. This would definitely be the worst day of his life.

Jake's cell rang and he thought, *Shit, not already.* Then he saw it was Ken, the Pirates owner calling, but he didn't want to deal, so he powered the phone off.

Then, a couple minutes later, someone started knocking on Jake's door. He ignored it, staying with his head covered, and then he heard the door open and his mother said, 'Jake? Jake?'

Jake didn't answer, hoping she'd go away, but she came over and tapped him on the arm and said, 'Jake? . . . Jake? . . . Your team owner's on the phone,' and he knew he had to say something so he said, 'Tell him I'll call back.'

'I think you should talk to him,' Donna said. 'He said there's some story in the news—'

'I'll call him back.'

Donna waited then said, 'He said it has to do with some girl accusing you of—'

'I said I'll call him back,' Jake said.

'Is it true? I mean, is what he said—'

'No, it's not true.'

'But he said it's on the news—'

'So you think everything you hear on the news is true? It's not true, all right? It's total bullshit, and I'll call him back later.'

'Okay,' Donna said. 'Whatever you say.'

Jake didn't feel like he fell asleep, but he must've, because when he rolled over and looked at the clock it was almost six thirty and there was a much bigger commotion outside. He didn't even want to go over to the window to look because he figured they had cameras aimed up there, and a grainy picture of himself hiding out in his parents' house, looking like he was afraid to go outside, was the type of photo op he definitely didn't need.

Even though he had to take a leak badly, he stayed in his room because he didn't want to get into it with his parents – especially his father. He knew his old man would flip when he heard the news. Actually, Jake was surprised that his father hadn't started banging on the door already to try to drag him out of bed to give him the lecture from hell about his partying and womanizing.

He turned on the TV, channel-surfing for a while. On ESPN, no one was talking about him, but on one of the channels there was a picture of him – a headshot from the Pirates yearbook, the one they always showed on TV – and the commentator was talking about how a fourteen-year-old girl had filed statutory rape charges against Jake Thomas in San Diego. Jake couldn't believe how bad it sounded, as if he were some kind of pedophile or something, and he turned the TV off in disgust.

He decided he had to see Christina as soon as possible, before she got too many wrong ideas about him. He packed a carry-on bag with a few outfits, and then, after poking his head out the door to make sure no one was around, he headed downstairs.

He went through the living room and dining room into the kitchen. He was starving and had to have something to eat, so he took out a bowl of chicken salad and, standing at the counter, had several quick bites. Then he put the bowl back in the fridge and guzzled down some Diet Coke straight from the bottle. When he closed the fridge, his father, standing right behind him, said, 'Where the hell you goin'?'

'Jesus,' Jake said. 'You scared the shit out of me.'

'Answer me. Where you runnin' to?'

'I'm not running.'

'You make me sick, you know that?'

'You don't know the facts.'

'I know enough facts. What do you think's gonna happen now? You run and this whole thing disappears?'

'I didn't do anything wrong.'

'So you gonna tell me you don't even know this girl? She's making it all up?'

'What difference does it make? No matter what I do you're

always gonna find some way to shit on it. Think whatever you wanna think.'

Jake went around his father and left through the back door.

'Go 'head, run!' Antowain called after him. 'Run all you want, but it ain't gonna get you nowhere!'

Jake took the secret passageway out to Avenue J. There was no one around but he walked fast, with his head down, so he wouldn't get spotted.

He thought there might be reporters or paparazzi at Christina's house, but there weren't – not yet anyway. He rang the bell, working out in his head what he'd tell her. He knew it would take a lot more than some bullshit about Leonardo DiCaprio and Enrique Iglesias to win her back this time.

Al Mercado answered the door and, seeming pleasantly surprised, said, 'Hey, what're you—'

'Is Christina here?'

'Yeah, sure, but how—'

'It's okay, Daddy. You can go.'

Christina had come up behind her father.

'Yeah, okay,' Al said. 'You two talk. I mean, I'm sure you have a lot to talk about. Go ahead.'

Al left, and Jake said to Christina, 'Look, it's not true, all right? I know it looks bad, really bad, but it's all bullshit. These people, the girl and the father, have been trying to extort money from me for months. I swear to God, you can talk to my lawyer and agent and ask them. I danced with that girl, that's it. Nothing ever happened between us. I didn't kiss her; I didn't even hold her hand. Hell, I didn't even know her name till her father called, asking for money.'

Jake expected Christina to curse him out or slam the door in his face.

He was very surprised when she said, 'Don't worry. I believe you.'

'Yo, Ry.'

Ryan had just made his way through the huge crowd in front of the Thomases' house. He looked over to his right and saw Jamal, the kid from across the street, with a friend of his whom Ryan had seen around the neighborhood before.

'Hey,' Ryan said.

'Crazy fuckin' shit goin' on here lately, huh?' Jamal said.

'Yeah,' Ryan said.

'You think J.T. did it, man?'

'Got me.'

'Yeah, he did it,' Jamal's friend said. 'Why'd she lie?'

'Girls always be lyin' 'bout that shit,' Jamal said, 'tryin' to get money.'

'Naw, he's gonna go to jail. You'll see.'

'Hey, that guy find you yesterday?' Jamal asked Ryan.

'What guy?' Ryan said.

'Yesterday afternoon guy came by asking where Ryan Rossetti lives at. He said he was a friend of yours.'

'So you told him where I live?'

'Yeah, I told him. Why? He didn't come to your house?'

'He was probably that guy who tried to kill me.'

'Oh, shit.' Jamal was scared. 'I woulda told the cops, man, but he said he was your friend and shit. I mean, I didn't mean to—'

'It's cool,' Ryan said. 'It's over now anyway. The cops shot him – he's dead.'

'Oh, shit,' Jamal said. 'That's fucked-up.'

'Yeah, but it's good fucked-up, you know what I mean?'

'Why was he comin' after you?' Jamal's friend asked.

'No idea,' Ryan said. 'But at least it's over now. See ya later.'

Ryan continued up the block, trying to decide whether to go to Christina's. He couldn't wait to be with her, but then he figured it would be a better strategy to give her a little more time. She was probably a mess right now, waking up and finding out that her fiancé was a child rapist. But once that all settled in she'd realize how she'd blown it with Ryan, the guy who really loved her, and beg him to take her back. He figured he'd get a phone call from her sometime today – tomorrow morning at the latest.

He walked along Flatlands to the Arch Diner and ordered a stack of blueberry pancakes and a ham and cheese omelette. For the first time in a long time he was excited about the future. Maybe he wouldn't get the fame and the fortune that Jake had, but he'd have a wife who loved him, a nice house, two great kids, and he'd own a successful business. After a while, he'd forget all about the fuckups of the past, and maybe someday he'd even realize that not making the big leagues was the best thing that had ever happened to him.

He wolfed down the food and then went to look for his car.

Although parts of Friday night were still hazy, Ryan was certain his car had to be near Vinny's Bar, and that the only reason he hadn't been able to find it that night was because he'd been so smashed.

Ryan explored the area near Vinny's, walking around for several blocks in each direction, but nothing looked familiar. Then he had an idea and called information on his cell and got the number for the city's parking violations office. He explained that his car was missing, and he wanted to find out if it had been towed. After talking to several people, he finally found out that his car had in fact been taken to the tow pound at the Brooklyn Navy Yard and that he could go pick it up tomorrow, Monday morning.

Ryan went home. He hung out in his room for a while, smoking cigarettes, listening to Big Tymers and LOX and checking out the latest posts on the AOL and BET boards. The same old bullshit was being discussed, so he went to iTunes and listened to tracks from the new SA Smash album and downloaded the joints he liked. Then, while listening to the downloads, he went into Photoshop and started designing a flyer for his new painting company. He came up with several possible names for the business: EZ Painting, Brooklyn Painters, Painting 4 You, Expert Painters. He wasn't crazy about any of them, but he knew the perfect name would come to him eventually. He surfed around and copied and pasted some images he liked into a file, then superimposed them onto an image of himself in a painting uniform that Christina had once taken. The flyer took shape quickly, and as soon as he had a good name for the company – maybe Brooklyn Painters wasn't so bad – he planned to print out flyers and start posting them around the neighborhood.

Ryan became so absorbed in working on his computer that two hours went by in what seemed like twenty minutes. At a little after one o'clock, he went down to the living room to watch the Jets game. His father was already there, in his easy chair. Rocco didn't look at Ryan when he came into the room.

Ryan sat on the couch. 'What's the score?'

Rocco continued staring at the TV. 'First possession. Jets're driving.'

They watched the game together, acting like yesterday had never happened.

Later, at around four thirty, Ryan went out to buy cigarettes. The crowd near Jake's was mostly gone. There were maybe ten or twenty people, including a few cops, and a Fox News van was parked in front.

On a lamppost on the corner Ryan noticed a couple of flyers – one for a plumber, and one for someone offering guitar lessons. The flyers were very plain – on white paper and no graphics. Ryan knew his flyers would really stick out, especially if he printed them on colored paper. But before he put them up he'd have to hire two or three guys to work for him. He wished he'd asked Jamal and his friend if they were interested. They probably would be, because Jamal had told Ryan a few weeks ago that he wasn't making a lot of money deejaying and that he was looking for something part-time. Hiring workers wouldn't be too difficult, and once Ryan had his crew and a first job, things would snowball. Before he knew it he'd have multiple crews, trucks, and plenty of money.

At a grocery store on Flatlands, Ryan bought a pack of Camels. He lit up in front of the store, cupping the flame with his hand. When he looked up he noticed a dark-skinned guy passing by who was looking at him in a funny way. The guy glared back over his shoulder at Ryan a few times, then got into a car. Suddenly Ryan felt like he'd seen the guy somewhere before, maybe recently, but he couldn't figure out where or when.

Ryan smoked half the cigarette, then tossed the butt away toward the curb and went a few stores down to the deli where Andre worked. He leaned close to the window to see through the glare of the streetlights, which had just been turned on, and saw Andre working at the counter. Ryan went inside and Andre, who was making a sandwich for another customer, saw him right away and said, 'Yo, what up?'

Ryan waited while Andre finished making the sandwich and rang the other customer up at the register.

When they were alone, Andre said, 'Yo, man, so what the fuck happened?'

'You didn't hear?' Ryan asked.

'I heard what's on the news, but what happened to you? They said you got shot or somethin'.'

Ryan explained how someone had shot at him and then how the shooter had been killed.

'Damn, shit's fucked up,' Andre said. 'And I can't believe what they sayin' about J.T. A fourteen-year-old girl?'

'It doesn't surprise me,' Ryan said.

'What? You knew he had it goin' on?'

'Nah, I had no idea. But I knew he isn't the guy everybody thought he was. It was hard to get people to listen to me when there're parties for him going on and everybody thinks he's this big hero, you know what I'm saying?'

'Yeah, now I know,' Andre said. 'When I go home tonight I'm gonna throw out all the shit he signed for me. I'm gonna throw out my Thomas jersey too. Paid a hundred bucks for that shit at Modell's, but I ain't goin' around dressin' like no child molester.'

A woman came into the store, and Ryan said to Andre, 'You're busy – I better go. But I just wanted to ask you – you like working here?'

'It's okay . . . . Why?'

'I'm starting a painting business. I thought you might wanna come work for me.'

'To paint?'

'Yeah. What do you make here, minimum?'

'Yeah, somethin' like that.'

'How'd you like to make ten bucks an hour?'

'That'd be cool. But I don't know how to paint. I tried to paint my room once – shit got all fucked-up.'

'Don't worry – I'll teach you.'

Ryan told Andre that he'd give him more details about the job once things got rolling, and then they high-fived over the counter and Ryan left the store.

Ryan lit another cigarette, took a couple of drags, then jaywalked across Flatlands. He heard the car before he saw it, and when he turned his head it was too late. It was speeding right at him, and the driver – the dark-skinned guy – looked insane. Ryan was starting to scream when the bumper slammed into him. He tumbled over the hood, against the windshield, and was catapulted off the side of the roof onto the street.

Twenty-one

When they heard the knock on the door, Jake said to Christina, 'Don't get it.'

He kissed her harder, his body pounding and grinding against hers.

There was another knock.

'Coming,' Christina said.

'Wait, I'm about to blow too,' Jake said.

'I was talking to my father.'

'What?'

'My father – he's knocking.'

'Ah, come on.'

'Wait one sec.'

'Jesus.'

Christina wriggled out from under Jake. He collapsed onto his stomach, cursing into the pillow.

'Be right there,' Christina said, putting on panties, then a long T-shirt.

Jake was still muttering as Christina opened the door.

'Sorry to bother you,' Al said, 'but I thought you'd want to know—'

'What is it?'

'Ryan was in an accident.'

'Oh, my God. Is he okay?'

'Yeah, yeah, his mother called and said he'll be fine – a car hit him and he broke some bones.'

'Oh, God, that's terrible . . . . Why did his mother call?'

'I don't know. I guess she just wanted to let you know.'

Now Jake came over to the door, naked, with a hard-on. Christina didn't notice it at first, but Al did and looked away quickly.

'What happened?' Jake asked.

'Put something on,' Christina said.

'Oh, sorry,' Jake said, and put his hands over his private parts.

Al repeated what he'd heard from Ryan's mother.

'Who hit him?' Christina said.

'She didn't say,' Al said. 'Anyway, I'll let you two get back to . . . See ya later.'

Al left.

'God,' Christina said to Jake. 'I can't believe it.'

'Shit happens,' Jake said.

'But I hope he's okay. Maybe I should call or something.'

'Oh, shit, look at the time,' Jake said. 'Better rock 'n' roll.'

'You're going *now*?'

'Gotta get to the airport, baby.'

'But it's' – she looked at the clock – 'not even eight o'clock.'

'I got a ten-something flight.'

Trying to look disappointed, Christina said, 'I wish I could come with you.'

'Me, too, but there's no reason to. I mean, I'm booked solid all week. And now, with all this rape shit coming down, I'll be on the phone with my lawyers all day, every day. You'll just be stuck in my living room, watching TV.'

'But at least we'd be together.'

'Yeah, but you have your job and your father and everything. Besides, soon we'll be married and see each other all the time.'

'That's true,' Christina said, 'and it'll give me something to look forward to.'

Jake went to the bathroom to shower, and Christina wondered if she was doing the right thing. Maybe when Jake came back she should just tell him she changed her mind, she wanted to call off the wedding. He could go back to Pittsburgh, and she'd never have to see his lying, rapist face again.

Yesterday morning, when she found out what Jake had done to that poor girl, she told her father that if Jake called to tell him to go to hell, and then her father said, 'Let's not be hasty.'

'What're you talking about?' Christina said. 'He raped a girl; he's the world's biggest asshole.'

'First of all, they're not talking about rape; they're talking about statutory rape. There's a big difference.'

'I can't believe you. You're actually defending him?'

'I'm just saying you can't rush to judgment. The media loves taking the victim's side in these types of cases. Jake's probably innocent.'

'I don't really care if he's innocent or guilty. Our whole relationship's stupid – I should've dumped him years ago.'

'You're not dumping him,' Al snapped. Then he smiled and said, 'I mean, I know you wouldn't do that to me. How would you feel twenty years from now if I get sick or I have a stroke—'

'Will you stop it?'

'—and you're married to some guy, some Brooklyn guy, a housepainter or whatever? If I get sent to some nursing home to waste away because we're both broke?'

'I can't believe you—'

'And you'll know things could've been different, a lot different, if you just went through with the wedding.'

'So you want me to spend the rest of my life with a guy I don't love just so you can have some money?'

'It's not me; it's both of us, and it doesn't have to be the rest of your life. Marry him for a year, maybe two years, then divorce him. You know how much you'll get in any settlement? Millions. And that's for what? Staying with a guy for a couple more years who you've been engaged to for six years. It's not exactly torture. I mean, you wouldn't've gotten engaged to him in the first place if you didn't like him, right?'

'I can't do that.'

'Yes, you can.' He forced a smile, then said, 'You're twenty-four. When you're twenty-six and you have all that money you can marry whoever you want to marry. Just do it, Christina. I'm telling you, if you don't you'll regret it someday. We'll both regret it.'

Christina knew her father was hitting her with another guilt trip, but she was starting to see his point. It would only be for a year or two, and Jake would be away most of the time playing baseball.

'But how do you know I'll be able to get a divorce?' Christina asked.

'That's easy,' Al said. 'The way he runs around, all you'll need is a detective with a camera and you'll get all the evidence you need for a big settlement.'

Christina felt like she had no choice. It was a once-in-a-lifetime opportunity and she had to go through with it.

So later, when Jake showed up at her house, looking like a mess, with bags under his eyes, begging for forgiveness, swearing that he'd never had sex with that Mexican girl, that it was all some big plot against him, Christina still wanted to tell him to go fuck himself, but instead she said, 'Don't worry. I believe you.'

Then Jake kissed her and she felt totally grossed out, but she put on a good act and made him think that she was into it. Later, after they had sex, she felt even dirtier and more disgusting, and she went into the bathroom and nearly threw up. She managed to get hold of herself and get back into bed, but she feared she hadn't been convincing enough. Jake couldn't be *that* stupid – he couldn't actually believe she wanted to be with him. He had to know she'd faked those orgasms and that he repulsed the hell out of her.

Jake returned from the bathroom with a towel around his waist and held up two linen shirts – one beige, one off-white. 'Which do you like better, the Boss or the Valentino?'

'The beige one,' Christina said.

'I like that one too. But you think it'll go with these shoes?' He held up his black Gucci loafers.

'Yeah, I do.'

He considered it, then said, 'Nah, gotta go with the Boss, baby. Gotta go with the Boss.'

Jake continued getting dressed, putting on a mustard-colored suit that looked like something a pimp would wear.

'I really wish I could come with you to Pittsburgh,' Christina lied.

'Me too, baby.'

A few minutes later the doorbell rang.

'That's my ride.'

Christina put on a nightgown and went downstairs with Jake. In the vestibule he held her and told her how much he'd miss her. She wanted to vomit in his face. Instead she kissed him as passionately as she could and even squeezed out a few tears.

Then Jake opened the door, and cameramen and reporters were

there, shouting questions. Christina was embarrassed to be on TV without makeup, and she knew Jake must have set this up, tipping off the reporters that he was at her house, but she didn't let her anger show. She played the part of the outraged, loving fiancée and told the reporters that the charges against Jake were ridiculous and that he was 'the best fiancé in the world.' Then she kissed Jake and held it for the perfect photo op.

After they answered some more questions, Jake walked away toward the limo. Before he got in, he turned back and blew a little kiss. Christina waved and cried some more for the cameras. Then, finally, Jake got in the limo and was gone.

Christina rushed upstairs. She brushed her teeth three times and took a long shower. When she got out she still felt dirty. She took the sheets off the bed and put them in the laundry – the smell of Jake's cologne was lingering, and she feared it would stick around forever.

As she was getting dressed, the doorbell rang and her father called out from his bedroom, 'Can you get that? I'm in the bathroom!'

Christina finished getting dressed quickly, then went down-stairs, figuring it was more reporters. But then she opened the door and saw a gray-haired man showing a badge.

'Christina Mercado?' the man asked.

'Yeah.'

'Detective Ed Noll, Sixty-ninth Precinct. Is Jake Thomas here?'

'No, he left for the airport.'

'Which airport did he go to and when did he leave?'

'What's going on?'

'I need to talk to him right away.'

'He had nothing to do with that girl in San Diego.'

'It's not about the girl; it's about something else.'

'What is it?'

Noll hesitated, then said, 'It has to do with the shooting in front of his house.'

'The shooting? But you guys solved that already. It was that guy from the projects, right?'

'We have two suspects in custody who claim that Jake Thomas shot Marcus Fitts on Friday evening.'

'What?' Christina said. 'That's crazy.'

'Were you with Jake that night?'

'No, I was home.'

'Did he tell you anything about the shooting?'

'No, but—'

'Which airport did he go to?'

'LaGuardia, but—'

'When did he leave?'

'A few minutes ago, but—'

'Airline?'

'I don't under—'

'What airline?'

'United, I think.'

Noll made a call, telling whoever was on the other end to pick up Jake Thomas at the United terminal at LaGuardia and to bring him back to Brooklyn.

When Noll hung up Christina said, 'Look, I don't get any of this. How could Jake've shot somebody? He doesn't even have a gun.'

'We recovered the probable murder weapon on Stillwell Place and we're still running tests on it.'

'So you have a gun. What does that have to do with Jake?'

'We just have to question him.'

'Why? I don't understand.'

'The suspects we have in custody, Kemar Nelson and Manny Rojas, are claiming that Saiquan Harrington, who was killed in a shoot-out with the police, told them that Jake shot and killed Marcus Fitts on Friday evening. Ordinarily we wouldn't believe a couple of punks, one of whom shot and wounded an officer, but we have a credible witness, a judge, who puts Jake at the scene. Look, Jake may very well have had nothing to do with the shooting, but we just need to talk to him and get to the bottom of all this.'

Noll left, and Christina went upstairs, deciding that this had to be a big misunderstanding. She knew Jake, and she knew he wasn't capable of murder. Statutory rape, yeah, but not murder. She took out her cell – noticing there were two missed calls from Ryan – and called Jake to warn him that the cops would be waiting for him at the airport. Jake's phone rang, but he didn't pick up, so she left a message.

Christina called in late for work and continued getting ready. As she put on her mascara, she realized that if Jake was even accused of murder and the story made it into the news, it would be a disaster. The thing with the girl was bad enough, but any involvement in a murder would be too much. People would assume he had to be guilty of something, and it would cost him millions.

The doorbell started ringing repeatedly, and she figured Noll had come back and was pressing the button again and again. Jeez, that guy was such an asshole.

Christina went down the stairs and marched toward the front door.

Twenty-two

The doctor at Brookdale, the one who set Ryan's right leg in the cast after the surgery, told him that it could've been a lot worse.

'If you tensed up when the car hit you, you wouldn't've gone over the side. But you must've been relaxed – that's what saved you.'

Ryan knew the doctor was only trying to make him feel better, but it wasn't working. Yeah, Ryan was glad he wasn't dead, but he was afraid it was only a matter of time. He knew that car hitting him was no accident. That guy was out to get him, he was sure of it, but he still had no idea why.

Rods and screws had been implanted into Ryan's leg and he was out of it; he couldn't think much about anything. While he was in recovery, his parents came to visit.

Rocco just said, 'Hey, kiddo,' and stood to the side, but Rose-Marie was crying and hugged Ryan and kissed him and told him again and again that she loved him.

Then she started to calm down and said, 'Did you hear they caught the guy?'

'What guy?' Ryan said, dazed.

'The one who ran you over,' Rose-Marie said.

'Who was he?'

'His name was Arturo Perez.'

Ryan had no idea who this was.

'The police caught him while he was speeding away,' Rose-Marie said. 'He got into another accident or something. But the police say hitting you wasn't an accident. He did that on purpose.'

Feeling nauseous and dizzy from the pain meds, Ryan said, 'What do you mean?'

'He said . . . he said you slept with his wife. Is that true, Ryan?'

Then it came to him – why the guy had looked so familiar. He was in the picture on the dresser at Elly's house – the guy in the Yankees cap.

Ryan realized his mother was staring at him, waiting for him to answer.

'I don't understand,' Rose-Marie said. 'You told me you were in love with Christina.'

'I am.'

'So why would you go sleep with some man's wife?'

'Okay, let's just let the kid rest,' Rocco said.

He touched Rose-Marie's arm, and she swatted his hand away.

'I didn't sleep with anybody's wife,' Ryan said.

'Then why'd he tell the police you did?' Rose-Marie asked.

'I have no idea,' Ryan said weakly.

A nurse came to check on Ryan; his parents went out to the hallway.

Ryan hadn't felt like getting into a whole thing about it with his mother, and he still wasn't sure what the hell was going on anyway. He didn't know how Elly's husband knew to wait for him outside the deli, or how he'd even recognized him, but he was too exhausted to think about it anymore. He had to stay at the hospital overnight for observation. He wasn't allowed to use his cell phone, so when Rose-Marie came in to say good-bye, Ryan asked her to call Christina, to let her know what had happened and that he was okay.

'And don't tell her about what that guy said,' Ryan told his mother. 'I mean, about me and his wife. And if she heard about it somehow, tell her it isn't true.'

Later Ryan managed to fall asleep, but he had awful nightmares. The nurse had told him that, as a side effect, Vicodin could cause dreams of being chased, and Ryan had them all right. He was running for his life from wild dogs, cars, and people with guns, and when he woke up he felt like he'd been through hell.

He closed his eyes again, drifting in and out of sleep, and when he opened them Detective Noll was looking down at him. Ryan thought he was having another nightmare.

'Remember me?' Noll asked, smiling.

'Jesus,' Ryan said, trying to get his heart rate under control.

'No, not Jesus – Noll, Sixty-ninth Precinct. This is getting to be a regular thing, huh? I see you more than I see my goddamn wife.'

'What do you want?'

'Actually, I'm here with some interesting news. You heard about our friend Arturo Perez?'

'My parents told me he was the guy who hit me.'

'Looks like he was also the guy who shot at you.'

Ryan still felt pretty dazed, and he wasn't sure if Noll was bullshitting, trying to get him to confess or something.

'What do you mean?' he asked.

'We found a gun on him when we took him in. We're still running tests, but it looks like we've got a match to the gun that was used in the drive-by.'

'I thought that guy from the projects shot me.'

'Looks like we made a mistake. It seems like a simple case of a husband looking for some payback. I guess his wife was that woman you scored with the other night.'

'Maybe it was; maybe it wasn't.'

'Come on, you told me she lived on Snediker Avenue – that's where Perez and his wife live. You also told me her name was Elly, which happens to be the name of Perez's wife. You're gonna tell me that's all a fucking coincidence? I also think you're missing a pair of boxers, am I right? Perez said that's how he found out about you, and then his wife told him your name and where you live. He drove over and tried to take you out with a couple of bullets. When that didn't work he went for the hit-and-run. Good thing we caught him. Third time might've been a charm, if you know what I mean.'

Ryan realized he must've told Elly where he lived, at least which block he lived on. Then Arturo, not Saiquan, must've been the one who'd asked Jamal which house Ryan Rossetti lived in.

'So does all this sound right to you?' Noll asked. 'I mean, am I missing anything?'

Ryan looked into Noll's eyes and said, 'All I know is somebody shot me and somebody tried to run me over. It's up to you to try to figure out who did it.'

Noll smiled widely, then he wished Ryan a speedy recovery and left. Ryan hoped he wouldn't go talk to Elly now and find out that

Marcus and Saiquan had been in the bar that night too. If he did that, Ryan knew he'd be totally fucked.

In the morning a doctor told Ryan that he'd have to wear the cast for four to six weeks and would need several weeks of physical therapy, but that he would probably have a full recovery. Then he was discharged and Rose-Marie drove him home.

When they entered the living room, Rose-Marie said, 'Go sit down on the couch. I'll bring you a nice warm plate of lasagna.'

Ryan settled on the couch and decided that, if everything worked out with the police, it was time to get the hell out of Brooklyn. He and Christina could move somewhere – anywhere. Florida, California, Arizona – someplace where the weather was nice and their sons could play baseball year-round.

He called her at work, disguising his voice by talking in a deeper tone, and Allison said that Christina had called in late today. He called Christina's cell a few times; her voice mail kept picking up, and he figured he'd keep calling till he got her.

Rose-Marie brought him a tray of lasagna and a cup of tea and asked him if there was anything else she could get him.

'No, Ma, thanks. But I really appreciate it.'

'You just let me know if there's anything else you need. I want you to relax, take it easy today.'

'I will, Ma.'

Ryan had a few sips of tea and a couple bites of lasagna and then maneuvered his leg in the cast up onto the coffee table and turned on the TV. He flipped around to the different sports channels, trying to find out the latest about the statutory rape charges against Jake. He figured that Jake was probably really feeling it now, terrified that his whole career would be ruined, and Ryan wondered if he was still hiding out at his parents' house. The first time around, he couldn't find any coverage of the story on the major news or sports channels, but after surfing the channels several times he turned to the MSG Network, and a reporter was talking about the case while the station was airing a Jake Thomas highlight reel. There didn't seem to be much new information, and Ryan was getting so sick of watching Jake hit home runs, steal bases, and make spectacular catches that he was about to turn the channel. But then the highlight reel stopped and there was footage of Jake standing next to Christina at the entrance to a house while answering questions from the media. At first Ryan was confused. He didn't know if the footage had been shot the other day at the party or some other time in the past, but then he realized that the house was Christina's house, and the reporter was saying something that included the words *earlier today* and *with his fiancée.* Jake had his arm around Christina, and Christina was saying that the charges against Jake were ridiculous and that he was the best fiancé in the world.

Ryan picked up the thing closest to him – the mug of tea – and flung it at the TV.

Then he struggled to his feet and started yelling, 'Ma! Ma!'

Rose-Marie came running from the kitchen and said, 'What happened?'

'Where're your car keys?'

'What? What's going on?'

'Your fucking car keys!' Ryan screamed, grabbing the crutches.

'Why do you need my car keys? What the hell's wrong with you?'

Stumbling on the crutches, Ryan went over to the side table where Rose-Marie had left her purse.

'What're you doing?' Rose-Marie said. 'You can't drive!'

Ryan went outside and struggled down the steps, and Rose-Marie followed him, trying to convince him to go back inside.

When he reached the car, she grabbed his arm and said, 'Please just tell me what's going on. What's happening?'

'Lemme go, Ma,' Ryan said.

'But where're you—'

'Lemme fuckin' go!' Ryan pushed her aside. He got into the car and sped away.

When he reached Christina's house, he left the car in the street with the motor running and went up to the door as fast as he could on the crutches. He rang the bell, then kept ringing it again and again. He didn't care if she didn't open up; he'd break the fucking door down if he had to.

The door opened and she was there, looking surprised, as if she were expecting somebody else.

'Get in the fucking car,' he said.

'What the hell're you—'

Ryan had both crutches tucked under his right arm and grabbed Christina with his left hand and tried to drag her out of the house.

'Let go of me,' she said.

'I'm taking you away from here,' he said, 'till you get some fucking sense into you.'

Christina started screaming and grabbed on to the door frame as Ryan continued to yank her other arm. Then she broke free and ran toward the staircase, and Ryan followed her on the crutches.

Al came out of the kitchen, cutting Ryan off, and said, 'Hey, the fuck's your problem?'

Christina went upstairs, and Ryan was screaming, 'Get back here! You're getting in that fucking car!'

Al grabbed Ryan and spun him around.

'You fuckin' little piece of shit,' Al said.

Ryan continued into the living room, yelling, 'Is he here too? Is the rapist here too?'

Al came at Ryan again and grabbed him. Ryan kept hobbling on the crutches, pulling Al along, saying, 'We're getting out of here! We're getting out of here right now.'

Ryan stumbled, and he and Al fell onto the floor, with Al partially on top of him.

'Christina, call the cops!' Al yelled, getting up.

'I know you love me,' Ryan said to Christina as he tried to get to his feet. 'You can't look in my eyes and say you don't love me.'

'She doesn't love you; she hates your guts, you moron. Why do you think she'd want you? You're a loser ... a fucking housepainter.'

Ryan, managing to stand, balancing himself on one crutch, said, 'I know you don't love him! I know you don't wanna spend the rest of your life with that asshole!'

'*You're* the asshole,' Al said.

'You have to come with me,' Ryan said. 'I love you!'

Christina came into the living room and said to Ryan, 'I hate you so much. Just get the hell away from me!'

'Please,' Ryan said. 'We just have to get away. Things'll seem different when we're away.'

'Didn't you hear her?' Al said. 'She hates you.'

'I know you don't mean that,' Ryan said to Christina. 'Look,

I don't care why you did it, okay? I'm not even mad at you. I just want you back, that's all.'

'Did you call the cops yet?' Al said to Christina.

'You better just get out of here,' Christina said to Ryan, 'before you get in big trouble.'

'I'm not going anywhere without you,' Ryan said. 'I just want things to be like they were before, when we were happy, before all this bullshit happened.'

'You really are a fuckin' moron, aren't you?' Al said. 'Christina's marrying Jake. She's in love with him. Why do you think she'd ever want a nobody like you?'

'Why don't you stay the fuck out of it?' Ryan said.

'You know it's true,' Al said. 'You're nothing. You're just some low-life scumbag whose life's going nowhere.'

'Just stay the hell away from me,' Ryan said.

'You come in here like a maniac, try to take Christina away, and you think she'd want to be with you? Are you out of your fucking mind?'

'Please just leave, Ryan,' Christina said.

'Just look into my eyes,' Ryan said, 'and tell me you don't love me. If you say you don't love me I'll leave here right now, and I swear you'll never see my face again.'

Christina stared at Ryan for a few seconds.

'That's it; I'm calling the fuckin' cops,' Al said.

Al headed toward the kitchen, and Ryan came up behind him and raised the crutch like a bat and swung it against the side of Al's head. Al went down like a bowling pin.

Screaming, Christina rushed over to her father. 'Daddy! Oh, my God, Daddy! Daddy!'

Christina turned her father over, hugging his head, and Ryan saw Al's wide-open eyes, and the blood dripping from his ear. Ryan just stood there, swaying, still holding the crutch above his head. Christina was hugging her father, wailing, as the noise of a police siren got louder and louder.

Twenty-three

Finally J.T. was riding in class, baby. The huge Hummer limo had fish tanks, a full bar, a DVD player, and L-shaped seating with plenty of room to stretch out. Best of all the driver was a real pro – a clean-cut, U.S. Marine-looking white guy who knew how to shut the hell up and drive.

As the limo rolled along Flatlands, past all the projects and graffiti and used-car lots and bums and drug dealers, Jake's cell bocked.

'Yep,' Jake said to his lawyer.

'Sorry, I had to take that other call,' Lufkowitz explained.

'No *problema*,' Jake said, thinking that after this whole Marianna Fernandez mess was resolved, one way or another, Fuckowitz was toast.

'So, like I was saying before,' Lufkowitz went on, 'I don't think any of this is as bad as it looks. Legally speaking her case is weak. It's early in the game and we have to wait to see what their side comes up with, but I think public perception is going to switch quickly on this. First off, she waited over ten weeks before approaching the DA, which is automatically going to make her story look suspect. We'll be able to characterize her side as money-hungry, out to blackmail— Shit, can you hold on for one more sec?'

'Yeah,' Jake said, annoyed. If the guy put him on hold one more time, that was it – he was hiring another lawyer.

'I'm back, sorry about that,' Lufkowitz said. 'Where was I? Right, the case against the girl. I think we can make a real strong argument that her father was out to extort money from you from the get-go. We have history – nothing in writing, unfortunately, but phone records – of him making a series of monetary demands. I think we'll have some strong testimony there. And here's the big news. The detective you hired, Mulligan, called me last night. He found two boys in Marianna Fernandez's school who say they paid her for sexual favors. There's a good chance other boys are involved, but bottom line, I don't think there's any way in hell the DA takes this to trial. There's too much ambiguity in the case, too much of a delay in making the allegations, and now it looks like the girl's the school slut. Their side'll probably try to cut a deal with us, ask for some kind of settlement.'

'No deals,' Jake said.

'I'm with you all the way on that. Why play ball if we don't have to? Now, of course, I don't want to give you the impression it's all hunky-dory, because their side's not gonna go down without a fight. They're probably going to produce witnesses and may even try to present physical evidence that sex took place between you and the girl.'

'Sex didn't take place.'

'Right ... And besides, if they had physical evidence they probably would've at least leaked that info to us already, so looks like we have nothing to worry about there either. Bottom line I really think this is all gonna go away fairly soon. It'll be a roller coaster for a few days, but I give the DA a week to drop the case. You know, one thing you might want to consider is filing a countersuit for defamation of character, but let's see what their next move is. Why shoot your load if you don't have to, right?'

'Good point.' Jake was starting to like this guy.

'Anyway, let's talk this afternoon when you get in,' Lufkowitz continued. 'Meanwhile, lemme get the ball rolling and make some calls. We'll probably want to do some kinda press conference from Pittsburgh later on. Whatever you do, don't make any comments without me present.... Shit, there's my other line again.... You have any questions?'

'Nah, it all sounds cool,' Jake said. 'And, hey, if this all goes as smoothly as you say it will, I'm sending you and your family on a vacation.'

'That's not necess—'

'Where do you wanna go, Bermuda, Saint Thomas, Martinique?'

'I don't—'

'You're going to Martinique. You and your family, first-class, five-star hotel. Seven days, or you want ten?'

'I—'

'Just do your job, take care of this mess, and my travel agent'll be in touch.'

As the limo approached Pennsylvania Avenue, Jake couldn't help feeling proud of himself. That Martinique bullshit was the perfect touch. There was no way in hell he was planning to give Lufkowitz any free vacation or pay him a penny more than he had to, but he figured he'd give the guy as much incentive as possible to win the case. You wanted people to work hard for you, you had to light a fire under their asses, dangle some carrots.

A call was coming in on his cell – from Christina. He figured she was just calling to tell him how much she loved him and would miss him, but he'd had enough of that for one weekend. He switched the phone to silent mode and let his voice mail pick up.

The limo passed through the slummy Spring Creek Towers housing project and entered the Belt Parkway. Jake kicked back and sipped his drink. Things had looked dicey there for a while, but now everything was starting to go his way again. Yeah, his public image had taken a beating these past few days, but people's memories were short. Before long some other big-time athlete would fail a drug test or kill somebody, and everybody would forget all about what J.T. had been accused of doing. He planned to string Christina along for as long as he needed her, but once the Marianna mess was officially resolved and his career was back on track and he didn't need the happy-fiancé photo ops anymore, he was going to dump her, pronto. By this time next year, when he scored his big multiyear contract and had all his endorsement deals firmly in place, the past few days would seem like a bad memory.

Jake saw a sign up ahead for Ozone Park and realized he was finally leaving Brooklyn for good. *Thank fucking God.* The place was a hellhole filled with losers and psychos – miserable sons of bitches with screwed-up dreams and lost hopes who deserved whatever they got.

As the Hummer continued toward the airport, Jake closed his eyes and rested, half smiling, feeling, finally, at peace.

Turn the page for a sneak preview of
Jason Starr's latest book,

THE FOLLOWER,
coming in August 2007
from St. Martin's Minotaur

Katie was so beautiful, so perfect in every way, that it was hard for Peter to stop staring at her. He loved the way her legs and arms moved as she ran, and the way her pony tail bobbed back and forth against her back. She had a great back—smooth, muscular, and lightly tanned. He forced himself to look away a few times, because he didn't want to make it too obvious, but she was just impossible to resist.

After her workout, she did some more stretches, then went over to the mats to do abs. As she did crunches on the exercise ball, he watched, loving the way her lips parted with each exhale. He was hoping she'd meant what she said about exchanging numbers and getting together sometime, that she wasn't just being nice.

When she finished doing abs, she did some isometric-type exercises, and then came over to him at the desk.

"Good workout?" he asked.

"Yeah . . . not bad."

Even sweaty she looked amazing, much better than in those pictures of her he'd seen on the Internet. Standing next to her he felt a spark between them, an energy that was so intense he knew she must've been feeling it as well. He had an impulse to screw all of his plans, to tell her straight off how he felt about her so that they could start their lives together, but he resisted it. He'd planned everything carefully and knew it would be crazy to try to rush things now.

They chatted for about five minutes about Lenox and about people they both knew—a typical what-ever-happened-to, I-wonder-where, oh-my-God-do-you-remember conversation. Then things progressed even faster than Peter had anticipated. Instead of having to ask for Katie's number, she spontaneously wrote it on the back of a Metro Sports Club business card and said, "You have to call me so we hang out sometime."

Peter, trying not to let his delight show, but trying not to sound too nonchalant either, said with the perfect balance, "Yeah, definitely."

The rest of the morning, Peter was so thrilled that he was barely aware of even being at work, at his silly job, and he felt like someone else was going about his duties of handing out towels, answering phone calls, and dealing with whatever mundane questions gym members had, and he was just sitting back, observing it all. At around noon, Jimmy introduced him to a guy named Todd, who relieved Peter at the desk; then Jimmy asked Peter if he could stay late today—even though it was his first day on the job—to stand on the street and hand out flyers to passers-by. Peter knew that Jimmy was pulling a power trip, telling the new guy to do the dirty work. Jimmy was really getting to Peter. It was so painful, listening to him go on and on about the "hot chicks" at the club, acting like he was some kind of Casanova or something, when he was obviously the type of guy who couldn't even get a girlfriend.

Normally, Peter wouldn't have had the patience to put up with a guy like Jimmy, but today he was in such a great mood that Jimmy could've asked him to scrub the insides of all the toilets and he would've happily said yes.

Peter stood outside and handed a flyer to almost everyone who passed by, giving the BS sales pitch—"A two-day free trial and initiation fee waived for today only," as if prospective members weren't always offered two free days with no initiation fee. He was so pepped up because of Katie that he managed to convince several people to walk in off the street and talk to the sales rep about a membership, and Dave, the sales rep, even managed to close a sale.

At the end of Peter's workday, Jimmy came over to him and said, "Great going, man. I didn't know you had sales skills."

Peter knew he easily could have felt insulted. It was as if Jimmy was treating him like a five-year-old who'd spelled his first word—*Oh, you made a sale, Peter Weter. I'm so proud of you. You're such a smart little boy.* But since Peter didn't really care about this job and wasn't even planning to keep it for more than a couple of weeks, he smiled and said, "I was just doing my job."

"Maybe you're wasting your time, trying to become a trainer," Jimmy said. "Maybe I should just train you to be a membership consultant."

Again, Peter felt like Jimmy was trying to get a dig in, but he just brushed the whole thing off, making it into a joke, going, "Yeah, maybe that's not such a bad idea."

"Hey, was that your girlfriend you were talking to before?"

"Yeah. Actually it was."

"I've seen her here before. Yeah, she's a babe all right. Well done, my man. Well done."

Jimmy told Peter what a great job he was doing so far and how happy he was to have him on board at the gym and then he finally said, "See ya tomorrow, bright and early," and walked away.

Peter was glad he would be quitting soon because he didn't know how much longer he could stomach working for Jimmy.

At around two P.M., Peter left the health club. Automatically he started toward Katie's apartment, where he'd been hanging out a lot every day for the past few weeks—in a disguise of a Yankees cap and mirrored sunglasses—but then he reminded himself that there was no reason to watch her anymore and, although he really wanted to see her again, going there could be a big mistake. If she spotted him it would ruin everything and there was no reason to risk that when things were going so well.

Instead, he walked down Third a couple of blocks, then cut over to Lexington and hailed a cab. He had the urge to call Katie from his cell and arrange a time to meet up, but he stopped himself. He knew that getting a girl was just like getting a job—attitude was everything. If he came off as desperate, impulsive, overzealous, it would turn her off and he'd take a major step backward. He had to stay cool, keep telling her what she wanted to hear. Every girl has a fantasy of their perfect guy. The trick was to transform yourself, to become the fantasy.

From observing Katie when she was a teenager and from watching her lately, Peter had figured out a lot about her. He knew that she was a good dresser and cared about her appearance. He also knew that she was very close with her father, and that she was looking for a strong, conservative, good-looking guy to protect her. At the ice-cream parlor in Lenox, she used to talk about her father a lot and Peter used to see her with Mr. Porter all over—at the supermarket, playing tennis, at the beach at Laurel Lake. Sometimes he'd see her walking down one of the side streets in Lenox, holding hands with her dad, or sitting with her arm around his shoulders at the movie theater at the Berkshire Mall.

From watching her in Manhattan, Peter had figured out that not much about her had changed. She wasn't ultra high-maintenance, but she liked to take care of herself—going to the nail salon on Third Avenue once a week, getting her hair cut and highlighted at Amor de Hair on Madison Avenue, shopping at Bloomingdale's, J. Crew, and Ann Taylor LOFT, and of course working out at the Metro Sports Club, which cost her seventy-four dollars a month. He knew that with the money she was making at her entry-level job there was no way she could afford this type of lifestyle and that her father, Dick Porter, was probably helping to support her. He was probably paying her rent and perhaps giving her additional money. Peter also got the sense, by Katie's mannerisms, such as the way she twirled her hair self-consciously and occasionally glanced in mirrors in a dissatisfied way, that she was insecure, that despite everything she had, she still felt like something was missing. Whenever she arrived at her apartment building alone, after going out with her friends, or when she came home from work, she'd look around nervously, obviously afraid that someone was going to try to follow her into the vestibule. Peter couldn't help thinking of her as a baby deer, alone in the dark, dangerous woods of Manhattan, desperate for a strong, secure guy, a father figure, to come along and protect her.

Peter knew that he could be that guy, that rock. All he had to do was play up to her fantasy, give her what she wanted. He was five years older than her, which already gave him a big leg up; girls who idolized their fathers were always attracted to older guys. She wanted a guy who was secure, mature, who could take care of her, make her feel safe, like she used to feel safe when she was daddy's little girl. She was probably used to dating guys in their early twenties who went on and on about themselves and treated her like crap, but what she really wanted was a more mature guy who cared about her, who *listened*. As for appearances, she seemed to be attracted to guys who had the same general features as her father. When she was walking along the street, or sitting at a restaurant or a coffee bar, or that time last Saturday night, when she went out with her friends to that bar in Chelsea, she seemed to notice the clean-cut, conservative-looking guys. When Peter came to New York, his hair was long, almost down to his shoulders, and he had a scraggly beard. But before he interviewed for the job at the gym he got a close-cropped, military-style do and trimmed his beard to a goatee. Afterward, when he looked in the mirror, he was surprised and delighted by how much he resembled Katie's dad, Dick Porter.

When Peter said hi to Katie at the gym he knew right away that his makeover had been successful. He could tell by the way she kept smiling and blushing that she was attracted to him. Because he knew she was insecure and would respond well to compliments, he made sure to tell her, in a very sincere way, how beautiful she looked. That scored a lot of points for him and he knew he'd also won her over big-time by hanging on her every word, being genuinely interested in what she had to say.

The traffic was stop-and-go in the East Sixties and it probably would have been faster for Peter to get out and walk. But then he had another thought—maybe he should just go for it and tell the driver to make a left at the next corner and head back uptown. Peter imagined going to Katie's building and buzzing her apartment. She'd wonder how he knew where she lived, but he could cover for it easily—tell her that he'd gotten her address from the health club's database. She'd invite him up and, since she'd just gotten out of the shower, her hair would be wet. She'd be wearing baggy sweats and a long, man's T-shirt, and would look great with no makeup. Although he'd never seen the inside of her apartment, he pictured the whole place being pink and very girly, like a teenager's room. And it would smell flowery, like potpourri, or the perfume she was wearing at the gym today. She'd look warm and cuddly and he'd want to give her a big, long hug. He'd look into her eyes, showing her how caring he was, and say, "I figured, Why wait? Let's go for that coffee right now." He'd have to deliver that line carefully, so he wouldn't sound too pushy or overanxious, but he was sure he could pull it off. Then they'd go out to a dimly lit coffee bar and sit next to each other on a fluffy couch and talk and laugh and look into each other's eyes for hours.

As long as he said the right things, treated her the way she wanted to be treated, she'd start to fall in love with him, and then they'd start seeing each other all the time, become inseparable, and when the time was right, he'd propose, giving her the Tiffany two-karat diamond engagement ring, and it would be the happiest day of their lives.

Passing Fifty-ninth Street the traffic thinned and the cab started moving at a steadier pace and Peter decided to hold off on going over there. It would be better to just relax, to let things take their course. Although he knew he could go over to her place and everything could work out perfectly, there was no reason to rush things. He'd stick to the plan and call her tomorrow night and suggest that they meet for coffee the following day—Monday.

He had taken out the business card with her number on it and now he stared at the handwriting. It was very neat and controlled; every letter in "Katie" and every digit in her number was easily readable. This was another sign that she was into him. If she didn't like him or didn't care if he called her, she would've scribbled her number; obviously she wanted to make sure there was no way for him to dial a wrong number and not be able to get in touch.

Zoning out, thinking of things to say to her on the phone when he called her and when they went out for coffee, he didn't hear what the driver had asked him.

"What?"

"What side?" the driver asked, annoyed. "Right or left?"

"Oh, left," Peter said, "across the street."

The cab pulled in front of the Ramada Inn on Lexington and Thirtieth. Peter gave the driver a twenty, which was nearly double the fare, and told him to keep the change. The driver seemed surprised and suddenly cheerful and told Peter to have a great day.

Hector, the young Puerto Rican guy, was working at the hotel's front desk. When he saw Peter he cupped a hand over the mouth piece of the phone and said, "Yo, Peter, I gotta talk to you. Hold up one sec."

"Sure," Peter said.

Peter knew what Hector wanted to talk about. Peter had been giving him advice on how to break up with his current girlfriend so he could get back with his ex. It was a sticky situation because the two girls lived in the same building in the Bronx and Hector didn't want his ex to know that he had been dating the other girl. Peter's advice was for Hector to be honest with the girl he wanted to break up with because when it came right down to it people always appreciated honesty.

Hector hung up and said to Peter, "Yo, you're a genius, man."

"It worked?" Peter asked.

"Hell yeah, man. I mean, I wasn't gonna do it. I went over to Jessica's place last night and I was, like, I gotta be crazy doin' this. She gonna be freakin', know what I'm sayin'? I gotta lie to her, make up somethin'. Then I was like, Naw, maybe Peter's right. So I tried. I mean, I did everything you said I should do, man, said everything you said I should say. I was lookin' into her eyes, being nice and sweet and all that shit, and I just told her, was like we gotta break up 'cause I'm in love with Lucy and that's just the way it is. I didn't say it like *that*, but that's kinda like what I was sayin', you know, and she was like, 'Yeah, you wanna break up. That's cool. I just want you to be happy, I wanna be friends.' I'm serious, yo, that's what it was like."

"I'm really happy for you, man," Peter said, consciously trying to talk like Hector, even taking on a bit of Puerto Rican accent.

"Yo, I owe you, man," Hector said. "Serious. Anything you want's on me. Tonight, do any pay-per-view, take whatever you want from the mini bar, whatever, and you won't get charged for nothing. . . ."

"That's okay—I'm just glad I could help you out. I'll talk to you later, all right?"

Peter took the elevator up to the twelfth floor and went into his suite. He was still very excited about how well everything had gone with Katie and he couldn't stop replaying their conversation in his head. There wasn't one thing he'd said that he regretted; if he'd written his lines in advance and read from the script it couldn't have gone any better. Again, he took out the business card with her name on it and, touching the writing gently with his forefinger, he had to resist calling her. He wanted to hear her voice. He wanted to know if he she sounded different on the phone than in person and he wanted to make sure she was okay. Of course, he didn't think anything *bad* had happened to her, but suddenly he felt protective over her, as if she were his child, and he knew it would make him feel better, more relaxed, if he could just talk to her.

But he reminded himself that this was only the beginning. There would be days, months, years, a whole lifetime of talking on the phone. Soon they'd have so many phone conversations that calling her would be something he wouldn't even have to think about or prepare for; it would come as naturally as eating or breathing.

Peter felt grimy from the city so he took a quick shower. Afterward, he opened the closet which he had filled with his new wardrobe—upscale, conservative clothes that he knew Katie would like—and picked out beige chinos and a black mock turtleneck. He didn't want to leave anything to chance. If something went wrong between him and Katie and things didn't work out as perfectly as he imagined, he didn't want to look back later and wish he had done something differently. He knew there would be a greater chance of winning Katie over if he looked and acted the right way.

He was planning to have a mellow day alone. He figured he'd take a walk downtown, hang out for a while at a Barnes & Noble or a Starbucks, grab some sushi for dinner, and then maybe go to a movie. He had to go somewhere because if he stayed in his hotel room all day, he knew he wouldn't be able to stop thinking about Katie and he didn't want to do something stupid that he'd regret.

It was a beautiful November afternoon—clear sky, chilly but not too cold, leaves whipping around on the sidewalks. On his way downtown, Peter decided to stop by the co-op he had purchased in the brownstone on East Twenty-second Street, to see how the renovations were coming along.

He opened the door to the building and went up to the second floor. The door to the apartment was propped open with a piece of wood and a worker was using a power tool in one of the back rooms. Peter checked out the dining room and kitchen, very pleased with how things were progressing. The crown molding was up and all the painting was done and the new Brazilian cherry strip floors had been laid down. The new silestone breakfast bar had been installed in the kitchen and all of the maple cabinetry was in place and looked great. The stainless steel refrigerator and Viking stove hadn't been delivered yet, but that was scheduled to happen sometime next week.

Peter went down to the main bedroom where two Mexican men were installing shelves in the walk-in closet.

"*Como estan?*" Peter said to the men.

"*Muy bueno,*" the older man said. "*Gracias.*"

"*Me gusta todos.* Seriously—it really looks great."

"*Gracias.*"

"*Cuándo usted acabará?*"

"*Dos dias. Quesas tres dias.*"

"*Ah, muy bueno. Muchas gracias. Estoy muy, muy feliz.*"

Peter peeked into the master bath, glad to see that the renovations were about halfway done and looked fantastic, and then he went across the hall to one of the bedrooms, which he planned to use for a home theater. The two leather chairs from Restoration Hardware had been delivered and were facing the wall where the sixty-four-inch LCD TV would be placed. He imagined he and Katie, wearing comfy sweaters on a cold winter night, sipping hot chocolate while watching a movie, a love story, and then he peeked into the room across the hallway that would be their first child's room. The room was empty now, but he imagined it filled with toys, a rocking chair, a crib. It was going to feel so great to sit in the rocking chair and rock his child to sleep, knowing that the baby was his *and* Katie's, that they had created a life together.

After spending another several minutes checking out other odds and ends, he left the apartment and continued downtown. He walked around Gramercy Park and then went along Twentieth Street for a few blocks before cutting over toward Union Square. Although he'd only been living in New York at the hotel for about a month, and before then had only been to the city several times— a few short trips with his parents when he was very young, and then, more recently, the trips in from Mexico to look at apartments and to close on the co-op—he already felt very comfortable in New York, like a native. This surprised him a lot because when he was growing up he could never have imagined living in Manhattan, or anyplace urban. He always imagined himself living in the mountains, maybe in Vermont or New Hampshire.

A few months ago, he'd been planning to move back to New

England, but then, surfing the Net one day in Guadalajara, he decided to Google Katie Porter. He didn't found out much about her, except that she had gone to college at Wesleyan and was living in Manhattan, but he knew he had to be with her, that he couldn't live without her. He also knew that he would have to reinvent himself in many ways to win her over, and becoming a New Yorker was one of them. Since she obviously viewed herself as "a city girl" nowadays, he figured if he was "a city guy" she would be much more likely to fall for him, and he also knew it would be nearly impossible for any single girl in Manhattan to resist a guy who owned a huge, spectacular apartment. So Peter shelled out the 975,000 dollars for the co-op, figuring he'd unveil it to her at the perfect time, when all the renovations were complete and their relationship was in full swing.

As Peter walked through the Saturday afternoon farmer's market at Union Square, he decided that waiting until tomorrow night to ask her out could be a big mistake or, at the very least, create unnecessary awkwardness. He knew, from following her around, that she usually went to the gym on Saturdays and Sundays. This didn't necessarily mean that she would work out tomorrow, but she was a very regimented person, sticking to a tight routine for most of her activities—leaving for work between eight-ten and eight-fifteen every morning, stopping at the same coffee cart outside her office for a breakfast of coffee and a raisin bagel "nothing on it," returning from work every day between five forty-five and six, except that one day last week when she went out to a bar after work with friends and didn't get home until later—so he figured there was a decent chance that she would be going to the gym tomorrow morning. If he saw her tomorrow and hadn't called her yet she might get the wrong idea, think he wasn't interested in her, and it would put him in an uncomfortable position.

He went to ABC Carpet & Home and did some shopping for the apartment, but then he couldn't take it anymore. He took out his cell and dialed Katie's number, which he had memorized.

"Hello?" God, her voice was amazing.

"Hey, it's me, Peter."

There was a pause. It only lasted a second or two, but it was plenty of time for Peter to get paranoid. He wondered if she wasn't really expecting him to call and was upset that he had, or if she thought it was weird that he was calling so quickly, or if she was with that guy she'd been dating.

But Peter's fears were alleviated when she said, "Oh, wow, Peter. Sorry, I just walked in the door and I didn't check my caller ID. What's up?"

"Not much. I was just wondering if you had any plans for tomorrow afternoon."

Damn, he sounded too pushy. He should've had a short conversation with her first. Why didn't he think all this through?

"No, I don't," she said. "Not really."

"Great," he said, relieved. "So how about we meet for coffee at around two?"

"Yeah, okay. That sounds great."

"Cool. I'll stop by your place after I get off work."

"I better tell you where I live."

"Yeah, that would be a good idea."

She gave him her address and he pretended that he was writing it down somewhere. He was angry at himself for making that slipup, implying that he already knew where she lived. He hoped she hadn't picked up on it.

"You know, I have a better idea," she said. "Since you're gonna be working, how about I just come by the gym and meet you there?"

Peter wasn't crazy about this plan, but didn't want to be difficult. "Okay," he said. "Whatever works best for you."

They exchanged some small talk about how they were going to spend the rest of their afternoons—she said she was going to do some laundry, which he expected because she'd done laundry on two other Saturdays at around this time, and he said he had to "do some errands around the neighborhood"—and then they said good-bye and clicked off.

Overall, he was happy with how the conversation had gone. He didn't think she was suspicious of anything and he was glad that she seemed excited about him calling and about their date tomorrow. Still, he wished he didn't have to be on eggshells with her, watching every word he said. He wanted to let loose, be natural. He knew that once she got to know the real Peter Wells she'd never even think about another guy again.

CPSIA information can be obtained at www.ICGtesting.com
Printed in the USA
239246LV00001B/66/P